**ALICE CAN**

# THE MURDER OF CAₖₒₗᵢₙₑ ᵦᵤₙₐᵧ

ALICE Campbell (1887-1955) came originally from
Atlanta, Georgia, where she was part of the socially
prominent Ormond family. She moved to New York
City at the age of nineteen and quickly became a
socialist and women's suffragist. Later she moved to
Paris, marrying the American-born artist and writer
James Lawrence Campbell, with whom she had a son
in 1914.

Just before World War One, the family left France for
England, where the couple had two more children,
a son and a daughter. Campbell wrote crime fiction
until 1950, though many of her novels continued to
have French settings. She published her first work
(*Juggernaut*) in 1928. She wrote nineteen detective
novels during her career.

# MYSTERIES BY ALICE CAMPBELL

# ALICE CAMPBELL

# THE MURDER OF CAROLINE BUNDY

With an introduction
by Curtis Evans

DEAN STREET PRESS

# ALICE IN MURDERLAND

In 1927 Alice Dorothy Ormond Campbell—a thirty-nine-year-old native of Atlanta, Georgia who for the last fifteen years had lived successively in New York, Paris and London, never once returning to the so-called Empire City of the South, published her first novel, an unstoppable crime thriller called *Juggernaut*, selling the serialization rights to the *Chicago Tribune* for $4000 ($60,000 today), a tremendous sum for a brand new author. On its publication in January 1928, both the book and its author caught the keen eye of Bessie S. Stafford, society page editor of the *Atlanta Constitution*. Back when Alice Ormond, as she was then known, lived in Atlanta, Miss Bessie breathlessly informed her readers, she had been "an ethereal blonde-like type of beauty, extremely popular, and always thought she was in love with somebody. She took high honors in school; and her gentleness of manner and breeding bespoke an aristocratic lineage. She grew to a charming womanhood—"

Let us stop Miss Bessie right there, because there is rather more to the story of Alice Campbell, the mystery genre's other "AC," who published nineteen crime novels between 1928 and 1950. Allow me to plunge boldly forward with the tale of Atlanta's great Golden Age crime writer, who as an American expatriate in England, went on to achieve fame and fortune as an atmospheric writer of murder and mystery and become one of the early members of the Detection Club.

Alice Campbell's lineage was distinguished. Alice was born in Atlanta on November 29, 1887, the youngest of the four surviving children of prominent Atlantans James Ormond IV and Florence Root. Both of Alice's grandfathers had been wealthy Atlanta merchants who settled in the city in the years before the American Civil War. Alice's uncles, John Wellborn Root and Walter Clark Root, were noted architects, while her brothers, Sidney James and Walter Emanuel Ormond, were respectively a drama critic and political writer for the *Atlanta Constitution* and an attorney and justice of the peace. Both brothers died untimely deaths before Alice had even turned thirty, as did her uncle John Wellborn Root and her father.

Alice precociously published her first piece of fiction, a fairy story, in the *Atlanta Constitution* in 1897, when she was nine years old. Four years later, the ambitious child was said to be in the final stage of completing a two-volume novel. In 1907, by which time she was nineteen, Alice relocated to New York City, chaperoned by Florence.

In New York Alice became friends with writers Inez Haynes Irwin, a prominent feminist, and Jacques Futrelle, the creator of "The Thinking Machine" detective who was soon to go down with the ship on RMS *Titanic,* and scored her first published short story in *Ladies Home Journal* in 1911. Simultaneously she threw herself pell-mell into the causes of women's suffrage and equal pay for equal work. The same year she herself became engaged, but this was soon broken off and in February 1913 Alice sailed to Paris with her mother to further her cultural education.

Three months later in Paris, on May 22, 1913, twenty-five-year-old Alice married James Lawrence Campbell, a twenty-four-year-old theatrical agent of good looks and good family from Virginia. Jamie, as he was known, had arrived in Paris a couple of years earlier, after a failed stint in New York City as an actor. In Paris he served, more successfully, as an agent for prominent New York play brokers Arch and Edgar Selwyn.

After the wedding Alice Ormond Campbell, as she now was known, remained in Paris with her husband Jamie until hostilities between France and Germany loomed the next year. At this point the couple prudently relocated to England, along with their newborn son, James Lawrence Campbell, Jr., a future artist and critic. After the war the Campbells, living in London, bought an attractive house in St. John's Wood, London, where they established a literary and theatrical salon. There Alice oversaw the raising of the couple's two sons, Lawrence and Robert, and their daughter, named Chita Florence Ormond ("Ormond" for short), while Jamie spent much of his time abroad, brokering play productions in Paris, New York and other cities.

Like Alice, Jamie harbored dreams of personal literary accomplishment; and in 1927 he published a novel entitled *Face Value*, which for a brief time became that much-prized thing by publishers, a putatively "scandalous" novel that gets Talked About. The story of a gentle orphan boy named Serge, the son an emigre Russian prostitute, who grows up in a Parisian "disorderly house," as reviews often blushingly put it, *Face Value* divided critics, but ended up on American bestseller lists. The success of his first novel led to the author being invited out to Hollywood to work as a scriptwriter, and his name appears on credits to a trio of films in 1927-28, including *French Dressing*, a "gay" divorce comedy set among sexually scatterbrained Americans in Paris. One wonders whether in Hollywood Jamie ever came across future crime writer Cornell Woolrich, who was scripting there too at the time.

Alice remained in England with the children, enjoying her own literary splash with her debut thriller *Juggernaut*, which concerned the murderous machinations of an inexorably ruthless French Riviera society doctor, opposed by a valiant young nurse. The novel racked up rave reviews and sales in the UK and US, in the latter country spurred on by its nationwide newspaper serialization, which promised readers

> . . . the open door to adventure! *Juggernaut* by Alice Campbell will sweep you out of the humdrum of everyday life into the gay, swift-moving Arabian-nights existence of the Riviera!

London's *Daily Mail* declared that the irresistible *Juggernaut* "should rank among the 'best sellers' of the year"; and, sure enough, *Juggernaut*'s English publisher, Hodder & Stoughton, boasted, several months after the novel's English publication in July 1928, that they already had run through six printings in an attempt to satisfy customer demand. In 1936 *Juggernaut* was adapted in England as a film vehicle for horror great Boris Karloff, making it the only Alice Campbell novel filmed to date. The film was remade in England under the title *The Temptress* in 1949.

*Water Weed* (1929) and *Spiderweb* (1930) (*Murder in Paris* in the US), the immediate successors, held up well to their predecessor's performance. Alice chose this moment to return for a fortnight to Atlanta, ostensibly to visit her sister, but doubtlessly in part to parade through her hometown as a conquering, albeit commercial, literary hero. And who was there to welcome Alice in the pages of the *Constitution* but Bessie S. Stafford, who pronounced Alice's hair still looked like spun gold while her eyes remarkably had turned an even deeper shade of blue. To Miss Bessie, Alice imparted enchanting tales of salon chats with such personages as George Bernard Shaw, Lady Asquith, H. G. Wells and (his lover) Rebecca West, the latter of whom a simpatico Alice met and conversed with frequently. Admitting that her political sympathies in England "inclined toward the conservatives," Alice yet urged "the absolute necessity of having two strong parties." English women, she had been pleased to see, evinced more informed interest in politics than their American sisters.

Alice, Miss Bessie declared, diligently devoted every afternoon to her writing, shutting her study door behind her "as a sign that she is not to be interrupted." This commitment to her craft enabled Alice to produce an additional sixteen crime novels between 1932 and 1950, beginning with *The Click of the Gate* and ending with *The Corpse Had Red Hair*.

Altogether nearly half of Alice's crime novels were standalones, in contravention of convention at this time, when series sleuths were so popular. In *The Click of the Gate* the author introduced one of her main recurring characters, intrepid Paris journalist Tommy Rostetter, who appears in three additional novels: *Desire to Kill* (1934), *Flying Blind* (1938) and *The Bloodstained Toy* (1948). In the two latter novels, Tommy appears with Alice's other major recurring character, dauntless Inspector Headcorn of Scotland Yard, who also pursues murderers and other malefactors in *Death Framed in Silver* (1937), *They Hunted a Fox* (1940), *No Murder of Mine* (1941) and *The Cockroach Sings* (1946) (*With Bated Breath* in the US).

Additional recurring characters in Alice's books are Geoffrey Macadam and Catherine West, who appear in *Spiderweb* and *No Light Came On* (1942), and Colin Ladbrooke, who appears in *Death Framed in Silver*, *A Door Closed Softly* (1939) and *They Hunted a Fox*. In the latter two books Colin with his romantic interest Alison Young and in the first and third book with Inspector Headcorn, who also appears, as mentioned, in *Flying Blind* and *The Bloodstained Toy* with Tommy Rosstetter, making Headcorn the connecting link in this universe of sleuths, although the inspector does not appear with Geoffrey Macadam and Catherine West. It is all a rather complicated state of criminal affairs; and this lack of a consistent and enduring central sleuth character in Alice's crime fiction may help explain why her work faded in the Fifties, after the author retired from writing.

Be that as it may, Alice Campbell is a figure of significance in the history of crime fiction. In a 1946 review of *The Cockroach Sings* in the London *Observer*, crime fiction critic Maurice Richardson asserted that "[s]he belongs to the atmospheric school, of which one of the outstanding exponents was the late Ethel Lina White," the author of *The Wheel Spins* (1936), famously filmed in 1938, under the title *The Lady Vanishes*, by director Alfred Hitchcock. This "atmospheric school," as Richardson termed it, had more students in the demonstrative United States than in the decorous United Kingdom, to be sure, the United States being the home of such hugely popular suspense writers as Mary Roberts Rinehart and Mignon Eberhart, to name but a couple of the most prominent examples.

Like the novels of the American Eber-Rinehart school and English authors Ethel Lina White and Marie Belloc Lowndes, the latter the author of the acknowledged landmark 1911 thriller *The Lodger*, Alice Campbell's books are not pure puzzle detective tales, but rather broader mysteries which put a premium on the storytelling imperatives of atmosphere and suspense. "She could not be unexciting if she tried," raved the *Times Literary Supplement* of Alice, stressing the author's remoteness from the so-called "Humdrum" school of detective fiction headed by British authors Freeman Wills Crofts, John Street and J. J. Connington. However, as Maurice Richardson, a great fan of Alice's crime writing, put it, "she generally binds her homework together with a reasonable plot," so the "Humdrum" fans out there need not be put off by what American detective novelist S. S. Van Dine, creator of Philo Vance, dogmatically dismissed as "literary dallying." In her novels Alice Campbell offered people bone-rattling good reads, which explains their popularity in the past and their revival today. Lines from a review of her 1941 crime novel *No Murder of Mine* by "H.V.A." in the *Hartford Courant* suggests the general nature of her work's appeal: "The excitement and mystery of this Class A shocker start on page 1 and continue right to the end of the book. You won't put it down, once you've begun it. And if you like romance mixed with your thrills, you'll find it here."

The protagonist of *No Murder of Mine* is Rowan Wilde, "an attractive young American girl studying in England." Frequently in her books Alice, like the great Anglo-American author Henry James, pits ingenuous but goodhearted Americans, male or female, up against dangerously sophisticated Europeans, drawing on autobiographical details from her and Jamie's own lives. Many of her crime novels, which often are lengthier than the norm for the period, recall, in terms of their length and content, the Victorian sensation novel, which seemingly had been in its dying throes when the author was a precocious child; yet, in their emphasis on morbid psychology and their sexual frankness, they also anticipate the modern crime novel. One can discern this tendency most dramatically, perhaps, in the engrossing *Water Weed*, concerning a sexual affair between a middle-aged Englishwoman and a young American man that has dreadful consequences, and *Desire to Kill*, about murder among a clique of decadent bohemians in Paris. In both of these mysteries the exploration of aberrant sexuality is striking. Indeed, in its depiction of sexual psychosis *Water Weed* bears rather more resemblance to, say, the crime novels of Patricia Highsmith than it does to the cozy mysteries of Patricia Wentworth. One might well term it Alice Campbell's *Deep Water*.

In this context it should be noted that in 1935 Alice Campbell authored a sexual problem play, *Two Share a Dwelling*, which the *New York*

*Times* described as a "grim, vivid, psychological treatment of dual personality." Although it ran for only twenty-two performances during October 8-26 at the West End's celebrated St. James' Theatre, the play had done well on its provincial tour and it received a standing ovation from the audience on opening night at the West End, primarily on account of the compelling performance of the half-Jewish German stage actress Grete Mosheim, who had fled Germany two years earlier and was making her English stage debut in the play's lead role of a schizophrenic, sexually compulsive woman. Mosheim was described as young and "blondely beautiful," bringing to mind the author herself.

Unfortunately priggish London critics were put off by the play's morbid sexual subject, which put Alice in an impossible position. One reviewer scathingly observed that "Miss Alice Campbell . . . has chosen to give her audience a study in pathology as a pleasant method of spending the evening. . . . one leaves the theatre rather wishing that playwrights would leave medical books on their shelves." Another sniffed that "it is to be hoped that the fashion of plumbing the depths of Freudian theory for dramatic fare will not spread. It is so much more easy to be interested in the doings of the sane." The play died a quick death in London and its author went back, for another fifteen years, to "plumbing the depths" in her crime fiction.

What impelled Alice Campbell, like her husband, to avidly explore human sexuality in her work? Doubtless their writing reflected the temper of modern times, but it also likely was driven by personal imperatives. The child of an unhappy marriage who at a young age had been deprived of a father figure, Alice appears to have wanted to use her crime fiction to explore the human devastation wrought by disordered lives. Sadly, evidence suggests that discord had entered the lives of Alice and Jamie by the 1930s, as they reached middle age and their children entered adulthood. In 1939, as the Second World War loomed, Alice was residing in rural southwestern England with her daughter Ormond at a cottage—the inspiration for her murder setting in *No Murder of Mine*, one guesses—near the bucolic town of Beaminster, Dorset, known for its medieval Anglican church and its charming reference in a poem by English dialect poet William Barnes:

> Sweet Be'mi'ster, that bist a-bound
> By green and woody hills all round,
> Wi'hedges, reachen up between
> A thousand vields o' zummer green.

Alice's elder son Lawrence was living, unemployed, in New York City at this time and he would enlist in the US Army when the country entered the war a couple of years later, serving as a master sergeant throughout the conflict. In December 1939, twenty-three-year-old Ormond, who seems to have herself preferred going by the name Chita, wed the prominent antiques dealer, interior decorator, home restorer and racehorse owner Ernest Thornton-Smith, who at the age of fifty-eight was fully thirty-five years older than she. Antiques would play a crucial role in Alice's 1944 wartime crime novel *Travelling Butcher*, which blogger Kate Jackson at *Cross Examining Crime* deemed "a thrilling read." The author's most comprehensive wartime novel, however, was the highly-praised *Ringed with Fire* (1943). Native Englishman S. Morgan-Powell, the dean of Canadian drama critics, in the *Montreal Star* pronounced *Ringed with Fire* one of the "best spy stories the war has produced," adding, in one of Alice's best notices:

> "Ringed with Fire" begins with mystery and exudes mystery from every chapter. Its clues are most ingeniously developed, and keep the reader guessing in all directions. For once there is a mystery which will, I think, mislead the most adroit and experienced of amateur sleuths. Some time ago there used to be a practice of sealing up the final section of mystery stores with the object of stirring up curiosity and developing the detective instinct among readers. If you sealed up the last forty-two pages of "Ringed with Fire" and then offered a prize of $250 to the person who guessed the mystery correctly, I think that money would be as safe as if you put it in victory bonds.

A few years later, on the back of the dust jacket to the American edition of Alice's *The Cockroach Sings* (1946), which Random House, her new American publisher, less queasily titled *With Bated Breath*, readers learned a little about what the author had been up to during the late war and its recent aftermath: "I got used to oil lamps. . . . and also to riding nine miles in a crowded bus once a week to do the shopping—if there was anything to buy. We thought it rather a lark then, but as a matter of fact we are still suffering from all sorts of shortages and restrictions." Jamie Campbell, on the other hand, spent his war years in Santa Barbara, California. It is unclear whether he and Alice ever lived together again.

Alice remained domiciled for the rest of her life in Dorset, although she returned to London in 1946, when she was inducted into the Detection Club. A number of her novels from this period, all of which were published in England by the Collins Crime Club, more resemble, in tone and form, classic detective fiction, such as *They Hunted a Fox* (1940). This event may have been a moment of triumph for the author, but it was also something of a last hurrah. After 1946 she published only three more crime novels, including the entertaining Tommy Rostetter-Inspector Headcorn mashup *The Bloodstained Toy*, before retiring in 1950. She lived out the remaining five years of her life quietly at her home in the coastal city of Bridport, Dorset, expiring "suddenly" on November 27, 1955, two days before her sixty-eighth birthday. Her brief death notice in the *Daily Telegraph* refers to her only as the "very dear mother of Lawrence, Chita and Robert."

Jamie Campbell had died in 1954 aged sixty-five. Earlier in the year his play *The Praying Mantis*, billed as a "naughty comedy by James Lawrence Campbell," scored hits at the Q Theatre in London and at the Dolphin Theatre in Brighton. (A very young Joan Collins played the eponymous man-eating leading role at the latter venue.) In spite of this, Jamie near the end of the year checked into a hotel in Cannes and fatally imbibed poison. The American consulate sent the report on Jamie's death to Chita in Maida Vale, London, and to Jamie's brother Colonel George Campbell in Washington, D. C., though not to Alice. This was far from the Riviera romance that the publishers of *Juggernaut* had long ago promised. Perhaps the "humdrum of everyday life" had been too much with him.

Alice Campbell own work fell into obscurity after her death, with not one of her novels being reprinted in English for more than seven decades. Happily the ongoing revival of vintage English and American mystery fiction from the twentieth century is rectifying such cases of criminal neglect. It may well be true that it "is impossible not to be thrilled by Edgar Wallace," as the great thriller writer's publishers pronounced, but let us not forget that, as Maurice Richardson put it: "We can always do with Mrs. Alice Campbell." Mystery fans will now have nineteen of them from which to choose—a veritable embarrassment of felonious riches, all from the hand of the other AC.

Curtis Evans

# CHAPTER ONE

It was the change in Miss Bundy herself which first excited Neil's curiosity, making him think something was amiss. Actually her home, Stoke Paulton, looked slightly different from his recollection of it, but that was because the stone lodge, for a time untenanted, now showed signs of habitation. In fact, people were just moving in.

From the greengrocer's cart blocking the gateway two corded boxes were being removed, together with household effects and, oddly enough, a big, professional-looking camera. A man in a badly fitting suit was tugging at the latter, while from the cottage steps a woman, his wife no doubt, offered suggestions. She it was who perceived the visitor's attempts to steer his two-seater round the obstruction, and beamed reassuringly.

"'Ere, Alf," she called in a flat Cockney voice. "You and 'Arry pull round a bit. Can't you see there's a gentleman wants to pass?"

Neil nodded thanks, whereat she smiled still more radiantly, and chirped, "Don't mention it." She was small, bustling and dreadfully bright, with a ruddy, rasped complexion and treacle-coloured hair braided in "earphones." Her artificial-silk jumper was sickly mauve in hue, and she wore black, barred shoes with heather-mixture stockings.

"Beg pardon, sir," apologised the toiler addressed as Alf. "I never noticed you was there. Now, sir—can you manage?"

Standing civilly aside he favoured Neil with a mildly vacant stare. He was an insignificant fellow, with a prim little waxed moustache, and colouring almost identical with the woman's. In his case the treacly hair was glued to his forehead in a low, sweeping curve, beneath which trickled rivulets of sweat. His manner was pleasant and by no means servile.

Who were these people? They had the air of petty shopkeepers—London sparrows, by the look of them, with some place like Brixton or Peckham Rye their habitat. Neil thought it odd to find such a couple taking possession of the lodge, for they were hardly the type one would expect Caroline Bundy to employ. Moreover, they seemed very curious about him, judging from the penetrating gaze which followed his progress along the drive. Both were still staring after him round-eyed when the rhododendron hedge shut them from view.

Primroses clustered in the shelter of the dark-green tunnel, daffodils on the lawn beyond tossed wildly in a boisterous gale. Here were the monkey-puzzle trees flanking the half-acre of shaven turf, and there between them the well-remembered house, early Georgian, spacious, with the secure dignity of a generous epoch. The westering sun warmed its rosy brick walls, glittered on every square-paned window. Wide, shallow steps led up to an impressive door.

"The owner of all this can afford to be independent," Neil inwardly remarked, with a connotation of the fact that the eminent Theodore, Miss Bundy's father, had been a man of substance.

A tight-lipped major-domo admitted him. It was the same butler he had seen six months ago when the mistress of the place had proved so tiresome about coming to a decision. However, if he recognised Neil he showed no sign of it.

"I fancy Miss Bundy's in the garden, sir," he announced guardedly. "In here, sir, if you please. I'll have a look round."

Neil hoped there would be no further difficulties. At all events, the letter he had picked up in Marseilles expressed a desire to resume negotiations at once. At a loose end now he would be glad to settle on a programme.

What a stubborn creature she was! His publishers had warned him what to expect. For ten years she had withstood every biographer's appeal, partly from absurd jealousy of her father's reputation, more, perhaps, because she enjoyed dominating the situation. One could not stir a step without her sanction, though, for she controlled all the data connected with the dead scientist's work.

Yes, she was dull-witted and exasperating. A good sort, all the same, even-tempered and dependable—rather like one of those calm, reliable plough-horses which bear the burden of the day without turning a hair. Very forcibly he recalled both her stodginess and her physical vigour, facts to be emphasised in order to appreciate his next impression.

The drawing-room he entered was serene with ivory panelling, glazed chintz and furniture of the Queen Anne reign. A log fire crackled on the hearth overhung by a Grinling Gibbons mantelpiece, and farther along glass doors framed a view of the garden. Through these, presently, he perceived a stocky, tweed-clad figure ambling towards him, eyes shaded by a battered felt hat, head bent with an air of intense preoccupation. It was Miss Bundy, but as she drew near he noticed with a shock how greatly she had aged and altered. Her frame was shrunken, withered; her lips moved as she muttered to herself. Why, he could hardly believe this was the same woman he had met only last autumn!

She came into the room unseeingly, and when she did finally look up at him it was without recognition. He was forced to speak first, to recall her to herself.

"How do you do, Miss Bundy? You see I've kept my appointment."

She gave a nervous start, blinked at him suspiciously with her small, near-sighted eyes, and woke to a realisation of who he was.

"Eh? Oh! It's Mr.—Mr. Starkey, of course," she muttered in a confused fashion. "Yes, yes, that's right. I wanted to see you."

She drew off a stained gardening-glove to shake hands in a perfunctory manner. About all her movements there was a sort of clumsiness, never more noticeable than now. She seemed not to know what to do with her guest now he was here, and pushing back her hat made an obvious effort to muster her faculties. As the light fell full on her face he could hardly repress an exclamation at the alarming alteration in her.

"Not feeling ill, I hope?" he ventured anxiously. "Perhaps you'd rather put off our interview till another day?"

"Ill?" She caught him up with disconcerting sharpness. "Nonsense—certainly not! I've been having some bad nights lately—nerves, I think, over—over certain matters, but that's nothing."

Her trembling hands belied her assurance, as did the sudden profuse perspiration which had broken out all over her wrinkled skin. Her clothes bagged on her; she must have lost quite two stone. Her colour was blotched, and gone was all the weather-beaten hardiness which had helped to mitigate her exceedingly plain looks. In short, she had become a broken old woman—a trying and querulous one, too, Neil began to believe, though perhaps he was wrong.

She sat down awkwardly, feet apart, and drummed with meditative fingers on a large alligator-skin handbag she had with her. Her mind was evidently engrossed in other concerns, but after a moment's silence she assembled her thoughts.

"It seems unusual," she began jerkily, "to choose an American to write my father's life, when there are so many Englishmen clamouring to do it. But I've been going through the reviews of your previous books, and it strikes me you are less prejudiced, more open to new ideas, than most of our literary people. Accuracy is indispensable, of course, but what is just as important is sympathetic insight into—into character. Be that as it may, I've decided not to postpone this biography any longer. I want to see the work completed under my eye, and if I keep delaying it—that is to say—" She floundered, and grew vague.

She was concerned about her condition, then. She was breaking up, and knew it. That was why she had hit on him, the last person to approach her on the subject. He had little belief in her critical discrimination.

Aloud he answered: "You are right about its being the very moment to bring out a life of Theodore Bundy. There's a new valuation of his achievements on foot. Our later men look on him as much ahead of his time."

Her dull eyes lit with a transfiguring gleam.

"Mr. Starkey," she said solemnly, "my father had great vision. Even you do not know how great. He was a seer. A man of science, but also a mystic. Ah, that astonishes you, doesn't it? I thought it would."

Neil was astonished. Bundy a mystic? None of his writings gave any indication of it.

"Few people recognise the real Bundy," she continued with triumph. "That is why I want to oversee certain portions of this book and supply you with facts known only to myself. We won't speak of that now, though. When the time comes, I will inform you. The great thing is to start immediately, do your preparation, and—but what are your present arrangements? Are you quite ready to begin?"

Puzzled by her eagerness as well as her manner of having some surprise up her sleeve, he declared himself at her command. He was free, and had put up the night before at a Glastonbury hotel.

"Glastonbury?" She shook her head. "That's three miles away. No, no, I propose you come and stay here, in my house. In that way you can spend long hours in my father's study, with all your material, letters, diary, notes and so on, where you can live with them, so to speak. It's better. I trust you will see that."

"Really, Miss Bundy, that is extremely kind of you. Quite certain I shan't be in your way?"

"Not at all. I should never suggest it if—if—What is it, Crabbe?" She broke off peevishly to the butler, who had just approached. "Why must you come on me suddenly like that? You know how I hate people creeping up behind me!"

"It's the new bailiff, miss," explained the man imperturbably. "Might he have a word with you outside?"

"The—the bailiff? Oh, certainly! I'll come at once."

She sprang up with quite amazing alacrity, her colour flared up, and her breath came quickly as she left the room in flurried haste. Neil looked after her, wondering curiously what had transformed the placid, phlegmatic woman of a few months ago into this excitable creature who started at the least sound and lost her temper over trifles. Greatly mystified, he finally decided she must be suffering from some unrecognised complaint.

Anyhow, she was very hospitable to invite him here. Not only would he be spared endless journeyings back and forth, but he welcomed the prospect of good food and a comfortable bed after last night's sample of what Glastonbury had to offer. Stoke Paulton, besides, was only a mile distant from two friends he hoped to see often—Giles Gisborne, vicar of the parish, and Rachel Gisborne, his sister. Yes, he would accept the invitation, and chance the old lady at close quarters. He would probably not need to see too much of her.

There was a longish wait. He examined a first edition of de Quincey on the table, strolled about, and picked up a fine piece of Irish silver to study its hallmark. It was while he was holding this in his hand and squinting at the tiny characters that he received his second shock.

A violent clamour broke out. Deep-throated barking of dogs and the bursting open of the glass doors caused him to jump guiltily as, with the force of a volcanic explosion a trio composed of a tall girl and a pair of gigantic Alsatians hurtled in, crashed down upon him. A voice cried out in stifled accents, "*You!* Oh, why did you come here? I warned you not to—oh!"

The beginning was a protest full of dismay, the last syllable a gasp of utter confusion. The speaker, seeing him face to face, fell back as though icy water had been dashed over her, staring at him transfixed. For an instant her hazel eyes were as fiercely accusing as those of the dogs, then a tide of crimson washed over her to the roots of her back-blown hair. She seemed positively seared by mortification.

"Sorry," she muttered under her breath, "you must think me mad. The fact is I took you for some one else . . . not that it matters. Quiet, Bistre! Wolf, be still, you fool!" Her strong hands gripped the spiked collars to cover her confusion, but all the time she was searching his face with the same uncompromising fixity. The pupils of her eyes had now narrowed to pin-points. "But I don't understand," she said with odd abruptness. "That two-seater outside—did you come in it?"

"I did," he answered, smiling. "Is there anything wrong about it?"

Clearly there was, for she remained unplaced.

"Who are you, then?" she demanded brusquely. "What are you doing in this house?"

## CHAPTER TWO

TAKEN aback though he was, Neil managed an even reply.

"My name is Starkey. I've come to see Miss Bundy on business."

Her rigidity snapped. She clicked her tongue in annoyed comprehension.

"How stupid of me! Of course, you're the American. But all the same I don't see—"

What baffled her remained unexplained, but if Neil had hoped she would laugh over the situation he was doomed to disappointment. All she did was to edge away, remarking ungraciously, "Then I'd better tell Miss Bundy you're here. She probably doesn't know."

"Oh, yes, she does," returned Neil, now slightly ironical. "I've seen her, thanks. She was called away for a moment, that's all."

"Oh!" She bit her lip, shook back her hair, and released the dogs, who bounded like springs uncurled into the open air. "In that case, I've made another blunder."

"A very natural one. Don't let it distress you."

She stood poised in the doorway, with the wind plastering her silk frock against her lithe contours. The thin fabric, coloured like a ripe corn-field and scattered over with black and scarlet spots, had to his eyes a savage suggestion, seemed in a way part of her, like an animal's skin. A human wolf-dog, he thought, with a flush of fantasy. Yes, there were three Alsatians who stormed in just now, all ready to attack—and she's the fiercest of the lot. . . .

She was not English, he decided. She couldn't possibly belong to this island, even though she spoke with no accent. He had seen features like hers in Hungary and the Balkans—wide cheekbones, almond-shaped eyes, the bridge of the nose ever so little flattened, mouth straight and sullen. Her hair, too—bleached and crinkled as though a hot sun had scorched it, and that warm skin, lightly freckled and tanned to almost the same shade. . . . She ought to be astride a half-wild horse, sweeping across blistered plains, with powdery dust clinging to that tawny mane of hers as it streamed in the wind. . . .

Unmannered, brutally direct—and yet with a touch of sophistication about her which piqued him. What was it? Merely that her nails were manicured, that her frock, with its rippling kerchief, was cut after a recent Parisian mode, or something subtle, deep-seated, which roused the male in him and made him say to himself, "Look here, this is the sort of girl you've got to watch out for." Young enough, too—not more than two-and-twenty at most—but for all that a look of self-reliance, the look that comes to those who have lived through a great deal. Altogether she stirred his curiosity, made him long to turn the sword of her own question against her and demand who she was, and what she was doing in this house.

The thread of his reflections was broken by her voice.

"Here's Miss Bundy back again," she murmured without turning, and swung off into the sunshine.

His hostess, on her return, seemed too flustered to concentrate, reminding him of a distracted hen crossing a road amid motor traffic. The arrival of the tea-tray was greeted with relief, and at once she began peering about petulantly, questing something or some one on whom she depended.

"Natasha!" she murmured fretfully. "Crabbe, find Miss Andreyev and tell her tea is waiting."

Natasha Andreyev! Appropriate as the name sounded, it increased his bewilderment. He had heard last autumn some mention of a secretary, but none had appeared, nor did the young person here a moment ago suggest any such prosaic appendage. She a secretary! Why, likely as not she would pick up the typewriter and hurl it at her employer's head! Not that he would altogether blame her, if Miss Bundy were often as wool-gathering and tiresome as now.

As though notified by telepathy, the girl strolled in again, without so much as the flicker of an eyelash in his direction. He rose, expecting to be introduced, but the old lady merely said, "Ah, there you are, Natasha. Will you pour out, please?" and subsided into her chair, gasping with the same unaccountable breathlessness he had previously noticed. No word of elucidation? None—but his chagrin gave place to covert amusement as he observed the grim efficiency of the unknown's movements, the tanned fingers clutching the silver teapot as though it were a scimitar. From downcast eyes and set mouth he deduced smouldering wrath against himself for both causing and witnessing her humiliation. Possibly she dreaded his mentioning the occurrence. If so, she could set her fears at rest.

Meanwhile, his hostess showed a ravenous appetite quite at variance with her shattered looks. As the hot tea took effect a cloud appeared to lift from her brain, and she began again eagerly to speak of the projected biography.

"I'm glad you are willing to work here under my supervision," she said, blinking at him keenly through scanty lashes. "Natasha, another cup, please. . . . Yes, it will be useful. You see, later on I hope to—to offer you an important contribution. Mind, I don't promise—I only say I may. But if I do, it will be something vastly illuminating, calculated to settle a great many disputes and—and add immensely to my father's fame. No, don't press me to be explicit. Wait. Be patient. One day you shall hear everything."

Off again on that mysterious tack! He let her ramble on, utterly at a loss to comprehend her veiled allusions. Suddenly he intercepted a scathing glance directed at the speaker from the girl's stern eyes—a look so full of scorn and denunciation that he grew positively uncomfortable. The very atmosphere seemed charged with hostility, as though he had stepped into the centre of a brewing storm. What was it all about? A moment ago the third member of the party had held herself indifferently aloof. Now, all at once she was watchful, contemptuous, and, unless he were grossly misled, apprehensive—but apprehensive of what?

Before long, however, he was brought down to practical matters.

"If you wish to move here to-morrow morning," said Miss Bundy briskly, "you'll find your room ready and, I hope, comfortable. That's settled, isn't it? And now, if you've finished your tea, suppose I show you where you are to work?"

Out of the corner of his eyes he saw the girl stiffen and stare at him in unfriendly fashion. Annoyed over his coming to stay, no doubt, though he could not conceive why. As he followed his guide out he felt her scrutinising them both, questioning, intent.

At the back of the house was a little cloak-room lobby, out of which led several exits. The first on the left, a baize-covered door, his guide swung back to disclose a second door, just beyond. She took a bunch of keys from her coat pocket, inserted the largest in the lock, and then did an odd thing. She peered suspiciously in every direction to make sure of not being overheard, switched on an interior light, and pausing on the threshold between the double doors addressed him in a guarded whisper.

"Mr. Starkey—after to-day I am going to entrust these keys to your care, and I particularly want you to return them to me personally each evening when you leave off. No one, you see, is allowed in this study without my permission. I don't want any one—any one, mind—prowling about amongst my father's papers, for which reason, if you have occasion to leave the room during working hours, even for a few minutes, can I depend on you to lock this door and take the keys with you?"

He promised, half-amused by her absurd cautiousness, and half-inclined to regard her waxing peculiarities with distrust. His former conclusions concerning her had now gone by the board, and he had begun to wonder if she were not a little unbalanced. Did that girl think so, too, and was that why she had given the two of them that penetrating look?

A strong, green-shaded lamp shone down on a mahogany table and a Chippendale arm-chair, but beyond its circle of radiance spread semi-dusk. Brown velours curtains hung from the windows, one of which gave on the back garden, the other on a rose-arbour. Two walls were occupied by glazed book-shelves reaching to the ceiling, a third was broken by a fireplace, while every intervening space was filled by filing-cabinets and cases containing specimens.

Over the mantel was a full-length portrait of the great man himself—bull-necked, aggressive, with fierce hazel eyes, and whiskers worn in the fashion of the 'eighties. So life-like, so compelling was it that Neil had the unpleasant sensation of being spied on by the late owner in person—more, that Bundy was still master here, brooking no interference, dictating commands as he had done for three-quarters of a century.

"Painted by Sir Aubrey Freyer," murmured the daughter in an awed undertone, "and presented to us by my father's old friends at Balliol. An excellent likeness."

It crossed his mind that she shared his feeling, and shrank a little from those accusing eyes. He glanced at her with a flash of insight. He had heard tales of the scientist's explosive temper, of quarrels with colleagues, and the disposition to crush those about him. Probably the devoted Caroline had been the chief victim, living here alone with the tyrant for so many years. Certainly there were things about her to suggest a thwarted personality tardily asserting itself.

"You were in close touch with his research, weren't you?" he asked tentatively. "Did you yourself have a scientific education?"

She blinked at him, surprised and, he thought, flattered.

"I? Oh, no! I was not considered clever enough for that. I was his secretary, though, from my nineteenth birthday. He trained me. I think I may claim to have been at least methodical, and in small ways helpful to him. If ever I achieve renown on my own account," she added hesitatingly, "it will still be only because I have carried to their conclusion theories he initiated. Some slight praise might be due me, but he would be the last to grudge me that."

Once again that fanatical gleam in her eyes! It told of a secret jealously guarded, yet so proud a possession that she must needs drop hints of it now and again. Was she indeed struggling forward with some line of work begun by Bundy? But no, such a notion was manifestly absurd. Either she had come on a hitherto unknown manuscript which she was trying to put in order—that was distinctly possible—or else what he had thought just now was true, that she was subject to some delusion, product of her physical condition. She could be business-like enough when it came to concrete details, as she showed by her next remark.

"You will see," she said, "that each of these bookcases and cabinets has its separate key. Here they all are"—she dangled the bunch before him—"and let me repeat, I rely on you to leave everything locked up at the end of the day. The room is at your disposal at any time, except from six o'clock onward, but after that I shall want it for myself. That's quite understood, I hope?"

It was six o'clock now, as it happened. The words were hardly out of her mouth when the bronze clock on the mantel struck the hour. Miss Bundy jumped, grew fidgety, and seemed to be listening for something. He realised she was anxious to get rid of him.

"I must not trespass on you any longer," he declared, moving towards the door and standing aside for her to go first. "As a matter of fact, I promised to go on from here to some friends of yours in the village—Giles Gisborne, you know, and his sister, whom I met in my own country last year. You remember I spoke of them."

She stopped stock-still. Her manner froze.

"Giles Gisborne! Indeed! No, I was not aware that you knew him. It's certainly the first I've heard of it."

She had forgotten, that was all. He was sure he had mentioned the vicar, since it was that person who, in the beginning, had put him on to the biography. Be that as it might, she had grown very red and was tugging at the hairs on her chin in marked displeasure. Some disturbance here, he knew not what, but the incident to follow was even more peculiar.

A bell pealed. His companion gave a violent start, trembled, and broke into fresh perspiration. Bundling him out, she dismissed him with an abrupt, "To-morrow, then. If you will excuse me, I have an important appointment," and left him in the hall, though he realised she had retreated only a few paces and was hovering in the background with expectant agitation. The butler handed him his coat and hat, afterwards passing on to open the front door.

At this juncture a voice, coldly disdainful, spoke to him from behind, and turning he found the Russian girl holding out the gloves he must have deposited in the drawing-room. Hardly had he thanked her when his attention was drawn to Crabbe, just delivering a measured announcement to his mistress.

"Mr. and Mrs. Tilbury, miss. Shall I ask them to wait or am I to show them directly into the study?"

The old lady's reply came with stiff dignity.

"I am quite ready for them, Crabbe—and mind"—in a low whisper—"no interruptions whatever. Not on any account are we to be disturbed till I ring."

A business conference, it seemed—but why did the girl's narrow eyes, involuntarily trapped by his, show again that mixture of angry scorn and humiliation? Why, for that matter, did their owner bolt from him without a word of leave-taking, as though she resented his knowledge of her annoyance? A second later he guessed the reason, or at least a portion of it.

Brushing past the two visitors, now divesting themselves of their wraps, he glanced at them with slight curiosity, confident of their being either county grandees or distinguished members of the scholastic calling, an impression derived from Miss Bundy's behaviour. Imagine his astonishment when he beheld a nondescript couple whose scrubbed faces and wetly-brushed hair he at once recognised.

In short, Mr. and Mrs. Tilbury were none other than the pair of incredibly vulgar Cockneys he had seen at the lodge!

## CHAPTER THREE

AMAZEMENT is too mild a word to convey Neil's reaction. He was utterly bowled over by the unexpected appearance of the two vapid little guttersnipes so incongruous in their surroundings, so exactly like lower-class tradespeople accidentally strayed into the wrong entrance. Ill at ease, yet complacent, the man reeking of foul hair oil, the woman perkily bright-eyed, her greasy braids coiled loathsomely round her ears—why, beside them, Crabbe, the butler, had the air of a distinguished diplomat!

Of course there was nothing peculiar in their having an appointment with Miss Bundy. Dozens of reasons could account for that. No, it was purely the old lady's manner which made the thing seem queer, her excited anticipation and badly-hidden defiance, as though she scented criticism and repelled it—and then, too, there was the girl's attitude, plainly revealing passionate disavowal of all responsibility. Something decidedly odd was going on at Stoke Paulton, something which perhaps went far to explain the changes he had noticed and felt.

His rather shabby two-seater turned his reflections into another channel. Why had the young woman addressed as Natasha fired that brusque question about the proprietorship of the car? The obvious answer was that she had recognised it as one familiar to her, the property of a friend, no doubt. Well, quite likely it had belonged to some one she knew, for as it happened he had purchased it only yesterday in Bath, second-hand, meaning to use it while he was in England and then get rid of it. Bath, of course, was no distance at all from this place. He wished now he had asked the garage man who the owner was. He had a grudge against him, anyhow, every time he started the wretched thing up. The engine was as tiresome as a balking mule. He had seen mules behave just like this along the rutted by-roads of Virginia, where he came from, stopping stubbornly and refusing to stir. He had thought of them often since the day before, and of the old man who had built a fire under his animal with the sole result of burning up the wagon.

Never mind, his immediate future was mapped out for him, and in a region he had always wanted to know. He spent the hour at his disposal trundling gently through the stone-bordered lanes, delighting in the unpeopled desolation and the beauty of the green hills, rolling smoothly one upon the other like waves of the sea. Yes, Somerset was a romantic, stimulating country, with something eerie about it in this soft half-light. He felt ready to believe all the legends grouped about its soil— King Arthur and his knights, Joseph of Arimathea and the blossoming staff, even the apocryphal story of the hidden Grail itself. Breathing in the cool, damp air with its scent of approaching spring, he responded gladly to his surroundings, and gave himself up to joyous contentment.

Neil Starkey was a born nomad. Since wresting a brace of degrees from Princeton University he had been in many quarters of the globe, contriving to do his literary work wherever, so to speak, he hung his hat. Conspicuous success in biographies, however, threatened to curtail his liberty, for writing people's lives is a stick-in-the-mud job. In the present instance, however, it was not so bad. He knew the South Sea Islands and Morocco, but the West of England was new territory, a fact which had possibly influenced him in his selection of Theodore Bundy as a suitable subject. Besides, he would make money out of the old man, his particular handling of this sort of thing being, luckily, much in vogue. His publishers had contracted to give him a thumping advance, on the strength of which he could set off, care-free, wherever he liked.

Stars pierced the dusk when he dipped into the hollow where nestled the village of Bishop's Paulton. Crossing a tiny market-place he passed between a lopsided inn and a Norman church to halt before a Tudor cottage with a thatched lych gate in front. This was the vicarage, and here was the vicar himself, throwing open the door and extending a large-knuckled hand in welcome.

"Ah, Starkey! Back from the sea and home from the hills? What about gathering a little moss in our midst by way of variety?"

"Just my intention. Miss Bundy has given in."

"Has she, by Jove! That's amazingly sensible of her."

Giles Gisborne's height towered above Neil's own six feet. Rough hair bristled on his arrogant head, grizzled brows overhung his irascible eyes, and his loose stride was nervously buoyant. He did not suggest the ecclesiastic, and indeed was rather more concerned over archaeology than religion.

"Not lecturing, I see," remarked Neil, as he was forcibly stripped of his Burberry.

"No, worse luck. Curate down with mumps. He would be, drat him! Rachel!"—in a thundering voice—"come and see the prodigal, burnt black as a Moor and altogether too dangerously fit to loose on the local hen-coops. How's that for a colour?"

A handsome woman of fifty answered the summons and surveyed the guest with penetrating dark eyes. She was dressed in warm crimson, with a band of old garnets round her smooth olive throat. Her straight lips twitched into an amused smile.

"It won't come off, will it?" she inquired, looking at Neil's bronzed complexion with approval. "Because I expect you'll be wanting to wash. Giles, show him the bathroom, and mind you give him a clean towel."

Neil felt instantly one of them. He laughed and followed his host, who clattered up the narrow stairs, talking incessantly.

"You've come at the right season. Spring's a miracle in these parts. Let me get Lent over, and I'll lead you to marvellous sights. Why, on our own glebe land I've been digging out third-century gravestones—Roman, you know, let into walls. You must look at my 'squeezings'—clean as a lino-cut. Somerset's new to you? That's excellent."

In the low-ceiled drawing-room a wood-fire flickered on waxed mahogany and early Staffordshire ware. Books sprawled open, a cat was curled up in the largest chair, and a maid was just setting down a decanter and glasses.

"Sherry? It's good stuff—comes from the cellars of my old college. Have some?"

As Neil sipped the amber liquid warm comfort so lulled his senses that the questions he had meant to propound slid into the background of his mind. Not till roast duckling, young peas, and apple-tart with thick cream had sunk into a dulcet past did he recall his recent experiences, and before he had mentioned them a diversion occurred. In the lane outside the engine of a powerful car whirred, and a second later the servant bent over her mistress with a whispered message. Rachel Gisborne glanced quickly at her brother.

"It's Tasha," she said, with a note of question.

"Well, why doesn't she come in? Fetch her in, Polly."

"She won't stop, sir," answered the woman. "She only wants a word with Miss Rachel."

The latter rose. "Coffee in the drawing-room, you two—and don't browse in here all night, will you?"

Tasha! That must be the girl at Stoke Paulton. Now, thought Neil, he was going to learn something, but although he waited patiently, consuming his final crumb of ripe Stilton with an expectant air, nothing was said. His companion was frowning moodily into a box of Coronas, and when he did speak it was at a tangent.

"So you think you can make an interesting book out of Bundy?"

"I ought to, now the public's waking up to his real value."

"Ah, quite so! Rum old bird in some ways, sort of Darwin, Gladstone and William Morris rolled into one. Went off the deep end a bit towards the last, though that needn't concern you. Always kept his daughter under his thumb, anyhow. Carrie worshipped the ground under his feet, but at the same time was terrified of him. What's your opinion of her, by the way?"

"I hardly know." Neil spoke hesitatingly. "Last fall I thought her absolutely calm and phlegmatic, but now she seems very excitable and full of crotchets. She looks ill, for one thing."

"Humph—you don't surprise me. Not that I've seen anything of her for months, but I've heard she was decidedly—broken." As the vicar said this he shot a keen glance at his guest.

"By the way," said Neil, "have you any idea who those two oily little Cockneys are who have moved into the lodge?"

"Moved into the lodge!" Gisborne exploded in an angry snort. "Do you mean to tell me she's actually got those people on the premises? In what capacity, pray?"

"There you have me, but if it's any help, I did hear the butler say something about a new bailiff."

"Bailiff—fiddlesticks! The fellow's a cheap photographer. Has, or did have, a shop in Glastonbury. Why, he knows less about running an estate than you or I. Bailiff, indeed! Carrie's stark, staring mad—absolutely gone off her chump!"

He continued to mutter till Neil interrupted him.

"And who is the foreign girl up there? Tall, good looking—?"

"Who, Natasha Andreyev? That's she talking to Rachel now. She's Carrie's niece."

"Niece!" It was Neil's turn to stare incredulously. "I can't believe it! What, with a name like that?"

"Precisely. She's half-Russian. You see, Bundy's second daughter, Sophie—attractive wench she was, quite another stripe from her sister— ran off with a temperamental Russian she picked up at the Sorbonne. Good family, but a spendthrift. There was a row, Bundy handed her over what money was coming to her and never saw her again. Chap murdered in the revolution, Sophie drifted back to Paris with two children, a boy and this girl to support. Ran a hat shop, I believe. Two years ago she died, the son stayed behind, and Natasha came to live with her aunt."

"Miss Bundy adopted her, did she?"

"Not at all. Tasha's a secretary-chauffeuse—works jolly hard for her keep. Not very happy, either, I'm afraid. Our people don't know what to make of her, and she despises them. I daresay it's very dull for her, especially now Carrie's behaving so peculiarly, but that's only hearsay, of course." He checked himself to clamp his teeth hard on a cigar. Neil got the impression he might have said much more, but for some reason was holding back.

"She didn't strike me as particularly docile," Neil threw out as a feeler.

"Docile?" Gisborne laughed. "Why, Tasha's as intractable as a wild pony. Good girl, though, and capable. . . . Stay where you are. I'm going to fetch those squeezings I spoke of."

He strode off into a little cubby-hole of a study, leaving his friend to meditate on what he had just heard.

He was meandering back towards Glastonbury along a tortuous lane when the blinding head-lamps of a car bore down on him, and he was barely able to swerve into a ditch to escape destruction. As the demon thundered past a familiar voice hurled an imprecation, well merited, since forgetful of English driving laws he had been on the wrong side of the road. Another blow to his pride, nor was he soothed by the brief glimpse of the face already present in his thoughts, pale, stern, with wild locks sweeping back like a Fury's from naked, beautiful ears.

She had not seen him. He was simply a nameless obstacle in her path. As the hum of the car receded two questions rose to trouble him: Who was this man she had mistaken him for? And why had she been so aghast at the idea of the unknown's coming to Stoke Paulton?

Silence and the Mendips closed about him. He shook his head, conscious of a disquieting sensation hard to define.

## CHAPTER FOUR

AT TEN next morning Neil slid his humble two-seater into Miss Bundy's garage beside the sleek, well-tended Austrian car which a few hours before had so nearly terminated his career. If he had known the important rôle the latter was to play in coming events he would have looked at it with greater interest. As it was, his eye roamed round in search of the chauffeuse, but she was nowhere in sight.

The butler conducted him to his bedroom, which was at the back of the house, directly over the study. It was gay with sprigged wallpaper, old-fashioned furniture, and bowls of primroses. There were pale-green chintz curtains, and big, comfortable chairs.

"If you'll leave your unpacking to me, sir," said Crabbe, "I'll take you to Miss Bundy. She's just finishing her accounts."

Neil was gazing out upon the dewy lawn where blackbirds and thrushes hopped about, picking up worms. The foreground was broken by an immense cedar of Lebanon, through the upper branches of which, on top of a slope, could be seen a group of ruined walls.

"What is that relic?" he asked. "Is it Miss Bundy's property?"

"Oh, yes, sir, that's what they call the Old Glebe House, though it's not much of a house now, as you can see. Hundreds of years old it is. A rare lot of sightseers come here to look it over."

Something in Gisborne's line, thought Neil, mentally resolving to inquire into its history. He followed his guide downstairs, where his hostess's voice reached him, peevish and peremptory. When the old lady joined him, he again noticed the trembling of her hands and the sweat which glued her short wisps of greying hair to her forehead.

"Oh, you've arrived, Mr. Starkey. That's right. Ready to begin work, are you?"

"Quite ready, but first let me thank you for my delightful room. The view is magnificent, and I've just discovered that interesting ruin of yours back there."

"Ruin?" The glance she gave him was quick and, he fancied, suspicious. "Has any one been talking to you about it?"

"Only the butler. He says it is very ancient."

"Ancient—yes. There are Roman materials in the walls, so it probably goes back to the early Christian era, but we know little except that it was inhabited by lay-brothers attached to Glastonbury Abbey. They collected the tithes hereabouts."

It struck him she was reluctant to discuss the Glebe House, though he could not imagine why. Almost at once, however, something put the matter out of his mind. Unlocking the study door she uttered a cry of intense annoyance.

"The carelessness of servants! Nothing in its place!" He could see nothing in the small gate-legged table she bundled hurriedly against the wall to rouse her ire, and again he wondered how it was she was turning into such a martinet. She stood looking about sharply at the clean and tidy room as though searching for other marks of disorder before opening up the bookcases to give him a brief inventory of their contents.

"Bound manuscripts—my father's diary in twenty volumes—notes on experiments—portfolios of correspondence. The published works you see above. Now let me show you the filing cabinets."

The latter proved a monument to patient industry. Here, neatly indexed, was all the help Neil would require—Family History under F, Controversies under C, clippings, reviews, voluminous references—the work of a lifetime. As he thought of how Caroline Bundy had slaved for her father and never emerged from his domination, words spoken by the vicar echoed in his brain: "No, Carrie never dared think for herself, and no one ever praised her. I don't suppose any man glanced at her twice, even when she was young. It's a bad thing when one's vanity has nothing to feed on. Somehow, one has to get even." Well, perhaps that was what she was trying to do now, very tardily—get even. Only what had the Cockney photographer and his wife to do with it? If the niece was right in declaring that the pair had been given employment solely to keep them at the old lady's beck and call, on what was the odd friendship based?

All the time his companion was pulling out drawers and running through files he kept wondering about this, and trying to link it up with the strange remarks let fall the day before. Was it possible Miss Bundy had discovered something of value among these papers, something she did not want an outside person to get hold of? If so, why did she not tell him about it at once? As far as any one knew, Bundy, who had lived to the ripe age of ninety-one, had produced no new work during his latter years. Even so, supposing there were a posthumous manuscript. . . .

The daughter's voice broke in on his reflections.

"There—have I made it all quite clear? If so, I'll leave you to get on. Lunch is at one—and please remember what I said about the keys."

When she had gone he lit a cigarette and began to forage. Two hours passed rapidly, and then, seeing it was nearly one o'clock he locked everything up according to orders, put the bunch of keys in his pocket, and sallied forth into the grounds for a breath of air.

Returning, he passed by the lodge, from the windows of which the succulent odour of roasting goose issued, together with a falsetto voice lifted in song.

> "Roses round the door,
> Kiddies on the floor—"

From an upper casement Mrs. Tilbury's rubicund features looked down on him, wreathed in radiant smiles.

"Nice day, ain't it?" their owner greeted him affably. "Having a bit of a stroll?" As the woman spoke, the duster she was shaking out slipped from her grasp and fluttered to Neil's feet. "Now, then, butter fingers!" she chid herself, and a second later emerged at the door to retrieve her property. "Ta," she murmured, accepting the cloth from him. "Haven't seen that man of mine, I suppose? If he don't turn up soon the dinner will be burnt to cinders. Fair treat I'm 'aving with that stove in there. Wants seeing to, it does. Oh—there's the young lady, now."

Neil turned to see the Russian girl coming in at the gates, the two Alsatians leaping about her. The bailiff's wife accosted her importantly.

"Oh, miss, will you be so good as to 'ave our flues looked at? Shocking state they're in. I'm all of a muck with soot."

Miss Bundy's niece paused, glanced at the speaker, then at Neil, the merest flicker of the lashes. Her voice when she answered was cold.

"Very well. I'll see to it."

She walked on, her head held high. Neil overtook her in the shadow of the rhododendrons, but she did not look at him. They paced on side by side for several seconds before she addressed him to ask if his room was all right and if he had what he wanted.

"Everything," he assured her. "I hope I'm not going to be a bother to you."

"It's no bother at all," she returned indifferently. "Only as it's my job to see to these things I like to know if you're comfortable."

This ended the conversation, for at the front door she deserted him, keeping to the path which led round the house. Slightly damped, he wondered if she had conceived for him a genuine dislike, or if she was merely embarrassed over yesterday's occurrence. As to her sentiments towards the denizens of the lodge, there could be no doubt. If the beaming Mrs. Tilbury had been a slug in the salad she could not have looked on her with greater loathing.

Hearing voices in the drawing-room, he entered the library beyond and picked up the day's newspapers, but the doors between were half-open, and almost at once he found himself listening to the querulous tones of his hostess, at that moment saying to an invisible companion: "I can't in the least account for it, unless it is this racking uncertainty which is preying on me. Why, I've never had these palpitations before—never in my life! I can't sleep and my heart behaves very queerly. Worry, that's what it is. I simply daren't do anything till I can get some absolute proof. If I'm not careful I shall turn myself into a laughing stock for all the neighbourhood."

"You, a laughing stock?" exclaimed a man's mild accents, which Neil immediately recognised as the bailiff's. "Why, 'ow could any one find fault with a lady like yourself? For the matter of that, wot's the hurry?"

"Only that we may go on like this for months, not getting any nearer—and it's of vital importance to—to my father's reputation that I should make sure. Think what it means—and think of the risk, if I go ahead without being sure of my ground."

There was a pause, broken by a rather sulky voice. "Oh, well, it's not me that's anxious to keep on with it. Just say the word, and we'll call the whole business off."

"No, no, don't misunderstand me," cried the old lady in evident alarm. "Please don't imagine I want to give it up now. It's not your fault at all, nor am I criticising you."

"In a manner of speaking, it's a waste of time for me," continued the man in an aggrieved strain. "Wot abaht my profession wot I've spent years on? Connie was at me only this morning over letting that place at Cookham slip through my fingers. Like me, she's soft-hearted, but all the same, we've our future to think of. This ain't getting us nowhere, now is it, if you'll pardon me saying so?"

"If you sacrifice yourself in my interests," declared Miss Bundy in a trembling tone, "I promise you shan't lose by it. I shall find means of making it worth your while."

"Well, no one could speak fairer than that," replied the other, mollified but still doubtful. "We'll go on for a bit, then, and 'ope for better luck. But there, now—here's your little drop of medicine ready waiting and you're about to forget it. Shall I pour it out for you? Doctor's orders, you know. Mustn't neglect your 'ealth."

The uncouth figure passed in front of Neil's line of vision and bent over to measure something into a glass. Two inches of standing collar and an obtrusive brass stud showed above the ill-fitting coat as its owner murmured soothingly, "Wot you want to do is to take it easy like. Save yourself, think of nothing at all, and come to it fresh. May make all the difference."

Come to what fresh? Neil was still asking himself what this cryptic discussion meant when the gong sounded, nor did Miss Bundy's haggard and worn face at the table help him to a solution. Strange to say, his hostess ate with the same voracity she had displayed yesterday at tea, a fact which appeared to puzzle her niece as well as himself, for several times he caught the girl looking across at the elder woman with a slight frown. An enormous appetite yet steady loss of weight. That in itself was odd. There was little talk, and the atmosphere again was decidedly strained. At the end of the meal Miss Andreyev spoke reluctantly to her aunt.

"You are going to lie down, aren't you? Dr. Graves said you must rest for two hours."

"Two hours! What nonsense!" Miss Bundy chafed visibly, but with a sigh gave in. "Well, if I must, I must, but don't forget to telephone Parkins to see to the lodge stove. If it's not attended to at once I shall take my repairs elsewhere."

Neil went back to his work. The house was quiet, there was nothing to disturb him. It must have been an hour later that, standing on the library steps to examine a volume from the upper shelves, he became aware of a draught blowing on his legs and heard just behind him a dry, tentative cough.

Some one had come in and left the door open. Looking round he saw on the other side of the big table the insignificant features and fixed, glassy stare of the bailiff, Tilbury.

## CHAPTER FIVE

THE green lamp, shining full down on the intruder's rather expressionless face, gave it the disconcerting effect of a spectre suddenly materialised out of thin air.

"Why, how did you get here?" inquired Neil blankly, still perplexed over not having heard any one enter.

The man coughed again, apologetically. "Beg pardon, sir, I do 'ope you'll excuse me barging in like this. I did knock, but as there was no answer I just ventured to come inside. It's my fountain pen I lost in here last night. Would it trouble you very much if I was to 'unt for it?"

"Not at all—only close the door, will you? The papers are blowing about."

"Oh, I'm sorry, sir! No, don't come down. I'll put it all tidy."

While Neil went on with his reading quiet movements proceeded behind him, the gentle shifting of furniture and the rattle of the waste-basket. Presently a low cry of triumph recalled his visitor's errand. The pen had been found, under the fender, but instead of taking an immediate departure its owner hung about, politely solicitous. He had such an ingratiating air that it was difficult to snub his efforts to be pleasant.

"Work going nicely, is it?" he asked, letting his pale eyes roam over the book-shelves with vacant wonderment. "Finding all you want, I 'ope?"

When Neil replied in the affirmative he went on conversationally: "Seems as 'ow this Mr. Bundy—or was it Dr. Bundy, sir?—was a big man in his line. Can't say as I know just wot his line was, though, and that's a fact. Pardon me asking—but wot did he do?"

"Science. He was a noted biologist."

"Ow, was he now!" The eyes protruded with awe. "Wrote books, I suppose. That one of 'is you've got in your 'and?"

"*This,*" answered Neil, showing the volume, "happens to be his earliest work, now out of print, and known only to a few specialists. It was withdrawn from circulation fifty years ago."

"You don't say! Why was that, now?"

"Because of its anti-religious tendency. The author repudiated the views held at that period, and did his best to erase the impression he had made. Except in his extreme youth, Bundy was deeply devout."

"Wot, Established Church, and that?"

"Yes, he was violently opposed to Rome."

That Tilbury could be interested in Theodore Bundy's tenets of faith was manifestly absurd, but at all events, he was pretending to be. Whether from idle inquisitiveness or the desire to please, he showed such effortless attention to explanations that Neil found himself giving out more than he would otherwise have granted. The man could not digest what was being said, yet he seemed a veritable human sponge, soaking up information. The questions he asked were naive, betraying utter ignorance, nor could Neil imagine where they were leading. Minutes ticked by, and altogether a quarter of an hour had passed before the man glanced at the clock, apologising once more for his intrusion, and humbly withdrew.

Left alone, Neil speculated afresh on Tilbury's connection with Caroline Bundy. Judging from the talk overheard that morning he was conducting some experiment with her, but whatever its nature it could hardly call for any intellectual ability. Why, the fellow did not seem to know what biology meant, while the distinguished Theodore's achievements were a sealed book to him. How he or his wife could be indispensable to any project was a mystery, and yet there was no doubt that Miss Bundy was overwhelmingly anxious to keep them with her.

The batch of correspondence Neil had been examining was neatly re-stacked on the table, but when he came to run through it the final page of a letter was missing. Had it been here before? He could not be sure. In any case, it was unimportant, merely an acceptance to a breakfast invitation from a colleague. After assiduous search he dismissed it from his mind and locked the other letters in their file.

He longed, however, to discuss the affairs of Stoke Paulton with some one, and consequently at four o'clock walked over to the vicarage, where he found Rachel Gisborne in the garden busy with a trowel.

"You look guilty," she greeted him with a smile. "*What* have you been up to since last night?"

"Eavesdropping," he confessed solemnly. "I'm going to repeat to you a conversation I listened in on to-day, and get you to tell me what you make of it." Whereupon he recounted what had passed in the drawing-room between his hostess and the bailiff.

Rachel stared straight before her with black brows knit.

"It's a complete puzzle to me," she said when he had finished. "The whole neighbourhood's buzzing about Carrie's intimacy with these vulgar little people, and about the extraordinary change in her, but neither Tasha nor I has any notion of what's going on. Giles knows something—or at least, I believe he does—but as he's been sworn to secrecy there's nothing to be got out of him. I dare say you've guessed that Carrie is no longer friendly with us. A pity, isn't it, after all these years? I don't understand the reason for that, either, except that somehow Giles has offended her. There's just one thing I can tell you. In the beginning it had something to do with photographs."

"What sort of photographs?" he demanded, recalling the fact that Tilbury was a photographer.

"I haven't a notion. Giles is annoyed if I question him, and only keeps repeating that Carrie's a fool. I suspect he told her so to her face. He's quite capable of it."

"But is she a fool?"

"Well, not very clever, certainly, but till recently she was sensible enough in a plodding sort of way. She never did anything stupid or irrational, which makes her present aberration all the more puzzling. You can imagine the wild stories that are going about."

"Just what are people saying?"

"Some think she's losing her mind, others contend—don't laugh—that she's infatuated with the bailiff man. Tell me, do you consider him personally attractive?"

"Attractive! Good God! Haven't you seen him?"

"Once, in Glastonbury. Rather an angle-worm, isn't he? Not that looks prove anything, and of course women of Carrie's age—and other ages, too, worse luck—do sometimes bestow their affections in the most amazing quarters. . . . Still, I've suspected all along it was less simple than that, and what you tell me confirms my belief. In a way it's reassuring to know she's urging them to stay there, for otherwise one would have been tempted to fear they had really obtained some hold over her. . . . And yet, I don't know," she went on, with a troubled face, "what to think of this extraordinary change in her health. Have they got anything to do with it? That's what one would like to find out, if one could."

"Do you mean you wonder if there's something disturbing about these nightly meetings of theirs?"

"Yes, either that or else—well, something is upsetting her very badly. According to Tasha she's had some alarming attacks which she tries to make light of. Several times she's been taken in the night with breathlessness and has seemed to be choking. Tasha's been in to her, and says she was quite purple and apoplectic; but again, oddly enough, she refused to have the doctor till the Tilburys persuaded her to send for him."

"That's what the fellow meant about not neglecting the doctor's orders. I saw him give her some medicine out of a bottle."

Rachel turned on him alertly. "You saw him give her medicine?" she repeated quickly.

"Why, you don't surely think there was anything wrong about it, do you?"

"Oh, it isn't likely, of course. Besides, there could be no reason for it. I daresay Dr. Graves is right and that it is high blood-pressure she's got.

That would explain her terrific energy and appetite, wouldn't it? But the trouble is Graves has no idea of this other business."

"Oughtn't he to be told?"

"Who's to tell him except Tasha? And if she does interfere there'll be a rumpus. Carrie's very high-handed these days. She might send the poor girl packing, and Tasha hasn't a penny but what she earns. You can see what a difficult situation it is, and if Tasha herself can't find out anything definite to go on there's no one else who can. Carrie has cut herself off from the entire neighbourhood, invites no one to the house, seems to be existing solely for this enterprise of hers, whatever it is. Hark!" She broke off as a Klaxon horn honked loudly in the lane. "There is Tasha now, calling for me to drive me over to Bath. Want to come with us? She's taking one of the dogs to the vet."

"No, no, I'll push off," he declared hastily, feeling sure the girl would not desire his company, but Rachel drew him along towards the gate, and cried out cheerfully:

"Tasha, my child, your guest has strayed here. Shall we hold on to him, or send him away?"

Under the edge of a scarlet beret the almond-shaped eyes gave him a fleeting glance. He fancied their owner's reserve was melting.

"Come along, if it won't bore you," she invited coolly. "Climb in at the back, but mind Bistre. He's got a hedgehog's spine stuck through his nose and is feeling very sorry for himself."

The Alsatian lay shivering under a rug, but when Neil gently spoke to him his big tail thudded softly on the floor. The car swung round to glide smoothly in the direction of Bath, and before long the old town came in sight, bathed in the golden radiance of sunset, with its arena of hills closing round it like the sides of a cup.

Leaving Natasha and her charge at the veterinary surgeon's, Rachel and Neil wandered about the broad streets so celebrated in eighteenth century fiction and finally approached the tea-shop agreed on as a rendez-vous. The dark-green car stood waiting before an archway, but there was no sign of its driver. Half-way across the street, however, Neil's eye caught a splash of scarlet well back in the shadowed entrance, and close beside it a man's figure of which he could make out nothing save a well-cut overcoat of Harris tweed and a slightly rakish bowler hat.

So the girl had met some one she knew—some one, moreover, in whom she took an interest, judging from the proximity of the two figures and a suggestion of tenseness in the whispered conversation going on. Rachel must have seen what he saw, which made her coming action somewhat peculiar. She caught him by the sleeve, pulled him along to the window of an antique shop, and directed his attention to a display of Spanish majolica within. Not till a step sounded behind them did she turn round, with admirably simulated surprise.

"Oh, there you are!" she cried as Natasha, unaccompanied, met them on the pavement. "How's Bistre? Did the vet get the spine out?"

"Bistre?" echoed the other absently. Her cheeks were the dull red of pomegranates, her eyes bright but thoughtful. "Oh, I left him being sick after the anaesthetic. I'll have to call for him to-morrow. Come along, let's get tea."

As they were leaving the shop the proprietress, a sandy-haired lady in a green smock, padded after them like an angular lioness and touched Natasha softly on the arm. Neil caught a suave murmur, beginning, "Your friend, Mr.—" the name escaped him—and ending, "said you would settle for his lunches, as he was waiting for a remittance to arrive. It's quite all right, isn't it?"

The whole thing happened with quick surreptitiousness, but though Neil pretended not to hear he could not avoid seeing the girl flush crimson, and with an air of guilty embarrassment slip two pound notes into the woman's hand.

## CHAPTER SIX

AT RACHEL'S pressing invitation, her two friends remained at the vicarage for dinner, which, as it was the maid's evening out, they all helped to prepare. In the present gay company Natasha showed herself a different being from the girl Neil had first known, high-spirited, with flashes of wit, and when occasion demanded, an ability to hold her own in serious conversation. She had, he noticed, the Continental woman's mind, while her Nordic blood gave her a straightforwardness he found oddly stimulating. It was hard to associate her with subterfuge or evasion, and this, in view of his belief that she did have something to hide, presented a puzzling paradox.

All during the evening he could not rid his thoughts of the episode in the tea-shop, which he kept turning over and piecing together with what had happened yesterday at Stoke Paulton. As a result, he arrived at the following conclusions:

One. The girl was in love with some one she did not wish her aunt to know about.

Two. She was defraying, or helping to defray, her lover's expenses.

Three. The man in question was the late proprietor of the two-seater car, sold because he needed money.

Four. Rachel knew and disapproved. (Quite naturally, for who could approve of a girl spending her hard-earned cash on a rotter?)

He told himself this summing-up might be hasty, also that it was sheer stupidity for him to concern himself thus over the affairs of a stranger. Still, there it was; and something Rachel said at parting made him think he was not far wrong in his surmises.

"I do hope you and Tasha are going to hit it off together," she whispered, drawing him aside on the doorstep. "I'm very fond of her, you know. Her mother and I were school friends. It's ghastly to think of what poor Sophie went through—Boris Andreyev shot down before her eyes, hideous indignities at the hands of the Soviets, and then poverty and struggle in Paris. I sometimes wonder what effect all that may have had on Natasha's character."

"Then you think it has affected her?" he asked.

"In a way, yes. For all her fine qualities, she's developed a sort of hard fatalism—a disregard for human life—I don't know how to put it, but it's rather frightening in one so young. She's headstrong, too, and difficult to influence. I only wish the right sort of man—you, for instance, could get her confidence and advise her. Do you think you could?"

"Thanks for the compliment," he answered, smiling; "but what about her brother? Giles told me she had one."

"Oh, Michael." She mused for a moment. "No, he's hardly able to be of much use. I believe she's deeply attached to him, but—"

"You mean he's not here? Well, I'll do my best, but somehow I don't imagine she'll turn to me very readily. I'll be willing to bet she freezes up as soon as we're left alone."

Nor was he mistaken. On the short drive back he sensed an immediate change, an erection of barriers barring every approach. She was friendly enough, but maddeningly impersonal, a fact the more irritating since he was now definitely aware of her attraction, and filled with curiosity to know just what Rachel's hints had meant.

When they had put up the car, Crabbe met them to say that Miss Bundy was still engaged in the study, but had told him not to wait up. Both glanced instinctively at the baize door beyond which was dead silence, but as though anxious to avoid any reference to her aunt's activities, Natasha went quickly through to the front hall. Neil hung up his coat in the lobby. As he did so the kitchen clock struck twelve. A lengthy session! He would have given a good deal to know what was going on in the closed room under old Bundy's stern eyes, and rather hoped his companion might talk it over with him, but when he joined her at the foot of the stairs her entire attention was centred on a thin grey envelope bearing a French stamp. She had just torn this open, and did not look up as he passed by into the drawing-room.

He had poured himself a weak whisky and soda, and was about to raise it to his lips when a smothered gasp made him turn in alarm. To his dismay he saw Natasha clutching her letter in her hand and staring straight ahead with an expression of agonised shock. For a moment he thought she was about to faint.

In a couple of strides he reached her to ask what was wrong. Had she received bad news? She did not seem to hear him. Her blanched lips parted to form the single word, "Michael," but she was speaking to herself, not him. He remembered, however, that Michael was her brother's name.

"Not ill, is he? Met with an accident?"

As she did not reply he tried to thrust the glass he held into her hand. "Here, drink this," he urged, but she pushed it away.

She had recovered sufficiently to glance wildly at the adjacent telephone, and even made a move in its direction, only to change her mind.

"Would you like me to put through a call to Paris for you?" he suggested.

For the first time she seemed aware of his presence, but looked at him as if he were something to be quickly got rid of.

"There's nothing you can do. Oh, please go away and leave me!"

Her distraught dismissal left him no choice but to obey. He went up slowly to his room, but had hardly got inside when a faint grating noise drew him to the window. There was just light enough to see the garage doors open and the car slide out, with Natasha at the wheel. Another second, and car and occupant had vanished round the curving drive. What—off again, at this late hour?

Struggling with astonishment, he sat down on his bed to think things out. Perhaps she had gone back to the vicarage, but he did not believe it. No, although she had seen this fellow in Bath last night and again this afternoon, he was confident she had dashed off post-haste for another conference with him. That must mean her brother's communication called for immediate discussion, or else—and a blank feeling came over him—she was running away for good and all. Why, he could not imagine, but when he realised how a moment ago she had made him think of an animal caught in a trap, he could not help fearing she was taking some desperate step.

Very soon he heard the bailiff and his wife slip out the back door, and Miss Bundy's tread mounting to her room, but although he kept awake for a long time straining his ears, he did not catch any sound of the returning car.

His theorising, as it happened, was entirely askew. Natasha had come home, and in the morning had finished breakfast before he appeared. Not till he saw the used coffee-cup being removed from her place did he admit how disturbed he had been, but now the very intensity of his relief served to infuriate him.

"Why should I mind what she does?" he scourged himself vehemently. "How can she mean anything to me? It's my blasted egotism, that's all. I'd like to make an impression on her, and I haven't succeeded. God knows I ought to see through myself by now!"

It was true he had his full share of vanity, and was not blind to the fact, but it was also true that at the age of thirty-two he had come seriously to doubt his capacity for strong or lasting attachment. Out of numerous affairs of the senses not one had held him long, nor had he any reason to suppose his present interest would amount to more than the most superficial emotion. One-sided, too, therefore how wise to nip it in the bud! He would have said the prospect of such an adventure bored him. In reality it threatened his pride.

Did Miss Bundy know of Natasha's midnight sortie? He wondered a little, ultimately deciding she was either too deaf or too absorbed in her own secret life to take note of her niece's movements.

On the lawn outside he caught sight of the new bailiff wrangling in a mild fashion with a grizzled, roughly attired man whom he rightly assumed to be the head gardener. There was an air of friction between the two, and when presently he saw Crabbe watching them with a furtive smile, he guessed that Tilbury was not destined to be popular with the staff. Servants are quick to resent an employee with an ill-defined status, and while the little man looked harmless enough there was a quiet persistence about him which boded mischief.

Inside the study, Neil opened the table drawer to take out his notes. A moment later he was holding up a sheet of yellowed notepaper and examining it with frowning attention.

"Hallo!" he muttered. "How did this get here?"

The heading on the sheet was "Stoke Paulton, Somerset;" the writing it contained merely a dozen lines of Theodore Bundy's scrawl, ending in a signature. In fact, it was the missing page he had hunted for yesterday and abandoned as non-existent. Perhaps he had inadvertently picked it up with his own jottings; more likely the maid had found it lodged in a corner and put it here for safety. As he gazed, a very slight suspicion came into his mind, but he instantly dismissed it as unreasonable. Who could want to borrow anything so utterly trivial? And besides, if the page were taken it could not have been returned through a locked door. Only—hold on! Tilbury was in here last night, with Miss Bundy. He could have done it then. . . . Still, the whole supposition seemed absurd. He consigned the paper to its file and from thence on, for many weeks, thought no more about it.

As he was yet curious about Miss Bundy's veiled allusions, he could not resist dipping into the last volume of the diary to see if the latter contained any illumination. Diligent reading, however, revealed nothing worthy of comment except certain poetic effusions, and, just at the end, a scattering of entries so obscure as to make no sense whatever.

The poems, sentimentally pre-Raphaelite in character, were rather amusing when one considered the author's militant type of religion. What era but the Victorian, thought Neil, could have produced this extraordinary paradox of a personality—a man of science who dined on roast beef and plum pudding, bickered with his associates, thrust forth an errant child because her marriage displeased him, and in the same breath, as it were, penned ballads full of white lilies, mystic numbers, and crowns of suffering? At one moment one pictured him as an angry volcano, fulminating in every direction to get rid of the fiery energy within; at another, one saw him straining wistfully after some vague beauty, sensed but ungrasped. Passionate egoist that he was, his violence was a matter of the adrenal cortex, pure and simple, even though he confidently invoked his God of Wrath to uphold his actions; but he had a strangely different side, as shown by his bad verses and also by the items set down in his ninetieth year.

Concise as the latter were, they disclosed tantalisingly little, suggesting that Bundy shrank from committing himself even in the privacy of his journal. Who and what was the mysterious Mrs. S., to whom frequent reference was made? Often a few words sufficed: *"Mrs. S. again. Poor, unsatisfying."* Or: *"Mrs. S. wonderfully dear. Must follow up."* These continued up to the final illness, and might, therefore, coincide with the breaking up of the writer's powers. In none was there any definite thing to lay hold on, so that Neil began to feel he was wasting time.

One passage, however, chained his interest for fully ten minutes. It was headed by the Scriptural quotation: *"And the old men shall see visions."* Bundy himself had seen a vision, the authenticity of which he did not doubt. His departed wife, usually designated as "my devoted Hannah," appeared at his bedside, spoke to him words of earnest encouragement, and adjured him to *"be brave, persevere."* Without specifying what this message meant to him, he dwelt at length on the reality of the dead woman's presence, describing her dress and the odour of lavender water which clung about her. At the last was a single cryptic line: *"She is right. I must not turn back. By this sign will the millennium be inaugurated."*

What sign? What millennium? Had the entry any real significance, or was it only the fantasy of a deteriorating brain? There seemed no means of deciding, even if one applied to Miss Bundy, but it was now possible to see some justification for the latter's statement that her father was a mystic. For that matter Gisborne, too, had said something about the old man's going off the deep end.

Late in the afternoon he saw Natasha crossing the lawn, clad in a green jersey, with her hair rippling in the wind like a blown cornfield. He had scarcely had a glimpse of her all day, and the desire to see how she fared after last night's contretemps proved too strong for him. Hastily locking up, he shouted to her to wait for him, which she did, in a patch of sunlight beyond the big cedar.

"I thought of taking a look at the ruin," he said as he joined her. "Want to show me over it?"

"Certainly, if you like. Not that I can tell you much about it. Mr. Gisborne is the one for that sort of thing." Except that she was a little pale, with a slight hint of stoicism in her expression, she looked none the worse for her recent distress. It occurred to him that she knew how to keep her feelings under cover, also that she would take it amiss if he mentioned what she wished to conceal.

All the way up the slope he was tinglingly aware of that quality in her which from the beginning had challenged his masculinity. Why, without making the slightest advance, she had more allure in her little finger than a hundred ordinary women put together! She was electric, vital. Perhaps it was this, together with the knowledge of her latent fierceness, which drew him. Never, at any time, had he responded to the milk-and-rose-leaves type.

On the brow of the hill they paused to look at the view. All about them, soft in the slanting light, rose the green Mendips, smoothed as by a giant hand. Here and there was the dark fold of a coombe, and in the distance a dim patch which the girl said was Glastonbury.

"That sticking-out bit is the famous Tor. The Holy Grail is supposed to be buried somewhere near there, but that's only a myth, of course. You can't see the abbey. Anyhow, there's only a fragment of it left, like this old building."

They walked on to the crumbling walls, in and out of which grew thorn bushes and a huge mass of ivy with a twisted trunk, thick as a man's thigh. The matted tangle clung to the ancient bricks, sucking its life from their crevices. Overhung by it was the remnant of a crude arch.

"Here was the refectory. Those flat stones are part of the original floor. There was a crypt underneath, but it's quite filled up. Shouldn't wonder if there are tombs down there now. This is a priest's hole—and look, here's the well the lay-brothers got their water from. It's terribly deep. Listen!"

Kneeling down beside a circlet of stone she dropped a pebble into the black shaft. Far below sounded a ghostly splash, coming apparently from the very bowels of the earth.

"It's a queer country, this," she went on. "All honey-combed with caves and springs. I'm told there are places where spray blows in your face and you can't see where it comes from. Makes you think of Alph, the sacred river, you know, and the caverns measureless to man."

The reference pleased him, even while, in a different fashion, he thrilled at the touch of her shoulder momentarily pressed against his. They remained for a bit gazing down into the well, then the girl moved away and stooping, began to examine the worn flags underfoot. The next instant she uttered a puzzled exclamation.

"At it again!" she remarked, frowning. "Do you see how some one's been loosening these stones? I've noticed it several times. I wonder if my aunt knows?"

"I should imagine a child is responsible," he answered, turning over one of the flags with his foot. "There's no sense in it, is there?"

"I don't know. Would a child carry a shooting-stick? Because whoever it is has stuck one in all about here. See these marks?"

Before he could venture an opinion on the neatly drilled holes she pointed out to him, a shadow fell across the ground between them. Straightening up he beheld Miss Bundy just topping the rise, puffing like a steam engine, and wearing her usual air of deep absorption. She hugged in one arm the alligator-skin bag from which she was never parted, while her right hand clutched a long steel contrivance with a spike at one end and a folded seat at the other. She had not yet noticed any one was near. Natasha touched Neil's arm and whispered, "Why, she's the one! It's her shooting-stick. What can she be after?"

A few yards away the old lady halted suddenly and saw them. A dingy red overspread her features, her small, wrathful eyes darted from one face to the other with unaccountable suspicion.

"Are you two looking for anything special?" She demanded this in a voice choking with spleen.

So accusing was her manner that Neil for the moment was dumb-founded. Natasha merely stared and turned away, leaving him to handle the situation as best he could. He went forward amicably, bent on ignoring the implied reproof.

"No, only prowling about," he answered easily. "All this is most interesting. Your niece has been telling me about the blocked-up crypt under here."

"Oh, so that's it!" Though evidently ashamed, Miss Bundy still seemed only partly appeased. "I wasn't aware that Natasha knew about the crypt—if there ever was one," she murmured, and to hide her confusion blew her nose with violence.

The handkerchief, dragged from her coat pocket, brought with it two objects which fell to the ground. Neil restored them to her—a long kitchen knife, and a yellow tape-measure. She stuffed them out of sight hastily, meanwhile directing another glance at the retreating girl. When the latter was out of earshot she spoke again in a pouncing fashion. "What have you done with my keys?" she said brusquely. "Are they in your pocket?"

"I'm so sorry!" he cried, producing the little bunch. "I've just come out, and didn't realise it was six o'clock."

She let the collection lie in the palm of her hand, but kept her eyes riveted to his face.

"Mr. Starkey," she said agitatedly, "I want to ask you something, and now is as good a time as any. Please think carefully before you reply." She hesitated, then went on with a mixture of embarrassment and eager-ness. "Have you done as I told you about locking the study? Or, what is more important, have these keys at any moment during the day been out of your possession?"

He reassured her positively on both points. No, the keys had been in his pocket all the time, except while he was at work, when they lay on the table under his eye. "Sure you've not left them on your dress-ing-table, or—"

"Quite sure. I've been just as careful as you told me to be."

She had hung on his words, and now a great sigh of relief escaped her. She mopped her heavily beaded forehead as though an intolerable load had fallen from her spirit.

"Thank God! Thank God!" she whispered. "In that case, everything is as it should be—only I had to make certain. . . . There, that is all. Continue with your walk. I have something I wish to do."

Thus dismissed, he left her standing motionless, with a spell-bound gaze fixed on the horizon. Her little dull eyes were filled with rapt wonderment.

## CHAPTER SEVEN

NATASHA was loitering about on the path ahead. In answer to her questioning glance he told her what had just occurred.

"Thank goodness I did carry out her instructions," he finished with a rueful laugh. "As it was she made me feel unaccountably guilty. Forgive me for asking, but frankly, is your aunt usually like this?"

Instead of replying she demanded quickly, "What sort of instructions did she give you?"

"Oh, about locking the room up and not leaving the keys lying about. I can't think why she should attach so much importance to the matter. When she saw I wasn't lying, she seemed frightfully relieved. She looked as though she were seeing visions."

"Half the time she's like that now," returned the girl slowly. "And the other half she's all nerves and irritability, with bursts of energy nothing can curb. See her now!" And she pointed back to the hill-top.

Sure enough the old lady was bustling in and out the ruin, bending low and prodding the earth with her stick. Once she got down on the ground and appeared to be taking measurements.

"It looks," he ventured with mock gravity, "as if she meant to dig for buried treasure. She brought a knife with her, I may tell you."

"A knife!" To his surprise she treated his suggestion quite seriously. "Maybe she does hope to find treasure. The Glebe House belonged to the abbey, you know, and the abbey was the richest in Europe. Still, after all this time you can't imagine—"

"I'm afraid I can't—much as one likes to believe in fairy tales."

"Then what is she after? And why all this sudden secrecy about the study? Can there be some clue among my grandfather's papers which she doesn't want any one else to get hold of? I never thought of it before, but perhaps she's conducting a search, with the Tilburys to help her."

"Why the Tilburys?" he objected, with a shrug.

"Why anything? Evidently there's some one around here she doesn't trust. Not you. Not those creatures." Her lip curled with scorn. "And I shouldn't think it was any of the servants. In fact, the only person left is me. Good heavens! Is that why she was so suspicious just now when she saw us together? I do believe it's me she wants to keep away from the room, and she was afraid you might have given me the keys!"

"That's obviously absurd," he returned in amusement.

"No, but is it? You don't know how queerly she's been behaving towards me lately. Oh, in lots of ways! So secretive, so—so critical. At times I feel she's a total stranger." She checked herself, as though fearful of saying too much. "Oh, well, I mustn't bother you with all this," she added, with an apologetic laugh.

"If I were you, I shouldn't dwell on it. If I may say so, your aunt doesn't seem quite normal. I noticed it as soon as I arrived."

"Three months ago she was sane enough. Now she behaves like a person possessed, driven by some idea that has got hold of her. I don't like it. It makes me—afraid." She shivered slightly and was silent. When she went on it was in a different tone, calculating, cool. "Be that as it may," she said half-lightly, "if there is any secret hidden away in that study, you're in a pretty good position to find it. Had that occurred to you?"

"Not till now," he replied, laughing. "Are you suggesting I prowl about and investigate?"

"You wouldn't, of course," she retorted, with a sidelong glance at him. "But I know what I'd do if I had your chance."

He could not quite make out whether this was meant jokingly nor not, but at a later date these words of hers were to haunt him in a singularly troublesome manner.

From now on Neil saw a good deal of her, and managed to draw her out on a variety of topics, without, however, getting one whit nearer to any understanding of her character. Indeed, it was amazing when he looked back on this period to reflect that, while he quickly accepted both his hostess's vagaries and the enigmatical position of Mr. and Mrs. Tilbury in the household, he still found Natasha Andreyev an unsolved problem.

Like her grandfather, she seemed a mass of contradictions. She worked hard, but loved pleasure—getting little enough of it, sad to relate; she had warm loyalties, generosity nothing short of quixotic, and at the same time a frankly mercenary regard for money, to the attainment of which she appeared to attach the greatest importance.

"If you don't believe people will do almost anything to get money," she once said to him, "it's because you've never happened to need it badly yourself. It's by far the biggest thing in life—when you haven't got it. It makes crooked ways straight."

"Sometimes the reverse," he reminded her.

"No, only the lack of it. Think of the men who go wrong when a little— oh, a very little!—help would keep them to the right track! And the rotten part of it is that those who can give that help refuse to do anything."

He guessed that she was brooding on a definite case, also that her frequent restlessness and look of unhappy preoccupation came from worry over the affairs of the man in whom she was interested, but not once did she let fall any hint which could clear the matter up in his own mind. Her reticence about her present life and even the later years in Paris was so pronounced that he soon despaired of learning anything about either. Whenever he brought the conversation round to matters which concerned her personally she turned the subject at once.

"There's nothing worth telling," she would say. "Just one long fight to keep alive—till I came here, of course. . . . I'd much rather you talked to me about your early days in America. I'm never tired of hearing what you did when you were a boy, and how you came to break away from that dull little town where you were born."

She seemed to be weaving romance out of the history which had never before been other than commonplace to him. She made him describe his home in the Chesapeake Valley, the big farm-house in which he had grown up, his father, the staid judge who had sat in the United States Senate and longed for Neil to follow in his footsteps, the whole life at Princeton University, and the chain of circumstances which had led to literature and wanderings.

"If you knew how I envy you!" she sighed wistfully. "All my life I've wanted to travel, to get away from monotony—and here I am, caged up, with one day after another stretching in front of me just like these tame, smooth hills. I mean to get out of it, though, sooner than you think. If I stay here much longer, I believe I shall go mad!"

Sometimes, without a word of explanation, she would drive off alone in the evenings, not returning till after midnight, on which occasions Neil conjured up scenes distinctly displeasing, though he stoutly refused to call his feelings by their proper name. What—jealous, when he was not in love? For he was determined to keep within the boundaries he had set himself, only rather annoyed at the entire needlessness of discretion.

He was now positively convinced of Natasha's infatuation for the unknown in Bath, and sure in his own mind what these excursions of hers meant. More, he imagined the letter from Paris which had so upset her had been a protestation on her brother's part against the entanglement the writer had got wind of, and wished to break up. Probably Michael was threatening to disclose the affair to Miss Bundy. Certainly the girl had been terrified at the thought of her lover's coming to the house. But what was wrong about this man? Once or twice curiosity drove him almost to the point of making inquiries at the garage where he had purchased his two-seater, but scruples forbade such a step. After all, what right had he to pry into Natasha Andreyev's private concerns? His activities in this direction were delayed till a later period, and so, wondering and inwardly chafing at the unanswered conundrum, he let three weeks drift by and bring him to the evening which, in more ways than one, represented a definite crisis in events.

Miss Bundy, for almost the first time since his arrival, had dined at her own table, a circumstance brought about by Mrs. Tilbury's cousin, from Cornwall, coming to spend the night. Lately the old lady, though still utterly absorbed in her project, had been slightly better tempered, but to-night she was as peevish as a child deprived of a treat. Possibly there was something more than disappointment to account for this. Neil was inclined to think so when, just as they were finishing coffee, Crabbe bent over her with a message which caused her to start as though touched on a raw spot.

"Peters wants to see me? What impertinence! Send him away at once."

"He won't go, Miss. He says he'll wait till you come."

Miss Bundy tugged mutinously at the hairs on her chin, looked about in angry indecision, and finally rose with a defiant set to her mouth.

"Very well, I will see him—though it won't do him any good. The man must be mad to think I have nothing better to do than go over his misdeeds!"

So saying, she trudged resolutely from the room, the living embodiment of a brewing storm. Natasha looked after her with silent apprehension, then bent her head towards the match Neil held out for her cigarette. The firelight glinted along the tarnished gold ripples of her hair, from which stole an indefinable fragrance, fresh and wild like the scent of daffodils. It was not the first time her companion had noticed it, and now, as always, it had an oddly intoxicating effect on him. How different, how much more truly an expression of her being than any of the heavy, exotic perfumes she might have used! He drew in a deep breath, and now they were alone let his eyes roam over her with open admiration.

Her green and yellow chiffon frock had a narrow belt defining her waist, and a fluttering shoulder-cape through which her arms showed slender and firmly modelled; her hair swept back boldly behind her small ears and lay on her neck in a smooth roll. She was so soignée, so exquisite, for all the free sweep of her carriage, that it was hard to imagine her as he had seen her a few hours before, clad in rough overalls, tinkering with the car—and yet she was as unstudied now as then. Like the scent which filled his nostrils, her garments at all times were a part of her.

"This looks like Paris," he remarked, touching the edge of the drapery nearest him.

"This rag? Yes, it came over with me, nearly two years ago," she replied, with rueful scorn. "All my clothes are ancient—not that it matters in the least in these wilds."

It did matter, though. He guessed how much from the disgust with which she suddenly eyed the neat darn on her silk ankle. No one could care more for beautiful clothes than she did, or wear them to better advantage. Was she denying herself in order to provide for another's wants? No good to keep repeating that his assumption rested on insecure foundations. The tea-shop episode stuck in his mind like a burr.

Perhaps his continued scrutiny conveyed something of what he was thinking. At all events, she turned away quickly, and going to a cabinet he had not noticed till now bent over to turn a handle. At once the warm strains of dance music flooded in upon them—saxophones and horns blended together in a seductive rhythm.

"Whence the radio?" he exclaimed in surprise. "I thought Miss Bundy hated it."

"So she does, but—well, other people can't exist without one. The two-valve set at the lodge isn't quite good enough, it seems. Connie likes tuning in to foreign stations."

Their eyes met, and they broke into surreptitious laughter over this new proof of the old lady's subservience to her favourites' whims. Not for Natasha, who long ago might have enjoyed this mild diversion, had the super-instrument been installed. No, it was for the little Cockney woman, now in and out of the house from morning to night. It passed comprehension.

The music swelled and pulsed till it became an irresistible invocation. Neil threw his cigarette into the fire and held out his arms with a gesture quickly understood. Natasha smiled, moved towards him, and in another second it was as though twin bits of magnetised steel had drawn together.

"She loves dancing," he reflected, and soon afterwards, with an odd exultation, "she loves dancing—with me." The triumph which surged through him was charged with immense potentialities.

If he had thought about it before, he would have expected to find her a little intractable, resistant—instead of which she yielded herself with the completeness of the perfect partner. Yet was there not more to it than this? So, at least, it seemed to the man whose treasured independence began to show alarming signs of capitulation. Till this moment some obstacle hard as flint had held them apart. Now that thing had fused in an intense heat, and in some strange fashion was welding them into one. Fantastic, possibly absurd, the conviction which stole upon him during the delirious interval of bodily contact—the idea that, however much he might distrust this girl, misunderstand her, hate her even, he could never again look upon her as quite separate from himself. There it was, he believed it, ready though he was to struggle against what it might portend.

They had come to rest on the hearthrug, with the enchantment still claiming them. Neil's arms, reluctant to withdraw, had slipped to a girdle round the slender waist. The eyes upturned to his were mistily bright, the voice which broke the new stillness softer than he had known it before.

"And I never guessed you could dance like that!" she marvelled, faintly reproachful.

He laughed, his gaze holding hers. "I can't, except with you," he began. "If you want to know the truth, I—"

He stopped, listening, for it was at this exact instant that the thing happened—a choking cry from the rear regions of the house, followed by a crash. Natasha broke from him in sudden fright. Her colour had ebbed, leaving her quite pale.

"Quick!" she gasped. "It's Caroline! Oh, something told me there would be trouble!"

With one accord they rushed for the door.

## CHAPTER EIGHT

THEY found Miss Bundy crumpled up on the floor of the little lobby, with Sally, the spaniel, whimpering beside her, and Crabbe and the gardener bending over. Though not unconscious, she seemed unable to speak. Her face was as red as a turkey cock, her eyes blinked confusedly up at the overhead light. Pushing the men aside Natasha knelt down and raised the inert head.

"Fetch some water," she ordered. "And ring up Dr. Graves at once. Peters! How did this happen?"

"I don't know, miss," stammered the gardener, badly frightened. His seamed features had a puzzled expression. "She just toppled over sudden-like—sort of a fit."

A dozen wild conjectures sped through Neil's brain as he examined the starting veins of the old woman's temples, on one of which was a slight cut.

"She struck her head in falling," he murmured; "but there's more to it than that. I'm afraid she can't use her tongue," he added as the stiff lips moved clumsily without any sound issuing from them.

Paralysis flashed on his mind, and as if answering the thought, Natasha whispered: "We were warned to look out for this. Blood-pressure. . . . Perhaps we'd better get her to bed and loosen her clothing."

The water had been brought. As the girl bathed the hot forehead there were already signs of recovery, and when Crabbe returned from the telephone to help pick up the heavy burden, an awkward gesture indicated that the old woman was quite alive to what was going on.

"She wants something. What is it? Oh, her bag, of course. Yes, Aunt Caroline, I'll bring it up. Don't worry." Midway the stairs an old-fashioned gold chain with a locket attached fell from the neck of her gown. On it dangled a tiny steel key, not an inch in length, and while Neil was wondering what this could belong to, and mentally commenting on his hostess's passion for locking things up, he caught sight of a corresponding keyhole in the clasp of the alligator-skin bag Natasha was carrying. The old lady seemed anxious till her property was laid beside her on the bed. She clutched it with one stumpy hand and drew it to her.

She was now making frantic efforts to formulate some command, which those about her interpreted as a question about the doctor. However, a violent shake of the head told them they were wrong, and in spite of injunctions not to exert herself, the struggles for speech continued till an intelligible mutter came forth.

"Tilbury—send at once. Must see him." Then as the butler looked doubtfully at Natasha the order was repeated with growing asperity. "I must be obeyed! At once. . . ."

"Certainly, he shall be sent for. Now keep quiet and rest."

Crabbe departed on his errand, and Neil helped the girl arrange the mountainous pillows and thick eiderdown quilt, meanwhile glancing round the ugly Victorian room. On every wall hung likenesses of Theodore Bundy, from infancy to old age; a large Bible lay on the bedside table, together with several historical and archaeological works on the West Country. Nowhere was there a feminine touch, or anything to suggest even a bygone vanity.

In a quarter of an hour a dour, spectacled man entered, set down his professional case, and cast a disapproving eye on the patient, who tried to sit up. He pushed her back firmly, inserted a thermometer in her mouth, and reached for her pulse. Neil now retired and descended to wait for news.

The strains of the "Blue Danube" poured from the forgotten radio. He crossed to switch off the instrument, and as he bent over it was startled by a flat, gasping voice behind him.

"Oh, I say! We'd ought to have thought of that!"

Turning, he saw little Mrs. Tilbury, clinging to her husband's arm, and looking like a frightened sparrow.

The tail of one of her braids had straggled loose, and her eyes, like those of her companion, were strained with anxiety. The two huddled figures made a curious impression on him. Somehow they seemed like a pair of childish conspirators caught playing a dangerous game, and terrified of the consequences.

He did not know what idea had been uppermost in his thoughts when he first heard Miss Bundy's cry and the sound of her fall, but now quite definitely the feeling of something wrong came over him. No good trying to analyse it. There it was, strong, instinctive. In that moment he could have sworn the bailiff and his wife had some connection with to-night's disaster.

The woman pressed forward, her teeth chattering. "Not really bad, is she?" faltered the shaking inquiry. "You don't think she's going to—to die, or anythink, do you, Mr. Starkey?"

"Silly!" the man chid her in an undertone, and pinioned her by the arm. "Course she's not. Nothink to worry abaht, is there, sir?"

But he, too, sounded alarmed.

"She's had a bad turn, but she's coming round," replied Neil, watching them narrowly.

"Oh, thank God for that!" Mrs. Tilbury broke into hysterical giggling, and she and her husband exchanged quick glances. The latter murmured soothingly:

"Why, of course it's all right, my girl. Don't you fret. Miss Bundy's a 'earty woman, she is."

Their intense relief made Neil think his recent suspicion an error of judgment. Why, how could the Tilburys possibly benefit by their employer's decease? The last thing either could wish was for their golden goose to come to harm. At the same time, wishing to be rid of their vulgar faces, he withdrew into the library till he heard Natasha accompany the doctor downstairs. The latter was saying in a grudging tone, "Yes, yes, let her see him, since she's so bent on it. Can't hurt her, if he only stays five minutes. To-morrow you and I will have our talk."

When the front door had closed, Natasha summoned the bailiff and coldly informed him he might go to Miss Bundy's room.

"Wot abaht the missus? Is she to come, too?"

"No, one of you is enough. You needn't wait, Mrs. Tilbury."

"Ow, very good, miss," answered a rather sulky voice, and in another moment the drawing-room was vacant.

Neil and Natasha met beside the dying fire. The girl looked anxious and white.

"Oh, she's much better already," she replied to the unspoken question. "The doctor didn't seem surprised. Says it's a mild attack due to high blood-pressure, and that she must keep in bed for a bit. But I'm not satisfied, and neither is he, over what's causing all this. You see, she's developed the tendency so suddenly. He wants to get at the basic reason for it—and that's where I come in," she added under her breath.

"Then you're going to give the show away?"

"I must. She'll be furious, but I'll have to risk that."

"Furious with you for wanting to take care of her? Come, after all, aren't you her niece?"

"Niece or not, I'm a paid dependent. Remember she never set eyes on me till two years ago—and I'm afraid she doesn't like me very much."

After a moment's thought he said: "It's unfair for you to have all this responsibility. Isn't there some old friend or relation who could relieve you of the task?"

"No. I'm her only near relative, and besides, no one about here knows what's going on. There is just one woman who has a lot of influence with her, but unfortunately she's in Gloucestershire. You've heard of Emily Braselton, the head mistress of Bellingham?"

"No. Ought I to know about her?"

"Well, she's very prominent, but, of course, as you're not English, her name won't mean anything to you. Anyhow, she's clever and determined, besides being very devoted to Caroline. If she knew what an idiot the poor thing's making of herself she'd soon find means of stopping it. The trouble is I don't like writing to her."

"Why not?"

"Because she hates me. I think she believes I'm some sort of adventuress, out to get Caroline's money. Oh, she practically told me so," went on the girl, as he looked astonished, "and naturally I let fly at her. As if I ever dreamed of inheriting a penny from poor Caroline! Of course, all this property will go to found a research fund when she dies. That's always been understood." She swept her hair back with an impatient gesture, and reached for a cigarette. "Still, some one has put my aunt against me lately, and it lies between Emily Braselton and—the Tilburys."

"Good Lord, they'd never dare—"

"Oh, wouldn't they? That's all you know about it. Listen!" She came closer and whispered with suppressed bitterness. "Old Peters got the sack this afternoon—after twenty-five years' service here. A good man too. I refuse to believe anything against him. That's why he came here to-night, to try to make her see reason. I had a few words with him while the doctor was upstairs, and it's just as I guessed. It's this slimy bailiff who's been making mischief."

"But what's to be gained by doing that?"

"Gained! Can't you see his game? He's set out determinedly to oust the old staff. Crabbe won't stand it much longer. Then my turn will come. Oh, he means to make a clean sweep, then he'll have undisputed power. Why, it's perfectly plain what he's up to."

This was a new view of the situation, though even now Neil could not see any reason in what she said.

"You forget Tilbury is keeping on his job under protest. I myself heard your aunt urging him not to go away."

Her glance withered him. "Can't you see through that dodge? The more reluctance he pretends the more benefits she'll heap on him to keep him here. That tin-pot photography business of his was about to go under. He and the woman are a couple of incompetents, with all eyes out for some one to impose on. In the ordinary way Caroline would never employ an unqualified person to run her estate. That's why it's so evident there's something queer."

She had never, till now, let herself go so freely. It was plain she was badly shaken over what had occurred.

"Do you still imagine the clue to it is among your grandfather's papers?" he asked, trying to get at her private opinion.

"That does seem a bit wild, doesn't it? And yet I don't know. . . . If there weren't something there, why should she hold on to the keys in this extraordinary way? You've not come across anything peculiar, I suppose?"

Before he could answer, the bailiff's step creaked on the stair. A second later, the prim, glistening face looked in on them.

"Well, miss, I'm happy to say your aunt's quieting down peaceful as a baby. Not much the worse for her little mishap, though I was a bit knocked over when that message came. Anythink I can do for you before I pop off?"

"Nothing at all. Good-evening." Natasha spoke between her set teeth.

"Good-evening, miss—and you, sir. I'll call in first thing in the morning to see how she's going on."

With this parting assurance, he flattened down his nauseous fore-lock with the palm of his hand, hitched into place the trouser-leg which had got caught up over his woollen underwear, and let himself out into the darkness.

Natasha shook with a spasm of loathing.

"Oh, if only I knew some way of showing them up! How can I, though, when I'm utterly ignorant and can't prove anything against them?" She stood with clenched hands on the spot where so short a time ago his arms had encircled her. It was some seconds before she drew a deep breath and turned to him a face still troubled but apologetic. "You really must forgive me for dragging you into this muddle. I'm rather ashamed at unburdening myself like this. Now I suppose I'd better go and look after Caroline."

She said good-night quickly, and left him to smoke another cigarette, and ponder on the evening's events.

Hours later, in bed, he was still turning over her interpretation of the Tilburys' motives, at one moment thinking it plausible and at the next exaggeratedly far-fetched. To get the old lady entirely at their mercy—that was how she had put it—could mean nothing worse than settling themselves in a berth which would serve just so long as their employer lived, but no longer. If she died, they would be up against hardship again. Therefore, why worry? And yet, what about that feeling he had had to-night, the dim notion that the couple were tampering with forces they did not understand? Was it purely visionary on his part? Connie's relief, too, had sounded just a trifle too hysterical. . . .

Gradually all this faded from his thoughts. Once more the music which had brought him and Natasha together pulsed through his brain like a delicious sedative. Half-asleep he felt again the yielding body pressed against his, inhaled the faint daffodil fragrance of the hair brushing his cheek. . . .

What was that? He woke with a start. From the study beneath had come a sort of thud, as though a piece of furniture had been overturned on the carpeted floor. He held his breath, but could hear only his heart-beats.

Still he was not satisfied. After a brief debate, he slid out of bed and with extreme caution crept down to look into the matter.

## CHAPTER NINE

SURREPTITIOUSLY he tried the study door, which was locked. Unbroken silence lay behind it. He waited a minute or two, but nothing happened.

Oh, well, he was wrong, evidently—though later, when he had regained his own quarters, it occurred to him that possibly there was some one inside the room with the door fastened for safety. The point was, who could have got hold of the keys, undoubtedly stowed away beneath their owner's pillows? Only Alfred Tilbury and Natasha—and of these two the latter alone would be able to return them before they were missed.

Had the girl snatched this opportunity to search the study, and if so, what was her object? There was hopelessly little chance of discovering anything against the bailiff and his wife, and still less of lighting on the clue to Miss Bundy's interest in the Glebe House. Yet it was this second matter which bothered him, and though there was nothing very wrong in her wanting to explore, he somehow hated to think she would take advantage of her aunt's illness to do so. He wondered again if she really believed there might be treasure buried in or about the site of the ruin.

Her face at breakfast told him nothing, except relief over the invalid's marked improvement.

"She's almost all right. Isn't it strange? Why, I've had a hard job keeping her in bed. Here are your keys, by the way. You are to take them up to her this evening, and"—with a laugh—"will you stay with the charwoman while she cleans the room? Even Mrs. Bebb's not allowed in there alone. Caroline undertakes to watch her."

This was news. On joining the lean old woman armed with dust-pan and broom he decided to question her as to the date when the vigilance commenced.

"Wot, this monkey business, sir?" She cocked an amused eye at him and sniffed contemptuously. "This is a new fad, this is. We began it—let's see—oh, 'bout the time you got here. Yes, now I count back, it was the very first morning, three weeks ago."

Then the precautions coincided with his arrival. Why, when he was permitted free access to everything the room contained? But wait! The Tilburys had come at the same time—to be exact, the day before. . . . No, that fact did not help. If any one was in Miss Bundy's confidence, they were; and in any case, they spent long hours here every evening. All the servants had been in service for months, in some cases years, before the new conditions arose; and Natasha herself had been entrusted with the keys only a moment ago! In short, he was as far from a solution as before. For that matter, perhaps there was no solution, except that Miss Bundy was the victim of an *idée fixe.*

Later in the day he learned the result of Natasha's conference with the doctor, who apparently was much upset over her disclosure.

"He declares these nightly meetings are responsible for her condition—intense nervous excitement, or perhaps something we don't know about—and that they've got to stop, or he won't answer for the consequences. This attack is only the beginning. There'll be others, if she isn't careful. She may even drop dead."

"How did she take all this?"

"Badly. She's livid with rage, but she's had to give in. I've expected all morning to get my marching orders, but so far she's only glared at me. She's got to lie up for a week, diet, and see no one for more than a few minutes—so temporarily, at least, I've outwitted those hypocrites!"

"What explanation did she give the doctor?"

"None, really. He tried to worm it out of her, but didn't succeed. I believe she stammered something about a line of research, and that it couldn't possibly hurt her, but that's all. I've been told to watch and keep him posted. He says she doesn't need a nurse."

Soon after this several minute incidents occurred which, at the time, meant little. The first of these concerned the alligator-bag, destined to figure largely in coming events.

On the second evening when Neil returned the keys, he surprised Miss Bundy going over a mass of loose foolscap sheets, which she quickly began stuffing into the receptacle just mentioned, locking the latter with the tiny key attached to her gold chain. In spite of her haste to conceal the scattered pages, Neil recognised on those nearest him the characteristic hieroglyphics of her father's writing, wavering and indistinct, like the effort of extreme age.

So there was actually a manuscript—though what it represented and why she clung to it so jealously no mental skill could fathom. Plainly it was something she deeply valued. When he had had time to think it over he realised that this discovery threw no light on the riddle of the study, which appeared to present a quite separate mystery—unless, of course, one impinged upon the other.

If Fate could have granted him the remotest insight into the horrors which were going to take place before he again set eyes on these scribbled sheets, he would have snatched them from the stumpy hands then and there, read them and thrown them into the fire. Unluckily no such premonition darkened his mind. Instead, pretending to notice nothing, he congratulated his hostess on her speedy recovery.

"Yes, yes, I'm quite well," she replied somewhat crossly. "Not that I was ever ill. I slipped and struck my head, that was all. If Graves were anything but an old fuss-pot I'd be up and about."

Her bravado did not deceive him. It was not easy to say how he knew she was secretly alarmed about herself, but for all that he was certain he was right. All her tremendous energy seemed to have been turned into thinking, planning. The look in her eyes told him this, and his belief was confirmed when she handed him a note she had ready, sealed and directed to Alfred Tilbury. Would he take it down to the lodge for her?

"If no one is there, just open the door and lay it on the table. I should like Tilbury to get it the moment he comes in."

He knew she had chosen him as emissary because she dreaded the servants' gossip. At the same time he was struck by her avoidance of his eye, and equally by her unwillingness to let a day go by without communicating with her favourites.

The lodge was empty, the small living-room, for all its gay cretonnes, in a state of squalid untidiness. Tilbury's camera occupied a large space, and beside it was a dusty safe, stacked up with account books and bottled stout. The table was such a clutter of unwashed tea things, socks to be darned, gramophone records and copies of *Home Chat*, that Neil had to clear a corner before setting down the note. In so doing he picked up a three-inch chemist's phial, partly filled with neutral-coloured liquid. A glance at its label made him frown and scratch his head thoughtfully.

Now, which of the Tilburys took thyroid extract? Hardly Connie, always bursting with exuberance. Alfred, to be sure, was a bit apathetic, though one would not have expected him to go in for this kind of preparation. Some friend must have put him on to it, with the view of boosting up his energy. Liquid, too. That was odd. Neil till now had not known of the stuff in other than tabloid form.

The matter did not occupy him long. What did stick in his mind with troublesome persistence was the information he happened on two days after this. It had to do with Natasha's situation.

Having broken his watch-crystal he had gone in to Glastonbury to get a new one. In the long, narrow jeweller's shop he came on the girl, whom at first he failed to recognise because she was unfamiliarly dressed in black, and standing with her back to him at the far counter. It was her voice, edged with keen disappointment, which revealed her identity.

"Only fifteen pounds for all these!" she was saying. "Surely that's frightfully little!"

The jeweller expressed regret. The stones were old-fashioned in cut, the settings, unfortunately, counted for nothing. Perhaps she would care to try elsewhere? There was a painful pause, fraught with indecision, ended by her pushing a little heap of ornaments across the counter.

"No, it's no use. I'll take the fifteen pounds—though it's a pathetic start towards the hundred I've got to raise, isn't it? What a pity I wasn't trained as a burglar!" She gave a quick laugh, in which the man politely joined, but there was a note in hers which, to Neil's ears, conveyed only dire distress.

He hoped to slip out unnoticed, but already she had turned, seen him, and drawn in her breath with dismay. Then she laughed again to hide her discomfiture, but her face as he came up to her flushed scarlet. No good pretending he had not heard. He did the next best thing, and fingered the pile of trinkets with frank curiosity. They consisted of odds and ends, chief among which were a small diamond cluster ring and a Russian cross of semi-precious stones.

"So you really want to part with these, do you?" he asked casually.

"I must. Even a small sum is better than nothing. Not that I mind. I never wear them."

The jeweller came from behind the partition to count some bank-notes into her hand. She crammed them into her purse and was about to leave when Neil detained her.

"Why rush off? Let's get tea and go to a cinema. I feel the need of diversion. Don't you?"

From the way she hesitated he knew how deeply embarrassed she was, but her state of mind was too wretched to let this weigh with her for long. For the past few days he had suspected something amiss, and now he was sure that a crisis in her affairs had arisen.

"Well, then. I'll come if you want me to, but I warn you not to expect me to be entertaining. I've a splitting head—for one thing."

They found an empty tea-shop with a high settle making an inglenook of the fire. Natasha sank down in the corner, her coat thrown back to disclose a scarf barbarically striped in red and orange. The close black hat she wore threw her Slavic contours into bold relief and accented the tawny pallor of her skin, to which, presently, the fire and the hot tea brought a tinge of colour. He banked cushions at her back, and when he saw she was eating nothing, lit a cigarette for her.

"Headache better?"

"Thanks, it's going off."

For some moments he puffed in silence, summoning courage to take a plunge. Finally he said as naturally as he could, "You won't be annoyed if I ask you something, will you? It's about this hundred pounds you mentioned. Is it very urgent?"

She winced and did not look at him. "Very, I'm afraid. I've tried every way I could think of to get hold of it, and now the time's getting short. It's got to be found, somehow—but I'd rather not discuss it."

"But I want to discuss it," he objected. "Good God, do you suppose I haven't been in tight corners myself? I usually find it's a help to talk it over with some one."

"That's just it. I can't talk this over with any one. Not a human soul," she answered in a low voice.

"Why on earth not? For that matter, what happens if you don't succeed?"

"Something quite ghastly." She whispered this to herself rather than to him. "Something which mustn't be allowed to happen. It's up to me to prevent it—before it's too late."

He realised she had reached a state of desperation. At her words a disagreeable suspicion grazed his mind. He leant forward and laid a firm hand on her rigidly clasped ones.

"Look here, my child. I've knocked about a good deal, and I may say it takes a fair amount to jar me. Why can't you let me in on this? What is it you're wanting to do?"

For a fleeting moment he thought she was going to blurt out the truth, but he was mistaken. She merely said, "Leave here. Go away."

"Where? Why? Is it necessary?"

She did not answer. He was right, then. She had a secret to hide, from her aunt, from all this small, censorious world in which she lived. Even though the idea hurt, her refusal to make the least bid for sympathy moved him more than any appealing outburst. She had pride—too much, perhaps, for her good. All the same, at the risk of a rebuff, he was resolved to try his luck.

"Now, listen to me, and don't misunderstand what I'm going to say. I can lend you that hundred easily, and it won't make any difference when you pay it back—if ever. Let me do it, please. I'll write you a cheque this instant."

He was almost alarmed by her reception of his offer. She had drawn back against the settle, was gazing at him with a sort of incredulous horror quite disproportionate to the circumstances—or so it seemed to him.

"Take money from you? Is it possible you thought I would? Oh! Can you imagine I'd have told you this if—if—" Speech failed her.

"No, no, of course not! What have you told me, except what I overheard by accident? Aren't you making a great fuss over quite a simple proposition? Be reasonable, please."

"I am being reasonable. I can't take your money. No, there's no use insisting. This conversation has got to end, now," She began gathering up her bag and gloves.

"Oh, well, don't annihilate me. Sit down. Let's thrash this out. I suppose you haven't thought of applying to your aunt?"

"Caroline? No. She's the very last person I could go to. Oh, I can't expect you to understand! Don't worry about me. I shall get it in one way or another. I've got to."

Something rather grim in her tone made him look at her quickly, but she did not notice the glance.

"Now," she said determinedly, "that's finished—except for one request I have to make. Don't, please, mention this to the Gisbornes. They know nothing about my troubles, and I don't intend that they should."

"Right—I promise. Now, let's go and see 'Love Behind Bars.' It looks just the kind of maudlin stuff that acts as a soothing-powder. Then we'll drop in at the King's Arms and see what sort of cocktail they can make."

Miss Bundy was in their midst again, physically greatly restored. She was still obeying the mandate about early hours and no excitement, though it was patent to all beholders how much she chafed under the restraint. She had a way now of slipping down to the lodge for private conferences, and only a few days after her reappearance Neil, returning from an early ramble and pausing to hang up his coat in the lobby, heard her sending a telegram which plainly showed how the wind blew. The name Braselton made him stop and listen. Wasn't Miss Braselton the head mistress Natasha had mentioned as her aunt's one close friend?

The guarded voice at the telephone continued: "Bellingham, Gloucestershire. There—have you got that correctly? Many regrets, have been ill and must ask you to postpone visit here. Writing. Signature, Caroline."

Yes, it was plain enough she was unwilling to have any one about who might pry into things and perhaps interfere. Too bad, if what Natasha believed was true, for the lady in question would probably prove an influence for good. However, the matter was not ended.

Late that afternoon he entered the drawing-room to find himself face to face with an imposing woman who, seated before the fire, was calmly disposing of a solitary tea. A travelling coat and gloves lay beside her on the sofa; a smart turban framed well-waved grey hair. He was about to apologise and retreat when she beckoned to him with authority, and fixing a pair of piercing brown eyes on him bade him sit down.

"You are Mr. Starkey, of course." Her voice, though magisterial, was admirably pitched. "You see, I know all about you—and I particularly want a word with you before Miss Bundy comes home. Perhaps I'd better introduce myself, I am Emily Braselton."

Afterwards he reflected that it was just as though she had said, "I am Mary, Queen of England."


## CHAPTER TEN

WHETHER the visitor had failed to receive the telegram putting her off or had come in spite of the message, he was left guessing. Meanwhile, with another look of worldly penetration, Miss Braselton plunged into her subject.

"Mr. Starkey, I am much concerned over the situation in this house. Miss Bundy's recent attack is not half so ominous as the rumours which have been reaching me. Tell me plainly. In what ways do you find her altered?"

Neil hedged a little, only to be pulled up short.

"No, no, this is no secret, I assure you. Every one knows something is wrong here. The whole point is, what?"

"Sometimes it's hard to separate cause and effect," he temporised. "You see, till my stay here I had only seen Miss Bundy once, so how can I judge what she was like before? Personally, I mean. High blood-pressure, of course—"

"That's neither here nor there." She sounded slightly impatient. "When I was here just before Christmas, I am positive there was nothing abnormal about her blood-pressure. Nervous excitement is all very well, but what is causing that excitement? Come, you have eyes in your head. Why need we beat about the bush? Should you say, for instance, that she is being subjected to some malign influence? There, I can't put it more plainly than that, can I? What I want is a direct yes or no."

Neil, not yet knowing Miss Braselton's reputation for calling a spade a spade, was decidedly disconcerted. This was no business of his. Had he any right to make assertions he could not substantiate?

"The possibility has occurred to me—but frankly I don't know how to answer your question. When you say malign influence—"

She interrupted him again with good-humoured scorn.

"You can't deceive me, Mr. Starkey. You know as well as I do that Caroline Bundy is being victimised, preyed upon. Blackmail is an ugly word which I hesitate to employ—but call it what you like, have you observed anything at all peculiar in her relations with"—she paused, looked about, and lowered her voice portentously—*"Natasha Andreyev?"*

At the unexpected name Neil almost jumped out of his seat. Natasha—! So this was what her innuendoes had been leading up to! The blood mounted angrily to his face. He could hardly trust himself to answer politely.

"I'm afraid I don't understand you," he returned stiffly. "Perhaps you'd better explain."

She shot him a shrewd glance. "Very well, I will. I have good reason to suspect the young woman I've mentioned is trying to extort money by means of pressure—more, that she remains here solely because of the hold she's managed to obtain. You, obviously, may be ignorant of this. I asked merely in case you had noticed any indication of such a state of affairs."

"Absolutely none. I may say the very suggestion is utterly dumbfounding."

His faculties were all at sea. The slight shrug which greeted his denial conveyed an infuriating judgment on the wiles of women and the blind credulity of his own sex, yet even as he met Miss Braselton's eye he wondered if and how she knew of Natasha's financial troubles. Her air of secret knowledge roused his hostility to such an extent that he cast off all caution.

"You'd like my real opinion," he said coldly. "Well, here it is: If Miss Bundy is under any evil influence, you must look elsewhere for the agents. Not far off, either. Do you know what I mean?"

"Perfectly," she nodded. "The bailiff and his wife. Oh, don't imagine I'm overlooking their part in this. Indeed that would supply just the leverage for a calculating third party to make use of. In other words, if one has committed some compromising folly, one will go to considerable lengths to prevent its being noised abroad. That is exactly what I fear to be the case—that poor Carrie has been acting stupidly, and that Natasha by threatening to make damaging statements is keeping her in perpetual terror. You must admit she's had ample opportunity to find things out."

Neil had now reached boiling point. "Please get this right, Miss Braselton," he said. "Miss Andreyev knows no more of the real situation than you or I. She's badly worried over Miss Bundy, and doing her utmost to keep an eye on her. I'm, moreover, quite positive she never receives a penny over and above what she earns."

"H'm," remarked the other, as though to say, "You believe that, of course. *You would.*" After a second she continued with a change of tone, "And now, as to the actual nature of these meetings with Mr. and Mrs. Tilbury. I myself suspect spiritualism. And you?"

"And if it is spiritualism," he retorted, "what of it? Why the exaggerated secrecy?"

"Ah! you don't know Caroline as I do. She is painfully sensitive to ridicule, like her father before her. The traditions of exact science, you understand, and in the present case the knowledge that her taking up with inferior people is sure to be criticised. Poor creature, she's like an ostrich hiding its head in the sand, though that, we're now informed, is a fallacy. Besides, how do we know there isn't some extra, dangerous feature, some definite thing which is wrecking her morale and making her an easy prey for the unscrupulous?"

She was thinking aloud. Her squared shoulders and set chin spoke of indomitable purpose.

"Anyhow," she pursued, "I shall make it my business to ferret out the truth. While she's surrounded like this I'm helpless, but if I succeed in persuading her to come away with me it will be another story. The doctor, I fancy, will uphold me. Meanwhile, Mr. Starkey, if I've trodden on your toes, I apologise. Please believe I don't venture blindfold on these assertions. I needn't say I rely on your discretion to—Hark! There's the car." Rising hurriedly she held out her hand. "If you wouldn't mind—the other door. It would be fatal if she thought we'd been discussing her."

Neil, disappearing into the library, saw her surge forward to greet her friend, who, shapeless and bulky in an old fur coat, stood in the entrance, gaping. The opening remarks of the two fell on his ears.

"Carrie, my dear! You didn't expect me, did you? Never mind, I've come expressly to carry you off to Rome. No arguments. Everything's arranged."

"Rome? But I don't want to go to Rome!" stammered the other, startled but obstinate. "I've no intention of—"

Let them fight it out, thought Neil, too angry to care about the outcome. As for that poisonous-tongued schoolmistress, she ought to be muzzled. A woman like that could do any amount of dam—

"Hallo! I beg your pardon!" This to the small, tousled figure which cannoned into him on his passage through the dark room. "It's Mrs. Tilbury, isn't it?"

"Would you believe it?" giggled Connie. "I popped in 'ere to 'ave a look at the papers, and wot must I do but drop asleep, sound as a church! Alf won't 'arf give me wot for!"

It occurred to him she might have been eavesdropping, with salutary effects, too, except for those beastly hints against Natasha. . . . Where was Natasha, by the way? Not till he went out to the garage did he come upon her, examining a big car and chatting with a chauffeur who touched his cap and withdrew. At once she turned, eyes shining.

"You know the head mistress I told you about?" she whispered excitedly. "Well, she's here. Stopping the night on her way to Paris, and planning to take Caroline with her."

"So I've just heard. The question is, Will Miss Bundy go?"

"There's that, of course." Her face fell a little. "But, oh, what a perfect solution it would mean! Emily Braselton's the one to tackle these people. If she can rid us of them, I'll go on my knees to thank her!"

So genuine did she sound that he felt ashamed of his doubt as to which prospect pleased her more—that of extricating her aunt, or of ousting the schemers.

"In the nick of time too," she continued in an undertone. "These visits to the lodge . . . I can't prevent them, but I know we shall have her crocking up again, worse than before. Do you think I ought to say anything to Emily?"

"Better not," he advised, wondering if he dared risk a word of warning. "No, if I were you, I'd leave them alone together. Why not come with me to the vicarage? Rachel complains you've not been near her for ten days."

She looked away, hesitating. "No, I can't manage to-night. Give Rachel my love, and—and—I say, those lamps are dim! Why don't you get your engine de-carbonised? You've no end of bother getting started."

No mention of her own tangle since their one futile discussion. He pictured her still struggling alone, an eaglet caught in a snare. Why, why was she so obstinate?

In the gloom of the double hedge some one scuttled, rabbit-like, across his path. The faint head-lamps lit for an instant the tear-swollen face and loose braids of Connie Tilbury, blindly fleeing in the opposite direction. Astonished, he gazed after her. She was gone now, but from the bend behind came a curious sound, half-sobs, half-chattering of teeth.

His brakes, violently applied, had swung him round so that the ineffectual lights bored into the shrubbery. Thus Tilbury, flinging wide the lodge door, did not perceive him, though he himself was clearly visible to Neil. His glassy eyes scanned the darkness, his spiky moustache bristled above teeth bared in a snarl.

"Con!" he called with cautious imperiousness. "You b— fool, wot's the idea? You come when I tell you. Wot, you won't, won't you? Well, then, my girl, I'm counting just five—see? And if you're not—"

Neil's engine whirred. The speaker gave a jump, peered into the shadows, and underwent a complete change.

"Oh! It's you, sir!" he cried suavely. "Just looking for the wife. Didn't 'appen to see her go past, did you, sir?"

"Yes, towards the house, I fancy."

"T'ck! Silly little tyke!" exclaimed the other, sprinting with lightning celerity up the drive. "Some gyme she's up to. Watch me catch her!"

The self-starter was again refusing to function when a creaking sound came from the hedge, and Neil beheld the two Tilburys approaching, arm-in-arm, convulsed with hilarity. A rapid volte-face, considering what he had just witnessed. Still, it was their own business, not his, and Neil would not have glanced at them twice, but for a lurking suspicion that the present scene was staged for his benefit.

"Gates, sir?" volunteered the bailiff jovially. "'Arf a mo'. . . . No, you don't, naughty!" Dragging the woman with him and giving her a playful pinch. "No more capering off at 'ide-and-seek. . . . Now, sir, drive ahead—nothing in front."

There was something, though, unseen till now. From the path which debouched between the gates and the lodge, Miss Bundy stumbled forth to run bolt into the mudguard and draw back confused. The sight of her heaving chest and dishevelled hair was as startling to the Tilburys as to Neil. Alfred recovered first, and pressing forward eagerly forestalled any speech on her part.

"Well, well! Taking a bit of a turn, eh, miss? Oughtn't to 'urry like that, though. Bad for the 'eart, if you'll pardon me . . ."

Midway his prattle the two-seater lunged forward, not preventing its occupant from catching the agitated words bursting from the old woman's lips: "This evening, as usual. I daren't put it off! Eleven—or it may have to be later . . ."

Through the side of the car Neil descried Connie, staring with fixed, red-rimmed eyes at the speaker's face.

## CHAPTER ELEVEN

FROM the vicarage Neil at once tried to telephone Natasha, and after several engaged signals, cut in on a conversation between her and a man. Try as he would, he could not put down the receiver till the concluding sentences had reached his ears. His whole skin prickled at the thought that now, at last, he was actually listening to the voice of one who had filled him with jealous rage for weeks on end. That it was an agreeable voice, well bred and with a definite charm, only made matters worse.

"Why aren't you here?" it said, with urgent reproach. "I've been at the Royal Pump over half an hour, waiting. I tell you, I can't bear this uncertainty any longer. We've jolly well got to come to some decision."

"Don't worry—I'm coming," answered the girl guardedly. "I'm more cheerful to-night, anyway."

"Why? You can't mean you really see a—"

"S'sh! Wait. I'll tell you presently." The click which followed told of a disconnection.

When, a few minutes later, he got through it was to learn from Crabbe that Natasha had just left the house. Foiled and furious, he banged down the receiver, well aware that his face had turned so swarthily red that Rachel and her brother were eyeing him with surprise.

"Anything wrong?" asked the former quietly. "You seem upset."

"No—yes." To himself he was saying: What decision did they mean? Why couldn't the fellow bear what uncertainty? Were they planning an elopement? Was the man already married? Aloud he explained briefly how he believed Miss Bundy was about to hold another seance, and that he considered Natasha ought to be told. "As she's dining out, there's nothing I can do except inform Miss Braselton—and I hate interfering to that extent."

The Gisbornes shrugged and exchanged glances.

"Really, now that Emily Braselton is there," said Rachel, "I should leave her to handle the situation. She'll look out for Carrie, never fear—though I must say it's odd for Carrie to do this the very moment her friend arrives."

"It's more than odd." His annoyance vented itself in a false direction. "Till now I've taken Natasha's suspicions with a grain of salt, but just now, believe it or not, I got the impression of something—well, sinister."

Rachel looked at him intently, but the vicar snorted with scorn.

"That photographer sinister? About as sinister as a white guinea-pig! He's out to get all he can, of course, but from what I know he can't have any genuinely evil intentions. It's impossible."

"But," objected his sister pleadingly, "if a word from you would put a stop to all this, don't you think it's your duty to speak it?"

"My dear Rachel, I said my say in the very beginning, and all I accomplished was to make an enemy. Carrie won't listen to me. Emily Braselton, now, may have better luck. I have some acquaintance with her, and I can confidently state that if there's any hocus-pocus going on she'll scent it at once. I expected sooner or later she would come to the rescue." He nodded with complacent triumph, as one whose prophecies had been fulfilled.

All the evening Neil felt Rachel watching him tentatively. When he took his leave she made an excuse to accompany him to the gate.

"About Tasha—" she whispered in a troubled voice.

"Do you think by any chance she's avoiding me? Is she unhappy, or anything?"

After his promise, it was hard to answer this. He rattled off an unconvincing explanation about the girl being kept busy over her aunt's illness, uncomfortably aware of his companion's steady gaze.

"Neil, you like her, don't you?"

"Very much," he replied, anxious to be gone.

"But I take it she's told you nothing about—herself?"

"I never expected she would. She's not the sort who bestows confidences freely. Why?"

"Nothing, only—Forgive an old maid's impertinence, but when you were at the telephone this evening I rather thought—that is, I got the impression you might be falling in love with her. Am I right?"

He flinched and grew hot in the collar. "Good God, no! See here, my dear, are you trying to steer me into matrimony? Because if so I must warn you it's a hopeless job. I'm in the difficult between stage, long past the calf-period, and nowhere near the dangerous forties. Not that it matters a damn what my inclinations are. She wouldn't look at me in any case."

"Well," she said, smiling, "we'll have to let it go at that. Only please don't give up trying to—to get a bit nearer. You needn't lose your heart over that."

"No, only my temper."

He gave a short laugh to hide his embarrassment. How was he to admit how hard he had tried, the nights he had lain awake endeavouring to solve the riddle of one who was not in the remotest degree interested in him? As he drove off an irritable touchiness laid hold of him. Hang Natasha and her cursed entanglements! If Rachel wanted them cleared up, let her do it herself. She knew something. Well, why didn't she act on her knowledge? The natural answer was that she couldn't, but at that moment it seemed to him that every person with whom he had contact was guarding some secret—the vicar. Miss Bundy, Natasha, Rachel, Emily Braselton. It grimly amused him to speculate on what would happen if all the lot got together and laid their cards on the table. . . .

And Alfred and Con—he was forgetting them. Did they, too, have something up their sleeves? He was inclined to consider this question very seriously when, at one o'clock, he heard the back door open softly and from his window saw their two stealthy forms slipping round the terrace. That meant Miss Bundy had pulled off what she had planned, after her guest was wrapt in slumber. He gloated over the surprise he was going to spring on Natasha next morning. Little did she realise how the old lady had stolen a march on her.

Yet on the following day events showed such a gratifying tendency to smooth themselves out that he felt his conclusions reversed and himself made to appear wholly ridiculous. He began, indeed, to share the vicar's belief that Miss Braselton's coming had put everything right.

"I don't suppose you know that your aunt had those people here again late last night?"

Having fired this announcement with brutal intent, Neil was unworthily triumphant to see his shaft take effect. Natasha lowered the bonnet of the car and fixed searching eyes on him.

"I went out. How do you know this?"

He supplied her with the facts, only to find her less perturbed than he had anticipated.

"Oh, well, it's probably the last time. You see, everything's worked out most satisfactorily—far better, indeed, than one could have hoped. We've had the doctor here, and he's told Caroline she must get away—that change is what she needs, and now's the opportunity to go with some one who'll look after her. To my astonishment she gave in like a lamb. I really don't know why, but there it is. She means to—s'sh! There's that chauffeur coming. Emily's leaving in a few minutes—has to be in Paris to-morrow for some conference."

"Then Miss Bundy's not going with her?"

"No, joining her on Saturday. She insists on a few days to prepare for the journey, and of course it will be better to get her strength back before she goes. What a gorgeous day! Like to come with me for a long drive? I've got to do some shopping for Caroline, right after lunch."

He despised himself for the alacrity with which he jumped at the invitation. Fool that he was! Utter, hopeless fool! He was slipping into quicksands and had not the will to put out a finger to save himself. All this could lead to no good, and well he knew it. Why hadn't he the strength of mind to stick to his job and put this girl out of his thoughts?

Miss Bundy, at lunch, wore that look of concentrated purpose he had noticed ever since her attack, while her midnight stance, far from harming her, seemed to have brought her fresh vitality. Not only was she apparently reconciled to the holiday she had so strenuously opposed, but she had the air of having settled harassing difficulties to her entire satisfaction. Why, she looked positively smug! The cat that has eaten the canary occurred to him as the correct comparison. He could not understand this complete change of front, and it was equally hard to see why she should urge her niece to spend the whole afternoon out and make the most of the sunshine. Never before had he known her display the least concern over Natasha's pleasure.

"Mr. Starkey's going too, is he? That's excellent. You must show him some of the sights. You won't mind venturing as far as Exeter, I hope? I've rather set my heart on some things from the Scotch wool shop there."

What had come over her? And for that matter what had turned Natasha into a being totally different from her recent self? When he met her at the garage she was singing "Sous les Toits de Paris" with carefree jubilance, her scarlet beret was set at a provoking angle, while her eyes sparkled in a manner which sent his own spirits soaring.

"By Jove!" he marvelled. "You look ready for any deed!"

"That's how I feel," she threw at him over her shoulder. "Funny, isn't it, how a little thing like a trip to London can brighten one's point of view? I'm driving Caroline there, you see, in order to speed her on her way. Just what I was banking on—only these events so seldom materialise. Come along, let's be off."

While he was cogitating on her elation, they came upon the Tilburys climbing into their neat Ford. Connie waved to them brightly.

"We've got the afternoon to ourselves too," she announced. "Alf and me are going to the Cheddar Gorge. Nice tea they give you at that 'otel by the caves. Ever been there?"

In the lane Natasha muttered vindictively: "Beastly little leeches! Why, to see them now you'd think they were glad Caroline was going away. They'd sing another tune if they guessed what a bloodhound Emily is."

"You seem quite confident this move will clear everything up," he remarked, far from envisaging how the sleuth propensities of Miss Braselton were to involve other people than the Tilbury couple in disaster.

"I am confident. I feel quite sure Emily will drag the whole mystery out and restore Caroline to a normal condition. The clever way she's handled her in these few hours shows what she can do. You wouldn't believe how quickly it was all settled. She's arranged for Caroline to spend Friday night at her flat in Kensington so as to break the journey, crossing by the ten o'clock boat Saturday morning. She's even getting her ticket and visa, so there'll be nothing to bother about. So that leaves me free to tackle my own problems," she finished in an undertone.

"And is the answer to them to be found in London?" He was thinking of the scrap of conversation heard last night over the telephone.

"I hope so, God knows!" She sighed, but seemed determined not to be cast down. "Anyhow, the way things are turning out is almost too good to be true—about the Tilburys, I mean." She said this hurriedly, as though to divert attention from personal matters. "I wasn't cut out for a watch dog, and I tell you I'm feeling the strain. Oh, you may laugh if you like, but this past week I've been absolutely haunted by the thought of some dreadful disaster." She shuddered and grew very grave. "I still can't get hold of a thing against those two smooth little people, and yet a sixth sense warns me Caroline is in their clutches and doesn't know it. They possess her body and soul, so much so that I should have been in terror to leave her alone with them."

While she was speaking his own thoughts had turned to the impression he had received of the Tilburys on two occasions, but her last sentence made him prick up his ears in quite another way.

"Do you mean you had intended to go away? You mentioned the possibility, I know, but I'm not sure I took it seriously."

"Well, you may take it seriously now. If things break well for me, this green and pleasant land shall know me no more. I shall vanish, that's all."

Even though she did not sound particularly happy as she made the announcement, he felt as if hit by a sledgehammer.

"But, hold on! You can't do that!" he cried in unconcealed dismay. "If you desert me, what amusement will be left? Expect me to spend my evenings doing crossword puzzles?"

She gave a ringing laugh. "And far more profitable, too," she retorted. "They can be solved, you know."

"I'm patiently hoping you can be solved."

"I advise you to give up the struggle." She glanced sideways at him. "I gave it up some time ago. Now I'm just letting Fate do as it likes with me. I've reached the point when anything's better than continually weighing right and wrong, even taking hurdles blindfold. One may break one's neck, but at least one will have had a good run for one's money. Isn't that so?"

The time came when he was to recall this reckless speech and read into it calamitous meanings. Now, however, he was too keenly responsive to the challenge of her mood to analyse anything closely.

Exeter—shopping—a visit to the cathedral. Where should they go for tea? It was at Natasha's suggestion they drove to Bath, the very name of which was now detestable; and that there was reason for the manoeuvre was speedily apparent. No sooner was the meal terminated than the girl rose, eyed him hesitatingly, and asked if he minded being left for twenty minutes.

"I shan't be longer. Where do you want me to pick you up?"

"Oh, here. I'll hunt up the American bar."

Two dry Martinis left him still ransacking his memory for new invectives to hurl at his own head. In the name of all moonstruck imbeciles, what spell had descended on him, Neil Starkey, of all people? When he thought of how, on that lovely stretch of road he had been about to declare his passion like any schoolboy he grovelled with shame. Yes, passion for an object he knew would have none of him! He reviled himself for straining after the unobtainable, and even more bitterly denounced his weakness in watching the clock as he pictured the scene being enacted somewhere not far off. He was about to command a third drink when the Klaxon drew him glumly to the pavement, to find the cause of his chagrin awaiting him.

As he expected, not a word of explanation. Her expression was indecipherable. He climbed in beside her, totally bereft of conversation, but aware that she, like himself, was wrapt in meditative thought. There was a touch of wistfulness in her subdued mien.

Just as they reached Stoke Paulton, a station taxi met them, chugging out of the gates. Inside was a sedate, elderly man, black-clad, with an open brief-case on his knees. At sight of him Natasha stiffened and gazed with intent curiosity.

"A visitor! He must have come by appointment, from the look of him. That's queer. I heard nothing of it." All at once she uttered a cry of enlightenment and gripped Neil's arm. "Tell me—what does he look like to you?" she demanded urgently.

"Possibly a medical specialist. More likely a lawyer."

"Lawyer! I knew it—it's her solicitor from London. So that's why she got rid of me this afternoon. I knew she didn't want one of those things we bought. Of course—fool that I am! That explains it. . . ."

"Explains what?" he inquired, mystified.

"Why, that she's up to something she doesn't want me to find out. As if it concerned me what she does! But she's afraid, all the same—afraid I might spoil her game."

However, what Miss Bundy's game was neither of them found out till the damage was accomplished.


## CHAPTER TWELVE

Friday, the twentieth of March—that day whose smallest incident was to be raked over again and again, and subjected to the most agonised scrutiny, but Neil as yet little dreamed it was to stand out red-lettered in his memory for the rest of time.

He was gazing blankly at the spot where the car had just disappeared into the shrubbery, getting used to the idea of Natasha's being gone and still feeling a bit staggered over his hostess's inconceivable whim of installing the bailiff and his wife in the house as caretakers and—crowning absurdity!—chaperons.

This latter suggestion was only too palpably an excuse for the couple's new promotion. With embarrassed avoidance of his eye the old lady had passed quickly to other matters. He, Neil, was to be given entire charge of the study keys, and lock up as usual. Mrs. Tilbury would take over the housekeeping, and she and her husband would have their meals by themselves.

No sooner had the announcement been made than the speaker left the dining-room, and half a minute later her outraged niece burst in like a cyclone.

"You've heard? Chaperons! Really, it's the last straw! Has she gone quite mad? That insufferable pair lording it over every one, making free of her personal belongings—!" For a moment breath failed her.

"Not that it affects me, for I shan't stop to see it. It's you I'm thinking about."

"You needn't. I promised to spend the month at the vicarage, so I shall come here only to work. I understand Rachel has invited you too. What about it?" He made no reference to her declaration of two days before.

She grew suddenly evasive. "I can't tell yet what I'll do. As I've got to bring the car back to Saunders's Garage in Glastonbury for overhauling I may turn up Sunday for a day or two. After that—*qui sait?*" She shrugged and returned to the source of her indignation. "Isn't there something uncanny about the way those two are creeping up, step by step, getting more power? If I wasn't so sure Emily was going to put everything right I'd say now they're coming into the house they'd never move out again. They will, though, sooner than they think. Thank God she's leaving in an hour. Why, even up to last night I felt something might happen to upset her plans. Do you know what happened?" she came a step closer. "After I'd gone to my room I heard her slip down here and followed to see what she was up to. She was in the lobby, just putting on her old leather coat to go out."

"What, in the rain?"

"Yes, and at twelve o'clock. She was quite nasty to me when I made her go to bed—said I was treating her like a child. I had to remind her that the doctor had said she was not to run any risks with her health or she would not be fit for her journey. After that I slept with my door open. Not that I've the least notion what she wanted to do, but there was some mischief afoot, never fear."

"Well, she'll be safe enough from now on."

Looking back he was struck by his comfortable faith in this statement. He fully shared the girl's confidence that Miss Braselton, little as he liked her, would find out the Tilburys' designs and expose them—although what hidden plan the latter could be nurturing was impossible to conceive. Two more empty-headed little people he had seldom come across. Even the single memory of Alfred's snarling temper and Connie's fright was now almost effaced by his recent sight of the pair as they raced after the car, waving handkerchiefs and shouting cheery farewells.

The staff, assembled to see their mistress depart, had, with the exception of Crabbe, shown a noticeable restraint, probably due to the unforeseen domestic arrangement; but Miss Bundy had seemed unconcerned over anything save the weather prospects. Flurried and anxious, she kept peering at the barometer till the bailiff jokingly pulled her away.

"Don't you bother abaht that glass, miss. See, overhead, 'ow the clouds is breaking up! Oh, you'll 'ave a good crossing to-morrow. Nothink to worry abaht, is there, Con?"

"Nothink at all," chimed in his wife. "She's just to leave cares behind and enjoy herself."

Miss Bundy, dressed in her musquash coat and a hat too small for her head, was heavily laden with an umbrella, a parcel, and, oddly enough, two shopping-bags, both hung over her arm by the straps. Neil took particular note of this latter fact, thinking it very like her to burden herself unnecessarily. The alligator-skin bag, of course, contained the precious manuscript. The other, of black leather, was unfamiliar, though he was destined to recall it later on at a time when every detail assumed enormous importance. That it held her money was proved by her taking from it various ten-shilling notes to distribute as Easter gifts among the servants. Its owner looked, he thought, ridiculously like one of George Belcher's drawings in *Punch*. Only a bird-cage was needed to complete the picture.

By striking contrast Natasha, who had delayed till her aunt began to grow impatient, appeared on the scene, the personification of chic serenity. Cool, detached, she descended the stairs, drawing on what was probably her one new pair of gloves—grey antelope, heavily stitched— saved, no doubt, for such an occasion. Her rough grey coat of Irish tweed was smartly cut, her little close-fitting hat of the same shade was carefully adjusted, while the neutral background of her attire was accented by a note of bright scarlet, matching her lips, in the shape of a flat bag tucked under one arm. Neil had never admired her more, and the thought that she was perhaps going from him forever sent a pang through him.

She paused beside him, an ironical glint in her eyes as she watched the Tilburys surging round the old lady to help her into the car and bundle her up with the rug.

"Well, we're off," she murmured. "Expect me when you see me. I can't say more."

In vain did he try to read what lay behind that calm mask of hers. All he could think of was the flying visit she had paid Wednesday afternoon in Bath, and his belief that she was planning to meet the man of her choice in London. His aimless remarks sounded hollow to his ears. She strolled down the steps and took her place at the wheel.

Still those clamouring Tilburys! Natasha ignored them, but the old lady looked pleased.

"Now, then, you're not to think of us. We shan't run off with the spoons, shall we, Con?"

"Not 'alf we shan't! And we'll see the plyce is kept clean and tidy, same as if you was here."

More giggling, urgent warnings against fatigue and draughts. The car started, the Cockney sparrows dashed in its wake, and Neil was left behind to struggle with the sense of emptiness which had descended on him like a pall. He was still staring at the green turf and the monkey-puzzle trees when the bailiff and his wife returned, encumbered with the first instalment of their personal effects. They dumped a pair of bulging kit-bags in the hall, and mopped their beaming faces.

"That's that," panted the complacent Alfred. "And now, abaht this little move of ours. Not going to put you out in any way, I 'ope?"

"Not at all. Why should it? It just happens, though, I shan't be staying here while Miss Bundy is away. Not at night, that is. I'm going over to Mr. Gisborne's, from this evening."

Their flushed faces fell. They exchanged hurt glances, and Tilbury exclaimed quickly: "Oh, I say! It's not on account of us, is it?"

Neil explained how he had accepted the invitation before he knew of their taking over the reins. He could not understand their apparent disappointment, nor the dead silence which greeted his remarks.

"Oh, I see. Well, you'll please yourself, of course." The man sounded sulky. "Only Con and me wouldn't like to think as 'ow—It's the missus's idea, this. I 'ope you know we 'adn't nothink to do with it."

"Miss Andreyev's clearing off too," put in Mrs. Tilbury, gazing hard at the carpet. "P'r'aps she's leaving because you are."

Neil froze. Even Tilbury noticed the blunder, for he gave his wife an admonitory nudge, whereupon she hurriedly chirped, "Oh, no offence! It's just that we seem to be breaking up the party, through no fault of ours. We have to do as we're told, you know."

Glad to escape, Neil started in the direction of his work, only to find Crabbe waiting to ask whether he would like his packing done and his lunch brought on a tray to the study. They conversed for a moment, and although the butler was as discreet as usual his volunteered admission that the two maids were just leaving seemed to bear out Natasha's prediction about the Tilburys' making a clean sweep. Be that as it might, the staff, during Miss Bundy's absence, was to be reduced to himself, the cook, and the daily char, Mrs. Tilbury undertaking to find new girls before the month was up. Neil rather thought he detected a scornful note in his informant's voice as it uttered this last detail, but perhaps he was mistaken. He shut himself up and plunged into his task, determined not to dwell on the blank hours ahead.

About five-thirty that afternoon he stopped by the drawing-room to collect certain of his books left there. Outside the door he fancied he heard a low mumble of voices mingling with the blare of the radio, but on entering, saw no signs of conversation between the couple now fully installed and very much at their ease. Connie, her short legs outstretched towards a roasting fire, lounged back rapturously, drinking in the tumult of jazz. Alfred lay on the Chippendale sofa amidst the scattered pages of an illustrated journal, a decanter and wine-glass beside him on a stool. A second glance, however, showed him to be pale and shaky, his hands pressed to his stomach. He uttered a faint groan as the door opened, but on seeing who was there struggled up with a wan smile.

"Rare good brandy, this," he remarked, motioning to the decanter. "Miss Bundy ordered me to take some to try and shift the nasty, grinding pain I've got inside. Started coming on about breakfast-time. Can I tempt you to a drop, sir?"

Though his voice was curiously husky, he was perfectly sober, nor, indeed, could one suspect him of bibulous inclinations. As Neil declined the refreshment, Mrs. Tilbury sternly adjured her husband to lie down again.

"He's come over quite bad, Mr. Starkey, and that's a fact. It's all this mucking abaht in the wet's done it—or else it's that game we 'ad yesterday. I never did 'old with 'igh game. Mustard plaster's wot he wants, and wot he'll get, soon as I can get him up to bed."

The whole room seemed polluted with their presence. Ashes strewed the hearth, the reek of hair-oil and cigar-smoke mingled in a sickly stench. As though dimly aware of the impression made on the onlooker, Connie bent down to button her gaping shoes, but paused alertly as the telephone pealed forth a summons. She switched off the radio, while Alfred, unmindful of his suffering, sprang into the hall to take off the receiver.

"Hallo, hallo. . . . Yes, this is Bishop's Paulton, two–six," Neil heard him say, and then followed a long wait. A trunk call, evidently. Connie came to stand close beside him, and the last thing Neil saw, as he let himself out, was the two holding their breath and eyeing each other with a sort of stilled eagerness.

How bitterly was he to regret not lingering to hear the result of that call! He did, indeed, stop a minute on the doorstep, thinking it might be for him, but as nothing happened, he thrust the bailiff and his wife into the background of his thoughts, and hastened to reach a less offending atmosphere.

None too happily he speculated on how and where Natasha would pass the night. Miss Braselton's flat being only a tiny *pied-à-terre*, she would probably go to an hotel and thus be free to seek amusement. If she were not alone, she would very likely go somewhere to dance and sup—yes, and pay for the entertainment out of her own pocket. At this revolting reflection he trod on the accelerator so violently that an unnatural burst of speed nearly ended the placid life of a Buff Orpington matron venturing for an evening stroll. Once and for all, thought he, let him close his mind to such futile conjectures. He must get on full steam with the cursed biography, and allow nothing to divert him till it was finished.

On his arrival at Stoke Paulton next morning he saw the doctor's brown Austin before the door, and a moment later learned from Crabbe that the bailiff during the preceding night had been alarmingly ill.

"What's wrong with him?" inquired Neil indifferently.

"Gastric attack, sir; food poisoning, or something like that. Mrs. Tilbury was in a rare state, up and down the whole time, fetching hot-water bottles and what not, and along about ten we had Dr. Graves round. I half-believed he was going to peg out, but he's easier now. Won't be up for a few days, I hear—not that it's any great loss to us, if you won't misunderstand me, sir."

For the first time Neil caught a gleam in the dead fish eye which showed very plainly its owner's real sentiments. A faint smile passed between the two.

"No word from Miss Andreyev, I suppose?"

"None, sir—but I didn't expect to hear from her. She won't come near this place, depend on it, unless it's to fetch her clothes."

All Sunday passed without news, and when Monday came, both Neil and Rachel began to wonder when the guest would turn up.

"I dare say she's so rejoiced to be in London she'll be in no hurry to leave," said Rachel. "Though I did think she'd drop me a line."

Neil said nothing, so tormented by the picture he had formed of Natasha's week-end that he smoked innumerable cigarettes and listened anxiously to the sound of every approaching car. After lunch he inquired at the Glastonbury garage on the chance that the girl had come back without notifying them. The answer received from the fat proprietor was quite unexpected.

"No, sir, she's not been in yet, and it so happens there's a telegram here waiting for her, since Friday. Don't know why it was sent to us. Seems you're not the only one trying to get hold of her. There's a lady been in twice, and a little while ago a gentleman called."

"What sort of gentleman?" demanded Neil, in sudden suspicion.

"Oh, a small, fairish person, with a little moustache. Drives Miss Bundy's old Ford. Name of Pilbury or Tilbury—something like that."

Tilbury! Why should he be asking for Natasha? How, for that matter, was he well enough to get out of bed? It seemed slightly peculiar and a little disturbing.

After dinner that evening Neil made unavailing efforts to fix his attention on a scientific treatise. The vicar was going through the galley-sheets of his latest book; Rachel was knitting. Just as the clock struck ten the door opened without warning, and Natasha, pale as a ghost, walked into their midst.

## CHAPTER THIRTEEN

ALL started up, one at least with ill-concealed relief. Rachel uttered a glad cry of welcome.

"Tasha—at last! We'd given you up for lost."

The girl made an effort to smile. There were dark circles under her eyes.

"Well, here I am—what's left of me," she replied, and after standing for a moment with sagging shoulders and a look of utter fatigue, sank down upon the sofa without removing her coat.

"Why, you are worn out! What have you been doing—dancing all night?"

"Driving all day is more like it. I've just walked from Glastonbury."

"Walked! But you could have brought the car here and let Saunders send for it."

"I suppose I could. I don't quite know why I didn't. . . . Oh, yes, there was a reason. Saunders was out, only that idiot of a boy looking after things, and he never gets anything right."

"Whisky and soda? Tea? You must have something."

"Thanks awfully. I would rather like some tea."

All this time Neil, his eyes fixed on her, kept wondering what was wrong. This was not mere physical exhaustion. The reaction of nervous shock occurred to him. She had so far not faced him directly, and scarcely glanced at the others. Now she pulled off her hat and cast it down beside her, without so much as troubling to smooth her hair.

The vicar knocked out his pipe and rose with a lazy stretch, bracing himself, unwillingly, for a tedious discussion with a vestryman.

"So Carrie's got safely off, has she?" he inquired with a yawn.

"I suppose so. I haven't heard anything."

"Why, didn't you see her off?"

"Not actually. She insisted on my leaving her alone from Friday afternoon."

"Hum. That's odd."

The door closed on him. Presently the tea arrived, and Rachel went up to look after her friend's room. Neil was now left with Natasha, who still did not speak to him. She leaned back with closed eyes, so spent that every drop of energy in her seemed drained away. The clock ticked. Neil could not take his eyes from her face. At last, without moving, she spoke in a low voice.

"It may interest you to hear that I got what I wanted."

"No! Not the hundred pounds?"

"More than that. So unexpectedly too. It almost makes me feel ashamed. You see, it was Caroline after all. Not that I asked her. I'll tell you how it happened—if you promise to say nothing."

She paused to moisten her lips, picking idly at the ruffle on the sofa.

"All the way up I kept thinking she wanted to say something, but she didn't bring herself to the point till just as she said good-bye. I had set her down where she asked to be left, outside the London Library in St. James's Square. She came round to the front and put a little package in my hand. In it were two ten-pound notes wrapped round—what do you think? A string of pearls!"

"Pearls!"

"My grandmother's. I'd never so much as seen them. She was quite awkward and confused. Said I ought to have them, as I was young and would wear them, while she never did. Then she said, 'I am doing this now in case anything should happen to me. I'd rather give them to you personally than leave them to you in my will.' Wasn't that funny? Perhaps she doesn't really hate me as much as I thought she did, or else she was trying to make up for the way she's acted towards me lately. I simply don't know. Anyhow, I was quite bowled over, almost speechless. The twenty pounds was for Easter. . . . They were nice pearls, small, but beautifully matched. I got three hundred and fifty for them."

"What, you sold them?" Neil felt a little shocked.

"What else could I do? I was ready to collapse with thankfulness. I told you how badly I wanted money."

He was silent for a few seconds. "Then I suppose you're happy?" he remarked conventionally.

"Am I? I'm too tired now to know anything. At all events, that affair's settled."

Closely studying her, he asked himself where and in what way she had spent the past three days. That they had not been given up to pleasure was only too apparent. His first impression, namely that she had passed through some shattering experience, returned with increased conviction.

All at once he recalled the telegram awaiting her at the garage.

"You got it, of course? Saunders says it's been there since Friday."

"Telegram?" The shadow of some fear dilated her pupils, to be replaced immediately by absolute blankness. "Why, who would send me a telegram there? I heard nothing about it. Maybe the boy didn't know. Well, I'd better go and find out what it's all about." She pulled herself up wearily.

"I'll drive you over in my car. It won't take a minute to get it."

"Thanks, it's good of you."

A short time after this Natasha was handed her message, which she tore open and read with a wondering expression.

"Look—it's from Caroline. She must have sent it here, not knowing where else to catch me. Soon after I left her, too."

On the slip he saw the following scrawl:

*"Alligator bag left in car deposit it at bank wire me Hotel Roblin Paris very important.—Bundy."*

The locked bag again!

"She had it over her arm when she left home," declared Neil. "I remember thinking how strange to carry two bags at once."

"I know. It was the black bag she kept her money in. I've no idea what was in this one. Have you?"

"Papers, I believe, in your grandfather's writing, though there may have been something besides. Well, shall we look? There's the Geisler over there."

The garage attendant, a loutish youth with oil-streaked hair, assured them the car had not been touched since it was brought in an hour or more ago. However, although they rummaged in every corner, all they found were some road-maps in the pockets, and the plaid rug, neatly folded on the back seat.

"She's mistaken, evidently. She must have dropped it in the street."

"Could it have been stolen from the car?"

"Not possibly. I was careful to lock up every time I left it. No, if the bag had been here it would be here now. Too bad. I shall have to wire her when we get back."

As they rounded the first corner on their return a Ford runabout passed them. Their own lamps shone for an instant on the driver's face, greenish-white, very drawn and intent. Neil turned curiously.

"That was Tilbury. Did you notice how ill he looked? He's been laid up since you left, poisoned in some way. Which reminds me—he's been inquiring for you at the garage. Very likely he's going there now on the same errand. Like to see what he wants?"

She came to from her reverie with a shudder of repulsion. "That slug looking for me? What for? No, I couldn't bear to see him. I hope I'll never set eyes on him again. . . . I expect I know what it's about. Caroline must have rung him up to tell him she'd lost her bag. It would be just like her to get into a frightful stew over a thing like that."

"Why—your teeth are chattering! Are you cold?"

"No. Just tired." She huddled her coat up about her neck. After an interval she said detachedly: "Did you ever strain every nerve to bring something off, and when you'd accomplished it suddenly begin wondering if it was worth the struggle? That's how I'm feeling to-night. Sick and—hopeless."

"I could understand better if I had a little more information," he answered quietly, but she merely shook her head.

"You'll know before long—in a way, that is. *Après moi le deluge*," she quoted under her breath, and to his dismay broke for a second into hysterical laughter. Very quickly, though, she recovered herself to say, "No, I'm not mad. Just let me be. All I ask now is to crawl into bed and sleep for hours and hours. I wish I might never wake up."

Her broken morale moved him deeply, nor could he help thinking the past days had brought some disillusionment which might be turned to his own advantage. He even had a brief moment of triumph when he pictured her as turning to him for consolation, but he soon realised there was little chance of this. She left him at the gate, and when he returned from putting up his car she was already upstairs. It was Rachel who met him, holding out a packet of cigarettes.

"Would you care to take these up to her? She's in the little blue room. I'm just going to send that telegram to Carrie."

In the dark passage above Natasha was waiting. She had slipped into her dressing-gown, and the ribbon of light from her open door showed a glimpse of amber and black striped silk hugged closely around her. Her tawny hair swept back in gleaming ripples from her white face.

"Here are your gaspers," he said. "Don't smoke too much, though. Give your nerves a rest."

As her fingers fastened on the packet her eyes met his, and something snapped in him. In an instant his arms were around her, straining the whole length of her body to his, while his lips found hers and took possession of them. For a space of pure rapture he recognised an uncontrollable response. As on that one former occasion, it was as though a hot flame had caught the two of them up together and was fusing them into one. Then, as quickly, she broke from him, fighting him off in wild panic.

"No—no!" he heard her sob. "Oh, God! You, too!" The anguish of reproach in her voice, amounting almost to hatred, was incomprehensible to him. Intent on recapturing the brief ecstasy, he pursued her blindly as she backed towards her room.

"Natasha—Natasha!" he whispered, finding delight in the repetition of her name. "Why do you say 'you, too'? Don't go. At least let me—"

It was too late. The door was shut in his face. He grasped the knob, but she had locked herself in. To his urgent supplications he got no reply.

Stirred to the depths, he descended slowly, to find the vicar just letting himself in. The tall figure was framed in the entrance, eyes turned inquiringly towards the gate.

"There's a small car stopped outside. Some one's coming in. By Jove! if it isn't that photographer chap! What can he want at this time of night?"

Sure enough it was the bailiff, pale, clammy browed. He seemed scarcely able to stand. The hand with which he removed his hat shook as with palsy, and when he spoke it was in a scarcely audible croak.

"Mr. Gisborne?" he whispered in a frightened manner. "You'll pardon me coming here and bothering you, but the fact is I thought—that is, the wife and me both did—I'd ought to ask if any of you'd had news of Miss Bundy."

"News?" echoed the vicar, amazed. "Why on earth should we have news? Is anything wrong?"

"Oh, I 'ope not, sir. I do sincerely 'ope not. But you see, this telegram's come, from the lady she was to meet, addressed to her, so we opened it. We supposed she was in Paris since Saturday evening, but—"

"Here, let me look at it. Starkey—Rachel—what do you make of this?"

The three heads bent over the paper. On it was written:

*"What has happened to you are you ill again have wired flat but no satisfaction let me hear immediately much worried.—Emily Braselton. Hotel Roblin, Paris."*

## CHAPTER FOURTEEN

"NOT reached Paris!" gasped Rachel. "Then where can she be?"

"That's wot we can't make out, miss. We 'oped you might know. I hear Miss Andreyev's back, stopping with you. Is that so?" The queer croaking voice brought out the question anxiously.

"Yes. I'll call her, but she knows no more than we do."

"So she is 'ere!" Tilbury's protuberant eyes watched Rachel with eagerness as she ran up the stairs. "We'd begun to wonder—"

"Wonder what?" demanded the vicar snappishly. He was still staring hard at the telegram.

"Nothink, sir, only that the two ladies being together like, I thought maybe Miss Andreyev could—" He stopped, swaying slightly.

"Here, man, sit down. You look badly shaken. Want a drink?"

"No, sir, thank you, sir," replied the bailiff, tottering to a seat. "Fact is, I've had a nasty turn with my inside. Affected my throat, it has, and with all this worry on top of it—"

"It's certainly very odd, but I dare say there's some natural explanation. What have you done about it?"

"We tried to get through to the mansions in Kensington where Miss Braselton has her flat, only we 'ad trouble making the porter understand. It was the boy at the garage wot told me Miss Andreyev was back, so I drove straight over here."

"When did this message arrive?" asked Neil suddenly.

"This afternoon—latish."

"But—" Neil was about to remark that Tilbury's first call at the garage could not have been inspired by the telegram, but Rachel's return checked him.

"What does Natasha say?" he asked.

"Only what she already told us. She hasn't seen her aunt since she left her at St. James's Square Friday afternoon."

"Wot!" Tilbury gave a little shocked exclamation. "Didn't she see Miss Bundy aboard her train? That's a bit of a stunner, that is. Why, I never dreamed such a thing!"

"Never mind that now," put in the vicar irritably. "I'll ring up those flats myself. She must be ill, another stroke, perhaps, in which case all kinds of a muddle may have resulted. What's the address?"

"Blessington Mansions, sir. There's a private number, but we couldn't get on to it. You won't mind me 'anging abaht a bit, will you, sir? I'll own to being all upset, wot with being left in charge, and all."

"Stay, naturally. We'll soon clear matters up. It's quite impossible for Miss Bundy to have disappeared." He picked up the telephone.

Natasha appeared in the doorway, so quietly that no one noticed she was there till her strained voice broke the stillness.

"I'm afraid the flat's empty, Mr. Gisborne. Miss Braselton has only a daily woman who comes when she's wanted."

Neil thought she sounded alarmed and bewildered—chiefly the latter.

Gisborne turned from the instrument to say: "But there must have been some one there on Friday, surely?"

"Oh, yes! Miss Braselton arranged for the woman to stay the night."

At last the bell rang, and the operator informed Gisborne she could get no reply from the Kensington number.

"You're right—there's no one there. I'll get on to the porter. He must know whether Miss Bundy came to the flat."

Another tense pause, filled by low-voiced discussion. Neil noticed that Tilbury kept his eyes glued to Natasha, who never once looked in his direction. Twice he started to speak, only to change his mind and mop his damp brow with a purple handkerchief. Quite evidently he was still suffering from extreme weakness; his strange greenish pallor indicated some physical disorder quite apart from mental inquietude. It seemed almost an act of heroism for him to have driven to Glastonbury twice since noon, and then over here. Only great anxiety could have strung him up to so much exertion.

"If she'd been taken to a hospital or nursing-home," said the vicar, "we ought to have heard long ago. And yet something of the sort must be the explanation. Supposing she met with an accident, there'd be no difficulty, would there, about identifying her?"

"She had her cheque-book with her, besides visiting-cards, and, I think, letters," replied Natasha, coming out of a dazed reverie. "No passport, of course, because Miss Braselton took that to get a visa and left it at the flat."

"And you can't say positively that she ever reached the flat?"

"How can I? She certainly intended to go there, in time for dinner. There's this wire I got just now. You don't know about that, do you? It was sent to the garage. I'm afraid it won't help us much, but anyhow here it is." She handed the torn brown envelope to the vicar, who took it eagerly.

"Alligator bag left in car. . . . Was that the bag with her money and so on in it—or her dressing-bag?"

"Neither. We deposited the dressing-bag at the flat on our way into town, and she had a black shopping-bag as well. This alligator one was extra. I don't know what she kept in it, but she always carried it with her everywhere."

No one had observed the sudden stiffening of the bailiff till his husky whisper made itself heard. "A wire from Miss Bundy, miss! Might I be allowed to look at it?"

As the girl took back the form and gave it into his hand she shuddered slightly as though at the touch of some loathsome insect. Neil saw this, and saw also the little man's eyes bulge as they devoured the script.

"It was sent from the main Victoria Post Office, which is just behind the Army and Navy Stores," remarked Gisborne, frowning. "Now, what was she doing in that neighbourhood? Shopping? The time marked on it is five-thirty."

Tilbury was trying to attract their attention. "I've just thought of another thing, sir. Along about five-thirty we 'ad a telephone call from Miss Bundy. She tried to tell us something, but the connection was so bad we couldn't neither of us make out what she said. I heard her say she'd got up to town all right, and then I caught the words 'car' and 'garage' and 'forgotten.' She kept repeating it over and over, but though I called the wife to the 'phone, she couldn't understand any better than me. Maybe this 'ere explains it."

"Why, of course it explains it! She wanted to let you know she had left her bag in the car. Why on earth didn't you mention this at once?"

"Well, sir—" An embarrassed look came over the pale, twitching features. "There seemed something a bit odd about the whole thing. Fact is, we weren't quite satisfied it was Miss Bundy speaking. Didn't sound like 'er voice."

"Didn't sound like her voice! What on earth do you mean?"

Natasha kept her eyes steadfastly averted. She seemed to be thinking deeply.

"I can't say, sir. It was certainly a lady, but it was so sort of breathless and far away . . . anyhow, both of us said afterwards we didn't feel sure it was the mistress herself. It worried us a bit. I'd been taken so bad I was obliged to go to bed abaht then, but Con—that's Mrs. Tilbury—went down to Glastonbury twice to ask if the car had come back. We thought—that is, we didn't know—" He coughed, and turned to Natasha with nervous eagerness. "You did find the bag, I suppose? Got it now, 'aven't you, miss?"

"No. It was not in the car," she returned to the room at large.

"Oh!" There was an exhaled breath, followed by a pause. "Then p'r'aps she was mistaken. I mean to say, maybe she didn't—"

"But what has the bag got to do with her disappearance?" interrupted the vicar impatiently. "My idea is she's had some sudden attack, that she's been taken off to a hospital, and that whatever messages have been sent have miscarried."

"I think so, too," said Natasha slowly. "Though I shouldn't wonder if losing her bag hadn't something to do with it. She's very easily upset these days."

At this moment the operator called through to say that the connection with Blessington Mansions had been established. Long before the vicar had finished speaking it was plain he had learned nothing useful. He replaced the receiver with a troubled air.

"The porter declares she didn't turn up at all, though Emily Braselton's maid waited, had dinner prepared and stayed the night. Deuced queer, this! I don't like the look of it. What's the best move now? It will take all night to get on to the various hospitals. The only sensible thing I can think of is to ring up Scotland Yard and let them make inquiries."

The words "Scotland Yard" struck a chill to all present. Only the trembling guest, however, gave utterance to his thoughts.

"You know best, sir—but, oh, I can't bear to think as 'ow anythink serious 'as 'appened. Miss Bundy 'as been a rare good friend to the wife and me." His voice broke.

Gisborne rounded on him with kindly exasperation. "There, there. Don't go looking for trouble! Why, even now there may be a wire at home waiting for you. Better hurry back and find out."

"Right, sir, I will. And you'll let us know, won't you, if you hear anythink?"

When the door had closed behind him, Rachel said: "How terribly distressed he looks! Why, he's all broken up!"

"Very naturally too," snapped her brother. "If any fatal accident has overtaken Carrie, he won't find another soft berth in a hurry, and well he knows it." He turned to Natasha with a puzzled expression. "Why, in heaven's name, did Carrie dismiss you like that? Any particular reason?"

She stared at him absently. "Not that I know of. I did certainly imagine she rather wanted to get rid of me."

"Any quarrel between you?"

"No, of course not. She seemed very much absorbed, and—and exalted, if you know what I mean. She's been like that a lot recently."

Now was the moment when Neil would have expected her to mention the pearls, but to his surprise she did nothing of the kind. He began to feel vaguely uncomfortable, especially as she seemed determined not to meet his eyes, although that, perhaps, might be accounted for by what had passed between them on the landing a short time ago.

"H'm! I confess I've often wondered if she wasn't going off the handle a bit, and this all tends to confirm my fear. Starkey, how did she strike you the last few days before she left home?"

"Exactly as Miss Andreyev says—keyed up, elated, but certainly not irrational. If she has lost her memory and wandered off, it must have come on very suddenly."

"Then where the deuce has she got to? Three whole days and not a word! A cursed nuisance Emily didn't communicate with us sooner, but I suppose she didn't dream anything like this had happened." He rumpled his stiff hair till it stood on end. "Tasha—Rachel," he exclaimed brusquely, "go to bed, and leave Starkey and me to attend to this. Don't worry. I expect it will clear up."

Until long after midnight they sat at the telephone, sending the necessary messages to put the machinery of investigation in motion, and hoping for some reply to come through. None did, however, and with the assurance that Scotland Yard would do everything possible, they had to be content.

By morning the first definite bulletins began to filter through. No trace whatever of the missing woman had come to light, and to make matters more baffling it was now known that she had not gone into the London Library after all. Natasha stuck to her statement of having set her aunt down barely a dozen yards from the door, the long line of waiting motors making it impossible to drive up to the building itself. She had then driven off quickly without looking back, confident that the old lady was about to carry out her intention. Why she had not done so remained a deep mystery. The vicarage household suddenly felt itself in a grip of fear.

Rachel insisted on keeping Natasha in bed. The girl was still in a state of exhaustion remarkable for one usually so vigorous, nor could she adequately account for her complete lassitude. Neil had her on his mind all the time he was helping with the unprofitable inquiries, haunted by the idea that there might be some obscure connection between her depressed state and Miss Bundy's disappearance. Had she told them quite all she knew? He could not help dreading she was keeping something back, though unable to imagine what it could be.

During the afternoon he went over to Stoke Paulton to find the Tilburys very distraught amid an atmosphere of hushed apprehension. More telegrams from Paris had come, but nothing to shed the least ray on the ever-darkening problem. Crabbe, closely questioned, shook his head and could offer no opinion. He looked very grey and decidedly older.

On his return Gisborne was just shutting the door on a rather sour-faced spinster who held her angular shoulders exceedingly erect.

"Devil take these busy-bodies!" he raged. "That's the third to come poking her nose in here and making unpleasant insinuations. It passes comprehension how quickly these matters get round. Why, the entire village knows Carrie is missing, and to crown all, some evil-minded person appears to have spread a most disagreeable rumour. I'm thankful Natasha came straight here to us. That, at least, is some protection against their poisonous tongues."

"Why, what do you mean?" demanded Neil uneasily.

"Well, no one's had the audacity to put it into words. It's just a general, nasty tone to the questions they're asking. Was there any quarrel between Carrie and the girl—did I know there was talk of Natasha's being sent away—and so on. That harpy you saw is the worst of the lot. She declares she's had it from—hallo! What's this? The local police calling."

True enough, two stout constables were turning in under the lych-gate. The foremost lifted his helmet and cleared his throat with portentous gravity.

"Sorry to trouble you, Mr. Gisborne, but a report's just come to us from Bristol. Lady's body found near there. We wanted to ask you and your friend to come along and look it over—in case."

"Bristol? Preposterous! Why, Miss Bundy was in London last Friday, on her way to Paris. This can't be she."

"I dare say not, sir, only there seems a faint chance. We've notified Stoke Paulton, too. In any case, I may tell you it's a matter of murder."

Above, from the top of the stairs, sounded a gasping cry. Neil and his companion wheeled just in time to see Natasha slump down in a heap on the landing.

## CHAPTER FIFTEEN

IN THE police car which whirled them towards Bristol, Neil could see nothing but the vision of Natasha's white face. What was it in her eyes—incredulity, horrified bewilderment? She had not lost consciousness, and on regaining her feet without assistance had said little, except to assure them she was all right, yet that some definite fear lurked behind her rapid resumption of composure was a belief impossible to conquer. She could hardly suppose this poor corpse they were about to view was that of her aunt. How could any one think so? The visit was one of routine, nothing more.

In the heart of the bustling city they threaded several crowded streets, to stop before a dingy building. Outside this a second car was just stopping, and from it alighted Crabbe and Alfred Tilbury, the latter very shaken and subdued. A sergeant met them and escorted the two parties along a passage to a small mortuary where, under a pitiless overhead light, a shrouded object lay stretched on a table. As they filed in, Neil caught from behind him the bailiff's strange, hoarse croak: "Why, 'owever could they think it was 'er? On 'er way to France she was—ticket bought and all!"

The words echoed his own thoughts. No, this was not Miss Bundy. No need to take so firm a grip on himself. Why should he suddenly be assailed by so shuddering a dread after the hundreds of mutilated dead he had seen in his time?

Creaking boots, heavy breathing. The sergeant looked round to make sure all were assembled, then drew back the enveloping sheet.

A long silence, charged with horror, then the vicar's low voice. "Yes, it is she. No doubt whatever. Poor creature—what a ghastly sight!"

It was indeed a ghastly sight. The short, greying hair was caked in blackened blood, which had spread downward on to the fur coat. The head, turned so as to show a purpled bruise on the temple, had been savagely battered in several places—battered and broken.

"Skull caved right in at the back," remarked the Bristol officer. "A regular butcher's job, as you may say."

Crabbe's thin lips were pressed tightly together. Tilbury's features twitched as with St. Vitus's Dance, his pale eyes starting from his face like glass marbles. He seemed shocked to the point of nausea.

Gisborne spoke again. "This seems quite inexplicable. When did it happen?"

"When, sir? Look at the clothes. There's your answer."

"They look soaked, as though she had lain a long time in the rain."

"Just so, sir—and what rain have we had except on Friday night of last week, between nine and twelve? Not a drop since. That pretty well fixes it, I should say."

"At five-thirty on Friday she was alive, in London."

"Was she, now? In London?" incredulously.

"Ah, but do we know that for sure?" came a hoarse, eager whisper from Tilbury. Every one looked at him. Neil, resenting the shrewd tone, felt his face flame with anger.

"What about the telephone call you had at five-thirty?" Gisborne reminded the speaker.

"True, sir, I was forgetting—if it was 'er." The bailiff said this under his breath, and again six pairs of eyes turned towards him inquiringly.

"The call can easily be traced."

"Oh, to be sure it can—and, anyhow, Miss Andreyev was with her a little before, wasn't she?"

No one troubled to answer this, and after a pause which, to Neil, seemed significant, the vicar asked if there were any theory as to the motive.

The officer hesitated. "Well, sir, on the face of it, robbery," he said. "Whatever she had was taken, though, of course, we don't yet know what it amounted to. All, that is, except her umbrella, and this here." He fished up from the sodden garments the gold chain and locket. "Not worth bothering about, probably. Picture of an old gentleman inside. Perhaps some of you can help with information. Do you happen to know what jewellery or money she had on her?"

Crabbe volunteered what they all knew—that Miss Bundy never wore jewellery beyond an occasional brooch. As for money, she usually carried no large sums, even when she was going on a journey, relying on travellers' cheques, and keeping only ten or fifteen pounds at most in her purse.

Neil said nothing. He was wondering if the two from Stoke Paulton had noticed what had instantly struck him, namely, that the tiny steel key was gone from its place on the chain. It was this key which belonged to the alligator-bag, but did any one outside the dead woman's household know of its existence? Neither face told him what he eagerly sought.

"Fifteen pounds," the officer was repeating. "Very little to commit murder for, but it might have been supposed she had valuables on her. For all we know she may have done. Elderly ladies are often a bit queer like that. My own mother carries every bit of jewellery she owns about with her in a little black silk reticule. Never leaves go of it. . . . Point now is, how did she get to Bristol? A high-powered car could have managed

it easy, of course, and that's the only guess we can make off-hand. . . .
Perhaps you gentlemen would care to look at the spot where she was
found? If so, one of our chaps will show it to you. It's about three miles
out of town."

Both the words "high-powered car" and the suggestion that Miss
Bundy might have had something intrinsically valuable in her possession added greatly to Neil's perturbation. Again he asked, why had
Natasha not mentioned the pearls to Rachel and the vicar? Supposing
her speedy disposal of the necklace became known, would she not be
placed in an embarrassing position? There must be witnesses who had
seen Miss Bundy after she parted from her niece, but if none were forthcoming, what then?

He was on pins and needles to apprise the girl of her possible danger.
Her startling collapse as well as the feeling he had had about her ever
since her return made him long to get back at once, but rather than call
attention to himself he decided it was better to accompany the others
to the scene of violence.

They followed the road by which they had come, but presently turned
aside into an expanse of waste land, scarred by gullies and dotted with
gorse. At a later season this desolate stretch was probably overrun by
motor cyclists, at least during the week-ends, but now it was singularly barren of life. Along a narrow lane they suddenly drew up, and
the constable in charge waved his hand towards a hillock about twenty
yards to the left.

"There, you see those gorse bushes? Just behind them, screened in
pretty completely, is a sort of scooped-out place. A natural grave it is
really. That's where she was lying, and she might have stayed there weeks
before any one found her. Shouldn't wonder if the spot was picked on
purpose by some one that knew the neighbourhood, with just that thing
in view—for it's well known the longer time goes by the harder it is to
track down a criminal. We've roped that bit off, as you can see. Not that
it's much use now. The rain made a clean sweep of any marks there might
have been. Those footprints running to and fro"—he pointed to a confused
mass of interlacing tracks—"was all made by the chaps that found her."

"How, exactly, was the body discovered?" inquired Neil.

"Pure chance, sir. These fellows, out of jobs, was knocking a ball
about early this afternoon, and one of them happened to be hunting for
it and saw a foot sticking up. Proper put the wind up him, it did. Come
tearing in to us on a push-bike."

Of the brief, halting discussion which ensued Neil heard little, rousing himself only in time to catch an inquiry as to when the inquest would be held.

"Can't say for sure, sir. This being Holy Week may postpone it a bit. You'll be notified, though, and I dare say some of you'll be called to give evidence."

In any case, it was several days off. Much could happen in that time....

As their engine started, Tilbury approached the vicar nervously. He looked like a hurt child about to burst into tears.

"Beg pardon, sir, but wot ought the wife and me to do? Move out?"

"Eh? Certainly not! Stay where you are and carry on as usual. Miss Bundy's solicitor will give you instructions, and if you get into a muddle, call on me."

"Yes, sir, thank you, sir. I just thought I'd better ask." As he climbed into the Ford they heard a hoarse wail. "Oh, dear! Oh, dear! Wotever poor Con'll say, I can't think! I don't know how I'm to break it to her."

"And I," muttered Gisborne, as they drove off, "don't exactly look forward to breaking this awful business to Natasha. Has it entered your head, Starkey, that she may be in for a bad time?"

"I don't see why," objected Neil, with pretended astonishment. "That telegram from her aunt safeguards her completely, doesn't it?"

"I'm not so sure. What if she can't prove she and Carrie didn't meet again?"

"At least the telegram shows they didn't expect to."

"However that may be," returned the vicar, dissatisfied, "I think I must try to prepare her for the sort of questions she'll be expected to answer. I shall do so this evening."

When they reached home, night had fallen. In the open doorway Rachel stood looking out with a mute inquiry.

"Yes," replied her brother shortly. "It is—though how the poor woman came to be in Bristol passes all understanding. Is Natasha able to bear talking about it? If so, call her."

There was no need for this. The girl was there, and had heard what was said.

"Caroline dead!" she whispered, and repeated the words several times as though to take in their meaning.

"I can't get used to it.... How—who—" She stopped to draw her hand across her forehead. "Tell me everything, please. When and where was she found?"

They went into the drawing-room, where she sat down rigidly on the sofa. It was not clear how much of Gisborne's account her brain absorbed. To Neil it seemed that her attention was divided between a paralysis of horror and a groping effort to think something out. When the vicar had finished, he fumbled for his pipe, only to lay it empty upon the mantelpiece.

"No," he said after a pause, "there's no good hazarding theories till we get hold of more details. Robbery, on the face of it, is quite absurd, but what other motive can there have been? However, what we must discuss, and that at once, is your own relation to the affair. You'll be called at the inquest, you know, and since you are the last person known to have been in her company, it seems wise to go through all your movements on Friday simply to get them clear in your mind. Suppose you tell us quietly exactly what you did from the time you said good-bye to your aunt?"

Natasha let her eyes rest on him for a moment, then she drew a long breath. "Very well. I'll do my best. Ask me anything you like."

"First, then," began Gisborne kindly, "what time was it when you left St. James's Square?"

"A quarter-past four. I remember looking at my watch."

"I see. Did Carrie give you any idea of what she meant to do after leaving the library?"

"None whatever. I assumed she would go straight to Miss Braselton's flat."

"How do you account for the fact that she never actually went into the library?"

"I can't account for it—unless at the very moment I drove off she missed her bag, and tried to catch up with me."

"That's possible." Gisborne considered the suggestion thoughtfully before continuing. "Now, just describe what you did during the afternoon and evening. Don't leave out anything."

She was a long time making a start. Her eyes, fixed on the row of Staffordshire figures over the fireplace, remained without expression. Is it conceivable, thought Neil, that she is not going to answer?

At last she broke the silence. "Does it matter so much where I went, as long as I didn't see her again?" she asked.

"It may. Unless the truth comes out, you'll be expected to furnish a detailed account of how you passed about six or seven hours. That's why I'd like you to review it while it's fresh."

Some inkling of his meaning had begun to dawn on her. She gave a slight start as she exclaimed: "Good heavens! You can't think that I—that she—Forgive me for seeming so dense. Of course, I understand now. Well, then, let me think." Once more that painful hesitation. "First, I attended to two commissions. One was at the Army and Navy Stores—a complaint about an order—and the other was at the Times Book Club in Wigmore Street. I had to return some books."

"Where did you go first?"

"The stores. It was easier to get through the traffic in the Victoria direction. Then I crossed back to the Times. From there I went to Hobson and Weaver's in Regent Street to do some shopping for myself. I was in the shop till closing time."

"Six o'clock. And afterwards? The important thing, of course, is to tell us what people you saw. Were you with friends?"

"No. I was alone the whole time." Her gaze had now centred on the middle figure of the Staffordshire series, a woman of the Nelson period, with a bonnet and market basket. "I stopped in at the Carlton and had a wash, and sat in the lounge reading the paper for perhaps an hour. Then I parked the car, had something to eat at the Corner House by Piccadilly Circus, and"—an infinitesimal pause—"went to the Coliseum."

"Oh, you went to the Coliseum! Didn't happen to keep the counter-foil of your ticket, did you?"

"I may have done. I'll look in my purse." She half-rose, to sink down again. "No—I remember. I threw it away."

"That's rather a pity." For the first time her questioner threw her a searching glance. He picked up the day's copy of the *Times*, and turned to the amusement column. "I see the Russian dancers have been at the Coliseum for the past two weeks. What ballet did you see?"

She made no reply. Slowly and absently she reached for a cigarette, held it poised in an unsteady hand. The others watched her closely. When she spoke her voice was low and apologetic.

"I hope you won't think me frightfully rude if I don't . . ." She trailed off, looking about as though for a match.

"Rude? Not at all. What I asked is extremely simple. I merely wanted to know what ballet—"

She had risen and left the room, so casually that not one of the three suspected her of any intention other than to light her cigarette. When the front door opened and closed they jumped as though shot.

"Why, she's gone!" cried Gisborne.

He and Neil sprang up startled. Already Rachel was in the hall, peering into the garden.

## CHAPTER SIXTEEN

THE street lay empty and dark. As the three gazed perplexedly up and down it, Rachel murmured, "It was wrong of you, Giles! You ought to have given her time to collect herself."

"Time to invent a better story, you mean." The vicar had gone an angry red. "If the girl has nothing to hide, why does she behave in this fashion?"

Without stopping to listen, Neil swung across to the inn, and fired a question at the mountainous blonde behind the desk.

"No, sir, I've not seen any one. Do you mean the young lady from Stoke Paulton, whose aunt's been—"

He banged the door. At the corner beyond, where the roads intersected, stood a red telephone-booth, with a shadowy figure just visible through the glass. He waited, and presently Natasha emerged, started a little, but recovered quickly.

"How clever of you to guess!" she remarked composedly.

Taking her by the arm, he drew her into the adjacent lane.

"My dear," he said, "don't you understand Gisborne's reason for asking you these questions?"

"Oh, yes, perfectly. That was a stupid lie. I wasn't prepared."

"But why lie at all? Is the truth so damaging?"

"It's quite impossible to explain—anything."

"At an official inquiry you'll have to explain."

"It may not come to that. At any rate, what I'm keeping back has absolutely no connection with this affair. I can't even imagine how my aunt came to be in Bristol. She knew no one there."

"There's another point you ought to consider. Does any one besides me know about those pearls?"

She trembled and drew in her breath sharply. "No, no one. I see what you mean . . . but I hardly think we need bother about that. She never wore them, you know. I doubt if any one knows she possessed a string of pearls."

"You can't be sure. What if it becomes imperative to—well, to prove an alibi?"

She grew very white as she gasped, "Oh, no! Why should that happen?"

"It may, unless they find the murderer at once. Would you still refuse an account of yourself?"

"I'm afraid so." Her voice was stubborn.

"Natasha!" he cried, exasperated. "This nonsense must stop! You know, and you may as well admit it, there's a man in this. You've been telephoning to him. Well, let me say this. Whoever he is, if he sits tight and lets you risk danger for his sake, he's a despicable rotter!" Her pinioned arm stiffened in his grasp. "Why do you assume," she retorted. "that I'm protecting anything except—my own reputation?"

"If you swear that's your reason, I shall be forced to accept it," he answered constrainedly.

"I've no intention of giving you my reason. For that matter, why do you feel obliged to meddle in my affairs?"

"Because," he blazed out, "I'm unlucky enough to be in love with you."

He had not meant to utter these words, which under stress of annoyance sounded oddly like an accusation. Half-regretting his confession, he saw her pupils contract, her lips part in a smile first incredulous, then ironic.

"Oh, no!" she denied coolly. "You're wrong. You may want to make love to me, but that's quite different from being in love. Why pretend?"

Was her diagnosis correct? Perhaps this was merely the oft-experienced emotion he had hitherto been too honest to call by a romantic name. Yet, abashed though he was, he argued the point hotly.

"Different or not, are you afraid to admit you have exactly the same feeling towards me? I'm thinking of last night."

"Afraid? No." She turned away in proud mortification, muttering in a tone which chilled his ardour. "You don't have to remind me I'm human. I was off my guard, that's all. I want to forget it."

His arm dropped to his side. "I understand. It's this other fellow."

She said nothing, but a tremor ran through her from head to foot. He drew a long breath.

"Well, then, now that you've spoken to him, I suppose you'll be going back."

"To collect my bag and move over to the George. If there's to be any sort of notoriety, I can't stay with the Gisbornes. It's not fair on them."

This intention, in spite of Rachel's protests, she proceeded to carry out, not even allowing her friends to accompany her, but Neil, silent about the call-box incident, followed her over, lit a fire in her fusty bedroom, and remembering she had not eaten, ordered up sandwiches and drinks. The food remained untouched, but she sipped a whisky and soda, sitting on her uninviting bed and with an air of stilled preoccupation removed articles from her bag.

"Pretty grim, this," commented Neil with a disparaging eye on the discoloured wallpaper and the lithograph of King Edward VII in coronation robes.

"There are worse places," she returned indifferently.

"I suppose you're aware that you are acting foolishly."

"I shall have to be the judge."

While he was still tinkering with the fire, one of her green morocco mules tumbled near him. He picked it up, and as he fingered the worn surface of the leather grew conscious of an utterly new emotion. Difficult to classify this, but at all events, far removed from his recent turbulence; different, too, from his longing to buy her beautiful clothes, wrap her in luxury. Odd that till this instant he had never wanted to protect a woman, assume responsibility for her ill-advised actions. That the woman in question repudiated all aid drove his feeling in upon itself, rendered him miserable, and apprehensive.

Presently, gripping the thick tumbler tightly, she bade him tell her all he knew about her aunt's murder. During his recital her eyes never left his face.

"It's like some ghastly trick," she murmured. "Out of a clear sky too— nothing to do with my suspicions, no connection with the Tilburys . . ."

"No, Tilbury was ill. Besides, what could he and his wife hope to gain? They are losing a fat living."

"Bristol!" she mused. "Why Bristol?"

"It's possible, you know, that her body was conveyed there after death. That's why it's important to get a clear statement of yourself. If you could furnish me with even a partial account which can be substantiated, I'll go to London to-morrow and check it up. What about it?"

He was somewhat surprised when, after brief cogitation, she nodded assent.

"Not now, though. Wait till morning. I warn you, it won't be complete."

"Right! Sleep over it. By the way, you know the little key Miss Bundy always wore round her neck? I looked for it, but it was gone. Does the fact mean anything to you?"

Although she shook her head, he fancied she had grown a shade whiter. However, before either could pursue the subject the church clock struck ten. Instantly she sprang up.

"Better leave me now. No, thanks, there's nothing I want. Tell Rachel I'm quite all right and not to bother."

At the head of the stairs he heard voices floating up from the lobby. The fat manageress was haranguing the barman and two commercial travellers with singular virulence.

". . . Cool as cool," she was saying. "Walks in here and asks for a room like as nothing's happened, and her own flesh and blood lying butchered not twenty mile off! I dare say the vicar's glad to see the back of her, but what I'm thinking is, s'pose the police comes down on us?"

"Well, and wot of it?" drawled a man's voice. "Put some life into the business. Young Ted here'll want help in the bar if it gets round you've got a murder suspect stopping with you."

How, in God's name, had the hideous rumour got started? For one moment Neil turned cold, the next he was so consumed with rage that he could scarcely restrain himself from plunging into the gossipers' midst and knocking the four heads together.

"S'sh—her gentleman friend," hissed the big blonde, as he descended and ran the gamut of hard stares accompanied by silent nudges.

Partly to cool down, but chiefly from unwillingness to encounter his host and hostess, he wandered into the churchyard, from which he could see Natasha's lighted window. When its rectangle of milky radiance blacked out he would go indoors, but not before, for to be quite candid he was not altogether satisfied over his abrupt dismissal. He had prowled for ten minutes amongst the gravestones and was just beginning his second cigarette when something arrested his attention, causing him to hide quickly behind the largest yew-tree. Natasha, wearing her coat and hat, had just issued from the inn door and was walking rapidly towards the crossing!

In a sickening flash he saw through her manoeuvres—her reason for going to the George, why she had got rid of him. Even the feint of unpacking—but no, she carried no bag. Anyhow, here was fresh deception, possibly of more than one kind.

Keeping in the shadow, he followed, intent only on ascertaining her coming move. What was she going to do? All life he felt, depended on it. At the top of the street he saw her poised, a solitary figure, eyes fixed on the lonely Bath road. Ages passed, and still she waited—for what?

Ah, now he knew! A ramshackle Daimler approached at breakneck speed, slowed, halted beside the telephone booth. He saw the girl jump to the running-board, saw the door open and a man's arm shoot out as though to draw her inside. Flight! Then it must mean—but hold on, what was this? A sharp bang, the car rattled on its way, and Natasha?

Quietly, with none of her former air of tense purpose, she was returning. Weary, listless, she reached the courtyard of the inn, and the darkness swallowed her up.

# CHAPTER SEVENTEEN

"MURDER AT BRISTOL—WELL-KNOWN SOMERSET WOMAN FOUND DEAD IN DITCH—DAUGHTER OF EMINENT SCIENTIST."

THE headlines leaped at Neil from the newspaper he unfolded aboard the London train. The two inches of small print following provided no new details, but half a column was devoted to Theodore Bundy. There was as yet no mention of Natasha.

He thought painfully of the incident he had witnessed last night, and of the girl's attitude when confronted with his knowledge. She had listened stony-eyed, neither denying nor explaining.

"Well," she had said at the end; "what do you intend to do about it?"

"Do? Keep quiet, of course. Only can't you imagine what came over me when I watched you, absolutely confident you were going away?"

"Oh!" with dawning comprehension. "So you thought—perhaps you still think—I'm concerned in this horrible affair?"

"What does it matter what I thought? It's other people's conclusions I'm bothering about."

"Other people didn't see me—or at least I hope not. Besides, if I hadn't told you about the pearls, would you be worried? Wait, you don't yet know the worst. What about the two ten-pound notes in my purse which the bank can identify? What about my being alone in London for so long a stretch that I might easily have driven to Bristol and back?"

"Then you were alone?" He had seized eagerly on the declaration, only to find her hard to pin down.

"Be that as it may, I can't produce one reliable witness from six o'clock onward. I've racked my brain, but it's no use."

"There was the waitress who served you at dinner."

"I said 'reliable witness.' I don't for a moment suppose I can count on her. If I've forgotten her face, why should she recall mine? The place was crowded. I can tell you approximately where I sat, but that's all."

"Never mind. Give me all the facts—as truthfully as you can. I want to know exactly how you spent your time."

Flushing, she repeated the items detailed the previous evening, up to the stop at the Carlton Hotel. From that point she showed noticeable reluctance.

"Both before and after dinner," she went on, "I—I drove about town. Between seven and eight, I went to Wimbledon—to pay a call."

"So you did see some one! Come, that's better."

"No, it isn't. My friend was away. I spoke to the hall-porter, but as the lights had gone wrong he'd never recognise me."

"He may. What's the name of the building?"

"Sorry. I can't give you that. It wouldn't help, really."

Again the stone wall! No persuasion would move her, and indeed, now he thought it over, he could not help wondering if this visit was an invention to which, later, she hoped to lend colour of truth.

"At any rate, where did you sleep?"

After a long silence, she countered his question with one of her own, wistfully ironic. "Would you believe me if I said I spent the entire night in the car?"

"Unless you can prove where the car was, you could hardly hit on a more damaging statement."

"Then I'd better not make it, had I?" She drew a long breath. "Well! At twelve o'clock I garaged the car in Greek Street, Soho. Afterwards"—she avoided his eye—"I put up at a beastly little pub called Bianchini's. That's in Greek Street too. If you insist on going there, I can't stop you, but they won't know me as Miss Andreyev. You'll have to say—Mrs. Addison."

Noughts and crosses—noughts and crosses—a double row across the envelope of jotted notes before he returned the dry comment, "Mrs. Addison. I see. So you're married?"

"No."

Desperately he waited for some embellishment of the denial, but none was forthcoming. Twice she opened her lips, only to say at last, "Why must you do this? You're sure to hate it."

"Need I remind you that my feelings aren't of the least consequence? What we've got to do is to find as many people as possible who can vouch for your presence in London—quickly, too, before they forget. Now, have you a photograph of yourself?"

"Only the one on my passport. You can take that."

As he opened the little book she handed him the purple stamp of a visa caught his eye. It was dated March 21st. That was the previous Saturday.

"What's this?" he cried, looking closer. "Good God—Persia!"

"Why not? I told you I meant to go away."

"But Persia! . . . What can you expect to do there?"

"What I've been doing. Drive a car."

He could get no more from her.

The time-facts relative to the London-Bristol journey were the reverse of reassuring. When he shut his *A.A. Guide*, the situation as he saw it was this: If he could satisfy himself that Natasha actually was in the Lyons restaurant from eight-fifteen till nine o'clock, he would breathe easily, not otherwise. Unhappily, he knew only too well how hard it might be to obtain the necessary proof.

Since Scotland Yard had extracted all possible information from the London Library, he need not inquire in that quarter. Miss Bundy, it seemed, had rung on Thursday to ask that certain archaeological works be set aside for her perusal, but she had neither claimed the volumes nor been seen by the doorman, who knew her well. The inference was two-fold; first, the old lady must have altered her decision on the very threshold, and second, her change of plan hinged on losing her bag. This was Natasha's opinion, with which he agreed, but had either of them got to the bottom of the dead woman's peculiar behaviour? Why had Miss Bundy refused to be accompanied to her friend's flat? Did Natasha guess the reason, or was it concealed even from her? For a moment this seemed to Neil the keynote of the whole affair, but almost at once the idea was routed by a startling discovery made at his first port of call, the Army and Navy Stores.

To the head assistant of the wine department he put the question: "Do you happen to recall a lady who was here last Friday to complain about an order sent to Stoke Paulton, Somerset?"

"Stoke Paulton, sir?" The man's professional suavity altered to hushed concern. "Beg pardon, but surely that's the address of the lady who's been—"

"It is. I am trying to establish certain facts previous to her death."

"I see, sir. Well, as a matter of fact, she was in here, though not to speak about the order. We were all discussing it just now."

"What, not Miss Bundy herself?" exclaimed Neil incredulously. "Sure it was Miss Bundy?"

"Oh, certainly, sir. She's one of our oldest customers—a stoutish lady, about sixty, near-sighted, rather a florid face."

Neil pondered the information. "What time did she come?"

"Round about five o'clock, sir. She seemed upset over something—wanted to know if a young lady, her niece, I think she said, had been here, but as I couldn't tell her, she hurried off. Later on I discovered the young lady had called, but that one of the other assistants had attended to her. If you like, I'll fetch him. Mr. Sanderson! Will you kindly step here a moment?"

A stripling with an engaging smile approached, took a look at the passport photograph, and recognised Natasha.

"That's the one, sir," he declared. "Tall, wore a grey coat, and carried a red bag." He beamed, adding with cheerful frankness, "Fact is, the red bag caught my eye. I'd wanted to give one like it for an Easter present."

"Do you think the two ladies could have met?"

The men exchanged glances, shook their heads.

"Hardly, in this department, sir," answered the elder. "The young one must have been gone a good half-hour before her aunt arrived."

An uneasy suspicion in his mind, Neil sped by taxi to the Times Book Company in Wigmore Street, mounted to the lending library, and put his questions to the woman at the first receiving desk. The clerk had no recollection of Natasha, though from her card-index she was able to inform Neil that Miss Caroline Bundy's books had been returned. Yes, here was the record—*Aspects of the West Country and Somerset—an Historical Review*, dated Friday last.

"Let me see, though," went on Neil's informant, with a frown. "I'm sure there was something connected with these books. . . . Oh, yes, now I've got it. That same afternoon, an elderly lady was here, inquiring if they'd been brought in. She appeared to be most anxious to get in touch with the person who'd returned them—quite agitated, indeed. She mentioned a valuable bag, left in a car."

"Did she succeed in finding this person?" he asked tensely.

"I'm sure I can't say. She may have done, for quite a bit later—nearly six, it was—she was back again, peering about as though searching for some one."

His suspicion was confirmed. Miss Bundy had done her utmost to overtake Natasha, for the sole purpose of recovering her bag. That the two had missed each other was easily explained, for while Natasha had gone first to the stores and second to the Times, her aunt had reversed the order. Suppose, however, they did finally meet? There was only Natasha's word to refute the suggestion, and her present evasions did not inspire much confidence.

It was then the terrible idea struck him broadside. What if the pearl episode came out, and the police put two and two together? How natural to assume that the bag contained a valuable necklace! It might justifiably be contended that the old lady pursued and overtook her niece only to find her property broken open and rifled; that denunciations and threats on her part were silenced by a murderous assault, following which her body was transported to a distant locality, in order to obscure the trail and, incidentally, postpone discovery. But for the merest accident, Natasha might have been out of England before anything definite was known. Had she not made plans for departure, plans which at any moment would almost certainly be dragged to light?

Neil cursed himself vehemently for thinking of all this, but it was to no purpose. Neither wrath nor reason could quell the tumult rising in his brain.

## CHAPTER EIGHTEEN

HE DASHED on to Hobson and Weaver's, in Regent Street, where Natasha had made certain purchases—a woollen pull-over, driving gloves, a leather coat, all obviously intended for use in Persia. Yes, during the week-end in town she had completed preparations down to the smallest detail, the one puzzle being that she had not immediately set off on her journey. And yet, there was an answer to that. Too hasty a disappearance would have attracted attention, whereas by spending a few quiet days at a country vicarage she would allay suspicion. Her aunt had vanished. If after a suitable interval she sought employment out of England, who could object? She must work, and to obtain a permanent post here presented difficulties, on account of her nationality.

In two departments of the store he learned nothing, but upstairs, in the cloak section, a young woman with well-waved hair readily identified the photograph. What day was it, now? Yes, it was Friday. The customer had tried on several coats, selected a dark-green one, and taken considerable pains over the fit. She was the last person to leave the floor. It was then six o'clock, closing time.

Neil's fears receded. It was near six that Miss Bundy had been seen half a mile away, and although the distance could be covered in a few minutes it was impossible to reconcile Natasha's calm dawdling in a fitting-room with a guilty consciousness. The two women might, of course, have encountered each other later on, but the chances, he felt, were all against an accidental meeting. There still remained the Persian venture, which had indeed an atmosphere of stealth about it, but perhaps it represented something quite different from a flight to escape consequences.

Next the Carlton Hotel, and an interview on the grillroom stairs with the white-haired woman in charge of the ladies' cloak-room. She listened acidly, and delivered a firm negative.

"There's a steady stream of ladies popping in and out, sir," she declared. "Unless they want sewing up or something in the toilet preparation line, I've no call to notice 'em. No, sir, I've not seen your friend, not that I know of."

With not one of the dozen waiters, all on duty last Friday afternoon, had he better luck. Slightly damped, he ascended the Haymarket to Piccadilly Circus, sought the second floor of the gigantic Corner House Restaurant, and put his case to the head waitress. What with the roar of jazz, the clatter of dishes, and the constant buzzing to and fro of maidens in black frocks and snowy aprons, he had some trouble making himself understood; but at last, friendly and helpful, the girl asked to be shown where Natasha had sat.

"It was either the fourth or the fifth table along that farthest row. She remembers being near a window."

"Friday," she mused. "Then it was Miss Douglas or Miss Pilcher who served her, and they're both gone. Miss Douglas has been transferred to our Hammersmith branch—you know, Hammersmith, Broadway; Miss Pilcher's got another post, or so I've heard. Here, Dolly!" She called to a soubrette tripping past with a tray of cutlery. "Know what's become of Gwen?" She lowered her voice. "Think Leslie's seen her?"

After a whispered colloquy, the soubrette, starry-eyed, informed Neil that although she was ignorant of Miss Pilcher's whereabouts, she might on Wednesday—her free day—be able to find out something from a gentleman who knew her cousin. She took Neil's address, promising to drop him a line.

Hammersmith, by underground train; another tea-shop, less imposing, but packed to the doors. Was any one of these harassed damsels, driven off their legs and obviously intent on private concerns, in the least likely to recall a diner seen but once, and that five days ago? Natasha was right. It was hopeless. Still, after tedious waiting, he found himself in conference with an ashen-haired wisp of a girl who poised beside him, impatient to be gone.

"Last Friday evening, between eight and nine," he strove to refresh her memory. "Grilled cutlet and peas—coffee afterwards—a grey tweed coat, small, close-fitting grey hat. Here is her picture. Ever see her?"

"What's this—a riddle?" Miss Douglas parried, with biting scorn. "My word, expect me to know a customer after all this time, unless she's a regular? No, never set eyes on her."

"Look again, please. This is important. She was reading a magazine. Isn't there anything at all familiar about her?"

"Afraid not. No good me pretending, is it? Might land me in a mix up," she added shrewdly. "Here, buck up, Gladys! I'm waiting for that buttered scone. . . ."

There remained Miss Pilcher, but, reflected Neil dispiritedly, would she prove any better than her colleague? He feared not. Natasha's story might be true as gospel, but he foresaw the ease with which it could be torn to bits. Six o'clock, and then what? An interval of blankness extending to midnight. Oh, well, he could at least try Pollard's Garage, in Soho, though there was not much to be gained from that quarter.

Here, at any rate, he met with confirmation. A young woman, admittedly the original of the photograph, had brought in a Geisler car at midnight on Friday, next morning took it out again for a few hours, and removed it finally on the following Monday. The car was fairly clean, considering it had done the journey up from Somerset—hardly any mud on the tyres, the sides not splashed. In London the weather had been dry.

This sounded hopeful. It did not look as though the Geisler could have passed through the deluged Bristol district, least of all along a by-road thick with mire, but the evidence was not conclusive. Cars can be cleaned.

Now for the last item on the list. Fighting down a sense of foreboding, he turned along Greek Street till he reached a narrow, dingy edifice designated as Bianchini's Family Hotel. Here it was, the "beastly little pub" of Natasha's description, sandwiched between a manufacturer of surgical instruments and a foreign comestible shop; windows unwashed, a reek of stale garlic clinging like a bad memory. Why on earth a girl like Natasha should have chosen this unsavoury abode when nearby there were hotels cheap, clean, respectable, defied understanding. Dreading the explanation, he plunged in.

The Italian slattern with scarlet combs thrust into her crinkled mop of hair made no attempt to cope with his inquiries. Shaking off the two sloe-eyed *bambini* who hung upon her skirts she shouted, "Antonio!" Whereupon a swarthy little man, the proprietor, no doubt, bounded forward, rubbing his hands.

Neil resorted to a mild fiction. Looking for a quiet spot in which to do some work—(Quiet! Children screamed in an adjacent court, a hurdy-gurdy operated in front, while a concealed optimist high up essayed "Scenes That Are Brightest" on a cornet)—and hearing from his friend, Mrs. Addison, of the quarters occupied by herself last week-end, he had come to see what could be arranged. Was Mrs. Addison's room free?

"Oh! So Mrs. Addison recommended us, did she?" The man's eyes, merry and shrewd, glowed with gratification. "A nice lady, sir—oh, a very nice lady! Yes, she stayed with us from Friday till Monday. If you'll come with me, I'll just show you." He bustled up the cramped stairs, talking steadily. "Unfortunately, the room's taken. Only for the week, though. Another couple came right in. Professional artists, on at the Holborn Palace—Vic and Mick, expect you know their turn."

The words "another couple" jarred through Neil like an electric shock.

"Mrs. Addison was not alone, was she?" he suggested with elaborate carelessness. "I believe she mentioned that—"

Was there a slight hesitation on Bianchini's part?

Perhaps he was only a little puffed with the stairs and forced to take breath before answering. "Quite right, sir. Mr. Addison was with her. They're not long married, I understand, but I expect you know more about that than we do."

"Yes, certainly—though it so happens I've not yet met Mr. Addison."

"You don't say so! Well, well! And he's the one we do know. Had him here all the month of January, and got quite attached to him. It was a great surprise to find he was married."

He flung wide a door, revealing a double room left in some disorder. Neil, with a stifled sensation, stared at the twin brass beds, each covered with a hideous flowered quilt, at the pink chemise drying over a chair, and at the littered dressing-table on which curling-tongs and eye-black mingled with a pair of striped braces.

"Nice and airy, eh, sir?" continued his garrulous host. "Yes, we hadn't heard from him since he left us. Seems they came up from the country separately, arranging to meet here, but Mrs. Addison arrived first. Her husband didn't turn up till quite late—oh, one in the morning—and she got rather worried."

"Nothing wrong, I hope?"

"Well, no, sir; not exactly what you might call wrong." Again the brief reticence, followed by a confidential burst. "The fact is, sir, Mr. Addison'd had just a small drop more than was good for him. You understand." With a tolerant wink. "Nothing against him, for I'm sure a nicer gentleman never was, but you see how it is, he's high-strung and nervous, and drink knocks him out a bit. Heart, sir, that's his trouble. Mrs. Addison, not being used to it, got quite frightened, but he pulled round safe enough."

Somehow Neil reached the street, sick with disillusionment. Natasha in that sordid bedroom with all its suggestion of intimacy and subterfuge—her trim coat hanging side by side with the Harris tweed one of hateful associations, her neat brogues ranged with those of a male companion who lay sunken in bestial stupor! Imagination revolted at the idea.

What had he accomplished? Married or not, she loved the blighter. He was a drunkard, but she meant to follow him into the wilds of Persia, and nothing could stop her.

"All I've done is to stir up mud!"

Mud that clung and sullied. No wonder she had hated giving him the name of this hotel, which, after all, was of no use towards constructing an alibi. Oppressed by his newly acquired knowledge, he shrank from the thought of the coming interview with her.

The latter came unexpectedly soon. As he was alighting at the Glastonbury platform, he caught sight of a familiar figure just slipping past the barrier. Natasha! So she, too, had been up to London. It angered him to think she had concealed her intention and even now was trying to get away before he discovered what she had done.

For a moment he decided to let her go, then suddenly, as she was signalling a taxi, he found himself touching her arm. She faced him with a faint, wry smile.

"I thought I might manage to escape your notice," she murmured, with a shrug.

"So I see," he returned grimly. "Well, as you haven't succeeded, you may as well let me drive you back. My car's at the garage."

## CHAPTER NINETEEN

THEY drove off homeward. Natasha volunteered nothing beyond the fact that she had taken a sudden decision to catch the twelve-nineteen train to London, while Neil, in no mood to beg for confidences, observed dryly, "Then if you've covered the same ground as myself, I don't suppose there's much I can tell you."

"You're wrong," she informed him. "I had quite another reason for going. What did you find out?" she inquired, with a hint of trepidation.

"Nothing of any use," he said brutally. "On the contrary, I got hold of something which may mean trouble. Are you aware that Miss Bundy tracked you half over the West End in order to recover that bag?"

"Did she? How do you know?" Surely her start was spontaneous! "I'd no idea—and yet I begin to see, up to a point, what must have happened. She tried first of all to overtake the car, and failing that followed on to the two places where there was a chance of meeting me. Somewhere between she sent the wire. But how can all this mean trouble?"

He hoped his crude announcement would wrest from her a full confession, but the silence following her single dismayed gasp showed her more than ever determined not to commit herself. She seemed to be weighing pros and cons with meticulous calculation, and let some time elapse before asking if he had gone to the hotel.

"Bianchini's? Oh, yes—I heard all they had to tell me. Need we discuss it?"

"I think not," she answered, low-voiced, but he noticed that her chin went up.

As they were nearing Stoke Paulton she coldly suggested a stop to collect her trunk, which was packed, waiting to be removed.

"Don't bother to come with me. Crabbe will see to it."

While she was in the house, Tilbury ventured forth and stood beside the car. His face was still pinched and wan, his voice croaked huskily.

"No news, sir? Nothink at all?" he inquired anxiously, and when Neil shook his head continued despondently, "It's a proper staggerer, sir. However the poor lady come to be way off there in Bristol—! If it was any one but 'er, I'd say she'd gorn off her 'ead, but Miss Bundy! Why, a more sensible lady never lived! Con and me can vouch for that—and the doctor, too." He paused heavily. "No, take my word for it, sir, she was done in first and carried there afterwards—and wot's more," he added in a meaning whisper, "whoever's responsible is some 'un as knows this section thorough-like. That there ditch would take a bit of finding."

"About the telephone call you received," said Neil suddenly. "Was there nothing about it which might suggest a clue?"

Tilbury's eyes lit eagerly. "Now you've mentioned it, sir," he returned in a hushed undertone, "neither the wife nor me was quite satisfied about that call. The connection was bad, and after the first bit we never got anythink plain, but we couldn't help thinking maybe the voice was kept low on purpose. Get my meaning, sir? Supposing it wasn't really Miss Bundy at all, but some other lady pretending to be 'er? You know, so we'd think she was alive when she wasn't. It's just a notion we've got, but all the same—"

He broke off pointedly to stare at Natasha, who in company with Crabbe emerged from the house, and presently withdrew, leaving Neil with an enraged comprehension of the source whence the disagreeable rumours had emanated. Bitterly did the latter regret not investigating the telephone call while he had the opportunity. The police were sure to do so, but meanwhile this fellow was spreading vile reports.

Having strapped on the trunk, Crabbe came close to Natasha.

"There's a matter I think you ought to know about, miss," he said respectfully. "You remember that last Wednesday afternoon when you and Mr. Starkey went to Exeter? Well, Miss Bundy had her solicitor down to draw up a new will. Mrs. Hickson and Pritchard acted as witnesses, and were told not to say anything about it."

"So that explains the man we saw in the taxi!" whispered Natasha, turning to Neil. "But why so much secrecy? And if witnesses were wanted, what was wrong with Crabbe and that man?"

"I don't know about myself, miss," replied Crabbe. "But she sent Mr. and Mrs. Tilbury off for the afternoon, and particularly didn't want them to know what she was doing."

Here was fresh matter for wonderment, though Neil, as they drove off, offered a partial explanation. "Beneficiaries, you know, are debarred from signing as witnesses. That would account, perhaps, for the cook and maid being called upon instead of these others, but the new will itself seems queer, coming as it did just two days before Miss Bundy's death. I thought all along, of course, that she was frightened about her health, but she could scarcely have anticipated what did happen."

"Unless she did know of a private enemy . . . I wonder! As I told you before, she meant her money to go to some research fund. She made no secret of that."

Before he set her down at the inn he asked if she had got her statement for the inquest clearly formulated.

"It's absolutely essential, understand, not to contradict yourself."

"If the truth comes out—as it may do any moment—they won't bother to ask me troublesome questions. Good-night, and thank you for all you've done."

He suspected the parting sentence to contain more than a grain of sarcasm, and suffered accordingly. That the facts he had dug up were in any case bound to appear did not ease a conscience which pricked him still more acutely when it came to auditing his recital for the Gisbornes' benefit. He studiously withheld all mention of Natasha's week-end companion, and also any reference to Miss Bundy's bag, but when he had finished there was uncomfortable silence. Rachel sat with averted eyes. Her brother stared gravely at him before remarking slowly:

"So Carrie followed the girl! The question now before us is, Did she or did she not succeed in catching her?"

"I see no reason for disbelieving Natasha on that score," replied Neil. "I take it she did not."

Gisborne continued ominously, "That alligator bag of Carrie's was lost or stolen some hours before the murder occurred. It must have been considered valuable, or she would not have taken so much trouble to recover it. Are you sure it contained only papers?"

"I'm sure of nothing, except that I once caught sight of what appeared to be one of Bundy's manuscripts. The bag may have contained something besides, or else the manuscript itself was regarded as precious. Personally, I incline to the latter opinion."

"You may be right. The unfortunate creature had a bee in her bonnet which would account for many vagaries." He bent forward, elbows on knees, face deeply furrowed. "Ah, well," he sighed, "she's dead now, poor woman, and since further silence on my part can't benefit her, I might as well give you the reason for her quarrel with me. It's extremely trivial, and sheds no light whatever on her death. I wish to Heaven it did!"

Exchanging glances, Rachel and Neil gave close attention to his narrative, trying to see if at any point it could be connected with the crime.

"It all dates back to something which occurred before Christmas," began Gisborne. "It seems this photographer chap, then quite unknown to us all, came to ask Carrie if he might take some views of the Glebe House, which, as you know, has a local interest. It was his intention to place these views on sale, to attract tourists. Carrie consented, saying she herself would buy copies, but although the pictures were taken she heard no more on the subject. Finally, after a fortnight or so, she went into the shop to inquire. She laid great stress on this, holding it as proof of the man's honesty that he did not attempt to foist his work on her. Indeed, he was reluctant to show her the pictures at all—quite embarrassed, according to her.

"Apparently something had gone wrong with the plates, an accident which he declared he could not account for; and sure enough, as she saw at once, there was an odd feature, common to the whole set of photographs. I myself examined both the plates and the negatives, so I can tell you what it was. Quite simply, it consisted of a transparent but fairly distinct shape or figure, superimposed on the landscape, always in the same spot. The affect was just what one sees in X-ray pictures. I considered it sheer trickery, but I'm going too fast.

"To explain what it meant to Carrie, I must tell you a bit about her father. Old Theodore in his last days—some would say his dotage—nurtured a pet theory regarding the Glebe House. There has always been a tradition that in former times the building was connected by underground tunnel with Glastonbury Abbey, though if such a passage did exist it was blocked up, possibly caved in, centuries ago. I have never come on any authentic record of it, but I know many people, including Bundy, believed in it. Well, Bundy went further. He believed that with the closing of this passage a relic of immense interest had been shut from human eyes. Carrie, it appears, had held an open mind on the subject, but was incapable of treating any of her father's ideas with disrespect. His lightest utterances were to her inspired gospel."

"One moment," interrupted Neil. "Had Bundy any foundation for his theory?"

"Not what you or I would call foundation. In the beginning he played with the notion, half-seriously—I've heard him discuss it by the hour— but towards the end of his life it was confirmed by communications supposed to emanate from his dead wife. You didn't know, perhaps, that he dabbled in spiritualism? He took pains to conceal the fact, afraid of his colleagues' ridicule, but he did, for a time, experiment with a medium in the person of a village seamstress. This woman, Mrs. Spencer, employed what is known as the direct voice, and the messages she issued made a deep impression on Bundy. Carrie was diffident about the whole business, so much so that when her father and the seamstress both died within a few weeks of each other, she let the matter drop.

"At the same time, she realised that if her father had lived he meant to have soundings taken and the tunnel, if any, excavated in hope of unearthing the hidden treasure. Her conscience troubled her to think she might be neglecting his wishes, but she was too timid to take active steps. Now you will see how she felt when, out of the blue, this ignorant photographer turned up with his weird pictures. She was thunderstruck, confronted by a miracle. Why, the man had never even heard of Theodore Bundy! The relic in question was a name to him, no more. She saw in him an instrument, employed by her father, to remind her of her duty."

"So that's why she was always poking round the ruin!" cried Neil, slapping his thigh. "And in the Bundy diary, too, there are entries which—"

"Wait. For all her father-worship, Carrie was a canny soul. Like Bundy, she had no wish to be laughed at. So she sought my advice, hoping, of course, that I would sanction the enterprise forming in her brain and thus enable her to go ahead without further scruples. She brought forward Bligh Bond's experiments at Glastonbury!—the lost Edgar Chapel discovered through supernatural means—arguing that what had happened once could happen again. Well, as you know, that business created a great stir. It was impressive, no getting round it."

He paused, mechanically stuffing tobacco into his pipe, then resumed. "Unfortunately for me, I threw cold water on the entire affair, which in my eyes was a clever charlatan's game, nothing else. The plates, I pointed out, could easily have been faked, while she had only the fellow's own word for his *bona fides*. How were we to know Tilbury was telling the truth in declaring that, though he attached no importance to it, this sort of thing was continually happening to him, becoming indeed a positive nuisance? How prove he was what he appeared—a well-meaning, untutored little man, ignorant alike of the Glastonbury legends and her father's beliefs? My arguments failed to move her an inch. She was already firmly convinced. She wanted to believe. The very way in which Tilbury seemed ashamed of his psychic powers—table-tippings and so on, occasionally indulged in to oblige his friends—indicated to her a character utterly incapable of deceit.

"Maybe she was right, but—well, I have lived too long in a wicked world not to view such goings-on with distrust. Furthermore, I reminded her of the total absence of historical support for her cherished myth, a myth probably originating in the minds of poetic visionaries. In my zeal to spare her from disappointment and humiliation, I went too far, assuring her that many serious students look on the great emblem as pagan, not spiritual in significance, but distinctly otherwise. Ah, that's where I blundered! I ought to have remembered the proverb about the tiger's cubs. Her virgin prejudices were shocked to the core; I mortally offended her, I was a sacrilegious vandal, a disgrace to my cloth. She flounced out of my study with a flea in her ear, and thenceforward regarded me with bitter hatred.

"Soon afterwards, I learned that she had taken up the Tilbury couple, was conducting seances with them, and heaping them with benefits. Knowing it was useless to interfere, and having given my solemn word to say nothing, I held my tongue. I could not see any grave harm in what she was doing, and even now I fail to perceive the remotest connection between these activities and her death. Can either of you find any?"

The two listeners sat silent. Neil was recalling the hitherto obscure reference in the diary—how did it run? *"By this Sign will the millennium be inaugurated."* No need to ask what sign was meant; yet he did ask.

Gisborne sucked hard at his pipe.

"Eh? Oh, you've probably guessed it. The shadowy form overhanging the ruin was shaped like a two-handled cup. What poor Carrie hoped to find in the ancient tunnel, placed there, presumably, by St. Joseph of Arimathea was the Holy Grail."

## CHAPTER TWENTY

THE coroner's court was crowded. Every class of society was represented—tradespeople, farmers, idle riff-raff, county grandees—and on
every face was the same look of morbid expectancy. Near the front the
Stoke Paulton servants formed a sedate group, with Crabbe at their head,
while a little apart from them sat Alfred and Connie Tilbury, stiff and
subdued in new, semi-mourning attire.

When the party from the vicarage entered, necks craned and a sibi-
lant murmur ran round. Plainly the dead woman's niece was an object
of intense interest, and at sight of her between the two Gisbornes many
eyebrows were raised questioningly. She, however, seemed unaware
of the stir her presence created. She took her seat with an air of steady
composure, and possibly no one but Neil fully realised how great must
be her inward perturbation.

A good deal of preliminary movement was going on. Various func-
tionaries pressed forward to consult with the coroner, a fussy, pompous
man who waved aside communications with impatience. It was easy to
see he intended to conduct proceedings in his own way, jealous, perhaps,
of his importance; but whether this fact augured for good or bad it was
difficult to foresee.

"Neil, look! She's come back in time for the inquest."

Rachel whispered this, directing her companion's attention to the
rigid, imposing figure seated across the aisle. It was Emily Braselton.
Her grief-stricken eyes, heavily circled, were hawk-like and vindictive,
her chin was set with a forbidding aggressiveness vaguely alarming in its
suggestion. Was she here with any definite purpose in mind? Neil stole
a glance at Natasha to see if she, too, had noticed the head mistress,
but she was staring straight ahead with a deadened indifference to her
surroundings.

As the coroner cleared his throat portentously, a police sergeant
creaked up to the platform and laid a folded slip of paper directly under
his eye. The good man glared affrontedly at the note, seeming to regard
any interruption as an offence to his dignity, waited till the unfortunate
sergeant had retired, and without opening the communication began
a prosy address. Neil saw Miss Braselton stir restlessly and grow still
more grimly stern. Her manner indicated contempt for the speaker's
long-winded periods, yet she listened to every word, watchful and alert.

The court doctor, by contrast, was dry and to the point. Having
performed a complete autopsy on the victim, he could state positively

that the latter's organs contained neither drug nor poison, and were indeed in a healthy condition. There were signs to show that a light meal had been consumed some two to three hours prior to decease, but whatever was eaten was of a harmless character. Death had resulted solely from the blows administered to the skull by means of some instrument, probably metallic, like a hammer or heavy spanner. No less than three deep fractures had been sustained, besides a number of minor injuries. She had, in fact, been literally battered to death, in what one could only characterise as a brutal, insensate manner.

Particles of dirt lodged in the mouth and nostrils indicated that the body had fallen face downward, probably after the initial blow, but this in itself furnished no proof of the attack having taken place near the spot where the victim was found. Quite possibly it occurred at a distance, the body being conveyed thither subsequently.

While the time of the assault could not be pinned down with exactitude, there could be little doubt as to the approximate hour of the body's consignment to the ditch. The saturated condition of the clothing showed that it must have lain in its hiding-place during at least part of the heavy rainfall which lasted from 9 p.m. to midnight on Friday, 20th March. After this date there had been no local shower till after the discovery of the crime. *Rigor mortis*, probably both accelerated and prolonged by reason of the cold and wet, need not be taken into consideration at all. The deluge, while removing other clues, had provided this single, indisputable bit of evidence. There were no marks of violence except those mentioned.

William Crabbe was called. Asked if during his seventeen years' service at Stoke Paulton he had suspected any one of cherishing malevolence towards his mistress, he gave a firm negative.

CORONER: "Then you don't know of any person bearing Miss Bundy a grudge, uttering threats, or in any way causing a disturbance?"

CRABBE: "No, sir. There was just a small unpleasantness lately, over a gardener she sacked. It wouldn't be worth mentioning, only Miss Bundy was upset and had a bad turn in consequence."

CORONER: "Indeed! I should like you to tell the jury exactly what happened and all about it."

The butler complied, obviously with reluctance. He was sure the gardener, an old man, had meant no harm. Miss Bundy had grown rather touchy of late, a little unreasonable, perhaps. He himself could venture no opinion as to the rights of the case, although he knew the gardener thought himself badly used.

CORONER: "Did the discharged man appear to brood or to harbour ill-feelings?"

CRABBE: "He certainly never used abusive language in my hearing. He's not that sort."

The name and present whereabouts of Peters were obtained. The other servants were then questioned without disclosing anything suggestive, and last, Alfred Tilbury was called.

The bailiff stood up promptly and in a low, husky voice repeated the oath, after which he was seized with such a violent fit of coughing that some time elapsed before he could go on. His air of fragility, combined with his assiduous efforts to control the spasms, roused sympathy in the onlookers. The coroner offered him water. He took a sip, and was able to speak again.

Modestly and frankly he described the circumstances which had led to his holding his present position A photographer by trade, he had had occasion to do some professional work for Miss Bundy, who, towards the end of February, had offered him the post of bailiff.

CORONER: "Then you did not yourself apply for the place?"

TILBURY: "Oh, no, sir! I'd no experience. I never even thought of such a thing, only Miss Bundy seemed to think I would suit. I almost believe she must have taken rather a liking to the wife and me. She said as 'ow she wanted some one good and steady as she could trust and train into her ways—some one to look after her interests. That was her fancy, more than the sort that knows it all, as the saying is."

He went on to explain that believing the open-air life would benefit him, he had somewhat diffidently accepted the offer, and that during his brief sojourn at Stoke Paulton he had been very happy. Miss Bundy was a lady in a thousand, a kind, considerate friend, the loss of whom in such distressing circumstances was more than he could bear to contemplate. Here he was momentarily overcome, while his wife was heard to sob. The coroner fumbled with his notes to allow him time to recover.

Asked if he knew of any enemies the deceased might have had, Tilbury emphatically denied the suggestion. True his late mistress had occasionally hinted that certain nameless persons were prone to take advantage of her good nature. He imagined something of the sort in the case of Peters, but could say nothing for sure. Of course, some people were all out for themselves, and if they couldn't gain what they wanted honestly were not above resorting to unworthy methods. Still, he had no definite knowledge, and it was not his place to cast aspersions. If Miss Bundy were anxious to secure reliable servants, that was only natural for one in failing health. He and his wife had been much worried over her recent illness and delighted at the idea that she was going abroad with the friend who would look after her properly. She had seemed in excellent spirits when she left home, perfectly cheerful with no sign of anything on her mind.

Neil listened expectantly for some mention of the seances, but none occurred. The coroner evidently had no knowledge of the couple's peculiar activities, which in any case seemed quite irrelevant to the murder.

The matter of the telephone call was thoroughly discussed. Tilbury repeated the fragmentary sentences he had heard, admitting, though with hesitation, his feeling of dissatisfaction about the identity of the speaker. He gave the slight impression of suspecting rather more than he cared to put into words, but did not overstress it.

CORONER: "That call has now been traced. It was put through from the main Victoria Post Office at five-thirty on Friday, 20th March, but the details concerning it are as yet incomplete. I suggest that the voice you heard used words similar to these: 'I am speaking for Miss Bundy.' Is that so?"

TILBURY: "Oh, no, sir—that wasn't it at all. What I did catch plain as plain was: 'This is Miss Bundy speaking.' It was about all that was clear. The voice after that was very faint like as if the person didn't want to speak up—or else it was a bad connection. I can't say which."

CORONER: "But you did understand some reference to an object left in the car?"

TILBURY: "I fancied so, sir. There was the words 'car,' and 'left behind.' Putting two and two together, we thought Miss Bundy wanted us to inquire at the garage and see if she'd left something in the car. Mrs. Tilbury went in to Glastonbury the next day to make sure, but the car hadn't come in. I was too ill to see to it myself." CORONER: "Yes, I am told you were under medical care for several days. When were you able to make personal inquiries?"

TILBURY: "On the Monday—though they was all very annoyed with me for slipping out when I was so bad. It was on my mind to try and catch Miss Andreyev when she got back to the garage, otherwise I might miss her altogether. I was anxious to find out how she'd left the mistress, and to see if she knew what the telephone message meant. I dropped in twice. The first time she hadn't arrived, and the second she had come and gone. By that time I'd had the telegram from Paris, and was properly worried to know what had become of Miss Bundy. So I hurried over to the vicarage, hoping I'd find the young lady there, and she was there—

but she didn't know no more than us. It was her that told me about Miss Bundy's losing her bag and telegraphing her to look for it. She'd hunted in the car, but it wasn't there."

CORONER: "Am I to take it you had no suspicion that any fate other than sudden illness had befallen Miss Bundy?"

TILBURY: "None of us thought anything but that. We all said she must have had another attack and been taken to a hospital."

Many additional questions followed without eliciting anything of importance. The coroner dismissed the witness and ran his eye over a list. Neil saw Emily Braselton lean forward to fix a compelling gaze on him, but he remained stolidly oblivious. A second later, with some hesitation over the foreign name, he called Natasha Andreyev.

There was a noticeable rustle as the girl took her place. Her three friends held their breath in dread anticipation of the approaching ordeal. Would her statement be pulled to pieces? Not one of them had the remotest idea of what she intended to say, nor did her pale, expressionless features give them any clue.

The coroner, plainly anxious to make things as easy for her as possible, addressed her in a softened manner, and the ensuing dialogue took place amidst tense silence.

CORONER: "Miss Andreyev, may I ask how long you have resided at Stoke Paulton?"

NATASHA: "A year and eight months."

CORONER: "And before that your home was—?"

NATASHA: "Paris. I was born in Russia."

CORONER: "Prior to your coming to England, were you well acquainted with your aunt?"

NATASHA: "I did not know her at all."

This answer produced a mild sensation. The coroner himself seemed astonished.

CORONER: "That is rather strange. How did it happen?"

NATASHA: "There was a family estrangement, caused by my mother's marriage. It was only when my mother died that my aunt looked me up and offered me the post of secretary-chauffeuse."

CORONER: "Just what were your duties?"

NATASHA: "I drove the car, of course, and I wrote all her letters for her, except a few personal ones. I did most of the housekeeping, too, and looked after the dogs. For six months, after the old bailiff died last summer, I collected the rents from the cottages on the estate and saw to all the tenants' complaints."

CORONER: "I see. H'm. . . . During your residence in the house, did you ever know of any person bearing your aunt a serious grudge?"

NATASHA: "No, never. I don't think she could have had any enemies."

CORONER: "Can you suggest any possible explanation of the murder, or account in any way for the body's being in Bristol?"

NATASHA: "No. If she had any association with Bristol, she never mentioned it."

Asked to relate what happened when she and Miss Bundy reached London, she did so collectedly, making it plain that but for the stop at Marlborough for lunch, her aunt had not quitted the car till they arrived at St. James's Square. On the way in they had passed by the flat where the deceased was to spend the night and left a small case containing her night things. From there they drove to Victoria Station to deposit her steamer trunk at the cloakroom, where it was to be picked up the following day. Then they went on to the London Library.

CORONER: "It has been ascertained that Miss Bundy failed to enter the library building. Can you give any reason for this?"

NATASHA: "It has since occurred to me that she must have missed her bag—the one described in her telegram to me—directly she got out of the car, and that she tried to catch me. I knew nothing about the bag, of course, till I got back to Glastonbury on Monday and found the message waiting for me."

CORONER: "And the bag was not in the car?"

NATASHA: "No."

CORONER: "Do you assume it to have been lost elsewhere or stolen?"

NATASHA: "Lost, perhaps—not stolen—or at least, not out of the car, because I never left the car without locking the door."

CORONER: "Would the bag's disappearance mean that the deceased was left without money and railway ticket?"

Natasha explained that this was not the case, also that she had no idea what her aunt kept in this particular bag. The telegram was now produced, read, and the place and time of dispatch commented on.

CORONER: "You say you did not receive this message till Monday evening. Was that because you passed the entire week-end in London?"

NATASHA: "Yes. I was given a month's holiday with no stipulations except that I was to drive the car back to Glastonbury some time or other to hand it in for repairs. My aunt knew I would go to the garage, but probably not to the house. That is why she sent the telegram to the garage, to catch me before I gave the car up."

CORONER: "I suppose you did not think to telephone your aunt on Saturday morning to see if she wanted you?"

NATASHA: "I did think of it, but as she had definitely said she didn't wish me to go to the station with her, I decided it was wiser not to bother her. She was a little odd in some ways. She might not have liked being called to the telephone when she was in a hurry to get off."

CORONER: "Might she, in your opinion, have had some private reason for wishing to be left alone? And you had positively not the least intimation of anything wrong till you learned of her non-arrival in Paris?"

NATASHA: "Not the slightest. The news came as a great shock."

The Coroner pondered. "Well, Miss Andreyev, unless the jury would like to put any questions to you, I don't know that there is anything more I can—Eh? What's that?" He broke off pettishly as the sergeant before mentioned tiptoed towards him and whispered in his ear. "Speak up, please. Note? What note? I haven't seen any—oh, that!"

In decided annoyance he picked up the neglected chit previously handed to him, and with an air of resentment, unfolded it. As he read its contents his expression altered, became both puzzled and displeased. He ran a furtive eye round the court, questing something or some one, pursed his lips, and tapped the table with a plump, freckled finger. When he spoke it was in a much less confident tone than he had formerly employed.

CORONER: "Before you sit down, I had better, I think, ask you one or two questions about—er—your personal relations with the deceased. Were you and she on—er—agreeable terms with each other?"

NATASHA: "Perfectly."

CORONER "Any little—er—differences, or disagreements?"

NATASHA: "No serious ones. We really got on very well."

CORONER: "Quite so. H'm. . . . Now I am afraid I must put a rather delicate query. Did you ever, on any occasion, attempt to borrow money from her?"

NATASHA (with an astonished intake of her breath): "Certainly not! I never dreamed of such a thing!"

CORONER: "Yes, yes, of course! But did you not at some recent time let it be known that financial assistance might be welcome, if not to yourself, then to some person in whom you were interested?"

NATASHA (coldly): "I don't quite know what you mean. I did once tell her about a person known to us both who was in difficulties, hoping she would offer to do something about it. As she showed no concern, I let the matter drop. I did not directly ask her for help."

CORONER: "Are you sure this individual you mention did not apply to her in person?"

NATASHA (flushing scarlet, with some asperity): "As sure as I can be of most things. If so, I never heard about it."

CORONER: "Very good. That will do. Would the jury like to put any inquiries to the witness?"

Apparently the jury had nothing to say, and after waiting quietly for a moment or two, Natasha resumed her seat.

The tottering bridge had been crossed. The girl's replies had been ready, explicit, and in no way calculated to invite criticism. If she had failed to speak of her aunt's parting gift or her own movements after the separation, there had really been no necessity for so doing. The Gisbornes looked intensely relieved, and Neil, to some extent, shared their feelings, only he could not help fearing Natasha had acted unwisely in keeping back what might be discovered before the inquiry ended. There was a vaguely ominous trend to the final questions, touching as they did upon matters the coroner would never have thought of without outside prompting. He had dealt with them lightly enough, to be sure, but might they not be followed up with disastrous results?

However, nothing further happened, and after a vast deal of unimportant evidence, the coroner summed up and instructed the jury to retire. Whispers ran round, guesses were hazarded as to whether or not an adjournment would be ordered. Those most concerned sat silent, tensely awaiting the outcome. From time to time Tilbury's hacking cough rang out sharply.

The door opened, the line of nondescript jurors filed back. The foreman, a small, dusky Welshman with a sing-song utterance, stepped forward impressively. With a great sigh of thankfulness Neil heard the verdict of wilful murder by a person or persons unknown.

A minute later, in the crowd, he came face to face with Emily Braselton, whose eyes, muddied with baffled rage, confronted him without the least recognition. In a flash he knew the truth. It was she who had sent that note up to the coroner, she who had proposed the line of investigation which might so easily have led to trouble for the girl she disliked. Now she was livid with fury against the incompetent who had had his chance and let it slip through his fingers.

Her unseeing gaze left Neil cold with fear. When she brushed him aside on her way to the exit, it was as though he had been swept out of the path of an avenging angel.

# CHAPTER TWENTY-ONE

On the way home little was said. In spite of the result of the inquest Natasha was still oppressed and subdued, possibly because she felt the aloofness of the vicar's attitude. Declining the urgent invitation to lunch with her friends, she went straight back to the inn, a lonely and listless figure.

"I can't understand what's come over her," remarked Rachel in a troubled voice. "It's as though some spring inside had broken. I've never seen her like this before, and it worries me."

Her brother forbore comment, changing the subject with what seemed a pointed abruptness.

"I can't help thinking it a bit extraordinary that nothing was said about Carrie's will. Haven't they got hold of any information yet? Easter holidays, of course, may have tied things up a bit, but even so—well, I admit I'm curious to learn what disposition she's made of her property, especially in view of this new will executed only two days before her death. That circumstance has a queer look, say what you like."

No one disputed this, but not one of the three was in the least prepared for the bombshell which burst in their midst that very afternoon. The bailiff called again and was closeted with Gisborne for a quarter of an hour, at the end of which time he departed, and the vicar returned to the drawing-room with a strange look on his face.

"Well," cried Rachel impatiently, "did he have any news?"

"News! Yes, and with a vengeance. You'll neither of you believe what I have to tell you. It's—grotesque." Words failed him. He had to pause to give himself time to simmer down. "Anyhow, here it is in a nutshell," he said brusquely. "Carrie's solicitor, a man called Powyss, has just been down for the purpose of reading the will. And what a will! After a few minor bequests, the residuary legatees of the entire estate are—Alfred Tilbury and his wife!"

The cigarette dropped from Neil's lips. He stared at the speaker as though doubtful of his sanity.

"Tilbury!" he burst out at last. "Why—you're joking! What in God's name do you take this to mean?"

"On the face of it, an infatuated woman's crowning act of folly," replied the vicar, with grimly set features. "If there's more behind it, who can say? One thing's certain—the fellow himself knows how bad it looks. He's knocked to bits. I had to give him brandy before he could stop dithering sufficiently to tell me about it. Declares he had no idea of such a thing—is afraid of what people will think, and all the rest of it. Came to me for advice."

"And what advice did you give?" demanded Rachel sharply.

"What could I say? If the will is legally sound, as it appears to be, he must take what's his and put up with gossip, that's all."

"Unless the courts can prove undue influence."

"Precisely, and that, I imagine, was his real reason for coming to me. He wanted to show me the letter Carrie wrote in Powyss's presence and deposited with the will—a queer document, but it pretty well disposes of any suggestion of influence. Evidently she foresaw the doubts which might be raised and repudiated them in advance. According to her, she was acting on her own carefully considered judgment, with neither the knowledge nor counsel of the beneficiaries, to ensure the carrying out of certain definite wishes. In short, she stipulates that the heirs shall open up the tunnel under the hill and conduct a thorough search for—the Holy Grail."

"Oh!" gasped Rachel incredulously, "so that's what it's all about."

"Quite. Her precarious health warned her she might not live to see the project through to its conclusion, consequently she has left it to this couple as a sacred trust, with her money to back it. Tilbury, acting in her behalf, is to be the Galahad of the twentieth century."

The picture evoked was so hopelessly comic that for a moment no one could do anything but laugh. When they had grown serious again Neil said confidently: "You may be quite sure the will won't stand."

"Who is there to contest it?" retorted Gisborne caustically. "The only near relatives are Natasha and her brother Michael. Are they likely to put up a fight, particularly as the other will—the one recently destroyed—left them each the same legacy as this new one? A thousand pounds apiece—that's all they would have got in any case. A woman may leave her money as she sees fit."

"But if she's mentally infirm—?"

"We can't prove she was that. Many an idiotic will has passed muster with the courts. I see no reason why this shouldn't."

"What a blessing Tasha gets something, anyhow," cried Rachel spontaneously, only to stop as she saw the cryptic expression of her brother's face.

"Is it such a blessing? I'm not sure."

Neil, distinctly uncomfortable, bridged the awkward silence by inquiring who were the executors.

"Ah, you may well ask! There's only one executor—Tilbury himself. Staggering, isn't it? A line at the end of Carrie's letter spoke volumes of fatuous trust. After a biting reference to those in spiritual authority ridiculing her idea—a dig at me, you understand—she said that throughout the ages God's work had been done by people of simple faith. Simple faith, indeed! Simple instruments to do her bidding, and incidentally see that the accruing glory goes to her. Pathetic, that touch of vanity. . . . Poor, misguided creature! Her one act of shrewdness was to make it a condition of inheritance that the legatees are to set about their undertaking at once and carry it through. If they fail to do this, the money goes to a fund for scientific research."

"But does Tilbury himself believe in this rubbish?"

"What does it matter whether he does or not?" Gisborne shrugged and began to refill his pipe. "He must have played up to the scheme while she was alive. Actually, I can't make him out at all. Something disarmingly childlike about him. He professes to have been in a trance during the seances, and says he has not the slightest idea what revelations have been made through his mediumship. I'm afraid I was too disgusted to question him very closely as to that part of the affair. He babbled a good deal about the wonderful thing it would be to restore what he calls the 'Oly Gryle' to the world, but he quite freely admits he's never been clear as to just what the Grail was."

"Is he faking ignorance?" asked Neil bluntly.

"Can't say. I tell you, he's a complete puzzle to me, but however that may be, he's shown himself remarkably practical in some directions. He's arranged with Powyss to obtain an immediate advance from the bank in order to start in on the digging, and he's offering a reward of five hundred pounds for information leading to the conviction of the criminal. I would hardly have credited him with sense enough for this latter move, but he declares he can't rest till the murderer is found."

"I'd like to hear what the solicitor thinks of it all," remarked Rachel, still dazed with bewilderment.

"I mean to see him to-morrow. Not that it's my business, but some one ought to inquire into matters." Suddenly Neil sprang up, declaring his intention of acquainting the girl with the new development.

"Of course—do," agreed Rachel eagerly, "and bring her back with you to dinner. She really mustn't be allowed to brood all alone."

Crossing the street he went straight upstairs, but as he neared the half-open door of number sixteen, low, angry voices issuing from it made him draw back and retreat into the adjacent bathroom. Who was with Natasha? He heard the latter saying with cold obstinacy:

"You have no right to question me like this. Surely you know I would tell everything if it had the slightest bearing on my aunt's death."

To his chagrin the unmistakable accents of Emily Braselton answered her—hard, accusing.

"Why should I know anything of the sort? I consider you capable of the basest deception. Don't forget I spent a day in Paris verifying the rumours which had come to my ears. Now I'm giving you your chance to explain. Are you going to speak, or shall I have to bring pressure?"

There was a stifled outburst of: "This is outrageous! What do you mean by rumours? Exactly what charge are you bringing against me?"

"I shall not put the whole of my idea into words," came the guarded retort; "but quite definitely I do accuse you of shielding the person who alone or with help from you was responsible for Caroline Bundy's death."

A cry of horror, followed by an indignant: "How dare you!" which sent a vibration along the listener's nerves.

"I dare anything for the sake of a lifelong friendship. If you had nothing to do with this, prove it—if you can. You think you can pull the wool over my eyes as you did with that stupid coroner, but thank God I am not a man!"

"Please go. I refuse to discuss this any longer."

"Very well, I will go—but you know what it means. You must face the consequences of your own wicked behaviour."

The speaker came out. Neil saw her sweep past, along the narrow passage, iron-faced, implacable, like some enraged Valkyrie on the war-path. When she had reached the lobby below he knocked softly on the bedroom door and without waiting for an answer went in. At sight of Natasha, white and frightened, with eyes narrowed to dark slits, his heart contracted with fear. The headmistress's visit had terrified her, that was plain. But why?

"I caught what that woman was saying to you," he said quickly. "What infernal insolence! She can't make trouble for you, can she?"

"I don't know," she whispered, with stiff lips. "If she can, she will— depend on it. I am powerless to stop her."

"But that is sheer nonsense!" he cried, catching her by the arms and trying to calm her. "Come, what can she do? She had no business bully- ing you, of course, but if a simple explanation would put things right, why not make it and clear yourself of all blame?"

"You don't understand. I can't."

"And whose fault is it if I don't understand? My dear child, this has gone far enough, but we'll talk of that later. Rachel wants you to come over at once and hear something quite astounding. You must share the new sensation."

"I can't go there. Don't ask me. Not that I blame Mr. Gisborne for feeling as he does about me, but—well, it's impossible for me to face him now. What is this news?"

"Simply that your aunt has left the Tilburys practically the whole of her fortune, on condition that they search for the Holy Grail. There— how's that for a stunner?"

From the blankness with which she stared at him she did not seem to have taken in his meaning. Then all at once a feverish excitement seized her. Crimson flooded her face. She gripped his arm with fingers of steel.

"What! Caroline left her money to those slimy creatures? Then it's they who murdered her, of course! One, both of them—it doesn't matter which, but, anyhow, they managed it between them. Oh, my God! to think we could have been such fools as not to guess it!"

## CHAPTER TWENTY-TWO

NEIL was still puzzled and annoyed over this interview when, early next morning, he repaired to Stoke Paulton. Natasha, in her refusal to face facts, was either wilfully obstinate, or else over-anxious to find scape-goats—an unspoken conclusion which must have communicated itself to her, for she had grown silent and aloof. However, here he was, bent on a personal investigation. If nothing came of it, it would not be his fault.

Tilbury himself opened the door, and though his eyes lit eagerly at sight of Neil, he seemed unduly careworn for one just come into an unexpected fortune. Overcome by his new responsibilities, perhaps, or apprehensive of what public opinion would say, but if a third element lurked behind his ill-concealed nervousness, it was impossible to tell.

"I was hoping you'd come, sir," he babbled hospitably.

"Poor Miss Bundy wouldn't want you to interrupt your work, and I needn't tell you 'er wish is law. Con and me was saying only this morning as 'ow you was to look on this 'ouse as your own. Your old room's ready for you, if and when you choose to use it."

Unable to keep his eyes from the band of crape on the other's arm and the strange trembling of his hands, Neil thanked him, adding that for the present he would stick to the existing arrangement. A moment later, shut in the study, he stationed himself by the window till he saw Crabbe go past, then signalled and whispered a few cautious words. In half an hour's time he was back in his car, waiting in the lane behind the estate. Here he was joined by the butler, to whom, as they drove off, he broached the subject of Tilbury's recent illness.

"I'd rather not be seen talking to you," he explained. "For obvious reasons, but I want you to give me a detailed account of what happened here last Friday evening."

"Yes, sir, I guessed it was that. The lawyer, Mr. Powyss, has already taken me over the same ground, and so has Miss Braselton. I'll tell you just what I told them—and God knows," he added with sudden vindictiveness, "I wish I could make it different!"

This did not sound hopeful, and the story which followed was even less so. The bailiff, it seemed, had complained of cramps off and on all day, though he made light of his indisposition and did not give in till late in the afternoon—in fact, directly after the telephone call from Miss Bundy.

"And, by the way, sir, did you notice how quick he was to get to that telephone? It's my place to answer it, not his, but he'd taken off the receiver before you could say wink. When I saw him in the hall I left him to it, but it crossed my mind he'd been waiting and listening, ready to jump to the line, if you understand me."

"Yes, I, too, thought he might have been expecting Miss Bundy to ring up, but I don't see that we can make anything of that. Go on. You say he then went up to bed?"

"At about a quarter to six, sir, and before seven Mrs. Tilbury came down to the kitchen to fill a hot-water bottle for him. At seven-thirty I took him up some Benger's Food, but as soon as he'd eaten it he was sick. I saw that myself. He seemed very bad."

"Did you send at once for the doctor?"

"No, sir. He said he must have eaten something that disagreed with him, but as he'd brought it all up he thought he'd soon feel all right. Then he had another bad turn, and about eight o'clock Mrs. Tilbury called the cook and me up to have another look at him. This time I may say I was quite shocked. He'd gone a nasty, green colour, was sweating and groaning, and his legs was drawn up right to his stomach."

"Not shamming, you think?"

"I don't see how he could have been, sir. Not but what he isn't as artful as the next, but he had all the signs, as you may say. Cook gave him some bi-carbonate and while she was mixing it his wife ran down to telephone to Dr. Graves. I heard her trying to get through, but the line was engaged pretty steadily, and finally she had to give it up. Then we went back to the kitchen, but even from there we could hear the groans. I remember saying to Mrs. Hickson—that's the cook—'Depend on it, that chap's got appendicitis bad. It would be our luck, with the mistress gone, and all.'"

"When did you next see him?"

"Not till about ten, sir, and by that time he was much worse—nearly unconscious, eyes rolled back, and shivering from head to foot in sort of spasms. I don't mind telling you it wouldn't have surprised me if he'd been gone by morning, and I believe the doctor thought the same, though he didn't say much. You know what doctors are. He got there while we was in the room, took a good look at him and gave him some sort of injection—morphia, I think, to relieve the pain. It eased off a bit, but not much. In fact, none of us got to bed till two o'clock, and even then, as my room is over theirs, I was kept awake for an hour or two by the moaning and so on."

"You don't think it possible, then, for either Tilbury or his wife to have been absent from the house without your knowing?"

"How could they have done, sir? I'm sure I've gone over it all with Mrs. Hickson a hundred times. Bristol's twenty miles away, but if it was at the bottom of the lane it would be the same. There wasn't a quarter of an hour that we couldn't hear him being sick or something, and Mrs. Tilbury was in and out the kitchen the entire time."

"You admit you did consider the possibility, though, even before you knew about Miss Bundy's will?"

"I did, sir, and that's a fact. It all comes of having a down on the man—no real reason, either, for till yesterday I couldn't see how he could benefit by having the mistress out of the way. According to my arguments, he'd have lost a good thing."

"One point more. Was the Ford car garaged as usual?"

"That I can swear to, for I helped put it up. Tilbury drove in to the village before lunch, and when he came back he was already feeling so queer he asked me to lend him a hand. I locked the garage door myself, and hung the key up in the back lobby, where it always stays. In the morning I wanted to get at a drop of petrol, and there was the Ford as I'd left it, clean, not a splash on it."

"Could it have been taken out secretly during the late afternoon or evening?"

"Hardly, sir, without our noticing. The kitchen window faces the garage, and one of the other of us was in the kitchen practically every minute of the time. Now there's only cook and me left we don't even use our dining-room for meals. We have them in the kitchen to save trouble."

Neil pondered the information despondently. At last he asked if Crabbe knew of any reason for his mistress's being in Bristol of her own volition.

"No, sir. Bristol's a place I've never known her go near, except maybe for a drive in that direction, all the years I've been here." He paused, and a curious expression came over his self-contained features. "In spite of all I've told you, I don't mind owning the thought of those two keeps nagging at me. Look at them—three months ago just the sweepings of the road, as you might say, and now the owners of all this!" He waved a bony hand towards Stoke Paulton. "I can't help wondering if they could have planned the murder and got an outside party to carry it out—though that would mean they knew about the will, wouldn't it?"

"You think they could not have known?"

"It seems she never said a word on the subject—and I'm positive none of us mentioned it. Why, Pritchard never spoke to them if she could help it, and Mrs. Hickson the same; and they were off the premises the whole afternoon when the will was drawn up. Yes, it's one too many for me, sir. Sometimes I've had a notion that Tilbury can read people's minds, or what's worse, that he puts ideas into their minds. If it didn't sound foolish, I'd say the mistress was bewitched."

Bewitched! It was Neil's own instinctive belief, crudely put.

"Anyhow," went on the butler with a grim set to his mouth, "I'm seeing the last of him and his to-morrow morning. I wouldn't stay under that roof another day, not if they was to double my screw. Let them get on with it, I say. They'll not be waited on by me." Hurrying to the inn to talk matters over, Neil received a distinct shock. Natasha declined to see him. Why? Had he unwittingly placed himself in the same category with Gisborne and forfeited the small claim he had on her confidence? This was evidently the case—unless. . . . But he shut his mind to the appalling alternative. That, at all events, was an idea he steadfastly refused to entertain.

Gisborne, following his intention, had gone to London to interview the dead woman's solicitor. Late in the day he returned, in a perplexed frame of mind. Neil met his train, and on the way home learned all he had to say.

"Oh, yes, we thrashed the whole thing out. I think Powyss was relieved to get it off his chest. I've seldom seen a man more outraged than he is—for, as I guessed, there's not a chance of upsetting that absurd will."

"No way of proving anything crooked?"

"There *is* nothing crooked. Legally, Carrie was as sane as you or I—sane, but deluded, as Powyss expressed it. Don't imagine he didn't exhaust every argument against such a disposal of her property. He says she finally got quite annoyed with him and threatened to call in another man. She wouldn't even consent to deliberate a little longer, as he begged her to do. No, her mind was made up. She was obsessed with the idea that she might die at any moment and that if she didn't make necessary provisions her plan would never be carried out. In the end he was obliged to draw up the document she dictated and get it witnessed."

"But he had misgivings?"

"Naturally. He felt certain these people were influencing her, even though she was unaware of it. When he read about the murder, it rushed on him at once that she had in some way been victimised and got rid of. He was in Essex, laid up with rheumatism at the time, but as soon as possible he hurried down here, as much for the purpose of looking into the case as of informing the Tilbury pair of their inheritance. He declares they showed every sign of amazement, but he wasn't taken in by that, of course. He got the servants aside one by one and questioned them, also paid a visit to Graves, but while he's still not satisfied, he's driven to conclude there's nothing he can do."

"Has he no theory about the murder?"

"He didn't have—but now, it seems, that Braselton woman has been to him with some cock-and-bull story. He was very close about it, wouldn't give anything away, but all the same—" Here the speaker looked embarrassed and fumbled with his tobacco-pouch. "I would feel easier in my mind if Natasha would come out with whatever she's keeping back. For there's something she's hiding. Every action of hers proves it. Have you seen her to-day, by the way?"

Neil, with the blood mounting to his face, admitted he had not.

"Humph! I don't half like it. I've had the feeling for days of walking on the brink of a volcano."

It was all a stupid mistake—a chimaera which at the first ray of truth would vanish into thin air. Neil kept telling himself this stubbornly, repeating over and over that by no chance could anything serious happen.

However, something did happen. On reaching the vicarage they learned that during the afternoon an inspector from Scotland Yard had called to see Natasha and been with her for an hour or more. The news had spread like wildfire. Rachel, who had been summoned to the outskirts of the village to visit an ill parishioner, returned to find a crowd of curious loiterers assembled round the inn. On ascertaining the cause of the excitement, she waited till the quiet, plain-clothes officer emerged, then sent up an urgent appeal to be admitted. All to no purpose. The girl, shut in her room, would see no one. Neil fared likewise, and Gisborne himself, sternly resolved to storm the citadel, had no better luck. When he came back to the vicarage he attacked his sister almost violently.

"See here, Rachel! I've known all along there was something between you and Natasha. No good denying it. Now, once and for all, are you going to be as great a fool as she is and hold your tongue when a simple explanation might clear things up?"

"But it wouldn't, Giles!" Her eyes were full of misery, she clasped and unclasped her hands with a distraught tensity. "Oh, can't you understand how I'm placed? If I say anything at all, it may only have the result of—of making it worse!"

The admission, wrung from her, told her hearers what they most dreaded—that she, perhaps with greater reason than themselves, was desperately afraid. . . .

It was not known how or when Natasha left the George. When Neil tried once more, later in the evening, to see her, she was not in her room. Gone for a walk, maybe, the manageress suggested with a rude stare and shrug. He hung about till midnight, but still the girl had not returned.

That same evening, on the point of boarding the Channel boat *en route* for Dunkirk, she was recognised, detained, and taken in charge.

## CHAPTER TWENTY-THREE

BRIEFLY, the misguided girl had committed the one folly calculated to bring the law charging down on her like an angry bull. Hours before her friends knew of her attempted flight she had been consigned to the Bristol jail to await examination before a magistrate. Throughout England millions of readers shook their heads over their morning papers, and said: "What did I tell you? So it was the niece, after all." Many added, with a shudder: "What a crime for a woman to perpetrate! But then, of course, she's half-Russian. . . ."

Possibly because she could not bring herself to ask favours of those who doubted her, she made no effort to communicate with either the Gisbornes or Neil. They, utterly stunned, felt an additional bewilderment over her continued silence, which they were forced to attribute to a different cause; yet nevertheless, they rallied their wits to meet the situation. In order to find out on what grounds the charge rested, Neil declared his intention of obtaining an immediate interview. Gisborne, without venturing any opinion, promised to arrange matters for him, but before anything could be accomplished a second thunderbolt fell. The evening press blazoned the following headlines:

### "WOMAN SEEN ON BRISTOL ROAD—BELIEVED TO BE NATASHA ANDREYEV AND VICTIM."

Impossible! Here, at least, was some ghastly error—and yet all the blood drained away from Neil's heart as he read the statement volunteered to the police by the proprietor of a filling-station a few miles on the London side of Bristol.

The man, Herbert Rowntree by name, gave an account of an eight-cylinder Geisler car which had stopped for petrol at some time between eight-thirty and eight forty-five on the evening of 20th March. The driver was a young woman wearing a light tweed coat and a small hat of the same shade, and carrying a red handbag. She had seemed much annoyed at having to wait while change for a pound-note was fetched from a neighbouring public-house. On the back seat of the car was a second woman, so enveloped in a rug and muffler—the latter wrapped round her head—that it was difficult to tell much of her appearance. She might have been asleep, but the proprietor was struck by something stiff and peculiar in her attitude. Shown a photograph of Miss Bundy's niece, he declared positively that she and the chauffeuse were the same.

Neil dropped the paper, and with a sensation of being stifled strode to fling wide the front door. As he stood in the cool air he heard a choking exclamation from Gisborne, and Rachel's voice crying imploringly: "Don't—don't say anything. Why should we believe this? You both know how many cases of mistaken identity there are."

"Mistaken or not," muttered the vicar, "it's her own refusal to speak that makes this statement so horribly damning."

After an agonised pause Neil turned. "These women were seen at eight-thirty, or thereabouts. Natasha was shopping in Regent Street at six."

"That's not quite good enough. It would be distinctly possible to reach that point in two hours and a half. She must prove what she did after six o'clock, or else the fat is in the fire and no mistake. Let's pray this new development will frighten her into telling the truth." He seemed about to add, *"if she can,"* but checked himself and closed his lips firmly.

The interview was arranged for eleven next morning. The vicar accompanied Neil as far as the prison, but did not go in.

"I shall only antagonise her, I'm afraid. Alone you'll have a far better chance of getting at the facts, but try to make her understand we are anxious to help her in every possible way."

After a short wait, Neil was conducted along cold passages to a bare room with a single barred window. Presently Natasha was brought in by the opposite door, and stood for a moment looking at him with cool, blank eyes. He guessed from her pallor that she had slept little, but for all that she was steady and composed, her shoulders erect, and her tawny-gold hair brushed with unusual care. He made an instinctive movement in her direction, whereupon the warder interposed, and assigning them seats at the two ends of a long table placed himself between.

For a second or two Neil's voice stuck in his throat. When he spoke it was to blurt out the question uppermost in his mind.

"*Natasha!* why did you try to get away?"

To his surprise she replied with singular evenness: "I lost my head, that's all. I was stupid enough to suppose I could leave England if I went at once. I wanted to do it before it was too late."

"Too late—!" He drew in his breath sharply.

"Then you were afraid?"

"Yes. You see, the Scotland Yard man told me they'd found out about the pearls."

"What made them suspect anything?"

"First they inquired at the bank in Glastonbury to see what money she had taken with her. It seems she had got the pearls out of her strong-box the day before she left. I didn't know that, of course. Then they made the rounds of the London jewellers, and finally discovered the dealer to whom I sold them. He's not a very reputable person, as it happens, and that, too, told against me. Also he identified my photograph."

It was much worse than he had feared.

"Why on earth did you choose a shady sort of jeweller?"

"Because I didn't want the delay and—and the publicity of having to furnish references. I knew I was getting less money in this way, but it was cash down and no questions asked."

Little as he doubted the truth of this matter-of-fact answer, he found it disturbingly unsatisfactory.

"But you told the inspector the necklace was given to you?"

"Naturally, but"—with a hopeless shrug—"if no one but my aunt knew that, what can I prove? It would, in a way, have been better if I'd make a clean breast of it at the inquest—but there again, I simply didn't dare. The coroner would have wanted the full facts, which I couldn't possibly have given. Now, of course, I can hardly expect to be believed, no matter what I say; but all the same I couldn't have acted differently."

"Tasha!" he groaned. "Then you must have known all along you were running your head into a noose. Why—why did you do it?"

She did not answer. After a torturing interval she glanced towards the warder, who, with bored detachment, was examining a splinter in his thumb-nail. When she spoke again it was with even greater quietness.

"I'm not quite such an idiot as you think me. You see, from day to day I've expected the real murderer would be found. It was after that inspector's visit that I was frightened to hold out any longer. The last thing I wanted was to run away, but it was forced on me, that's all. I did my best, picked out the most unlikely crossing to escape notice, though even so I didn't dream the authorities had been warned to watch out for me. It looks now as though they'd been on to me from the first. You may have guessed it, but I didn't."

Her confident reference to the real murderer eased him slightly, but then all at once the filling-station proprietor's statement rushed upon him, upsetting every other conclusion. Did she know of this damaging evidence? Apparently she did, and was inclined to dismiss it with scorn.

"You don't take that seriously, I hope? He can't have seen me, because I simply wasn't there."

"But if he sticks to his identification, can you prove you were elsewhere at the time?"

"I don't know. I'm much afraid that depends on the Lyons' waitress."

Leaving this point for the moment, he explained what the coming examination would mean and how she might still avoid a formal indictment for murder. She listened attentively, but refused to commit herself in any way. Evidently her reasons for silence were as strong as before. Only when he announced his intention of going at once to London to secure legal advice did she display any emotion. Faint red tinged her cheeks, and she made a gesture of shamed protest.

"You? I can't, I won't permit it! This is my affair. Please keep out of it."

"I'm afraid you can't help yourself," he said dryly. "If this does result in an indictment, Gisborne and I"—he had hastily decided it was wiser to couple the vicar's name with his—"mean to see that your defence is placed in capable hands. However, let's not discuss that now. I merely mention it because—well, it's up to you to help us. We can't work blindfold."

A pleading look came into her eyes, now softened by a hint of moisture.

"That's exactly why I'd rather be left alone. I can't guarantee to do what you expect of me."

"You mean you still refuse to give us full information?"

"I'm afraid that's it."

Although they talked for some time longer, the interview came to nothing. When the wardress reappeared to marshal her charge back to the cell, Neil was left just where he had been at the beginning, his mind a confused mass of unanswered questions.

At three in the afternoon he was seated in the private office of Pettifer, Pettifer and Grew, urging his belief upon the junior member of the firm.

He gave a brief resumé of the facts in his possession, at the end laying on the desk a typed sheet containing the sum total of his own investigations into Natasha's movements on the day of the crime. Mr. Archibald Grew, a dry man of forty, wiped his horn-rimmed glasses, and re-adjusted them with a disparaging shake of the head.

"Too bad, too bad!" he murmured. "Some of the facts you've told me are almost as regrettable as the young woman's attempt to fly the country. You are right in supposing that the prosecution will instantly seize on this unknown man as an instigator and accomplice. Coupled with the pearl incident, it looks very grave. . . . H'm—a Persian visa? Worse and worse! Dated—? March 21st! Why, good heavens, that's the day after the murder!"

A chill penetrated Neil as he caught the undercurrent in the solicitor's voice. Until this moment he had not fully grasped how black the case against Natasha could be made to appear.

"Suppose we find this man Addison also secured a visa for Persia?" went on the other dryly. "If so, we shall have our work cut out for us in earnest. The point is, who is Addison? Where has he got to, and why must he be protected? Those are questions we must be able to answer right away. Of course, the case may not come into court, but all the same you were wise to begin preparations. I am only surprised that up till now the police have not. . . . Hold on! What have we here?"

He had broken off as a clerk entered to lay before him a copy of the *Evening Standard*. He picked it up, glanced at the front page, and gave an exclamation of triumph.

"Ah! What did I tell you? Look at this."

In glaring print Neil saw the announcement:

"SEARCH FOR MISSING MAN IN BUNDY CASE" beneath which ran the explanatory line:

"Police Engaged in Hunt for Maurice Addison."

In breathless silence he devoured the three inches of small print.

"Antonio Bianchini, proprietor of a small hotel in Greek Street, Soho, states that Addison, with whom Natasha Andreyev passed the week-end from 20th March to 23rd March, is well known to him, having spent the month of January at his establishment. On the recent occasion he arrived, not in company with the accused, but a full hour later, at one in the morning. He was then in an advanced state of intoxication. The taxi-driver who deposited him at the hotel has been found. He declares he picked up his fare in Charlotte Street, near the Tottenham Court Road. Addison was then on the verge of collapse from drink, but was able to give the necessary directions.

"According to Bianchini, Miss Andreyev was expecting Addison, whom she stated to be her husband, but so far no record of the couple's marriage has come to light. The two occupied a double room on the first floor, and Addison for two days was in a condition grave enough to cause considerable alarm, though no doctor was called. On Monday he was sufficiently recovered to take his departure. He and Miss Andreyev drove away in the Geisler car belonging to the murdered woman, but did not mention their destination.

"No trace of Addison is forthcoming, and it is thought he may have quitted the country. He is described as good-looking, of well-bred appearance and manner. Age, about twenty-seven; height, nearly six feet; hair and eyes brown but not dark, complexion clear, clean-shaven, nose straight, teeth good. When last seen he was dressed in a suit of brownish homespun, a dark-red tie with a yellow pin-stripe, a Harris tweed overcoat, Raglan shape, and a bowler hat. He carried a suit-case marked with his initials: 'M.B.A.'"

The solicitor drew in his breath between his teeth. "Not much to show who he is or where he's stowed himself," he remarked. "But of course the search has only begun. The man must be known to some one besides this hotel-keeper."

"I can suggest a probable source of information," said Neil, rousing himself from the stupor into which he had momentarily fallen. "Six or seven weeks ago I bought a second-hand two-seater in Bath. I have some reason for believing it was formerly Addison's property. Here is the number of the car"—he wrote it down on a leaf torn from his note-book—"and when I get back I may be able to find out something definite. If so, I'll telephone you."

"Let me have the engine number as well. The licence and so on may have been changed. As things stand, we must get all the facts obtainable about this young man, who quite likely represents the crux of the affair. I myself will go to Bristol to-morrow to try my persuasions on the prisoner. If you care to meet me there, we can talk over the result."

That evening Neil dined at the Corner House, where he sought out the girl called Dolly who had promised to apprise him of the missing waitress's whereabouts. She was full of apologies. No, she had not forgotten, but the truth was Gwen Pilcher had gone on a holiday to Margate, leaving no address. Her former landlady knew nothing about her, and though she could doubtless be traced by means of her employment card, that might take time, if she was no longer working.

He spent the night in town, and early next morning sent out for the papers. His first glance brought a violent shock. Headed by the words: "JOINT SUSPECT IN BUNDY CASE" the ensuing paragraphs met his eye:

*"An official in the passport bureau at Dunkirk volunteers information concerning Michael Boris Andreyev, who crossed by the night-boat on 27th March, en route for Persia. The surname struck him at the time because it tallied with that of the young woman mentioned as Miss Caroline Bundy's companion. Furthermore, the man states that Andreyev's appearance strongly suggests the Maurice Addison for whom the police are searching. The initials of the two names, it will be noted, are identical. Natasha Andreyev is said to have a brother called Michael, supposedly resident in Paris."*

Michael! Good God! Why had he not guessed this sooner? Was it Michael she was shielding? The accompanying item left no doubt on the subject.

*"Our Paris Correspondent states that a warrant has recently been issued for the arrest of Michael Boris Andreyev, who some two months ago disappeared from the city having taken funds from the stockbrokers' firm with which he was associated. As it now appears that on 21st March the Persian Consulate in London granted a visa for Andreyev as well as for the young woman under arrest the aggregate of facts is highly significant. It is understood that extradition papers are being prepared for the purpose of recalling Andreyev to England."*

All Neil's ideas underwent a swift readjustment. For a moment he felt an overwhelming relief to know how utterly he had misjudged the entire situation. Natasha had no lover. It was for her own flesh and blood she was sacrificing herself. Poor child! What a harvest she had reaped, through no fault save the desire to help her brother!

But—that brother was a criminal, fleeing from justice! His exultation collapsed, as one by one a succession of stark facts rose to smite him in the face. What were those facts? He forced himself to examine them in the light of pitiless logic, view them as they would appear when set before a jury.

First: Natasha's desperate need of money. Why? In order to save Michael from prison.

Second: The sale of her aunt's pearls—how obtained, no one but herself knew; sold, moreover, under suspicious circumstances.

Third: Her sending the miscreant to safety, refusal to furnish any information regarding him, and her own attempt to follow where he had gone. Plan made before her aunt's death, details executed immediately after.

Fourth: The Geisler car with its two occupants seen near Bristol—one woman identified as herself, the other carefully concealed—inference, dead.

At this point he drew back appalled. The discovery of Michael a blessing? No, on the contrary, it supplied the one missing piece in a ghastly pattern—a convincing motive for the crime.

## CHAPTER TWENTY-FOUR

ON THE journey back Neil reviewed every incident of his acquaintance with Natasha, beginning with the moment when she had rushed in on him with her breathless: "You! Oh, I warned you not to come!" Yes, it was Michael she had expected to see—Michael, then hiding under an assumed name and carefully kept from contact with her aunt. Almost certainly Miss Bundy had never guessed he was in England. Rachel Gisborne, on the contrary, was aware of it. Just what information did she possess? He meant to tackle her and find out.

Then came the letter from Paris which had thrown its recipient into a panic, the letter he, in his blindness, had assumed to be from Michael himself. That, of course, was the mistake which had sent him racing off on a false scent. Next, his growing suspicion of financial worries, later confirmed by the girl's own admission. For three weeks she had tried hard to raise money—but how? Nothing could induce him to accept

Emily Braselton's theory of threats and extortion, but strangers might prove less difficult to convince. . . .

Particularly did he dwell on that afternoon in Bath when Natasha left him to make final arrangements with her brother—for that undoubtedly was what she had done, and on two further matters equally suggestive. One was the girl's collapse on hearing that a body had been found; the other, Michael's drunken condition on his arrival at the hotel. Inevitably did this last point to the sequel of a horrible experience. Would not nine out of ten men drink themselves blind in the effort to wipe out the memory of a murder?

Yes, it was easy to see the logical theory to be evolved from this collection of facts. First, the penniless girl, egged on by her brother's peril of arrest, seeking by every possible means to secure money for his escape; the turn of the wheel by which a valuable string of pearls came into her possession; murder to cover up theft, and plans for speedy leave-taking. There it was, simple and complete, with nothing, so far as he knew, to give appearances the lie.

"And yet it's not true—it can't be true!" he groaned. "I refuse to dwell on it for a moment till I've heard what she has to say. She must have some reasonable explanation, and now Michael's known about she'll be forced to give it in full."

Rachel was sitting in the little drawing-room, her eyes glued to a newspaper, which, as he threw open the door, dropped from her nerveless hand. With an expression as distraught as his own she sprang up, trembling in every limb.

"Rachel, you knew Michael Andreyev was here. Now, how much did Natasha tell you about him?"

Her knees gave under her. She sank on to the sofa, pressing her fingers over her eyes.

"Very little," she whispered, "and even that I'd given my word not to mention. He turned up unexpectedly in London, about three months ago. He'd given up his position—or so she said—on account of nerves and ill-health. I swear to you I never dreamed he'd stolen money. I find it hard to believe she knew it either—or at least not at the beginning. . . ."

"It seems impossible for her not to have known of it."

"I—you may be right. My mind is utterly confused. You see, Michael has always been restless and unstable—extravagant too. That is why Tasha got him down here, where she could keep an eye on him. She was worried, of course, because being an alien he couldn't hope for settled employment, but still, here he was, and she had to make the best of it. I'm afraid all her earnings lately must have gone towards supporting him."

"I guessed as much."

"Because of what happened that day in the tea-shop? I longed to explain, but didn't dare abuse her confidence; but now you can see why I spoke as I did to you. I thought she needed some one sensible and normal to take hold of her and—and keep her from doing anything foolish. I'd begun to be afraid Michael was preying on her, morally as well as financially, that is—oh, it's very difficult to put it into words!" Her voice shook.

"In what way was he preying on her morally? Do you mean he was influencing her actions?"

"I don't quite know." She hesitated. "She's the strong one, of course; he's weak and capricious, but lovable, and with a sort of flighty brilliance that must be very captivating. She looks on him as a child, even though he's five years older than herself. She's inclined to give in to him, and to make allowances for his faults. It would have been a bad thing, I feel, if she had gone away with him as she intended to do. I argued hard against it, but it was no good."

"Why did she want to go with him?"

"I don't believe she did want to—not altogether, that is. She's obsessed with the idea that without her to look after him he'll come to grief. Her sense of responsibility towards him is—well, fanatical. Sophie, when she was dying, entrusted Michael to her care—begged her keep him out of trouble. It's something she can't forget."

"You met him, of course?"

"I? Never. She seemed to think he was in such a neurasthenic condition he was better left alone. I didn't even realise he wasn't using his own name. What I've just learned is a terrible revelation."

All this was far from answering Neil's doubts. He nerved himself to put one more question.

"What precisely did you mean by saying you were afraid to tell us anything for fear of making matters worse?"

She started guiltily. "I—oh, nothing definite. I suppose it was just an intangible dread that—that—"

He finished it for her. "In plain language, you considered it possible that Michael committed this murder. You thought that Natasha knew about it and that if such were the case it was safer for her sake to say nothing. Isn't that what you had in mind?"

She made no reply. Her head sank as she murmured despairingly: "Oh! to think one should have such thoughts, now of all times, when the poor child needs all our trust and help!"

He probed no further, lest he should entrap her into some admission best left unspoken.

He was pacing the lounge of the Bristol hotel agreed on as a rendezvous a full hour before the solicitor arrived.

"You've seen her? What has she told you?" he asked anxiously.

Grew led the way to a quiet corner and dropped into a seat. He drew one hand reflectively over his chin and did not speak till Neil had repeated the query impatiently.

"Eh? Oh, rather more than she told you," he answered slowly. "That was inevitable, now this business about her brother has come out. It's unsatisfactory, though, most unsatisfactory. . . . An odd experience," he mused in a puzzled tone. "I don't believe I've ever dealt with a client who was so much more concerned over another person's fate than her own. First of all, she flatly declines any assistance towards bringing Andreyev back."

"Declines! But she must be made to! Good God, it's sheer insanity!"

"Insanity or not, she won't, and that's that. Declares she has no notion where he is—there, I expect, she's speaking literal truth, but that even if she could produce him it would do her no good. Oh, she admits helping him to escape—says she put him up to it and gave him money. According to her he was quite ignorant of the murder till she rang him up from the call-box last Tuesday night."

"Did she furnish this information readily?"

"Not quite. The driver of the Daimler car which carried Andreyev to London has now come forward with a statement. That circumstance forced her hand."

"But, surely, if the worst happens, they won't try her alone? Won't they wait till the brother is caught?"

"Most unlikely. These extradition cases have a way of dragging on for ever, and as Andreyev had more than a week's start before anything was known about him, he stands a fair chance of getting off altogether. No, it looks very much as though she'll have to face the music by herself, which, to be perfectly candid, is what she wants. She said to me quite definitely, 'I can stand this. He can't. I don't intend to have him ruined for something he didn't do.'"

"Meaning—?"

"That if her brother is brought back, whatever else happens to him he'll be clapped into a French jail for theft. He is guilty of that offence, of course, but she is determined he shan't pay the penalty. Yes, it's only too apparent she's thought it all out beforehand, foreseen the chance of being arrested, and prepared to meet it. Cool, collected—" He shrugged, giving it up. "Even when I told her she was doing her utmost to prejudice her case, she said yes, that might be so, but that it couldn't be helped. What is one to do with a woman like that?"

After a pause he continued, "Briefly, the situation is this. She still declares positively she never went near Bristol, and that the filling-station man has simply confused her with some one else. Be that as it may, we must do our best to build up an alibi for her. She's given me some additional material to work on. I shall go ahead and test it. Perhaps it may prove sufficient."

Although his voice sounded dubious, Neil felt suddenly relieved.

"Thank God for that!" he exclaimed, gulping down the whisky before him. "But why on earth didn't she come out with it sooner?"

"For fear of implicating her brother. Just as long as there was the slightest hope of keeping him in the background, she held her tongue, even though by doing so she was risking her reputation in other respects."

Yes, she had allowed it to be supposed she had spent the week-end with an unknown lover rather than give Michael away.

"You yourself are satisfied that was her only motive?" demanded Neil, catching an odd expression on his companion's face.

"Well," replied Grew cautiously. "I can only repeat it's a degree of quixotism I'm not very familiar with. In moments of danger most people are out for themselves and devil take the hindmost. However, let's get on. It appears there are three Russians we've got to hunt up—the only persons in the whole of England who knew Andreyev by his own name. That, of course, is her excuse for not mentioning them before. The first"— he consulted his note-book—"is a man called Wassilieff—runs a motor business in Great Portland Street, and lives at 6 Midlothian Mansions, Wimbledon."

"Then that's the friend she called on early in the evening."

"And failed to see. He was in Amsterdam, not due back for a week. The porter, a new man, had never seen her before, and actually he didn't see her on this occasion, for the lights had gone out. Unfortunately, she didn't leave a card, or say who she was—so all things considered, she can't expect much from him as a witness. It was after this she had her dinner at the Corner House—roughly from eight to eight forty-five, or it may have been from eight-fifteen to nine. If we succeed in finding a waitress who can recall her, it will smooth out a lot of difficulties. If not—" He stopped with ominous abruptness.

"But you mentioned three Russians. Who are the other two?"

"Yes, of course. You see, after going to Paddington Station and finding her brother was not on the train she'd expected him by, also that there was no other train except the two-forty, she concluded Andreyev was motoring up. It was the sort of thing he would do in the excitement of getting her telegram—"

"So she sent him a telegram!"

"Certainly. Hadn't I mentioned that? Soon after she left her aunt she wired him to join her at once."

"But doesn't that bear out her story of receiving the pearls as a gift?"

"Hardly. As there was no reference to the necklace in the message, a different interpretation may be put on it. However, to return. She then decided to call in at a little restaurant in Rupert Street, Soho, known to them both, and run by some people named Kosloff, former servants of her family in what was then St. Petersburg. She rather expected Michael would arrive at any moment, in which case he would come to this place to look for her. She stayed talking with the Kosloffs from eleven till twelve o'clock, up in their private rooms, but Michael didn't turn up. Finally, she began to think he hadn't received her wire."

"She was with this couple for an hour before midnight?" cried Neil excitedly. "Well, then, there's proof for you. What more do we want?"

Grew shook his head. "It's not quite as good as you suppose. There are two reasons why the Kosloffs' word may be discredited. First, they are devoted partisans, ready to swear anything to help their old master's daughter. These expatriates, you know, stick very close together. Second, Miss Andreyev admits going to them after the murder was discovered to beg them to say nothing unless it became absolutely urgent. That, at least, is her statement, but it may be held she had a totally different motive for her visit. In short, she may have wanted them to pretend she was with them on Friday when in reality she didn't go there at all. You see?"

"But there must have been other people at the restaurant?"

"No, not as late as that. She saw no one but the Kosloffs themselves, but on the second occasion she was seen by a waiter. Makes it a bit difficult."

The clouds regathered. Much as Neil shrank from the supposition that Natasha had primed her allies to manufacture false evidence, he began to see how the thing would look to prejudiced eyes. She had gone to London on the same day as himself, but had not told him why. . . .

"I'm afraid, Mr. Starkey," continued Grew, lowering his voice, "there is worse in store for you. What I am now going to disclose accounts very plausibly for the prisoner's reluctance to speak, but unfortunately it casts black doubt on all her present assertions. There's no good mincing matters. You may as well know how we stand. You see, this is what happened. . . ."

For some minutes he talked in an earnest strain. Neil, listening, felt as though icy fingers were closing round his throat, choking him by inches.

During the coming week there were two adjournments. At the second of these a true bill was found, and Natasha was committed for trial at the approaching sessions, on the charge of Wilful Murder.

## CHAPTER TWENTY-FIVE

"THE charge is one of murder, in a way that is peculiarly dangerous and peculiarly cruel. To a very large extent the material available is circumstantial evidence. Human testimony is liable to all the defects of human nature, forgetfulness, want of observation, partiality, leading persons unwittingly very often to present a version that is inaccurate. These infirmities, rather than wilful falsities, more frequently colour and weaken the value of human testimony. Real circumstantial evidence is evidence of fact. If these facts point unmistakably in one direction then they are not less reliable but more reliable than human testimony.— MR. JUSTICE ROCHE."

SIR Henry Challenge paused and let his deceptively torpid eyes run slowly over the crowded room. His coarse wig rested slightly askew, showing the pendulous lobes of his ears; his loose, dried skin was like the over-lapping armour-plates of some prehistoric saurian. In marked contrast to his desiccated appearance, his voice, now stilled, was full and reson-ant. For half an hour it had held his audience charmed, even those who were most antagonistic. It continued after a brief stocktaking, with even greater assurance and the power which comes from direct simplicity.

"Gentlemen of the jury, I ask you to dismiss from your minds anything you may have heard or thought on the subject of this case. I ask you to be influenced solely by the facts about to be placed before you. Do not forget that the annals of crime hold many instances of women who, though endowed with beauty and attraction, have none the less shown themselves capable of greed, callousness and insensate cruelty. It is for you to decide, having considered the evidence, whether Natasha Andreyev's name can be added to the list.

"I ask you to weigh the fact that in over five weeks' time the united efforts of the Somerset police and Scotland Yard have failed to discover any other person to whom suspicion may attach. The blameless life of the victim so foully butchered can show among countless acts of public and private benefaction not one calculated to rouse hatred or enmity. The very manner in which Caroline Bundy befriended her niece, removing her from hardship to ease and security speaks for itself.

"Picture the young girl, hitherto clinging to the ragged fringe of society, transplanted to dignified surroundings, amply remunerated for light labours, and treated as the daughter of the house. Would you not expect the recipient of such favours to respond by affection, by warm-hearted gratitude? I shall prove to you that on many occasions Natasha Andreyev showed herself unsettled, resentful, arrogant. Frequently she expressed a desire to get away—perhaps, shall we say, craving the excitement, the meretricious pleasures of the French capital left behind?"

The speaker halted a moment to let this sink in. He resumed in tones coldly judicial:

"You cannot have failed to be struck by the gross dis-similarity of the two statements issued by the accused at separate times. Can you honestly believe that the woman who evaded truth, suppressed evidence and contradicted herself again and again has no guilt to hide? Accepting the latter version as the one now authorised, let us look into it carefully.

"On Friday, 20th March, having driven the deceased from Somerset to London, the prisoner parted from her at St. James's Square. She declared that her aunt refused to be accompanied the following morning to her train. Do you or do you not consider this likely? An elderly woman, just recovered from an alarming attack, desirous of setting off on a journey alone when her own car and the niece in her employ are close by to render assistance? You may perhaps incline to the belief that Miss Bundy gave instructions to be picked up later in the afternoon, conducted to her friend's flat, and called for next day. If so, your assumption will be a reasonable one.

"You will note that the deceased carried two bags—one of black leather, said to contain money, traveller's cheques, and personal belongings; the other, brown alligator skin, remains a mystery to us. It was locked, and the key worn on a chain round the owner's neck. Both bags have disappeared, but it is with the second one we have now to deal. That bag, gentlemen, was missed directly after the separation in St. James's Square. That it was valuable is clearly shown by the fact that Miss Bundy turned back at once, followed her niece by taxi to two places where she hoped to overtake her, mentioning her loss to various witnesses and betraying marked agitation. At the Times Book Club she appeared for the second time, having dispatched a telegram to Glastonbury requesting that the car be searched on its return, also having put through a trunk call to her home. There is no doubt whatever that the alligator bag contained something very precious to its owner.

"You may say that these actions confirm the prisoner's statement of a final parting. Is it not conceivable, on the other hand, that Miss Bundy had a lurking fear that her niece was not to be trusted? That she did succeed in catching the young woman only to find her bag rifled and a pearl necklace gone? That just accusations and threats of exposure led to the assault which cost her her life?"

A ripple passed over the closely packed court-room. It was quickly stilled, and the steady voice pursued its inexorable course.

"Consider what followed. Six hours elapse, during which we know nothing of either victim or accused. The latter may produce witnesses who will affirm her continued presence in London. If so, it is for you to say whether such testimony is reliable. Meanwhile, we have to deal with the statement of an eye-witness on the subject of a Geisler car with two women occupants, seen near this city between eight-thirty and eight forty-five. The younger of these two women strongly suggests Natasha Andreyev. The other, inside, leaning in the corner in a stiff and unnatural attitude, had her head concealed in a scarf of muffler. There is much to indicate that this hidden figure was the murdered corpse of Caroline Bundy."

A shudder greeted this dramatic assertion. Neil Starkey felt the scene melt into black-meshed haze, in which nothing stood out save the dominating profile of the prosecuting counsel. He sensed, without seeing them, the commonplace jurors, awedly attentive, the judge in his heavy robes, all the dim rows of faces morbidly alert, stretching to the doors where officials watched to keep order. Somewhere facing him Natasha herself was seated, but he dared not let his eyes stray in her direction.

The voice began again, with a new note of sternness.

"I have purposely omitted till now the evidence relating to the accused's brother, Michael Boris Andreyev. That evidence, you will agree with me, is of a distinctly unsavoury character. I will mention first of all that on three occasions he applied to the deceased for financial help, that in one instance Miss Bundy responded generously, but that after acquainting herself with her nephew's unstable habits she declined further assistance. Soon after the third demand, four and a half months ago, Michael Andreyev quitted Paris for London, later removing to Bath. In this country he went under the name of Maurice Addison, and although in constant communication with the accused, kept his aunt in ignorance of his proximity.

"Why? Simply because in Paris he had been guilty of an intrigue with his employer's wife, had inflicted personal violence when discovered, and had defrauded the firm for which he worked of a considerable sum of money. In short, he was in danger of arrest and imprisonment."

Renewed sensation. The jurors leaned forward, the tension throughout the court grew still more acute.

"Impossible to gloss over these appalling circumstances. Andreyev's record is that of a thief, a sponger on women, a gambler and a drunkard—and yet the accused supported and upheld him in his evasion of justice, schemed to accompany him to a distant country where he might lose his identity, and when the murder became known provided him with the necessary funds to precede her to safety!"

Neil, while now aware of Michael's history, could not repress a momentary recoil at this bald summing-up. How, he asked himself with an inward groan, could Natasha have supposed it possible to preserve a secret so easily laid bare? He could not understand such apparent blindness on the part of an intelligent woman, and indeed it darted through his brain that even now her reasons for concealment were not wholly disclosed. No doubt she had meant to thrust Michael out of danger before the storm broke, but was this all? The next words uttered by Sir Henry furnished a sinister solution to the problem.

"It does not enter into my province to speculate on the part Michael Andreyev may have played in this drama of brutal crime. The accused refuses to reveal his present hiding-place, or to shed any light on his movements prior to his arrival at the obscure hotel where, in her company, he spent the two nights following the murder. However, the fact that he left his lodgings in Bath at about 7.45 p.m., was partly intoxicated at the time, and was seen no more till he reached his final destination in a state of sodden inebriety may strike you as significant. You may even form the opinion that by just rights he should be standing in the dock beside the woman undergoing trial. . . .

"If you are satisfied that in sending her brother away while she herself remained behind the prisoner was serving her best interests, you will have gone a long way towards being convinced of her guilt. If you consider that a man not known to be in England could reasonably expect to get away without causing excitement, but that a woman with an established place and a definite relationship to the victim would be unable to make a similar move without causing adverse comment, you will doubtless form a correct estimate of Natasha Andreyev's mental processes. She would show wisdom in staying where she was till a later date, knowing that there was an excellent chance of eluding discovery, whereas if it became known that she was harbouring one already a criminal any statement she made was likely to be discredited. Remember that she did not at first know where her aunt's pearl necklace had been kept, or even that any living person was aware of its existence. In regard to this matter she committed her initial mistake. The second and even more serious one was her self-condemnatory attempt to flee the country. . . ." The room had grown insufferably close and hot. The mingled hues of women's headgear swam against the sickly drab walls; a shaft of sunshine streamed through a window full upon the judge's heavy wig. Neil found his attention wandering, his strained eyes taking note of first one irrelevant detail, then another—a purple birthmark on a juror's chin, the fat, goggle-eyed face of a reporter industriously bent over his pencil, a ghoulish old woman who punctuated every point in the discourse with a sniff. Suddenly he was recalled to acute awareness by the following sentences, uttered with arresting clarity:

"Doubtless you will be told that a crime of this kind is incompatible with a woman's physical strength and nature. Your attention will be called to the savage brutality of the attack, to the needless number of blows literally rained upon the victim's skull, and to the fact that three of these blows caused deep fractures. You will be asked if it is reasonable or likely for this violent, insensate assault to have been accomplished by one of the so-called gentler sex. Let me remind you, first, that the prisoner is a young woman of superior muscular force, good at tennis and golf, and accustomed to handling heavy cars; second, that in the absence of fire-arms or other lethal weapons, the present method of death-dealing is precisely what one would and does expect from a female terrified at the thought of exposure and driven to an extremity of passion. The very way in which the murderer struck and struck again indicates that touch of hysteria so often met with in the emotional crises of women."

Here Challenge leant forward. His hooded eyes drew together every other eye in the dense assemblage as, lowering his voice to a vibrant whisper he delivered his culminating stroke:

"Has any one of you ever seen a woman kill a rat? I have. In a village in Dalmatia I saw a peasant woman slay a rat with an iron bar. She felled it instantly, but before her insane panic had spent itself she had battered the animal to a pulp. . . . In such manner was Caroline Bundy slain. I ask you to bear in mind what you yourselves know of feminine attributes before deciding whether the action in this case was that of a man or a woman."

The entire room shuddered. Neil himself was so paralysed with horror over the picture presented to him that he registered nothing more till the concluding words jarred him out of his stupor.

"If, having heard the evidence, you consider the summarised facts as satisfactorily established, it will be my duty to ask you for a verdict that Natasha Andreyev is guilty of the wilful murder of Caroline Bundy."

## CHAPTER TWENTY-SIX

MASS-consciousness has its responses set on a hair-trigger. In the present instance there was small doubt that the prosecuting counsel had released a full charge of hostility against the girl who, from first to last, had sat motionless, hands in her lap, quietly facing her accuser. Here and there, perhaps, a sympathetic eye sought hers, but an onlooker would have had to search painstakingly to find it.

One after another Natasha's tools had failed her. Serge Wassilieff, eager to help, promised meagre support. He either had not known or dared not admit knowledge of Michael Andreyev's misdemeanour, hence the conclusion that Natasha had deliberately deceived him. Worse, it was now established that on the memorable Wednesday after the murder the girl had hurried to him to implore his silence. In view of this fact, any deposition he made was likely to prove injurious to her cause.

The Kosloffs threatened an even greater disappointment. Warmly loyal as they were, their parrot-like repetitions suggested only too strongly a fiction dictated by Natasha herself. If they were lying, they would not stand a rogue's chance when raked by Sir Henry Challenge's pitiless fire.

One witness only remained, and on her the defence centred their hopes. This was the waitress, Gwendolen Pilcher, difficult to ensnare and, now they had got her, a most uncertain quantity. Would she recognise the prisoner? There was simply no means of knowing. After long and doubtful study of Natasha's photograph she had refused to commit herself, and though her indecision might vanish when she was confronted with the living girl, it was just as likely she would say No as Yes. Yet if she let them down, what was left? Only a faintly possible reluctance on the part of the jury to convict on circumstantial grounds; and unhappily one knew of many trials where the death sentence had been delivered on evidence less substantial than that arraigned against the present accused. Motive weighs heavily—and no one doubted that Natasha had a powerful incentive for committing murder.

Pricked by the word "motive," Neil ran his eye along the witness benches to the insignificant couple now staring with strained intentness at the judge. Motive indeed! There sat the two beings with the real, indisputable motive for removing Caroline Bundy—Alfred and Connie Tilbury, inheritors of virtually all the dead woman possessed, schemers in the opinion of many, yet with not one iota of legal proof against them. With cynical bitterness Neil thought of the effort wasted in trying to penetrate the seamless respectability which encased the pair like a suit of mail. At sight of their smug, ingenuous faces he was scorched by uncontrollable hatred.

No, it had come to nothing. All these past weeks he had had them shadowed by a private detective, and what had he learned? Only such facts as might have been guessed by the most unimaginative observer, the worst being the verdict that they were drifters, having moved from one town to another for the space of twelve years. A large number of decent folk had been found who could and did vouch for their honest character. In Chester a chemist with whom they had shared lodgings spoke highly of their affable qualities, their mutual affection, and of Alfred's serious, inquiring turn of mind. On several occasions they were reputed to have been on fairly close terms with elderly women of means, and these periods undoubtedly coincided with unwonted prosperity, but as these women were now dead—in inconspicuous circumstances—there was no way of determining what, if anything, the friendship had gained them.

Meanwhile, the excavation, well on its way, was the talk of the countryside, and scarcely a day passed that some antiquarian did not come to prowl about the ancient crypt and propound theories as to the probable location of the tunnel, which as yet was shrouded in mystery. One could not pick up a Sunday paper which did not contain either views of the work, or some reference to the Glastonbury legend. Gossip over the will had dwindled as interest gathered round the trial of the dead woman's niece, and in the circle of their immunity the Tilburys sat serene—or so one supposed—intent on minding their own concerns.

Yet, eyeing them at this moment, Neil had a fleeting notion that the public, like a vast pack of hounds, had been drawn off pell-mell on a false scent, while directly under their eyes the real quarry merged into the landscape. Was this so? One voice within him clamoured loudly in favour of it, but another, equally strong, argued that his belief rested on prejudice, set going in the first instance by Natasha herself.

He came to with a start to find Inspector Mayo of Scotland Yard detailing his interview with the prisoner, following this detrimental evidence by a description of Miss Bundy's car as seen in the Glastonbury garage. The interior had shown an entire absence of blood-stains, and no fresh scratches or abrasions. Reassuring, but was it conclusive? The woman noticed in the car near Bristol had had her head wrapped up in a scarf.

Crabbe, Mrs. Hickson, and Pritchard, upper housemaid, spoke loyally of Natasha, denied quarrels between her and her aunt, and declared her to be just, efficient and, though sometimes moody, never disagreeable. Crabbe admitted the young lady's frequent excursions at night, though where she had gone he could not say. He knew she had full permission to use the car when she liked, and had never heard her questioned on the subject. Once or twice in his hearing she had spoken of her wish to leave England, but this he attributed to the dull life she led and her unaccustomedness to English ways. He knew of no definite plan in this direction.

All three servants had noticed the prisoner's depression during the weeks preceding the crime. Pritchard averred that from the beginning of the year Miss Andreyev had become "very saving" and had once remarked that from now on she was not likely to want many new clothes. About a fortnight before her aunt's death she had either put away or disposed of a quantity of old-fashioned jewellery which used to lie in a tray on her dressing-table. Pritchard did not know what had become of it, but it was unlike Miss Andreyev to lock up her own belongings. For her part, Pritchard had always found Miss Andreyev kind and considerate. When she, Pritchard, was suffering from an infected knee, the young lady had supplied her with hot fomentations all through the night. If anything went wrong with the dogs, she would go to endless trouble. She had certainly tried hard to persuade her aunt to look after herself—not an easy task, either, for Miss Bundy had been very self-willed of late.

Generally speaking, a point scored, but it was speedily neutralised by what came next.

Mrs. Ivy Grace Woods, of 12 Magellan Road, Bath, stated that early in February the prisoner, calling herself Miss Addison, engaged a room for her brother, said to be ill with a nervous breakdown. When the gentleman arrived, he looked surprisingly fit, though it soon appeared his nerves were not what they should be. He was temperamental and highly strung, either very gloomy or almost hilarious. At the same time he was very likeable and attractive, having, as the witness expressed it, "a way with him." She and her daughter had instantly taken to him, even though his habits were so distressingly erratic. He had no sense of time, stayed up all night and lay in bed by day if it pleased him, and now and then drank far too much. Whether his sister was aware of this or not, she was unable to say.

Miss Addison visited him several times a week, usually in the evening, always coming in a big, dark-green car which she drove herself. On one occasion she turned up long after midnight, rushed up to her brother's room and flung open the door in a distraught manner. Mrs. Woods caught a storm of what sounded to her like reproaches, though as it was in a foreign language she could not be sure what sort of things were being said. Eventually the conversation died to whispers which went on for a couple of hours.

COUNSEL: "What was the date of this occurrence?"

WITNESS: "I can't say exactly, but it was the last week in February— round about the twenty-sixth or seventh, I think."

COUNSEL: "On which side were the reproaches?"

WITNESS: "The young lady's. She was terribly upset—crying and sobbing at first, but at the last I fancied she was laying down the law and her brother giving in in a sulky way."

COUNSEL: "After this did you observe any alteration in either?"

WITNESS: "Yes; Mr. Addison seemed very jumpy but sobered, if you understand my meaning. His sister looked worried to death, but with a set to her mouth as if she'd screwed herself up for something. We all spoke of it."

On March 18th, late in the afternoon, the accused drove up, and her brother went out to speak to her. Both seemed eager and secretive. Mrs. Woods, from the upper window, heard the young lady say at parting, "If I see the least hope of bringing this off, I'll send you a wire."

On the afternoon of the 20th Addison received a telegram which threw him into intense excitement. Informing his landlady that he would be gone for several days, he quitted the house at seven o'clock, carrying a suit-case. Although there had been but a brief interval between the arrived of the message and his departure, he had managed to consume a whole bottle of whisky. This the witness could positively state, because the bottle had been fetched in at noon, and was empty when she went into the bedroom to tidy up.

The week-end passed without news, but on Monday evening the two Addisons drove up together, both looking exhausted, and the brother in a really shocking state—blue under the eyes, every inch of him shaking as with ague. The young lady explained that he had caught a severe chill and must stop in bed. He did so all next day, scarcely touching food and starting at the slightest sound. The witness wondered if she ought not to call a doctor, but in the evening, about nine, her lodger was summoned to the telephone, held an agitated conversation with his sister, and as a result pulled himself together in an astonishing way, as was shown by what immediately followed.

COUNSEL: "One moment, Mrs. Woods. How much of this conversation can you repeat?"

WITNESS: "None, because it wasn't in English. Sometimes he spoke to his sister in English, and sometimes in French or another language. But I can tell you this much—he was scared. There was no mistaking that."

A quarter of an hour after this, Addison, fully dressed and carrying his suit-case, presented himself to the witness and asked for his account. With that and a hurried word about sending back for his things, he was out of the house before the bewildered woman could ask a single question. Gone in a moment, with no explanation—and his trunk and golf clubs still in her back hall.

COUNSEL: "Did you make no inquiries?"

WITNESS: "How could I, when I'd never known the sister's address? Besides, though I was pretty sure something queer was going on, it wasn't till the police called that I guessed what really was wrong."

During the examination which followed, Neil uncomfortably speculated on the hours preceding Michael's arrival at the hotel. Was it true he and his sister had not been in each other's company till one o'clock, and if so, how to prove it? Challenge's shrewd questions showed a determination to suggest connivance between the two Andreyevs—an idea impossible to uproot once it was planted in the jurors' dull brains. That Natasha and Michael had made a plan was self-evident, and from this belief to the other sinister one was but a single step.

His wrath fell upon the craven who at the first peal of thunder had taken himself out of reach. Incredible that any one calling himself a man should leave his sister in the lurch like this, unless—paralysing alternative!—he could not improve matters by coming forward. Neil turned cold at the thought that here indeed might be the explanation. The true facts defied pursuit, and meanwhile, guilty or misjudged, these two were bound together so firmly that no ingenuity could sunder them. Bound together by a steel cable of circumstance—and yet, grotesque fatality, the girl alone had to suffer.

Suddenly he told himself that without Michael this whole business was a tragic farce. Michael must be dragged back. If the verdict went wrong, as it well might do, he himself would obtain an appeal and search diligently for the miscreant. What, was a man to vanish utterly, in an age when papers were scrutinised at every frontier, in spite of every aid furnished by those twin searchlights, the press and the radio? Absurd, unthinkable! . . . There was, of course, that peculiar feature which Grew had spoken about. He did not know whether to believe it or not, but at the moment instinct cried out brutally that whatever the case the brother must be made to shoulder his part of the burden. . . .

Emily Braselton mounted to the stand. Her important presence commanded awe; she was as composed as though addressing her eight hundred girl students at Bellingham. Except that her eyes occasionally flashed, she betrayed no emotion.

In tones which penetrated to the farthermost benches, she told how last autumn Miss Bundy had shown her a letter from the nephew in Paris. The third of its kind, it embodied an urgent appeal for money, and was couched in reproachful phrases because its predecessor had been ignored. The recipient by her own account had answered the first request with a cheque for fifty pounds, but was determined not to accede to further demands. She had heard tales of Michael's extravagance and unreliability. There was bad blood in him, she said, from his father's side.

COUNSEL: "Kindly tell us how you first came to hear of Andreyev's present situation."

WITNESS: "To begin with, I had reason to believe he was in this country. A Frenchwoman of my acquaintance, living now in Bath, informed me she had seen him driving about the neighbourhood with his sister, but thinking she might be mistaken and having no wish to worry Miss Bundy, I kept the matter to myself. However, directly news of the murder reached me in Paris, I set out to make certain inquiries into the antecedents of both Michael and Natasha Andreyev. I found that the girl, previous to her appearance in England, had been dismissed from two positions, and that her brother had recently left the city under suspicious circumstances. Limited time forbade my obtaining complete details, but I heard enough to convince me Michael was in hiding from the police."

COUNSEL: "Is it true you advised Miss Bundy against employing the prisoner?"

WITNESS: "I did, most strongly. I foresaw that the arrangement would be entirely unsuitable—and I was not wrong."

Questioned as to the relations between aunt and niece, Miss Braselton affirmed continual friction kept under cover from the outside world. The Russian girl was secretive, jealous and predatory. Perhaps because she saw certain cherished hopes of inheritance daily dwindling, she had become increasingly restless and resentful of authority. When a new bailiff was installed she displayed a sullen temper, although she herself was singularly unfitted to carry on the duties she had temporarily assumed.

Here the judge interposed. The witness must confine herself to first-hand knowledge, not offer opinions on hearsay. Miss Braselton retorted with dignity that she had actually heard the prisoner inveigh against the bailiff, hinting that her aunt had some ulterior motive for employing any one so incompetent. Furthermore, she stated that her own reason for urging Miss Bundy to accompany her to Rome had been to get her away from the niece who was making her miserable.

Again Mr. Justice Warlock vehemently protested. The witness must on no account put ideas into the jury's minds unless she could produce proof of their correctness. With quiet defiance Miss Braselton proceeded to quote chapter and verse. Miss Bundy had said to her such things as, "Don't tell Natasha I am alarmed about my health." And, "I don't wish Natasha to know I am mentioning her in my will. It is never good for people to get notions of that kind." Also, in the girl's presence, Miss Bundy had been ill at ease, apprehensive. Once when the accused entered the room the older woman broke into a profuse perspiration, trembled violently and showed every sign of fright and dismay.

COUNSEL: "Did Miss Bundy inform you of her intention to present the prisoner with a string of pearls?"

WITNESS: "Never—and I am quite positive she did not dream of doing so. There was no liking or sympathy between the two, only a staunch sense of duty on Miss Bundy's side. My friend was a loyal and conscientious woman."

In spite of the judge's two reproofs, this testimony had a damaging effect. The speaker's reputation and authoritative manner gave an *ex cathedra* stamp to her utterances which carried immense weight. Only Neil was aghast at the vindictiveness which warped appearances into caricatures, falsely distributed emphasis, and deliberately suppressed all mention of the Tilburys' real function. Emily Braselton could hold no brief for the couple, yet so convinced was she of Natasha's guilt, that she would go to any lengths to carry her point.

The court now adjourned. Neil's eyes followed Natasha as, moving like an automaton, she disappeared under escort. The crowd stretched their necks, a buzz of comment broke forth. Over a choppy sea of heads he saw Gisborne signalling to him, and stoically resigned himself to the encounter.

Some one touched his arm. Turning, he found the solicitor, Grew, close beside him with a curious expression in his lashless eyes. Instantly he guessed that something had happened, but of all conceivable eventualities the one about to be disclosed was farthest from his thoughts.

"What is it?" he whispered tensely.

The lawyer took hold of him and drew him into a cleared space.

"Simply this. Michael Andreyev is dead—two weeks ago, in Teheran. The news has just come through from Scotland Yard."

## CHAPTER TWENTY-SEVEN

MICHAEL dead! It was a blow full in the face, and yet Neil's first reaction was one of illogical thankfulness. Who could lament the removal of the troublesome entity for whom Natasha was sacrificing herself? The feeling passed at once, however, as a horrid doubt entered his mind.

"Not—suicide?" he muttered.

"There's only the bare report of his death, but I fancy it's not suicide." The solicitor set his teeth. "Of all hellish calamities, that this should happen—now!"

"It's as bad as that?"

"Could it be worse? Just look at it for a moment. Our alibi's shaky enough in all conscience. It's quite likely the whole thing will tumble down—and the way the case is going every turn brings us up dead against this brother. Don't you see how Challenge is working that fact to his own advantage? As it was before, there was little chance of finding out what the fellow was doing during those six hours. There's none at all now."

This seemed fatally certain. Advertisements had drawn blanks, no railway official or car owner had admitted so much as a glimpse of Michael from the time he quitted his lodgings. To all intents and purposes he had vanished from the sight of man—as Grew said—for six hours. Neil listened in stupefied silence while his companion outlined the situation.

"It was bad enough having him disappear till one in the morning, but while he was alive there remained a faint chance of getting some testimony we could trace and substantiate. At least it would have created a doubt. Now if the prosecution bullies the jury into believing the two spent that interval together—or even part of it—we're powerless to refute the suggestion. . . . Oh, we'll do our best. Cairnes is able enough—only we can't expect him to make bricks without straw."

"The Kosloffs—?"

"Don't bank on them. Even if they pass muster, eleven at night is too late. It's just possible for the journey to Bristol and back to be managed in five hours, barring hold-ups, and now the jury's ready to consider Michael as an accomplice, they may snatch at the idea of his helping to dispose of the body and getting drunk afterwards to wipe out the impression. He may have had a car of his own and bribed the owner to keep quiet."

"They can't prove anything of the sort."

"Nor can we disprove it. Don't forget we've no sure evidence regarding our client after six o'clock, and there's all that ticklish business of the victim's following her niece about to get back her property. No, it's as I warned you in the beginning. Everything hinges on those waitresses, Douglas and Pilcher. If one of them turns up trumps, it will knock a hole clean in the middle of the dangerous period. Nothing else will."

"Neither girl recognises the photograph," said Neil dully.

"You can't tell by that. Colouring, speech, dress, make a big difference in identifications. Anyhow, we'll go on hoping."

However, there was no doubt that Grew feared the worst and was trying to prepare the other for absolute defeat.

Before the court opened on the second day, Michael's death was public knowledge, and, with the realisation of the problems raised by it, interest became still more acute. On every side speculation was rife as to what effect this new debacle would have on the outcome.

Evidence continued. A clerk from Lloyds Bank (Glastonbury) described the removal of the pearls from the owner's strong box on the morning of Thursday, March 19th. The witness saw Miss Bundy place them in a bag which he believed to be brown, though he could not state this definitely. The deceased was unaccompanied. She obtained seventy pounds in traveller's cheques and cashed a self-endorsed cheque for forty, receiving payment in the form of two tens, two fives and ten one-pound notes.

Marcus Katz, dealer in second-hand and wholesale jewellery, of 99 Hatton Garden, gave an account of the prisoner's visit to him on March 21st. The pearls purchased from her showed signs of not having been worn for a lengthy period. He paid her by cheque the sum of three hundred and fifty pounds, which she cashed the same day. The prisoner, whom he readily identified, seemed anxious to make a quick sale and furnished neither references nor address. She did not appear especially nervous, rather less so, indeed, than many ladies bent on similar business.

The telegram sent by the dead woman to her niece was read and given over to the jury for examination. The time of dispatch indicated its having been handed in at some time between the deceased's two calls at the Times Book Club. The jury was asked to note the wording: "Alligator bag left in car," going to prove absolute certainty in the owner's mind as to where her property was to be found. Definitely, then, this bag had been left behind in the car, not lost in the street. The point was emphasised as having especial importance.

Assistants from the Army and Navy Stores described the visits of both prisoner and victim. The counsel laid stress on the latter's agitated inquiries for her niece, but was unable to secure evidence to show that the prisoner had betrayed any unusual emotion. The young man who attended to the prisoner knew her at once, even recalling her attire, which had struck him as smart and effective; particularly had he noticed the red bag she held in her hand.

Doris Marjory Stearns, from the receiving desk of the Times Library, told of the elderly lady who, on the afternoon of March 20th, had put to her some rather distressed questions regarding a lost bag and a young lady she appeared to connect with the bag. The witness had not seen the young lady, who probably came in while she was having her tea, though no one seemed to have any recollection on the subject. It was fairly certain she did come in, for the books in her possession were returned on that date. Of course some one else might have brought the books. Later on, towards six o'clock, she had again noticed the old lady, who was hovering near the stairs and peering down towards the entrance. On this occasion nothing was said.

The jury was here informed that after this second appearance of the deceased at the Times premises there was no further record of her as a living person. It was also pointed out that as she spent a considerable amount of time hanging about, it was not unreasonable to infer a meeting between her niece and herself. No eye-witness of such an encounter could be produced. It was entirely a question of probabilities.

Clerks from the Victoria Post Office verified the telegram previously shown; and testified concerning a trunk call put through to Bishop's Paulton 26 by an elderly, stout lady with a florid complexion. The applicant rambled about impatiently while the connection was being obtained, and eventually, at about five-thirty, spoke from one of the booths.

Sir Benson Fincastle, medical expert, gave a detailed confirmation of the facts outlined at the inquest. In his opinion the head injuries were not at all incompatible with a vigorous woman agent, particularly one actuated by violent emotion. Probably only the initial blow was administered while the victim was in an upright position; the rest, delivered after the latter was partly or wholly unconscious, could easily have been managed by an arm of average strength. What was needed was a free swing and a heavy weapon, not great muscular development.

The witness could not fix the time of death with any greater precision than the former doctor. It remained as before at some time between 9 and 12 p.m. on Friday, March 20th. Chemical analysis of the dirt found in the mouth and nose revealed it as identical with the soil surrounding the ditch, but as rigidity did not commonly set in for several hours this circumstance proved nothing except that the body had been dragged for a short distance, probably from the road to the hiding-place. From a medical point of view there was nothing to invalidate the theory of the murder having taken place somewhere else, even two or three hours away.

On being shown the spanner belonging to Miss Bundy's car, he declared it to be the sort of instrument he had in mind. The jury were then handed the spanner to inspect. It was clean, oiled and bore nothing beyond the scratches of ordinary usage, but as counsel pointed out, the prisoner had had ample opportunity to put it in order before parting with the car.

James Pollard, garage owner, of 36 Greek Street, Soho, gave evidence relating to the eight-cylindered Geisler car left at his premises on the evening of March 20th. Generally speaking, the exterior was clean; it did not suggest having been driven in the rain or along muddy roads. The interior he did not see, except for a cursory glance through the windows, as the young lady who brought it in locked the door before leaving. The time of this was just about midnight. He had not supposed he would recognise the young lady, but now he saw the prisoner he could declare without hesitation that she was the one.

COUNSEL: "It would be a simple matter, I imagine, to wipe off any splashes from the sides of the car?"

WITNESS: "Oh, certainly, especially before they dried."

COUNSEL: "Did you observe anything unusual in the lady's manner? Did she strike you as perturbed or apprehensive?"

WITNESS (considering this): "No, only tired. She told me she had driven up from Somerset and all about town."

COUNSEL: "When did you see her next?"

WITNESS: "On the Saturday morning. She took the car out and brought it back early in the afternoon. It stayed with us till Monday, round about two o'clock."

COUNSEL: "On any of these occasions did she seem agitated?"

WITNESS: "Well, not exactly; more quiet than agitated, but she looked all in every time I saw her, worse after the first time."

COUNSEL: "Describe exactly what you mean by the expression 'all in?'"

WITNESS: "Worn out—dark under the eyes. Depressed and worried, or so I remember thinking."

Much was made of this, the witness being called on to explain to the nth degree his idea of the prisoner's appearance. When he withdrew it was to be replaced by another witness whose intense nervousness was in such total contrast to his unimportant evidence as to draw Neil's attention.

This was none other than the youth employed at Saunders' garage in Glastonbury—Albert Stokes by name, a big, loose-jointed lout of stupid aspect. Neil, on the few occasions when he had conversed with him, had received an impression of a low intelligence linked with easy good nature and rough manners. There seemed no reason for him to gasp and stammer over his simple statement, but the fact remained that he did so, glancing this way and that and sweating till his shelving front hair was streaked with moisture.

According to Stokes, the prisoner had come in with Miss Bundy's car on the evening of March 23rd, and an hour later returned to fetch the telegram about which he had known nothing. Stokes had then helped her search for her aunt's bag, but without success. He could swear the car had not been touched during the hour between her two visits. He himself had been washing down a very dirty roadster only a few yards away from the Geisler, so he would have known if any one had been around. The prisoner had not seemed much concerned over her aunt's loss. She appeared too tired to bother. There was a gentleman with her the second time, Mr. Starkey, who had been staying at Stoke Paulton. Soon after the two of them left Miss Bundy's bailiff came in, and on hearing about the telegram, took a good look at the car to make sure the bag had not escaped notice.

Having got through what evidently was a trying ordeal, Albert Stokes shambled to his seat, where he mopped his forehead with a shaking hand. Only Neil followed his departure, for at this juncture a new sensation arose in the calling of Alfred Tilbury.

The audience strained forward eagerly to catch sight of the much-discussed man. Many used opera glasses. Whispers were heard:—"There he is!"—"Pleasant-looking chap, eh?" and, "Nothing to write home about, is he?" Meanwhile, slightly self-conscious under the eyes fixed on him, the former bailiff took the oath and waited with unobtrusive deference for counsel to begin.

He admitted having been vaguely disturbed over his employer's telephone call, mainly because of his inability to catch what was said. Although he felt sure Miss Bundy had lost something she valued, he could not make out what it was. It was to relieve his mind that his wife had gone to Glastonbury the following morning and again on Sunday, he being too ill to get out of bed. On Monday, still so weak that it was in defiance of the doctor's orders he was up at all, he determined to make inquiries in person for Miss Andreyev, hoping she might shed some light on the matter which was troubling him. Not until he learned about the telegram did he realise how it was the alligator bag which had caused the excitement, and as this was after his own knowledge of Miss Bundy's non-arrival at her destination, he became extremely worried. He could not help connecting the lost bag with Miss Bundy's disappearance, though he had not worked out anything satisfactory in his own mind. He was greatly astonished to hear Miss Andreyev had not seen her aunt off after going all the way to London with her—indeed, could not understand it at all.

Questioned as to his impression of the prisoner's manner when he encountered her at the vicarage. Tilbury replied that he was too taken up with his own feelings of alarm to notice her much. She might have been as shocked as he was. He really couldn't say.

COUNSEL: "Was there any ill feeling between you and the prisoner?"

WITNESS: "Not on my side. I sometimes got the notion she wasn't keen on my being at Stoke Paulton. I fancied it was because she'd been collecting the rents and so on for about six months, and didn't like giving up the job to a stranger."

COUNSEL: "Did she show resentment when you and your wife were installed as caretakers?"

WITNESS (hesitating): "Well, sir, I don't believe she liked it, and that's a fact. I heard her say 'Damnation!' and declare she wasn't going to stay under the roof with me. She didn't say it to my face, of course. Soon after the murder she fetched her box away."

COUNSEL: "I am told that you and your wife were engaged in some sort of occult research with the deceased. Had this anything to do with the prisoner's attitude towards you?"

WITNESS (with the utmost candour): "I shouldn't wonder if it had. You see, Miss Bundy never discussed her private affairs with the young lady, and as Miss Andreyev never knew we was only doing it to please Miss Bundy, she may have got wrong notions in her head. I for one never believed as 'ow she tried to spy on Miss Bundy though some do think that, I've 'eard. I only suppose she was put out like, owing to her aunt's taking a liking to us."

The witness throughout did not deviate from his mild-mannered impartiality. Not once did he indicate a wish to injure Natasha, though there was no doubt that his quietly dropped denial about the spying had the full effect of a denunciation. Having created an impression of frank simplicity and earnest desire to acquit himself justly in a painful situation, he left the stand amid murmurs of approbation.

Following this came a lengthy analysis of the prisoner's telegram to her brother, sent soon after her arrival in London. It ran thus: *"Can get money meet me according to plan spend night Bianchinis,"* and was signed *"Tasha."* The jury's notice was drawn to the phrase "according to plan;" also to the fact that no train was mentioned, counsel's inference being that here was evidence to show a carefully arranged scheme dependent on given conditions. The whole thing tallied perfectly with the landlady's statement that Andreyev had been told to expect a wire if a definite event materialised. This event did materialise, and Andreyev received his message per agreement. As to the construction to be put on these facts, the jury must decide for themselves.

A deposition from the Paris police was read and comments on it given. Michael Andreyev was accused by his employer, M. Joseph Waldemar, a stockbroker, of inflicting personal violence on him and of absconding after using clients' money for private speculations. M. Waldemar had at first refrained from taking action, but on learning the extent of the defalcation, reported the matter to the authorities. A rumour reaching him that Andreyev was in England, a warrant for the fugitive's arrest was issued.

The morning was wearing to a close when the last and most important witness was called. It was the proprietor of the filling station near Bristol. Breathless attention greeted his appearance in the box. Neil took an iron grip on himself and looked. What he saw did not reassure him—a beefy, bull-necked man with a bristling moustache and round, staring brown eyes, not easily intimidated. The coarse hands which grasped the book showed no sign of a tremor.

The supreme moment for the prosecution had come—yet photographs are deceptive things, the one used by the police in this instance being three years old, faded, and showing Natasha in evening dress. The witness, confident as he was before, might falter when it came to the test. If he did not—but no, one must not allow oneself to think. . . .

No one stirred while Natasha was handed the coat and hat she had worn on the fateful Friday. She put them on, tucking her hair under the little felt cap and adjusting her collar with steady hands. If terror lurked behind those spent hazel eyes, she gave no indication of it. To see her now one would think her mind preoccupied with matters entirely remote from the problem of life and death confronting her.

Sir Henry Challenge waited patiently. When he spoke, his voice was suave.

COUNSEL: "Herbert Rowntree, I wish you to look closely at the young woman in the dock. Take plenty of time. Is she or is she not the driver of the Geisler car which stopped at your establishment on the evening of March 20th?"

WITNESS (staring hard and sucking in his breath): "Yes, she's the one. I recognise her clothes, and I recognise her face."

The packed listeners swayed. Somewhere at the back a woman's hysterical laugh broke out sharply.

COUNSEL: "That, my lord, is the case for the prosecution."

The judge enjoined silence. When the turmoil had subsided a new figure rose and surveyed the court.

MR. GREGORY CAIRNES, K.C: "My lord, I call the prisoner. . . ."

She was there, motionless, the target for bulging eyes, a girl of twenty-two, with a straight, firm bearing, and a pale Slavic face.

Neil Starkey, however, did not see her. What he did see was a peasant woman, features contorted, lashing blindly at a rat.

## CHAPTER TWENTY-EIGHT

SLOWLY Neil shook off the evil spell and forced his attention upon the defending counsel. Cairnes, an Edinburgh Scot, who had fought his way to the front rank by a series of brilliant victories, was burly and unprepossessing to look at, his face a rough country of hillocks, in the depths of which small twinkling eyes hid behind sandy lashes. His gestures were clumsy, his accent marred by a burr, his utterance occasionally stammering; yet his very unawareness of these defects together with a heavy dynamic vigour, endowed him with a curious charm. The unruffled blandness with which he set about his unpromising task commanded a tribute of respect, but for all that the prevailing attitude towards him was one of commiseration. Sharp he might be—no one disputed it—but he was not a prestidigitator who, by a turn of the wrist, could transform black into white.

Neil, sunk in despair, shared this general opinion. All he now dared hope for was a disagreement, and that not unless their own chief witness came up to the scratch. He knew that since yesterday Cairnes had spent long hours in consultation with Natasha; that by placing her in the box he was banking to a large extent on her youth and personal appeal, but that this decision was an error of judgment was painfully apparent. How could the girl, shattered by the news of her brother's death, be expected to win back sympathy long since alienated? A single glance at her deadened exterior showed how useless it was to seek in her those qualities which sway emotions. She might perhaps tell a more complete, story now there was no need of concealment, but after the last witness's knock-out blow would any statement of hers be believed?

When, without any warning, her brother arrived in England, he told her nothing of his real reason for leaving Paris. Depression, nerves, general fed-upness was his excuse. Above all, he must find some new job, far removed from familiar scenes. Natasha was feeling much the same, weary of monotony, longing for change. It occurred to her the two might strike out together, particularly as she sensed in Michael an instability which needed a strong guiding hand. Her affection did not blind her to his shortcomings. She knew him to be a spendthrift and a little inclined to drink and to take gamblers' chances, but he was clever and versatile, and with her to keep him in order might be steered into a useful career.

With this in mind, she sought out her father's old friend. Serge Wassilieff, a Russian now living in London. Wassilieff promised to secure work for them both in the motor transport in Persia, provided they could find money for their fares. He himself, being hit by the falling market, was not able to aid them financially, though in an emergency he would have done what he could. However, Natasha was determined not to call on him. She planned to set aside her salary for the purpose, and in time could have managed very well if her brother's resources had not come to an abrupt end. From this event onward she had Michael to support, always hoping that if the latter found even temporary employment the situation might be eased.

Thinking to lessen his expenditure and remove him from the temptations of London life, she persuaded him to take up his residence in Bath. She quite understood his unwillingness to inform their aunt of his proximity. From the first Miss Bundy had taken what seemed an unreasonable dislike to Michael, and would have strongly disapproved if she had known her niece was taking care of him.

COUNSEL: "Then you did not know your brother had applied to her for money?"

NATASHA: "Absolutely not. I only thought it wise on general principles to avoid friction."

COUNSEL: "Can you explain why you did not introduce him to any of your friends?"

NATASHA: "If I had done so my aunt would have got to know about him. Besides, he was really in no fit state to meet strangers."

She had been, in fact, rather troubled about Michael's pronounced neurasthenia, indications of which had been noticeable from an early age. She attributed it to the shock sustained when, a boy of thirteen, he had seen their father butchered by the revolutionists. Even his calling himself Addison—a family name, incidentally—was to her mind a symptom of his morbid wish to dissociate himself from the past, although he rationalised it by saying how difficult it was for a foreigner to obtain work in England. He could only, of course, have held a position for three months at a time on account of labour regulations. Actually, he did try to secure several posts, but without success.

Towards the last of February she received from a friend in Paris a communication of a staggering nature. In plain language she was informed of Michael's embezzlement, and warned if she knew where he was hiding to get him out of England as soon as possible. It was a terrible unveiling of much which had vaguely puzzled her. Now, in a flash, she knew why Michael had left France, why he was using a false name, why he was so desperately anxious to seek a distant country. His depression, his nervous condition, all were explained.

COUNSEL: "He was in immediate danger of arrest?"

NATASHA: "It was merely a matter of finding him."

Frantic with misery and shame, she rushed to confront him with the accusation. He denied nothing, but declared that rather than serve a term of imprisonment he would kill himself. She knew Michael. The threat was not an idle one. He had a revolver ready loaded, which she wrested from him, and later that night threw into the Severn. Before they separated she made him swear to do nothing rash, but to leave matters to her.

The situation demanded quick action. Even if Michael did not take his life, he could never stand up against the disgrace of imprisonment. To brand him as a thief was to finish him utterly, of that she had not the slightest doubt. Yet she had faith in his good qualities, believed that with an entirely fresh start he might pull round and amount to something. It was up to her to get him to safety before he was captured, and equally important for her to go with him. Both her practical knowledge of car mechanics and her moral support were essentials to him in this crisis.

Money must be raised—but how? She dared not approach her aunt, who would have denounced the offender and exposed him to punishment. The family trinkets she sold fetched only a trifling sum. As the danger increased with the passing of every day, she was forced to consider applying to Mr. Wassilieff, but she hesitated to write, preferring to speak to him in person. She did not know how she could tell him the truth, yet she shrank from securing a loan under false pretences. In any case, she must see him—and her aunt's decision to go abroad made this easy. As things turned out, she had no need to ask favours. Miss Bundy, at parting, presented her with a totally unexpected gift—her grandmother's string of pearls. Overjoyed, she telegraphed Michael, whom she had already advised to hold himself in readiness to join her if their Russian friend supplied them with funds. The words *"according to plan"* meant simply that she would meet the first train by which her brother might arrive, and if he did not come on it she would first wait for him at the restaurant run by the Kosloff couple, and later go to Bianchini's Hotel.

Next followed the movements known to us—visits to the stores and the Times, the shopping expedition, stop at the Carlton, and the excursion to Wimbledon, only to find her fellow-countryman absent from town. She then returned to the West End and dined at the Piccadilly Circus Corner House, afterwards taking an aimless drive in Richmond Park till time to meet the ten twenty-five train at Paddington. Michael failed to arrive, and there was no other train that night except the two-forty. She therefore dropped in at the Samovar Restaurant in Rupert Street to spend an hour chatting with the former cook and butler of her childhood, always hoping Michael, who might be motoring up, would come and find her, but he did not appear. Incidentally the Kosloffs, except for Wassilieff, were the only people who knew who Michael really was. This fact explained the suppression of them in her first statement, issued when it was not yet discovered that Michael had been in England.

At midnight she put up the car at a neighbouring garage and repaired to the hotel in Greek Street. Again disappointment—Michael was not there, and as luck would have it, there was only one available room. Certain she need not expect Michael till the morning, she took this room, but before she had undressed she heard a commotion below, and through the window saw her brother being helped out of a taxi-cab. A glance told her the distressing truth; he was hopelessly intoxicated, a condition in which she had never seen him.

She was horrified, also in a sore quandary as to what to do with him. Impossible to seek a strange hotel, which very likely would not take him in—yet where to put him? In the stress of the moment she invented the only story she could think of. She explained to the proprietor that she had been married to Mr. Addison a few days before, enlisted his aid in getting the stupified man to bed, and for the remainder of the night sat up, badly frightened by her brother's alarming symptoms—for even without previous experience she could see that his heart was affected, and that he was in danger of collapse.

Now comes the most perverse feature of the entire affair. Michael, on regaining consciousness, was not only very ill, but quite ignorant of the evening's events. In riotous relief over his sister's summons he had begun drinking at once, with the result that from seven o'clock onward his mind was a total blank. Drink, he admitted, had sometimes served him in this way, but never with quite such devastating effects. He was probably bordering on *delirium tremens*, though how he had got hold of the intoxicants which supplemented his own whisky he could not say, any more than he could account for his arrival in town or his movements thereafter. It was a mystery to him that he had been able to direct the cab driver to Bianchini's—yet evidently he had done so. When he was recovered sufficiently to keep down some strong coffee, Natasha left him in the proprietor's charge, and set forth to make preparations for their coming journey.

These she could not complete till Wassilieff's return from Holland, but she did dispose of the pearls to a jeweller Michael told her about, inquired into the tickets, and obtained the visas from the Persian Consulate. For two days Michael was not well enough to get up, but on Monday she drove him back to Bath, thinking that by the time their friend was home again he would be in a suitable condition for travelling. She devoutly hoped the experience would frighten him into sobriety.

She garaged her aunt's car at Glastonbury, learned at the vicarage of the telegram awaiting her, and went back to fetch it. The bag could not be found. To Mr. Starkey, who already knew a little of her financial needs, she confided about the pearls, but did not mention them to Mr. and Miss Gisborne, simply because she wished to avoid a painful explanation which would burden the latter with knowledge of her brother's guilt. They could not be expected to applaud her resolution, so, as she was resolved to go through with it, the less said the better.

Later that evening she learned of Miss Bundy's disappearance, but while puzzled and distressed, had no suspicion of grave disaster. If she collapsed on hearing that a body had been found, it was chiefly because she was worn out from lack of sleep and anxiety over Michael. She did not seriously imagine her aunt had been murdered, nor when the awful fact was revealed, did she see it in relation to herself until Mr. Gisborne began his interrogation, but then, with a shock, she realised her position. To tell all she had done in London meant giving away Michael, who at any cost must be got clear of the country before his presence became known. Refusal to speak looked bad for the moment, but as the truth about the crime might come out before her movements were closely examined, she must simply remain silent while she could.

At the first opportunity she rang her brother up on the telephone to bid him go immediately, warned him to hold no communication with her for the present, but assured him she was in no danger. If necessary, she could always reach him through the French Consulate at Baghdad, and in any case, she would join him at an early date. An hour later he motored past the village. She met him with money for his journey and sped him on his way.

At the inquest there had been no need to mention the pearls, but when the Scotland Yard inspector told her of the information gathered from the bank and from Marcus Katz, she was obliged to yield up a portion of her secret. In her efforts to keep Michael's name out of her account she made a bad hash of things, and with sudden fright saw not only that the whole truth would soon be dragged from her, but that it was going to be exceedingly hard to convince the police of Michael's lapsed memory. Since her brother was already sought on a minor charge, how natural to fasten on him the guilt of this other, far graver crime! If tried, he might be acquitted, but he would automatically be handed over to the French authorities, convicted for theft and sentenced to prison. In short, panic-stricken at the thought of a second and fatal interview with the police, she resolved on the flight which led to her arrest.

Here the tale concluded, and the long cross-examination began. By every device Sir Henry Challenge tried to wear down the girl's resistance and trap her into admitting she had been in Bristol. As time passed it seemed she was being bullied and harried into a condition where she would be forced to contradict herself, but although towards the last she became so dulled that questions had to be reframed in order to reach her intelligence, she stuck immovably to her original statement. Again and again she repeated that she had all along seen the weakness of her position, but had chosen the lesser of two evils, confident that no jury would condemn her for something she had not done.

Once the judge addressed her:

"It is quite understood, then, that you fully grasped the gravity of your offence, that you were setting out deliberately to defeat justice?"

"Legal justice—yes," was the low rejoinder. "I certainly knew I was defying the law, but I considered it a worse wrong to ruin my brother for all time. I would do the same again."

This brought a gasp. There appeared to be a few amongst the audience who inwardly applauded the prisoner's courageous refusal to sacrifice the being nearest her, but others, the great majority, wore a sceptical expression. The story, utterly different from the first she had told, savoured too much of cool after-thought. It hung together remarkably well, but what did that or anything else matter when the fact remained that at eight-thirty she had been seen near this city in company with a woman presumably dead? Amid murmurs of strong disbelief the court adjourned.

On the following day the Gisbornes were called, strove hard to throw a favourable light on their friend's conduct, and one after the other were subjected to a merciless grilling. Most of the former witnesses were recalled and questioned anew. Out of a mass of small evidence little emerged save the undeniable fact of the prisoner's having warm supporters.

Neil's turn came. He made the most of Natasha's refusal to accept his proffered loan, and of her efforts to safeguard her aunt's health. His disclosures regarding the alligator bag scored a mild triumph. Yes, he himself had seen what it normally contained—a manuscript in Theodore Bundy's handwriting. The latter was evidently looked on as a valuable treasure, for Miss Bundy kept the bag in question locked, the key on a chain round her neck, and always carried the bag with her wherever she went. It did not at all astonish him to learn of her distress over its disappearance. He himself did not believe she would have shown half so much concern over losing a string of pearls. Lastly, he declared that when he had viewed the victim's body the chain was in its usual place, but the key gone.

On these points Mr. Cairnes dwelt heavily. Bag known to contain manuscript but nothing else; key taken from body after death. Did this combination of circumstances agree with the prosecution's theory? Decidedly not. If the bag was stolen by the present accused, it must have been broken open and rifled at once, or else there would have been no occasion for denunciations and subsequent violence. Yet, if this was the case, why remove a key from the dead woman's neck? To do so would be not only needless but a dangerous waste of time. If on the other hand, the key was taken by the murderer, it must have been because the latter did not yet possess the bag, but hoped to get hold of it later and open it in an unsuspicious manner. Obviously it would be easy enough to slit the leather with a knife, or force the lock. If the murderer hesitated to do this, he or she must have had some important reason.

This minute detail, went on counsel, might yet serve to put a rope round the criminal's neck, but not round the neck of Natasha Andreyev, who, if she had unexpectedly found herself in possession of the bag, would certainly not have waited till she had committed murder before ascertaining the contents of her prize. The whole assumption was manifestly absurd and untenable. At the same time, the key was taken—and for what purpose, if not to open the bag? That meant that the bag at the time of its owner's death was still unlocked, also that it was in some other locality, but not considered irretrievably lost. The prosecution might argue that the victim herself removed the key to place it elsewhere, but if so, they would find difficulty in supporting their contention.

A new and interesting matter was now brought forward. Why did the prosecution take it for granted that Miss Bundy reached Bristol by car? The six-thirty Paddington express would have got her there in precisely two hours and twenty-seven minutes. Possibly, for a hidden reason of her own, she did actually travel by this train. The six-thirty is often crowded, so that a passenger arriving by it could easily escape notice at the barriers. At the same time the first-class carriages are not always filled, occasionally empty. If, as might have happened, the deceased had occupied an entire compartment to herself, she could have made the journey without being observed by fellow-travellers. On March 20th the to-half of a first-class ticket was handed in at Bristol and it was a singular fact that the return half, though extensively advertised for, had never come to light. Where then, was this ticket? Was it not natural to suppose it to have been destroyed with the other contents of the victim's black bag?

Nor was this the only circumstance suggestive of a voluntary journey. While at the Victoria Post Office Miss Bundy tried to get on to a Kensington telephone number, but failed to receive a reply. The number, recorded at the time, was that of Miss Braselton's flat in Blessington Mansions. What if the attempted call was for the purpose of informing her friend's maid that she would not arrive for dinner? True, she could have left a message to this effect when she passed by the building two hours before. If she did not do so it must have been either because in the interval she altered her intention, or because she was unwilling to acquaint her niece with that intention. Counsel himself inclined strongly to the latter opinion, which was bolstered up by Miss Bundy's refusal to allow her niece to remain with her. This in itself argued the existence of some secret plan, nor was it straining probabilities to assume that plan to have been directly or indirectly responsible for the victim's ultimate fate.

Serge Wassilieff, a handsome, grey-haired Russian of fifty, described his encounters with Michael Andreyev, and denied knowing anything about the Paris trouble till the newspapers blazoned it to the world. He had been unaware that Michael was using a name other than his own. Of Natasha Andreyev he had the highest opinion. He had known her as a child, and had occasionally seen her in Paris. He could state positively that she was one in a thousand—high-principled, loyal, dependable. For this reason and also because of his deep attachment to her dead father, he had been only too anxious to help her in any way possible, much regretting his inability to hand her outright the money for the Persian enterprise. He had, however, told her to come to him if she could not otherwise raise the needed funds, but as she was very independent about asking favours, he was not surprised at her failure to do so. He did not see her at all from their first discussion of the project till her appearance at his place of business in Great Portland Street on March 26th. It was then that she told him the difficulty she was in over Michael, and begged him to keep the whole thing secret. She did not seem alarmed for her own safety, only terrified lest her brother should be hauled into the inquiry.

Patrick Healy, janitor of Midlothian Mansions, Wimbledon, failed to identify the prisoner as the lady who called to see Mr. Wassilieff of the evening of March 20th. He did remember passing a lady on the stairs, when he went up to mend a fuse wire, but as the lights were out he had no idea what she looked like, nor did he recognise the prisoner's voice. A number of people, men and women, inquired for Mr. Wassilieff while the latter was in Holland. Mr. Wassilieff was very popular, and his flat seemed a general meeting place for Russians, all of whom spoke English almost or quite without accent.

An electric fuse gone wrong! Was the tale of impish fatalities never to cease? On a faulty bit of wire a girl's life hung—and that wire had chosen this one moment of all others to blow itself out!

The saleswoman from Hobson and Weaver's identified the prisoner, and gave details of the latter's unhurried selection of a coat. Three waiters and the cloak-room attendant from the Carlton Hotel declared they had never seen her before. Mabel Douglas was called, and Neil saw before him the waspish, flaxen-haired damsel from the Hammersmith Lyons. She surveyed the accused with antagonistic deliberation and gave a decided negative.

The Clerk of the Assizes called Miss Gwendolen Pilcher.

Neil's collar choked him. For the second time the room dissolved in a haze, through which nothing was visible save a pallid, spectacled girl in a brown coat and skirt, who took her place in the box and fidgeted nervously with her rolled-up cotton gloves. Timid conscientiousness gazed forth from her near-sighted brown eyes. She bit her lip to stay its trembling, and in a faint awed whisper repeated the oath.

COUNSEL: "Miss Pilcher, I want you to take a good look at the prisoner, and tell us if you served her at dinner at the Corner House on Friday, March 20th. Consider every detail of her appearance and try to give us a definite Yes or No."

The witness's distress was painful. Her eyes stared fascinatedly at Natasha; she flushed a dingy red, then paled to a sickly hue. A minute, two minutes passed, and still she remained tongue-tied. The audience held its breath.

COUNSEL (encouragingly): "Don't be upset, Miss Pilcher. Take your time. . . . Now, do you recall this lady's face?"

GWENDOLEN PILCHER (in an agonised gasp): "No—oh, no! Oh, dear, I—I wish I did, but . . ."

She gave way utterly and left the box in a flood of tears.

## CHAPTER TWENTY-NINE

WHAT was left to be said? The prisoner's statement stood forth as a concoction of lies from beginning to end, the facts refuting it sufficient to damn a saint, still more one who by her calm behaviour recalled all the historic instances of criminal callousness. Even at the waitress's denial and weeping collapse she had remained like a creature made of stone.

The parking of the car created a bad impression. How was it that on two occasions—from eight to nine-fifteen and again from eleven to twelve—Natasha had left the Geisler, not at a regulation parking place, but along a side street in Soho? Her answer was simple enough.

"I often do that, to save time. If you leave a car in front of an empty house and take the key, it's perfectly safe, and no policeman will bother you."

Safe—but had she done this? It was obviously the sort of story to be invented if the car and herself with it were miles away on the Bristol road.

Surprise was felt at the recalling of Herbert Rowntree. Here, at any rate, was a witness best left alone—yet he was back again, bull-necked, stertorously breathing, staring out upon the court with hard, unimaginative eyes and a look of defiant preparedness, to repeat his former declaration. With matter-of-fact urbanity Cairnes addressed him.

COUNSEL: "Mr. Rowntree, I take it you are familiar with many makes of motor cars. About the one seen by you on the evening of March 20th—you are, I suppose, quite certain it was a Geisler?"

WITNESS (confidently): "Oh, yes, quite."

COUNSEL: "The Geisler is an Austrian car. I understand that, like a few others of foreign manufacture, it is less commonly seen here than, shall we say, the Sunbeams, Chryslers, Armstrong-Siddeleys, and so on. Do you get many of them your way?"

WITNESS: "Well, not what you'd call many. I know 'em, though. I can pick out a Geisler saloon fifty yards off on a dull day."

COUNSEL: "Ah! yours is a practised eye. What colour was this one?"

WITNESS: "Dark green—a very dark green."

COUNSEL: "And the power?"

WITNESS: "Eight cylinder. Wire wheels it had. Offhand, I should call it a 1930 model."

COUNSEL: "Might it have been a 1929 model?"

WITNESS: "Maybe. They're much of a muchness."

COUNSEL: "I wonder if you have ever noticed the strong resemblance between the 1929 eight-cylinder Geisler such as you describe and the same powered Getz car of that year?"

WITNESS (slowly): "Can't say as it's struck me. We don't get a rare lot of Getz cars down here. Maybe they're a bit alike."

COUNSEL: "The similarity was remarked on at the 1929 trade show. The standard colour of both was the same shade of dark green, and at a short distance one might have been mistaken for the other. In fact, they frequently are confused, as I happen to know, my own car being a Getz. If on this occasion you chanced to notice any feature which can put the matter beyond a doubt, please mention it. Don't be afraid to be technical."

WITNESS (aggressively): "I didn't take a squint at the badge, if that's what you mean. The general look was enough. I said to myself, There's a Geisler that's not brand-new, but it's been well handled. I said—"

COUNSEL: "One moment, Mr. Rowntree. Did you make these observations at the actual time, or later?"

WITNESS (puzzled): "Things go through your head, even if you don't put them into words then and there."

COUNSEL: "Ah, to be sure. Now let us consider the question of petrol. Can you recall what sort was purchased, and the amount?"

WITNESS (promptly): "Fifteen gallons of Tex. I remember thinking, she wants to be prepared for a good run without stopping, for she's got a fair bit left now."

COUNSEL: "Tex! It may interest you to learn that on the sworn statements of four separate people Miss Andreyev confined herself entirely to Shell. She thought the Geisler ran better on Shell. You are quite sure it was Tex she asked for?"

WITNESS (doggedly): "Tex is what she asked for, and what I gave her."

COUNSEL (after waiting for the judge to suppress a murmur): "Describe the lighting at your station, and the position of this car in relation to it."

WITNESS: "Three big standard lamps in a row. The Geisler drew up just between the second two."

COUNSEL: "So that the third lamp shone directly on the driver's face?"

WITNESS: "That's it. I could see her plain as plain."

COUNSEL: "But I dare say the interior of the car was less clearly illuminated. Kindly inform the jury just what you saw of the inside occupant."

WITNESS: "I saw a lady covered up with a rug to about here" (indicating a point near the shoulder). "She had her face and head wrapped round in something dark. She didn't stir—lay close up in the corner, propped stiff-like."

COUNSEL: "Which corner?"

WITNESS: "The one towards me."

COUNSEL: "Oh! Then if the person was on your side, and you were standing near the bonnet, I cannot think you had a very good view."

WITNESS: "I saw just what I'm telling you. I thought she looked queer."

COUNSEL: "One other point. If the person was almost completely enveloped in rugs and so on, why do you assume that it was a woman and not a man?"

WITNESS (surprised and displeased): "Why, she looked like a woman; that's the idea I got."

COUNSEL: "Can you describe any essentially feminine article of dress? A hat, a bit of fur?"

WITNESS: "I didn't see any hat or any fur. She was too covered up."

COUNSEL: "Yet with a matter of six inches or so of the shoulders showing—I refer to your own statement—you must have noticed if the person wore a fur coat."

WITNESS: "I never noticed it. I can't tell you what sort of coat she had on."

COUNSEL: "Miss Bundy is known to have worn a musquash fur coat. It was on her when her body was found. In consideration of the fact that you saw none, I object to your use of the feminine pronoun. It strikes me, and I think the jury will agree, that you are not at all positive on the question of sex."

WITNESS (cogitating, very much on the defensive): "Anyhow, I saw the driver like as I'm seeing you now, and she was a woman." (Laughter.) "She was that young lady in the dock."

COUNSEL: "A blonde lady?"

WITNESS: "Betwixt and between. These little tight hats don't show much hair. Hers didn't, no more than now."

COUNSEL: "I was coming to the subject of headgear, which seems to me important. As I look round this room, I see about two dozen hats of the same general type as that worn by Miss Andreyev. I can count six with not a pin-point's difference in the matter of shade—beige, I believe it is called. Also there is a marked tendency with the present styles to conceal the hair. . . . Now, what about her coat? Can you furnish us with any distinctive details—material, trimming, shape of lapels or cuffs?"

WITNESS: "All I noticed was that it was a rough, lightish tweed, fawn or grey. Little tufts of dark wool sticking out."

This was an accurate description of Natasha's Irish tweed. Whispers of confirmation had to be silenced.

COUNSEL: "At one time you stated that the driver showed great impatience to get away. By what signs did you notice this?"

WITNESS: "When I told her I'd run out of silver and would have to send the boy round to the pub for change, she got very annoyed. She hunted through her purse, turned round to look at the person inside—"

COUNSEL: "Stop! You say she turned round to look at the person inside?"

WITNESS: "That's right. Then she clicked her tongue and came back at me snappish-like. She said, 'Oh, well, send along—but be quick about it.'"

COUNSEL: "She seemed, in short, to have considered the advisability of calling on her companion for change, but finding the latter asleep, altered her mind?"

WITNESS (taken aback): "In a manner of speaking, she did."

COUNSEL: "Not what one would expect if the other person was a corpse, is it? One doesn't turn to a dead body for change."

WITNESS: "Mind you, she might have been thinking something different."

COUNSEL: "We cannot concern ourselves with surmises. What we want is a clear account of the lady's actions and your own instinctive interpretation of them. You declare that the driver turned impulsively, as though uncertain whether her companion were asleep or not, decided the latter was asleep, and told you to go ahead. Am I right?"

The audience stirred in their seats. Some showed impatience. After all, why this combing over of non-essentials when the bald fact staring them in the face remained unchanged? A few, however, and among them was Neil Starkey, bent forward, watching every flicker of the barrister's veiled eyes with rigid attention.

COUNSEL: "Now then, Mr. Rowntree, you say the lady hunted through her purse, and in your original deposition I think you stated that the bag she carried was red. Can you give us a further description of that bag?"

WITNESS (sure of his ground): "Yes, I can. It was dark red, what you call wine colour. I can't name the leather, but it was stamped all over in an irregular pattern. My wife had one like it once, that's why I noticed it."

COUNSEL: "Good! Anything more?"

WITNESS (most cheered): "It was worn at the edges, not over-clean, and bulgy, like as if it had a lot inside it. A nice bag, but old. It fastened with a metal clasp, with two little knobs to open it by, and there was a handle to go over the arm."

COUNSEL: "Gentlemen of the jury, you have heard the witness's remarkably clear description. The bag he saw was dark red, stamped in an irregular pattern, and fastened with a metal clasp. It was rather shabby and overcrowded. Have I got this correct, Mr. Rowntree?"

WITNESS: "Quite. I'd know that bag anywhere. I can see it before me now."

COUNSEL: "That will be exceedingly useful. It so happens that Miss Andreyev took only one bag away with her, and used it the entire time. It is sufficiently striking in appearance to have been mentioned by a former witness. I shall produce her property and ask if you can identify it."

Tense silence while Natasha's red bag was handed to Cairnes and by him given into the witness's hairy paws. The whole audience craned and twisted. Twenty people in the rear stood up, but were sharply ordered to sit down. A glimpse, however, sufficed.

Wine coloured, shabby? No, the smooth rectangle was bright vermilion in hue, fresh as paint and without decoration, either of metal or stamping. It had no handle but a flat strap against the back, and closed with a tongue thrust through a narrow band of its own material.

COUNSEL: "Mr. Rowntree, you seem surprised. Is not this the bag you saw?"

WITNESS (dumbfounded, as though a trick had been played on him): "Why—why—the fact is—"

A precipitous movement along the witness benches. A girl in brown scrambled to her feet and cast herself blindly in the direction of the prisoner's solicitors. It was the waitress, Gwendolen Pilcher.

THE JUDGE (sternly): "Order! There is no occasion for this disturbance."

COUNSEL (imperturbably): "Mr. Rowntree, I repeat the question. Have you or have you not seen this bag before?"

WITNESS (injured): "No, it's not the same. Not anything like it. I—"

COUNSEL (to the judge): "My lord, I see that one of our other witnesses wishes to say something. As I have now finished with the present gentleman, I should like to call Miss Gwendolen Pilcher."

Gibbering with excitement, the girl in brown took the box. Gone was her tongue-tied embarrassment, the torrent of speech which burst from her sent a thrill along every listener's nerves.

GWENDOLEN PILCHER (explosively): "It is her bag! I know it. I know her, too, now. It all comes back to me, everything. I never noticed her particular because—well, you know how it is with customers coming and going all day and every day, but I did look at that bag of hers, close, whenever I passed her table. I'd wanted one like it to go with my new costume, only when I saw one in Bond Street I found it was sixty-three shillings. My word, I ask you! When I was making out her check—"

COUNSEL: "Go slowly, please, Miss Pilcher. Can you give us the date when this happened?"

GWENDOLEN PILCHER: "Why, of course, it was my last evening at the Corner House. I was going to Margate the next day to stay with my aunt, so it was the Friday evening—yes, 20th March it was, because you can see by my insurance card I left on the 21st."

COUNSEL (to jury): "I have a sworn statement to the effect that Miss Pilcher did leave her employment on this date. . . . You are positive, then, Miss Pilcher, that you saw the prisoner on the evening before the 21st?"

GWENDOLEN PILCHER (as though to a stupid question): "Why, naturally, that's why I wanted a new bag, to take with me. I bought one next morning, but not half so nice. Here it is." (She displayed a bag red and flat like Natasha's.)

COUNSEL: "At what time did you see Miss Andreyev?"

GWENDOLEN PILCHER: "Round about eight-fifteen or eight-thirty, but she stayed a long time reading—I should say an hour at least. The bag was lying beside her plate and—oh, don't stop me! I can tell you just what she had inside it—things that don't come with it, you understand. . . ."

COUNSEL: "Just a moment, Miss Pilcher. Are we to take it you are referring to accessories purchased independently, not bought inclusive with the bag itself?"

GWENDOLEN PILCHER (impatiently): "Why, certainly! You don't buy a yellow chiffon handkerchief with a powder-puff attached, and a square, nickel-plated lipstick with a bag, now do you?" (Laughter.) "Well, that's what she had. She took them out and used them. And wait—I'll tell you something more. When she was finishing her coffee she spilled a drop on the red leather, right in front. She wiped it off, but I'm certain it left a mark. Look—don't you see a faint stain?"

A hundred faces, mouthing, giving their disbelief, surged before Neil. They were trying to tell him what scores of scarlet bags there were exactly like this one, counters, shops full of them. If the accessories corresponded, but they would not. It was impossible. Gwendolen Pilcher had not seen Natasha. The coffee mark, of course—but to his straining gaze the red surface was without blemish.

Mr. Cairnes held the bag again in his clumsy fingers. He loosed the tongue, reached inside, fished out—what was this? A tiny, square-sided tube which glittered in the sunshine—a lipstick! A second more and a gauze cloud, primrose-tinted, fluttered aloft.

A noise like rushing waters. Through it sounded a far-off, triumphant voice with a strong, North-of-Tweed burr.

"Gentlemen, I am going to pass this bag round for your inspection. Please examine the two objects I have just replaced. Look, also, at the small brown mark on the front. I think you will say that it might well have been caused by a drop of coffee. . . ."

Nothing dear after this. Of what importance was it that the twelve jurymen trooped out under escort to examine two eight-cylindered cars, a Geisler and the counsel's own Getz; that endless parley over mechanical details ended in Herbert Rowntree's crushing humiliation? A powder-puff and a drop of Lyons' coffee had turned the scales. It was a foregone conclusion for the jury to return the verdict of Not Guilty. Natasha was free.

Free. . . .

She was close beside him, with policemen clearing a pathway to the car. Enthusiasts scrambled and cheered, photographers clicked their shutters, some one threw a bunch of faded violets, some one else—but no, it was a trick of his fancy. Nothing here but congratulation, hysterical sympathy. . . .

Then it was that a woman's voice poured a thin stream of vitriol in his ear.

"She's a lucky one, she is! Not many would a shinned out of it like that. Tell me she's innocent!"

"My aunt!" agreed a second. "Ask me to believe she 'adn't a 'and in it? Wot abaht that brother of 'ers, popping off so convenient-like? Lost his memory, did he? S'pose I listen to my old man of a Sunday morning when he comes up with that tale? Innocent—pah!"

The door banged, but not in time to shut out a furtive, ominous sibilance. It sounded strangely like hissing.

## CHAPTER THIRTY

"No," Natasha said lifelessly. "I can't marry you. Not possibly. You must be quite mad to suggest it. When you've thought it over you'll see why."

Her passionless tone chilled him. If the cold hands still remained in his clasp it was because she was too nerveless to remove them.

"Do you dislike me then?" he asked. "I know I've no business to bother you now, only I can think of nothing but getting you away from here, now, at once, into the sun and warmth. Italy, Algeria—it doesn't matter where, so long as it's far enough for you to forget all this has ever happened. Look at me! If I'm distasteful to you, say so plainly, and I'll let you alone."

She brought her eyes back from their unseeing tour of her flower-decked room, to which, in spite of the welcome prepared for her across the way, she had insisted on returning. A spasm of pain twisted her mouth.

"Distasteful? After all you've done! No. It's exactly because I'm more grateful to you than I've even been to any human soul that I can't link up my life with yours." For an agonised moment she searched his face, then burst out, "Oh, are you absolutely blind? Don't you see what this verdict means? Every one knows I'm let off not because I'm innocent, but because they can't prove I did it. Not ten people believe in me—and they won't unless the murderer is caught."

Those foul women! He knew she had heard. . . .

"No," she went on, answering his thought, "don't blame any one. It's just circumstances. As soon as I heard of Michael's death I guessed how it would be—that even if I got off I'd still be under a cloud of suspicion. Oh, I'm thankful to be alive!" She put her hand to her throat and laughed shakily. "But you see we can't possibly prove Michael and I didn't murder her together. You know that as well as I do."

"If I grant your assumption—which I don't—how can it affect you and me?"

"How? Listen. The way you feel about me now can't last forever. . . . No, don't stop me. When it's over, you'll still be tied to a woman whom you've always just a little bit doubted. It's true. At this moment, you're not entirely sure. Soon you'll loathe the very sight of me. You'll try to hide it, and that will make it worse. I'll know—and I shan't be able to help myself. At night you'll look at me when I'm asleep and ask yourself: Did she do it? Did she scheme to murder a harmless old woman for the sake of a string of pearls? Then there'll be nightmares. Over and over you'll dream of a creature with my face, lashing at a rat with an iron bar."

"Natasha—be quiet! Stop this horrible nonsense!" He seized her by the shoulders and shook her. She submitted passively, and presently his hands dropped to his sides. They measured each other, face to face, and once again he knew himself confronted by a resistance nothing could break down. He might argue all night and all day. At the end things would remain unaltered.

For a single second there was wistfulness in her eyes. She touched his hand timidly and then drew away.

"I'm being beastly, I know, but I have to put it in a brutal way to make you understand. One day you'll see and be glad. . . . What am I going to do? Don't ask me. Go away by myself, I suppose, somewhere where no one knows me. It will have to be very far. I shall make over the money

Caroline left me and Michael—it will be nearly two thousand pounds, but first I shall have to pay back what he owed—to you. Oh, not as repayment—just to make it more bearable for me, that's all." She drew her hand slowly over her eyes. "And now, please leave me. I'm rather—tired."

In his thwarted consciousness one insistent idea hammered. Somehow, by hook or by crook and without delay, Caroline Bundy's assassin must be tracked down. It was the only means by which to attain happiness. If the solution came too late, he might wake one morning to find Natasha flown. But what chance was there? None, as far as he could see. Everything that could be done had been done, yet all the same he must try again. . . .

A figure detached itself from the group in the vestibule. Supposing it to be one of the reporters constantly dogging him, he strode rapidly on, till a hand on his arm made him turn.

"You, Crabbe? Back from Bristol already?"

"Sir James Curwood's chauffeur dropped me here, sir. I'm working up at Pethbridge, you know."

They walked out together. When they had reached a quiet spot the butler continued, "Well, sir, thank God for that verdict. I'd lost all hope. Did you ever see a man crumple up like that Rowntree? It just goes to show how little the best of us can trust our own senses. I only wish Mr. Cairnes had the handling of some others I could mention."

"What have you heard?" demanded Neil suspiciously. "Do you mean there's dissatisfaction over the verdict?"

"Well, sir, you know the sort of talk that goes on if a thing's not cleared up quite to every one's liking. It's that brother, you know. People will say he murdered Miss Bundy, with his sister to tip him off and help him. They're even saying he committed suicide because he saw from the papers how matters stood."

"There's nothing to prove it was not a natural death. Besides, by no stretch of imagination could he have reached London in time and then get to Bristol and back before one o'clock."

"No, but he might have met Miss Natasha half-way and carried on from there, giving her a chance to go back. I hear it said he hired a car and that the owner's afraid to come forward. I almost knocked a man down for making that suggestion, but what can you say when there's that gap of two and: a half hours for Miss Natasha, and a six-hours' blank for her brother? The telegram too. It allows people to think what they like. Oh, I dare say it will pass over, but it's hard now to stop their tongues."

Natasha was right, then. In his exultation over her release he had shut his eyes to the true situation.

"If it was just the ignorant riff-raff, sir, I wouldn't mind so much, but when my own people, Sir James and Lady Curwood, keep harping on it—"

But Neil had heard enough. Had he not till to-day battled with these same formless doubts which every one in England would now be wrangling over?

"Anything fresh from Stoke Paulton?" he asked, simply to change the subject.

"I was going to mention that, sir." The butler dropped his voice. "I've been going by there now and then to chat with the workmen and see how that hole in the hill is getting on. What I hear makes me wonder a bit—not that it's much. It's mainly the other side a certain party's showing, how he's lording it, so to speak. Regular slave-driver he is. It's just nag, nag, hurry and fault-finding from morning till night. Not one has a good word for him."

"Oh, he's in a hurry, is he? Is the work going all right?"

"Not half quick enough, it seems. They've struck some snag, and it's going to cost a lot more than was expected, besides taking longer. The two of them are forever fidgeting like cats on hot bricks. Something's wrong, or I'm very much mistaken, but I can't make out what. Some of my information comes from Mrs. Bebb, our old char, who's the only servant there now. She says they've no interest in the place, that half the rooms are shut up, and the rest like a pig-sty. Just marking time, I should think."

"I'm told Tilbury has subscribed decently for the church and local charities," remarked Neil absently.

"He'd have to do that, sir, to keep up appearances, but all the same he's busy interviewing agents and getting men up to make valuations. That don't look like settling down, now does it? You watch, sir. Once the terms of the will are complied with, he'll clear out. I shouldn't wonder if he left England."

"Because the neighbourhood is antagonistic?"

"Not that. His skin's thick enough. It's my private opinion he's worried out of his wits. Scared to death. What about? Ah, now you're asking!"

Neil eyed him curiously. Was there something in this after all? By Jove, if any hope remained. . . .

"What gives you this idea?" he asked quickly.

"Well, sir, there's something I've never told you. What do you think they did the very morning after the lawyer called? Got a locksmith to make keys to every blessed cupboard and drawer that was fastened. Far into the night they was turning things out. Once I caught them at it, overhauling the mistress's bedroom. They jumped like mice in a pantry. Searching for something, and I don't believe they found it. The nervous way they've acted tells me that."

"Have you any notion what they were looking for?"

"No, sir. But here's something else I noticed. When Tilbury was in the box yesterday, why did he keep quiet about that original statement he made? You know, when he pretended not to recognise Miss Bundy's voice over the telephone?"

"He knew how foolish it would sound. The post office evidence proved it was Miss Bundy."

"Then why make such a song about it in the first place? Why cast suspicion on Miss Natasha, for that's what he was up to right enough, unless"—here Crabbe looked about him cautiously—"unless it was to turn attention from himself?" He paused to let his suggestion sink in. "Oh, he knew all along it was Miss Bundy. What's more, he was expecting the call. Believe it or not, Mr. Starkey, there's more in that conversation than meets the eye. I myself believe it's the key to the whole business."

"I've thought of that, too, Crabbe. I even had a private detective working on it, but not one of the operators overheard a word. If they had done, how can one get round that infernal alibi?"

"I don't see that we can, sir, but I still think they may have worked it by means of a third party. Here's something. Why does Tilbury keep going up to London? For the last two weeks, except for the trial, he's been popping off every day or so, just going there and back again, not spending more than an hour or two at a time. He's there now. The minute the verdict was delivered he left his wife to come home by herself while he took a taxi to the station. I heard him tell the driver he wanted to make the four-thirty train."

Neil considered this and shook his head.

"I don't know that there's anything suspicious in that."

"Maybe not, but it just struck me he might have got into deep water of some kind. It's that worried look of his that makes me think it. Anyhow, if there's anything queer going on, now's our chance to find out and see where it leads us."

They had stopped in the shelter of a hedge. Neil turned the matter over in his mind, but could see no illumination in it. However, anything was worth trying.

"Thanks for telling me, Crabbe. You might ask that charwoman to keep me posted as to when he sets out for London the next time. I'll have him followed. That at least we can do."

"Right, sir. I'll drop by Mrs. Bebb's place now and leave a message, and if I hear anything worth while, you shall know about it."

Two minutes after this Neil dispatched a telegram to the firm of detectives lately employed by him, notifying them to hold a man in readiness for immediate orders.

## CHAPTER THIRTY-ONE

AT TEN in the evening he rang the bell of Dr. Hilary Graves' mid-Victorian dwelling, and was ushered into a library filled with stuffy furniture and execrable ornaments. There he stood, looking about dully, still suffering from the deflated feeling which had come upon him as the result of Natasha's refusal of his suit. An hour of intoxicated relief over her acquittal—and then emptiness.

In vain did he rack his brain for overlooked clues. The strain of the past weeks had left him so depleted that any effort at mental activity was like flogging a dead horse. Possibly some vital incident had been missed, but where to look for it?

Three witnesses, none especially willing ones, had vouched for the bailiff's illness. If there was a flaw in their evidence, how to find it? And yet what Crabbe had said about the best of us not being able to trust our senses struck him as somehow significant. It was solely because of the faint doubt raised by this aphorism that he was here now.

The doctor entered, listened to his visitor's remarks, and made a sour grimace.

"What—not again?" he snorted. "Do you realise, Mr. Starkey, just how many times I've been interrogated over this tiresome affair? First Miss Bundy's solicitor, then the police, then some private detective from God knows where—and now you come to drag me over the same ground! Well, then, let's get on with it. What do you want to know?"

"Merely your personal impression of Tilbury's attack. To put it baldly, I want to hear from your own lips whether there is the slightest chance of its having been an imposture."

"Imposture? Certainly not. A man may sham illness up to a point, no doubt, but no one can produce nausea, convulsions and diarrhoea at will—not even the worst hysteric. I found the patient literally doubled up with cramps—legs drawn up to his stomach, stiff as pokers. He was barely conscious, clammy as death, and suffering to such an acute degree that I was forced to inject morphia."

It appeared unanswerable, but Neil persisted.

"You saw him, I understand, shortly after 10 p.m.? How long should you say he had been in this condition?"

"Hours, probably, though I admit that's guess-work. His wife told me he had been pretty bad since before noon, but had got much worse during the evening. It seems she'd been trying to telephone me from eight o'clock onward, but my line was in use."

"It really was in use? You are sure of that?"

This was a point the detective had gone into as thoroughly as possible without determining anything beyond the fact that the local operator had succeeded twice in putting Mrs. Tilbury through, and that each time the connection was severed. This sort of thing frequently occurred. The Bishop's Paulton service was notoriously bad.

"Well, as it happens the 'phone was rather busy that evening," answered the physician with a shrug. "I had several calls myself, and my daughter was ringing up friends for a bridge party."

"Now, about this illness again. Could it by any chance have been self-induced?"

"You mean could the patient have taken something?"

Graves hesitated. "I can't swear he didn't, of course. There are drugs which would produce a similar condition, though it's suicidal to tamper with them. In this case, though, I can't see that it matters, so long as the result was total incapacity. The man couldn't have stood alone, much less ventured out and driven a car."

For some inexplicable reason the word "drugs" stirred a chord in Neil's memory. Irrelevant, obviously, and yet he suddenly saw before him a littered table, and in the midst of the clutter a small inconspicuous chemist's bottle.

"Had you ever supposed," he hazarded at random, "that Tilbury was in the habit of taking thyroid extract?"

"Thyroid extract?" The doctor glared at him with an outraged expression. "You don't surely mean that suggestion seriously? No, decidedly not! I have not the least knowledge of Mr. Tilbury's medical history, but if for one moment you imagine that thyroid, even in enormous quantities, would bring about the symptoms I have described, you must have scant acquaintance with its properties. Thyroid, indeed! Utter nonsense!"

"What effect would thyroid have if taken in over-large quantities?" asked Neil curiously. He did not quite know why he put the question, or why he stipulated the "over-large." Possibly now, as before, he found it a little strange for either of the Tilburys to be indulging in the stuff. At any rate, he felt he would like to get to the bottom of it.

"That would depend a good deal on the subject's constitutional tendencies," replied the other with a look of boredom. "The usual thing would be hot flushes, shortness of breath, perspiring fits, greatly increased energy and nervous irritability, augmented appetite, loss of flesh. If the person by nature possessed a sufficiency of thyroid secretion, the results might be disastrous. In certain cases the heart would be affected. I need hardly tell you Mr. Tilbury shows none of these signs."

Neil's mouth fell open. He leant forward excitedly.

"No," he exclaimed, "Tilbury doesn't, but all you mention applies most amazingly to Miss Bundy's state of health prior to her death. Had it occurred to you that—"

"That she might have taken thyroid?" the doctor finished the sentence for him with scathing indignation. "Preposterous! Really, I don't know how you get such ideas. Do you suppose in my maddest moments I would have dared prescribe such a remedy for one in her condition? Nor was she the woman to meddle with patent preparations on her own. In her case thyroid, at any rate much of it, would have precipitated the very crisis we were trying to avoid. It might easily have killed her. Good God, what insanity!"

He paused, eyed Neil aggressively, and tightened his lips.

"It is quite plain what you're hoping to get at," he said in a dry tone, "and my advice is—leave well alone. I may even tell you, without unduly committing myself, that a number of persons are not at all satisfied justice has been done in the matter of this trial. They contend that if a certain individual now dead—I won't mention names—had been put into the dock these past three days we should have secured a double conviction. I say no more. . . . Is that all? Then I'll wish you good-evening."

It was some minutes before Neil could master the impotent rage roused by this accusation. When his brain cleared he was back in his car, driving blindly out amongst the hills. By slow degrees he took stock of the little he had just learned, and in a half-hearted way considered the possibilities raised by the discussion of thyroid.

Not once had he ever thought to connect Miss Bundy's failing health with the properties of the gland extract. Even now there might be nothing in it, but Graves, quite without realising it, had detailed the old lady's symptoms with extraordinary accuracy. Was it dimly conceivable that the victim, unknown to herself, had been fed on thyroid? And if so, for what purpose? Not, surely to bring about her death? The Tilburys' absolute panic over her one bad attack was a complete refutation of that idea. At the same time there was something provocative in the train of conjecture set going, something he resolved to follow up, even though at this late date it could lead to no useful conclusion.

He had turned into the narrow lane which formed the rear boundary of the Stoke Paulton grounds. On top of the hill close at hand the vague shape of the Glebe House stood out against the night sky. Moodily curious to know what progress was being made on the excavation, he stopped his engine, vaulted the stile and climbed the slope.

A few hundred yards away the wide Georgian house lay shrouded in darkness. He looked towards it for a moment, then picking his way over the loosely turned earth past a workman's shack, peered into the hole which yawned beneath the refectory pavement. A sickle moon lit up the entrance. The ivy leaves rattled in a light breeze, the odour of fresh soil mingled with a stale, dank breath coming up from below.

This, then, was the crypt about which antiquarians were talking— this low cellar, black as Tophet, reached by an incline of muddy planks. Little to see when one got inside it. The few human bones which had been found, together with some beads of broken rosaries and a couple of silver vessels, had been removed to a museum, and nothing remained but a rubbish heap of flints and crumbled brick.

Striking a match, he saw a series of shallow niches, in three of which attempts had been made to burrow into the hill. The central one of these was blocked by a rude door, on which was chalked, "DANGER—KEEP OUT." He wrenched it open to look within.

Utter blackness met his eyes, but presently he made out a flight of narrow steps cut in the soil. Slimy and insecure, they descended steeply between wet walls in a slit barely two feet across. He ventured down them, one cautious step at a time, counting as he went. Ten—eleven— twelve—then his match died out. He could not in safety get at another, for the last tread shelved ominously and his exploring foot grazed the edge of a void. From an unseen source a current of damp air blew on his legs. He had the sensation of tomb-like, subterranean space opening up below, and fancied the drip of seeping water.

Horrible! With a shiver at the creepiness of it all he retreated to the top, cleared the incline and under the moonlit sky filled his lungs with pure air. Moisture hung upon his coat, his very skin was beaded with cold drops. He had found out, though, why the excavation had assumed unexpected proportions. If, as he imagined, there were underground springs and caving limestone only a few feet from the surface, Tilbury might easily foresee thousands of hard cash disappearing into the fool's project forced on him as the penalty of wealth. How soon would the law allow him to abandon the attempt? It was a question no one could answer off-hand. Probably, though, the next few weeks would show whether or not there had been a passage, and if no sign of one appeared, what was to stop the owner from selling up and clearing out? It was evidently what he intended doing at the earliest possible date.

Next morning Neil crossed the street and asked for Natasha. The manageress with a jerk of the head and a cold glance from her little pig's eyes replied that her guest was in the coffee-room.

"Go in—you'll find her. There's a gentleman calling."

Another reporter, of course. Why in God's name couldn't the hyenas leave the poor girl in peace? So thinking and resolved to make quick work of the intruder, he threw open the door, and in so doing ran headlong into Alfred Tilbury.

## CHAPTER THIRTY-TWO

OF THE two, the ex-bailiff was the more disconcerted. He opened his lips for an explanation, but Neil pushed past him into the coffee-room and strode straight to Natasha. "What's that fellow been saying to you?" he demanded.

She was standing motionless with angry spots in her cheeks. Her manner was puzzled as she answered:

"He may have meant to be kind. If so, then I was rude, that's all. This is how he put it: Knowing my legacy won't be available for several months yet, he, as trustee of the estate, offers to advance me money in case I want to leave England at once. He even hinted pretty broadly that, of course, I wouldn't care to stick it here now, on account of what people are saying."

"The infernal scoundrel! He actually had the impudence to say that! And you told him—?"

"That I didn't want his help. I may have said more than that. It's that soapy manner of his that makes me see red—and besides, though I may be imagining things, I got the idea he himself is desperately anxious to get me away. You too. He asked if you meant to go on with your work here, or if I thought you'd like him to box up my grandfather's library and send it somewhere else to suit your convenience."

Neil swore softly. "No! Did he say that? Maybe he knows I've been having him watched, and is afraid I may start in on him again! By Jove, what you say cheers me immensely, though what he's nervous about at this stage passes comprehension. Is it just faintly possible there's a weak spot in his armour?"

"If there is, we'll never find it," she replied hopelessly.

"Never mind, I intend to try. I've thought of another way too, of clearing things up as far as you are concerned. Has it struck you that all we want is one single witness who saw your brother during those uncharted hours? It's only the not knowing about him that makes all this doubt possible. What I must get hold of is a good photograph. You have one, I suppose?"

Her quick glance of gratitude told him he had hit on the one means of rousing her from her lethargy and shaking off her obsession. He resolved forthwith to work it to the fullest extent.

"All I can give you is a snapshot, but it's fairly like him. Nothing will come of it now, though. It's far too late for any chance person to remember him."

He tried gently to draw her out on the subject of Michael's death. Although she had not yet had any definite details, she was certain in her own mind as to what had happened. It must, she said, have resulted from another drunken bout, which his weakened heart was not able to withstand.

"He drank because he couldn't bear knowing what I was up against," she whispered, dry-eyed. "He was torn between the feeling that he ought to come back, and the certainty that if he did it would only make the situation more impossible. He was right there, of course. He couldn't have done me any good. What jury would have believed him?"

"And you never realised till that night in Soho what a hold drink had got over him?"

"No. It made me see how absolutely necessary it was for me to stand by him. I don't even know if I could have pulled him round, but I'd have done my best."

Poor girl! She must have guessed, then, how she was staking all she had on a lost cause. He saw clearly why, on her return from London, she was so shattered, so utterly spiritless.

"One thing more—not that it matters, of course. That car of mine did belong to Michael?"

"Yes." She flushed slightly. "He bought it second-hand when he reached this country. He had a little money then, you know. Afterwards he sold it to settle up with a bookmaker, but I'd not yet heard, and when I saw it in front of the house I supposed—"

"You needn't explain. Tell me this. What was your brother like?"

"Utterly disarming. When one was away from him, one could get very angry over his—his irresponsibility, but the moment one saw him again everything was forgotten. Some people are made like that. Here is the snapshot you asked for. Do you think he looked like me?" And she put the little picture into his hand.

Like her, yet with a difference; the same enigmatic charm, but much less decision and strength. Darker, too, and with something rather farm-like about the slanting eyes. Studying for the first time the well-formed features of the wastrel who had caused such dire disaster, Neil felt a curious and resentful idea rise within him. This creature was only half-human. He was an incubus who while alive had sucked his sister's blood, and now he was dead clung on to her tenaciously, dragging her down with him. . . .

"You'll see Rachel to-day?" he asked as naturally as he could.

She shook her head. "No, I'd rather not."

No need to demand an explanation for her morbid shrinking from companionship. With a stab at his heart Neil saw how impossible it was for her to become herself while this shadow of doubt overhung her. Arguments fell on deaf ears. She merely looked at him and said nothing. In the end he pressed her hand and set off to carry out the intention he had formed overnight, stopping on the way to post Michael's photograph with instructions to the private agents.

An hour later, in a chemist's shop in Glastonbury, he was leaning over the counter asking for liquid thyroid.

"Liquid, sir?" The assistant smiled regretfully. "I'm afraid we don't stock it. Won't the tabloids do?"

"Then you never keep it in liquid form?"

"No, sir, simply because there's so little call for it. I don't remember but one customer wanting it in—oh, all the years I've been here. That was about three months back, if I'm not mistaken. We can get it for you, of course. It'll take a couple of days."

"Don't trouble, I'll try somewhere else."

"I feel certain you won't find any in Glastonbury, sir. It's not at all in demand."

As by an after-thought, Neil made another inquiry.

"I wonder if you happen to recall who ordered the last lot? I was thinking it might be the friend who recommended it to me."

"I'm afraid I can't, sir. He wasn't a regular customer."

At three other establishments Neil met with similar replies. None of the chemists stocked liquid thyroid extract, and all declared that about three months ago a gentleman had obtained some through them. In the second shop a record of the purchase had been preserved. The date was February 8th, and the applicant's name set down as Mr. Tracey. No address was given, the preparation having been called for in person. The last chemist, an old-fashioned, garrulous man with mutton-chop whiskers, volunteered some conclusive information.

"I'll tell you who it was, sir," he said confidentially. "It was our local celebrity, Mr. Tilbury, of Stoke Paulton. At that time I didn't know him, though I believe his photographer's business was just along at the end of this street. It was at the inquest on Miss Bundy that I saw him again and recognised him. Shocking affair that, eh, sir? Doesn't look as though we'd got to the bottom of it yet, and not likely to, either, now this young Russian scapegrace has taken himself out of reach."

Neil hid his indignation and steered the talk back to the thyroid. Did the proprietor know why Mr. Tilbury preferred the liquid sort?

"Why, yes; it was because he'd a rooted objection to swallowing tabloids. Now and then you find some one like that. The sole advantage of the other is that you can mix it in soup, tea, milk, whatever you choose, and as it's practically tasteless you don't know you're taking it. It's just a matter of convenience, that's all."

This explanation set Neil thinking furiously. Practically tasteless—could be given in anything liquid. . . . His mind flew back to the time he had seen the bailiff measuring out a dose of Miss Bundy's medicine. Suppose at that actual moment thyroid was being poured into the glass, or, better still, into the bottle itself? If the fellow had wanted to play this game, he must have found ample opportunities, made childishly easy by the old lady's short-sightedness. Neil himself had seen covered bowls of soup on the tray carried each evening to the study—and then what about the victim's excessive thirst?—incidentally a symptom of thyroid poisoning, which had made her consume quantities of tea and lemon-squash at all hours of the day? He recalled this, as well as the bailiff's habit of dancing attendance on her, never allowing her to wait on herself if he was at hand.

Oh, undoubtedly it could have been managed, and whether it was or not, the fact remained that four bottles of the stuff had been ordered on or about the same date, all called for personally, and in no case with the right name or any address supplied. Stupid, unnecessary precautions, but why any precautions, unless the purchaser had something to hide?

And yet there seemed to be no clear object in all this. The prolonged administration of thyroid might, indeed, have brought about an untimely decease, but unless the schemers knew they would benefit by it, they could hardly have wished to kill so useful a benefactress. Nor was there the slightest reason to think they did know either that a new will was contemplated, or that its terms would leave them rich. It had been definitely ascertained that not one of the servants had mentioned the matter to them, and they themselves had gone out for the entire afternoon. In short, the problem was just as inexplicable as before—possibly more so.

He set himself laboriously to reconstruct, step by step, the events leading up to the crime, hoping to read into them some fresh meaning. First, Miss Bundy's attack. (Note.—If Alfred and Connie showed terror over this, could it indicate fear lest their victim should die without complying with their secret wishes?) Next, the week in bed with a complete cessation of nerve strain—and thyroid?—followed by recovery. Then Emily Braselton's arrival and the hurriedly planned séance; and on the ensuing day, the agreement to go abroad and the solicitor's visit, carefully timed to coincide with the Tilburys' absence. After this a blank, and forty-eight hours later the murder, to all intents and purposes totally unrelated to all that went before.

Ah, here was the damnable stumbling block! If Caroline Bundy had died of high blood pressure—but no, she had left home in good health and spirits, to be found with her skull shattered, twenty miles from Stoke Paulton, and more than a hundred from where she was last seen! There was something perverse and provoking about it—no sequence or logic.

True, the old lady had been afraid of dying suddenly. Powyss mentioned her anxiety in this respect, while he, Neil, had noticed the same thing. Her actual words when presenting Natasha with the pearls, "in case anything should happen to me," revealed a state of uncertainty regarding the future. Granting this, it was reasonable to believe she was unwilling to set out on a journey without leaving her affairs in order, which very likely meant seeing that her wishes concerning the excavation were sure of being carried out in the event of her death. The Tilburys, reckoning on her remaking her will under given conditions, might indeed have set about manufacturing those conditions, but it was certainly a bit fantastic, and utterly impossible to prove. Besides, they could not in any case have had a direct hand in her death. Graves's account had squashed all hope of that.

The stone wall again—nor did it help to consider the idea of a third, concealed party as being the active instrument employed, since in the course of many weeks neither Scotland Yard nor private detectives had found any trace of such a person. The whole affair remained exactly as it had been at the beginning, and all this dexterous theorising over the thyroid was simply waste of energy. If Tilbury were faced with the anonymous purchase of a medical preparation, what charge could be brought against him if the murdered woman's organs showed no sign of poison or drug? Thyroid, anyhow, was neither of these. No autopsy could detect it, no matter how much had been absorbed.

As for shadowing Tilbury, he had not the least hope that it would lead to any result. The man had surely no need to compromise himself, and, guilty or not, was quite safe from the clutches of the law. Oh, for something to go on, some infinitesimal strand of evidence left lying about and neglected! But there was none. Why hope for the impossible?

And yet his prayer was answered unexpectedly soon. Hardly had he returned to the vicarage when Crabbe was announced and, shutting the door carefully behind him, took a folded newspaper from his pocket.

"I found this, sir, in the servants' hall at our place half an hour ago," he said in a dry whisper, pointing at the same time to the personal column of the advertisements. "Just cast your eye over it and see if it means anything to you."

What Neil saw was this:

*"Lady's alligator-skin bag lost or taken from car in West End of London March 20th, ample reward for return with contents intact, no questions asked. Address C.L., Box 53, Daily Express."*

"Well, sir—is it, or isn't it—?"

Their eyes met in a sharp glance.

## CHAPTER THIRTY-THREE

NEIL's skin prickled. Alligator-skin bag—lost or taken from car—March 20th. . . .

"If it's not, Crabbe, it's an extraordinary coincidence. The description, the right date—"

"Don't overlook the bit about no questions asked," interrupted the butler softly. "That's meant to keep whoever's got it from being frightened to come forward. Oh, I'm convinced it's the one, sir. The point is, who's so overpoweringly anxious to get possession of it, and why!"

Without answering, Neil picked up *The Times* from the table and turned to the "Agony" column. Yes, here was the same appeal, but it was signed with other initials.

"I saw that, too, sir—and it's in the *Telegraph*, and last Sunday's *People*. Our footman says he's noticed it several days running."

"The police made a thorough search for this bag at the time of the murder," said Neil doubtfully. "If this had appeared two months ago they would have investigated it like a shot."

"It didn't appear then, sir. I can swear to that. That makes me think the person, whoever it is, didn't like chancing any move till the police had turned their attention elsewhere. Don't forget Miss Natasha was supposed to have stolen the bag and got rid of it. No one was interested in it after it was known she'd had the pearls."

It was certainly true that during the trial the actual bag had been almost forgotten. It was the pearls which counted, and if, as he himself believed, the pearls had never been in the bag at all—

"You said something about a manuscript, sir, didn't you? Well, none of us know what that manuscript represented. Isn't it possible it has a value for some one?"

"Not to any casual thief, who would very probably destroy it."

"This C.L. evidently hopes it hasn't been destroyed. If he doesn't think there's some chance of getting hold of it, why is he making such a fuss?"

"There's something in that. Yes, he must either want the manuscript, or else something we don't know about—for, of course, there may have been other things in the bag. . . . And yet, I don't know. Miss Bundy took nothing but the pearls out of her strong box. . . . By George, I shouldn't wonder if it is those papers he's after! Why, I can't imagine. However, one thing's sure—we must follow this up for all it's worth, now, at once. I'll hand on this information to my detective chap, tell him to get busy. If it's Tilbury who's advertising, we'll soon find out. By the way, have you seen that charwoman again?"

"No, sir, but if you want to know when Tilbury goes up to London again, I can suggest a way of finding out. He always leaves the Ford at the garage—Saunders' place, in Glastonbury. Why not get Saunders to ring you up the next time this happens? You could get on to your man within the hour, and have him pick up Tilbury at Waterloo."

It was a useful expedient, even though it involved taking Saunders into partial confidence. Neil pocketed the newspaper and, filled with excitement, started back to Glastonbury.

Saunders was out, and the one visible appendage of the garage was the young employee, Albert Stokes, whose ill-warranted nervousness in the witness-box had so struck Neil a few days ago. With his loose-jointed frame bent over the racing model he was washing down, he did not notice the visitor's approach, and this gave the latter a chance to observe him closely. Everything about him, even to the slack movements with which he swished the wet swab up and down, betrayed a low mentality, probably arrested at the age of fourteen. At the moment he appeared not to have a care in the world. With the moist stump of a Woodbine clinging to his lower lip, he was whistling, inaccurately, the tune known as "Peanuts," and now and then pausing to wipe back his shelving hair with an oil-streaked hand.

Still unheard, Neil drew nearer, and as he did so, something caught his eye. It was the open pages of the *Daily Express*, outspread on the concrete floor beneath the pail of dirty water.

Hardly had he observed this when something odd happened. In the rear creaked a firm, heavy tread, and turning, he beheld a blue-coated constable, solemn-faced, important, coming in his direction. At the self-same instant there was a stumbling noise, the crash of an overturned pail, and streams of water flooding the floor. Albert Stokes had met with an accident. Nor was this all. He was glaring, transfixed with some sudden emotion—was it fear? not at Neil, but over the latter's shoulder. His gooseberry-green eyes started from his head, his greasy skin had turned quite remarkably pale.

"Mr. Saunders about?" boomed the constable's deep voice. "No? Oh, well, I just popped in to see if he or you would take a ticket to our garden fête? Two shillings. Booked for June 5th."

Stokes' relief was spectacular. A foolish grin widened his mouth as he explained that Mr. Saunders had gone up the street for tobacco. The policeman, pleasantly off duty, dawdled for a few minutes, sold Neil a couple of tickets, and departed, saying he would call in later. Stokes wiped his hands on a bit of waste and, still looking weak, inquired what Neil wanted.

Neil, however, had swiftly altered his decision. He purchased some oil, got back into his car, and in a quarter of an hour was hammering on Natasha's bedroom door. Without ceremony he burst in, to find the girl beside the window, listlessly mending a silk stocking. She turned haunted eyes on him, but before she could speak he had plunged head-long into an announcement.

"My dear, I've made a stupendous discovery! It's been staring me in the face for two months, but, blithering ass that I am, I never saw it till now! First, though, look at this advertisement. It's appearing in all the daily papers." So saying, he thrust the copy of the *Express* under her eyes.

She scanned the printed lines, looked up, startled.

"Can it be Caroline's bag? But who—why—"

"That's what we've got to find out. Never mind for the moment who wants it. It's who stole it I'm talking about. Can't you guess?" As she stared and shook her head blankly, he brought out the triumphant words, "That lout at the garage—Albert Stokes."

"Bert?" incredulously. "So you think he's the thief?"

"Of course. He took it just after you brought the car in. He was alone, wasn't he? And the car was unlocked? Hold on a minute, though—at every other time are you perfectly sure you left it so that no one could get inside?"

"Oh, yes, absolutely There are so many motor-thieves in London one has to be careful. There was a rug there, if nothing else."

"Exactly, and when we opened the door that night I remember seeing the rug folded up on the back seat. Who folded it—you or Michael?"

"Neither of us. We were too tired to bother. It was on the floor in a heap, just as it slid from my aunt's knees."

"That clinches it! Bert folded it up, and took the bag he found under-neath. You always said your aunt must have dropped her bag in the street, but I never thought that seemed likely. The average passer-by's instinct, especially in a decent neighbourhood like St. James's Square, is to pick up what he sees dropped and hand it back to the owner. Besides, the telegram said plainly, 'Bag left in car,' showing Miss Bundy had no doubt in her mind. Well, then, it was left in the car. It slipped off her lap, the rug fell on top of it, and what with her preoccupation over one thing and another, she didn't realise it till you had driven off."

"It sounds plausible, but—"

"It's more than plausible—it's what happened. Naturally Bert lied to us, but he had the bag then, only hadn't been able to open it. He believed it had something valuable in it, and was waiting till he got home to inves-tigate. Now I understand the funk he was in at the trial when they were cross-examining him. I couldn't see any sense in it at the time, but when I saw him staring at that policeman just now, the whole thing flashed on me." He gave a rapid account of the incident.

"Can he have seen the advertisement?"

"I don't know. Of course, if there were only meaningless papers in the bag, he probably got rid of them right away and the bag as well, for fear of being caught with it. If that's so, he couldn't claim this reward, but somehow I don't believe he has done that, or else why should he turn green with fright when a constable walks in? One thing's certain, though. He can hardly have answered the appeal yet, for this is to-day's paper. C.L., whoever he is, is keeping on persistently, which means either that he has something to gain by getting the bag into his hands, or else"—he stopped thoughtfully—"he's afraid of some disclosure."

"Always assuming it is Caroline's property and not some quite irrelevant bag. I must say it's a strange coincidence, if it isn't hers. So you think those papers inside it may constitute a menace?"

"Again I don't know, but what we may take for granted is that it's extremely unlikely for any person outside Stoke Paulton to have any interest in the bag one way or the other. If neither you, I, nor Crabbe knows anything concerning those manuscript sheets, who else is there who could have any ideas on the subject? There's only one answer to that question."

"Tilbury," she whispered. "But why should he upset himself over a thing like that, when he's got practically the whole property by law, and no one disturbing him? What you saw can't be another will throwing him out of possession."

"No, it can't be a will, but if there wasn't something underhand about his intentions, he or any one else would apply openly to the police, not go inserting advertisements with this clause about no questions asked. Anyhow, I'm catching the next train to London to start a thorough investigation—and you, my child, had better come along with me. We'll hunt up a restaurant with a good jazz band, take in a musical show, and—"

She shrank back against the window. "No, I can't do that!" For a second she could not speak, then went on with an effort: "Listen. This morning I slipped out for a walk, just to get some air. On the road I passed three lots of people I knew, and all of them—just didn't see me. It's not good enough, is it? I don't intend to go out of this place till I leave it for good."

"The beasts!" He caught her to him angrily. "Tasha, why—why won't you be reasonable and let me take you away from all this? Somerset isn't the world, you know. It's just a little censorious backwater. If this thing has got to be fought, let's fight it together. I can't bear to think of you being subjected to these humiliations."

"Do you imagine marrying you would make it any better? On the contrary, it would be worse, for I'd always be miserable over dragging you into the mire with me. Promise, please, not to say anything more about it. . . . I'll drive with you to the station, though, and walk back. You're right, I mustn't stick here in this room all the time." She shivered, looking about at the brown figured walls. "I get such horrible ideas when I'm here alone! Wait, I'll get my hat."

"And coat," he advised, glad she had given in to this extent. "It's chilly towards evening."

He helped her into the grey tweed which had been through each stage of her turbulent drama, little knowing the important part it was to play in the last act of all.

"That's right, put on your red beret. It looks like old times."

As she reached for the beret a pile of letters tumbled from the cupboard shelf to the floor.

"You seem to have a good many correspondents," he remarked, gathering up the collection.

"Correspondents?" she echoed scornfully. "Money-lenders, requests for my autograph, three offers from single gentlemen to go abroad as companion-chauffeuse—that's a good line, isn't it? I forget how many proposals of marriage, and a rather larger number of anonymous denunciations. I shan't open any more."

"And travel booklets, I see. Have you been studying these?" he demanded, turning over a heap of highly coloured literature setting forth tours of the Greek Isles, Norway, Tahiti, New Zealand.

She seized them guiltily. "No—yes. One must do something."

"But not run away, Tasha! My dear, you wouldn't do that without giving me at least a chance? I've a right to ask that surely?"

"If I went without telling you, it would save us both a great deal of misery."

"No, it wouldn't. Here, look at me! Let me see your eyes! Give me your solemn word not to make any decision without consulting me first."

"Nothing will come of this, you know," she murmured unhappily. "But—I'll do as you say. There, are you satisfied?"

"Good girl! I trust you."

On the way to Glastonbury he returned to the momentous subject.

"Why did the Tilburys, before the murder was found out, keep dropping in at Saunders' place to inquire for you? It strikes me it was the bag they were so anxious about, that they wanted to get hold of it before you did. Crabbe declares they turned the house upside down hunting for something. Doesn't that look as though they thought there was just a chance that what they wanted wasn't in the bag after all?"

"It does, rather. I'm afraid to hope, but it almost seems as if we were on the right track at last. If something will only come of it!"

"Something must come of it. By this time to-morrow I may bring back some really startling information. I'll tell you what—keep the old bus, make use of it, and meet the four-eighteen to-morrow afternoon. Then we can go back together and thrash the whole thing out."

She nodded. His train was already at the platform. He dashed into the station and, turning for a last glance, saw her almond-shaped eyes resting on him with a still, inscrutable gaze. His heart gave a great surge as he flung down money for his ticket and leaped into a compartment.

## CHAPTER THIRTY-FOUR

CRADDOCK, the private agent, wore an aggrieved expression. Whitsun week-end, the sun blazing from a flawless sky, and a holiday on the river gone west! A detective's lot is not an easy one.

Ignoring distress signals, Neil pushed a batch of newspapers under his eyes.

"See this? That's yesterday's issue. Advertisements coming out for days on end, and now this morning not in a single paper. Stopped dead. What does it mean—that C.L. has got what he wants?"

"Can't say." Craddock gloomily unhooked a brown bowler from the door. "May mean he's given up hope. Only thing to do is to make the rounds of the newspaper offices and see what facts we can collect. You'll come with me, I suppose? Right, but stay in the taxi outside, in case the person turns up and is the one you suspect."

At each port of call—*The Times, Telegraph, Express, Evening News*, and two of the illustrated journals—they elicited the same information. All the insertions had been handed in over the telephone a fortnight ago, scheduled to appear daily till further notice, and instructions given for replies to be forwarded to Mr. Charles Lomax, at an address in the Kilburn High Road. Payment had been made by post-office order, and in no case had the applicant come forward in the flesh. Yesterday the item was cancelled.

"Looks queer, but you can't judge by appearances," commented Craddock resignedly. "Plenty of people do this sort of thing over the 'phone. Anyhow, I may tell you this fellow Lomax is not in the directory. This address probably represents a shop of some kind. We'd better run out to Kilburn and see if I'm right."

The surmise proved correct. In the crowded High Road they halted before a combined tobacco and sweets establishment, run by one Henry Buxton. One half of the showcase was occupied by cheap and lurid bon-bons, the other displayed cigarettes, lighters, leather pouches and articles of imitation tortoiseshell obtainable by means of coupons. The detective left Neil in the taxi and lounged into the door with a nonchalant air.

Racked with suspense, Neil asked himself whether Charles Lomax was a real person in search of some bag totally unrelated to the Bundy case. If so, the present clue led up a blind alley. As the minutes dragged by it seemed to him that his entire future hung on the conversation taking place behind the assortment of Turkish delight and goldflakes. Twice he started to join his companion, and with difficulty restrained his impatience. The third time he was half-out of the taxi when Craddock reappeared and stood chatting with a spectacled woman in a knitted jumper.

"Sorry I can't help you," the latter was saying obligingly. "If Mr. Lomax does drop in again I'll give him your message, but he did say as 'ow he was off to Southend and wouldn't be back for some time. It's not as though he 'ad any regular address, moving about as he does. Oh, it's no trouble at all. Thank *you*, sir. Good-day."

"Well?" cried Neil, bursting with anxiety.

"Just as I supposed," announced the other, lighting a cigarette moodily. "This Lomax is or pretends to be a travelling salesman with no fixed abode. For a short time he arranged to have his letters sent here and has been calling in several times a week to collect them. Nothing came, though, till yesterday morning."

"Yesterday!"

"Exactly. One letter, and he got it. As the advertisement's stopped, it must have been the one he was hoping for. If he's your man, he won't come back."

"One day late!" groaned Neil. "But did the woman say what he looked like?"

"Yes, or tried to. Might be Tilbury, and again it might not. England's full of small, fair men with moustaches. She examined the envelope, too, before giving it up. It was directed C.L., care of the *Express*, and the original postmark, almost effaced, began with the letters G-l-a."

"Glastonbury!"

"Don't forget there's Glasgow, Glassford, and Glasbury, to name a few."

"It is Glastonbury—I'm sure of it. The letter was from the garage employee I've got my eye on. God! If only I'd known of this sooner!"

"Too bad. If both men live in the same town, your chance to catch either of them is gone now. It wouldn't take twenty-four hours for the property to change hands and be destroyed—if it is a case of getting rid of evidence."

"I'm afraid you're right. What's the next move?" urged Neil, feeling a professional sleuth ought to be ready with suggestions. However, Craddock, looking remarkably unsleuth-like, shook his head and consulted his watch, obviously calculating trains.

"Ah, that's a hard question. Neither of those two will admit anything, and you may be sure there were no witnesses to their deal. If money's been paid, it would be in cash—nothing to trace. We could haul this tobacco woman down to Somerset to identify Tilbury, but where would that get us? All he need say is he was doing a spot of private detecting on his own, and there'd be no means of proving him a liar. The man has a perfect right to try to get back something Miss Bundy lost. He's her heir and trustee."

"Can't we arrest him on suspicion?"

"Suspicion of what? We've got to have a formal charge. No, the law can't help us there. I can shadow this garage chap and see if he's spending any large sums, but, even so, how can we make sure how he got the spondulicks if—"

"If—if—!" broke in the exasperated client. "Oh, I quite see it's no use. The scoundrel's slipped through our fingers and there's an end of it. Carry on with the other line. It's all we've got left, I'm afraid."

"Meaning the lady's brother?" The tone sounded disparaging.

"As you say. Of course I'll do my best, but don't be disappointed if it doesn't get us anywhere. The ground's been pretty thoroughly covered already, you know. It's like looking for a needle in a haystack. . . . Waterloo for you, I suppose? If you keep clear of the traffic, you can just make the twelve-forty."

Alone in the west-bound train Neil once more cursed the perverse fate which had brought him knowledge too late to turn it to account. What if Tilbury and Charles Lomax were the same? By no conceivable device could he now hope to trap the offerer of the reward, or force Bert

Stokes into a damaging admission. Craddock was right. Whatever had been planned was already accomplished. In short, the trail was cold.

Still, even as the bearer of ill tidings, he was soon to see Natasha again. He must hold on to her with might and main, and if she fled from the scene of her wretchedness, go with her. On no account must he allow her to face life alone in a strange land. At least he could be near her, and possibly by slow degrees he might alter her present attitude towards life and him.

Four o'clock. . . . Why was the engine slowing? Four-eleven . . . four-fifteen. . . . Were they behind time? He fixed his eyes on his watch.

Events even now were cannoning to a close. One hair-breadth's swerve to left or right would spell hideous catastrophe. The whole outcome depended on one man's approaching actions, and that man, totally unaware, swore only at the train for being late.

Four-eighteen . . . four-twenty. The platform at last! He sprang out, reached the street, looked eagerly around. No Natasha—no familiar two-seater. Never mind, she would come. He would wait for her here.

A quarter of an hour's vigil found him less confident. With dampened spirits he betook himself to the garage to see if his car had been left there. No, apparently it had not. Perhaps the girl had not dared brave the neighbourhood after all. He jumped into a taxi and hurried to Bishop's Paulton to find out why she had not met him.

The Gargantuan female at the George stared hard at him.

"Miss Andreyev? Haven't set eyes on her since she left with you yesterday. I supposed you knew where she'd got to. We don't."

"You mean she's not been back?" he roared at her.

The cool announcement stunned him. He wanted to argue, to smite his supercilious informant, make her eat her words. She elaborated, maliciously.

"Taken nothing with her, left no message. I'm sure I don't know what to think. Car? If it's yours, you mean, I've not seen that either. Look if you like, but I promise you it's not on our premises."

Gone, without warning, without explanation. Knowing him away, she had seized the opportunity to vanish. Why had she done this thing? In Heaven's name, why?

# CHAPTER THIRTY-FIVE

DAZED, benumbed, Neil crossed the street to the vicarage. Against a whirling background of blue seas and red-funneled ocean liners a single black certainty stood out. She did not love him, she could not bring herself to love him. She was taking this way out to avoid explanations. Wounded though he was, he did not blame her, only it was not in his own nature to understand evasiveness. Deucedly odd, not taking any of her belongings. Perhaps she hoped in this manner to make the bolt without letting even the inn people know. She could buy what she wanted in London, of course. . . . Where did she mean to go? Where was she now? Would she have the grace to drop him a parting word?

Rachel was digging in an herbaceous border. He spoke to her dully. "Natasha's gone. I left her in my car at the station yesterday afternoon, and she's not been seen since. Do you know about it?"

"Gone?" Her startled eyes betrayed bewildered ignorance. "Why, she can't be! And yet—I wondered why I got no reply when I sent over some lilac to her. You don't think she's—"

The telephone pealed. She darted indoors, answered it, and handed the receiver to Neil. "It's for you—a man speaking. . . ."

It was Saunders, from the garage.

"Mr. Starkey? . . . A two-seater's been brought in. We think it's yours. Constable noticed it standing empty between here and Stoke Paulton. Want it sent along?"

Empty! What did this mean?

"No, I'll come. Keep the constable there." With a perturbed face he imparted the news to Rachel. "I don't like the look of this. I must report it right away."

She uttered a cry. "Oh, Neil, not that! You can't really think—"

He was already out of the gate and jumping into the taxi he had left unpaid. "Glastonbury again," he shouted, and before many minutes was threading the busy High Street. At the entrance to the garage Saunders met him with a square-jawed policeman, who touched his helmet and explained:

"You know the stone bridge, sir, where the Stoke Paulton lane branches off? I saw the car there this morning when I went past on my push-bike. I supposed the driver had got out for something, but when I came along twenty minutes ago and it was still in the same spot, I drove it back here to see if Mr. Saunders knew anything about it. It's yours, I take it?"

It was. Neil examined the petrol tank, to find it almost full. She could not have driven far.

"Which direction was it facing?"

"This way, sir—towards the town."

Then she had started homeward and turned back. Had she abandoned the car to walk to the station? Bidding the officer wait, he drove to make inquiries of the guard and ticket seller, both of whom knew the girl by sight. Their answers were negative. However she had got away, it was not by rail from this point.

"Constable," he announced a moment later, "a young lady, Miss Andreyev, had this car from four o'clock yesterday afternoon. She's now missing. I want an immediate search made, the whole neighbourhood scoured."

"What, sir—not *the* Miss Andreyev?" exclaimed the man, only to be interrupted by Saunders.

"Why, Mr. Starkey, she called in here about four o'clock. I talked with her myself."

Neil turned on him swiftly. "You saw her then? What did she want?"

"She says to me, 'Where's Bert?' Just like that. Bert's the boy. I tell her he's gone to his lodgings, feeling bad. She says, 'You're sure he is bad?' And I says, 'He says so, anyhow, and has got the afternoon off.'"

She had asked for Stokes! Had she some project in her mind?

"What else did she say?" he urged impatiently.

"Why, sir, she asked me where Bert lived, and I gave her the address—17 Briarcliff Villas. She nodded her head and went off."

A dozen formless conjectures flooded the listener's brain.

"Constable, please report this at once. I want every garage, every telephone booth, every"—he hesitated—"every chemist's shop canvassed as quickly as possible. Find out if she's been seen and when."

As the officer departed on his mission, Neil turned back to Saunders. "Have you by any chance seen Mr. Tilbury to-day?" he demanded.

"Mr. Tilbury?" The proprietor showed surprise. "No, sir, not since Thursday, when he left his Ford here on his way to the station. He fetched it again in the evening."

"If you do see him, don't mention anything about this, will you?" And slipping a ten-shilling note into the astonished man's hand, he set off post-haste for Briarcliff Villas.

Presently, on the outskirts of the town, he drew up before a row of dingy, two-storied houses, each with its few feet of garden and its aspidistra in the front window. The door of Number 17 gaped open, to reveal shabby linoleum and a flight of worn stairs. A woman in a dirty apron answered his knock.

"Does Albert Stokes live here?"

"Yes, sir. He's laid up. Was you wanting to see him?"

"Are you his mother?"

"Oh, no, sir. He's a lodger—friend o' my boy's."

"Perhaps you can tell me if a young lady called to see him yesterday afternoon?"

She blinked inquiringly. "A young lady, sir? Why, yes, there was one come in a small car. She asked for Bert, but he'd gorn out. Got home about three he did, 'ad a wash and changed into his plus fours."

"Then he was not ill then?"

"No, sir, I don't think so—just going somewhere. It was when he come in again about nine that he was so bad. Sick like anything. Been in bed ever since."

Out of the thickening tangle one fact stood clear. Bert had given illness as an excuse, possibly to keep some appointment. If he had met Tilbury, he must have got money from him in exchange for the stolen bag, but all that was irrelevant now. It seemed fairly certain he had not met Natasha.

Parting with another ten shillings, Neil cautioned the woman to say nothing of his visit, and struck out on the road leading to the stone bridge. A dreadful doubt was gnawing at his vitals. He must satisfy himself on one score before going further.

Here was the bridge, and here, plainly shown in the thin layer of mud, were the tracks of his own tyres. He leapt out and scanned the sluggish stream which wound between dipping willows. Scarcely anywhere had the brown water any great depth. In most places the flat stones were visible, while there were so many sedges and out-cropping roots that a body could not drift far without being caught and held.

Racing down the incline, he followed the footpath in both directions, peering into every pool. Downstream he covered several hundred yards, then gave it up. No, nothing here. Why then, had she left the car in this spot? For that matter, what reason to abandon it at all? Almost he was ready to believe the poor girl in a fit of aberration had strayed off across the hills, not caring what became of her; yet even so, some one must have seen her. Human beings cannot vanish into thin air.

All the same, her aunt had vanished without rhyme or reason, to be found days later dead, in a place where no one would have thought to look. The list in yesterday's paper assured him that every few weeks some similar atrocity occurred.

He pulled himself up frantically. No, impossible!

Twenty-four hours ago she was well—sane. She could not have been attacked while in the car, nor could she have left the car, except of her own free will. That meant she must have hired another car from one of the several garages in the town. Of course—the obvious solution!

Half an hour later he knew this was not what had happened. She had hired no vehicle of any kind, and over the telephone he learned from Rachel that nothing but the clothes she wore yesterday were missing from her bedroom. This annihilated the bare chance of her having slipped into the George and out again without being observed. The vicar was busy with the village police and would presently join him. He had already communicated with Scotland Yard, but in his own mind believed Natasha had simply chosen this way of going off, to avoid argument.

In desperation, Neil rang up Sir James Curwood's place and spoke to Crabbe. The latter, who had heard nothing, could offer no suggestion, and unfortunately, as a dinner-party was in preparation, he could not get out to aid in the search.

"You say she knew about that advertisement, sir?" The butler's voice sounded strained. "In that case, mightn't there be some connection between—?"

"All I know is she tried to get in touch with the boy at the garage and failed. We'd both decided it was he who stole Miss Bundy's bag, so it's possible she hoped to find out something from him. Also, the boy himself went off yesterday on what may have been an appointment, but that's only a wild guess."

"Maybe it's not so wild, sir," whispered Crabbe with sudden tenseness. "There may be much more in this than meets the eye. I'll tell you what—I'll send word down to Mrs. Bebb, and tell her to take the bus along to the King's Arms directly she leaves off work. You can find out from her exactly what a certain person's been doing these past two days—if she knows, of course. In the meantime, why don't you get hold of that boy and put the fear of God into him? For all we know, he may have something to tell."

"You're right, Crabbe. It's the one line I haven't tackled."

Little as he expected from this particular quarter, he recognised in Bert's panic at the mere sight of an official uniform a possible means of forcing his hand. At the police station he enlisted the services of the same placid constable who had sold him the tickets to the garden fête, explained what he wanted, and with some difficulty obtained the other's consent.

"You need do nothing but show yourself on the pavement outside. I'll do the talking. I'm not asking you to arrest this Stokes, you understand."

Slow comprehension dawned over the broad face.

"If that's all that's required, sir, I'm willing to oblige—though I don't just see what's in your mind."

The landlady of Number 17 acceded to Neil's request without demur. She mounted the stairs, closely followed by the visitor, and rapped on a door at the rear of the upper floor.

"Bert, there's a gentleman to see you. Am I to let him in?" she called, and without ceremony turned the knob.

There was the sound of a flying leap, and the door was barred by the impact of a body. A hoarse voice muttered in tones of fear.

"No, I won't see him! Keep out, I tell you!"

"Why, Bert!" exclaimed the woman reproachfully, and in a whisper explained, "There's no key, sir—he can't lock himself in." In a persuasive manner she continued aloud, "It's only some one as wants a word with you, stupid. No 'arm meant."

A pause. At last a sulky voice returned, "Right-o. Give me two minutes to pull on my trousers."

"That's it, sir," confided the landlady reassuringly. "I expect, being it's so warm, he's got nothink on. He'll let you in a second." She retreated down the stairs.

Neil waited. The two minutes lengthened to three, then five. Finally he cried impatiently:

"That will do now. You've had long enough."

So saying, he flung open the door and stared round. The small tumbled room was empty. Its occupant had escaped through the open window and down the drain-pipe.

## CHAPTER THIRTY-SIX

YET, thought Neil, since the room did not overlook the street but only a tiny enclosed garden, it was not the policeman who had caused the flight. On the contrary, it was he himself—a fact which confirmed his instinctive fears.

Clattering to the ground floor, he shouted to the constable, and with the amazed officer lumbering behind, swiftly surveyed the back premises. No Bert. The two men scrambled on top of the low, crumbling wall which separated Briarcliff Villas from the adjoining row of houses, and from this vantage point gazed sharply this way and that over stunted lilac bushes, lines of washing, and untidy dust-bins. Only a few cats, sunning themselves. The fugitive had taken cover, probably plunged straight through one of the villas and out into the neighbouring street.

Suddenly from a ramshackle shed sounded a crash of flower-pots, followed by an ancient's annoyed protest: "'Ere, come out of it, you young scoundrel! Wot're you up to, spoiling of my geraniums?"

The constable with one swoop threw himself over the wall on to the shambling figure just extricating himself from a mass of debris. Two arms like flails hit out at him wildly.

"Got him, sir! Would you mind lending a hand?"

At sight of Neil the violence abruptly ceased, and an expression of abject consternation overspread the youth's face. From the way in which his loose mouth fell open Neil knew it was not himself who was responsible for the exhibition of terror. Bert looked puzzled and suspicious, but no longer tried to escape. Quite submissively he stumbled back into the kitchen, darting furtive glances from one to the other of his two captors. His greenish pallor and trembling limbs showed his illness to be genuine enough. When Neil shoved him into a chair and stood over him truculently he made no resistance, merely muttering with weak defiance: "You can't pinch me. I've done nothing—see?"

"Then why did you skin off like that?" Neil motioned the officer to withdraw, and left alone with his victim continued in a mollified strain: "Now, then, Stokes, I don't mean you any harm so long as you tell me the truth. One lie, though, and you'll find the bracelets on you."

"What for?" Turning a still more sickly hue. "What have I done?"

"I can give you in charge on two counts—stealing, and the suppression of evidence in a murder trial." As Bert winced and shifted his eyes he went on with assurance: "You know quite well what I'm referring to, but if you make a clean breast of things I'll promise to spare you. The whole point is this. Where is Miss Andreyev?"

There was not the slightest doubt that the question was wholly unexpected. In utter blankness Bert stammered, "Miss Andreyev? Why, how should I know where she is? I've not seen her since the trial—so help me."

"She was looking for you yesterday. Didn't she find you?"

"No, sir. They told me she come here, but I never seen her. I swear to God—"

"That will do." Inwardly Neil recoiled from this fresh blow, but he went on determinedly: "All the same, you met some one yesterday. You came home pretending to be ill in order to do it. Who was it? If you don't tell me, I'll call in that constable."

"I—it was nobody at all. I—" The gooseberry eyes wavered guiltily. "That is—well, I did mean to meet a party, but—he never turned up."

"Quick—who was it? I'll give you ten seconds—"

"Hold on, sir—" The boy gave a spasmodic gasp.

"I've no call to keep anything back. You see. I had a letter from a gentleman in London about a chauffeur's job. He was to come on the four-eighteen train, and I was to wait on the platform for him. Well, I waited, near on an hour, but I never set eyes on him. That's the God's truth, as I'm sitting here."

"Not the whole truth. What happened then?" Neil was bluffing, little dreaming what his question would bring forth. "What did you do after that until you got back at nine o'clock?"

Eyeing his inquisitor uncertainly, Bert licked his dry lips. After a pause he stammered: "It was like this. A chap—that is to say, a gentleman I'm acquainted with come along—been seeing his wife off to Cornwall. He chats with me a minute, then asks if I'd care to drive up to his place with him and have a look round. It seemed I was wasting my time hanging about any longer, so I went."

"I want the name of this man. Who was he?"

Another doubtful glance, then the hesitating admission: "Mr. Tilbury, of Stoke Paulton. For weeks he's been saying I ought to come and see that hole they're digging up there. This time I thought I might as well go."

So Neil's guess had been right, though he could not tell if Bert were lying about the accidental nature of the encounter, or if the incident had a bearing on the one thing which mattered.

"What happened when you got to Stoke Paulton?"

"We stopped in at the lodge and had a few drinks. Port wine it was, and it turned me queer. Maybe I took a drop too much. Anyhow, the last I remember is walking up the hill to get some air, and the next I knew I was in the house, with Mr. Tilbury putting cold water on me. Soon as I come round a bit, I footed it home, him not liking to leave the place with nobody there."

"Then the two of you were absolutely alone?"

"The char was in the kitchen, but she left about six. I seem to recall him going by to give her money, but I didn't see her."

"And that's all you have to tell?" demanded Neil, sick with disappointment.

"That's all, sir. I've been laid up ever since. That port wine done it. I wish to God I'd never seen it—nor him," he muttered under his breath with bitter loathing, and something which suggested fear.

The involuntary betrayal told Neil that one thing was fairly sure. If Bert had parted with his treasure he had got little, possibly nothing, for it. As though in answer to his thought the youth added with a cunning glance: "You mentioned the word stealing just now. Well, I've not taken nothing that didn't belong to me—see? And you can't prove nothing against me, because there's nothing to prove. Search me, if you like, turn out that room of mine. You won't find a scrap that's not mine."

Then the bag and its contents had gone from him to Tilbury. Full of despair at the hopelessness of further parley, Neil dismissed him.

"All right, go back to bed, but if this isn't straight goods, I warn you what to expect."

Bert, released, lurched towards the open door, violently overcome with nausea. As Neil rejoined the waiting constable, the kitchen clock struck seven.

"No good, officer. He hasn't seen her. I'll come along with you to the station to see if there's any news."

There was none. Natasha's last known action was the call at Briarcliff Villas, twenty-six hours ago. Once more paralysing dread set in. Neil told himself that the girl, finding the situation more than she could face, had made an end of things. How, where, remained a mystery at present insoluble, but one would soon learn the worst.

The May sun shone on holiday-makers—shock-headed young men with rucksacks, trudging beside giggling girls, bicyclists with sheafs of bluebells tied on behind, perspiring families in side-cars. A ponderous green char-à-banc blundered along, filling the street, and all but ran down the meandering two-seater in which Neil sat, stony-eyed, seeing only a horrifying vision of dead eyes, upturned to the sky.

He was abreast of the King's Arms when a voice screeched shrilly: "Mr. Starkey! Mr. Starkey!" A parrot? No, a gaunt female in a battered bonnet, making frantic signs to him with her black-gloved finger. It was Mrs. Bebb, whom he had quite forgotten.

She whispered confidentially: "I got your message, sir, and come right along in the bus."

She accompanied him into the dim lounge, where Neil mechanically ordered her a bottle of stout.

"Thank you kindly, sir. Wot with the 'eat and the jam, I am a bit dry. But about this business, sir—"

She sank her voice lugubriously. "Am I to understand as 'ow Miss Tasha's gorn and 'opped it?"

"She's missing. That's why I wanted to see you. I'd like to know if anything out of the ordinary has happened up at your place of work, either yesterday or to-day. Anything, mind, no matter how trifling. What have you noticed?"

Mrs. Bebb cocked a bleared eye towards the approaching waiter.

"Well, sir, I don't know as I've noticed anything, but I've not been there since ten o'clock this morning. Now you speak of it, that's out of the ordinary, if you like—'im paying me full wages and giving me the week-end off till Tuesday." She bestowed a humorous wink on her companion. "The missus gorn, too, and nobody to lend him an 'and; but 'e said never mind, 'e could manage on cold am, and the like."

"He's alone, then?"

"Not a soul on the place but 'im. Workmen knocked off too, till the middle of the week."

"Before you left yesterday—six o'clock, wasn't it?—did you see any one about, either in the garden or up by the excavation?"

He was thinking it might be useful to verify Bert Stokes's account, but the charwoman shook her bonneted head.

"No, sir, can't say as I saw any one. Early on there was plenty of sightseers prowling over the 'ill, but the last of 'em went before I did. Wait, though—there might've been somebody there, too, because about the time 'e—I can't rightly call 'im the master, sir—come to give me my money, I did 'ear the dogs up in that direction, making no end of a row. Barking like mad they was—you know, them two big Elstayshions."

Neil looked at her sharply. "What did it sound like? Were they angry, or—?"

"Oh, no, sir—pleased, like as if it was some 'un they knowed. That's why I noticed it. I says to myself: 'Now, wot's come over them dogs? They 'asn't carried on like that since Miss Tasha went away.' I don't know wot they meant by it, I'm sure."

He was leaning forward eagerly. "Mrs. Bebb, think hard. You're quite certain you saw nothing? Any movement in the distance, anything bright red, any—" An idea shot through his mind. "Any sort of car in the lane when you went along to your cottage?"

"Car, sir?" A look of surprised recollection crossed her seamed features. "Why, sir, now you mention it, there was a small car, something like yours, standing close to that there stile at the back. No one in it. I never took no notice, because there's often a car—there, now! Wot 'ave I said? You don't suppose as 'ow—?"

He was out of the door and dashing up the street, the blood pounding in his temples. A terrible feeling of suffocation had come over him. Natasha—the Alsatians—his car in the lane. . . .

Ten yards away he cannoned into Gisborne, coming to look for him, and poured out an incoherent story which the other greeted with troubled disbelief.

"Sheer, utter nonsense! Natasha would never dream of going there. There are hundreds of cars like yours!"

"It was she. I know it. I'm going to get hold of a posse to search the grounds. Let me go, for God's sake! Can't you realise every second is precious?"

"I'll come with you, of course, but the police may decline to assist us. They can't swear out a search-warrant on flimsy evidence like this."

The sun slanted low over the monkey-puzzle trees when a party of four alighted at the steps of Stoke Paulton and hammered on the knocker. Peaceful, dormant, the rose-red house stretched before them, with windows rather smudged and curtains not over-clean. From the neglected borders the fragrance of wallflowers and Virginia stock stole forth on the warm summer air.

The rat-tat echoed within. Was there no one here? Two of the group, those in uniforms and helmets, waited imperturbably. A third, wearing a clerical collar, looked sternly anxious, while the fourth was hatless, dishevelled, his black hair clinging in moist wisps to his brow.

"You won't find nothing, sir," muttered the elder officer, with a shake of the head. "It's my opinion he's—but no, I'm wrong. Some one's just spied us out of that window."

He indicated a chintz drapery which still swayed from an unseen touch. The next moment the door opened to frame the owner's harmless-looking figure.

"Mr. Gisborne I This is a surprise. And you, sir?" with a glance at Neil. His eyes strayed glassily towards the two constables. "Why, what's up? Anything I can do for you, gentlemen?"

Two strips of court-plaster adorned his cheeks, yet he had not recently shaved, for his chin showed a bristly stubble. . . .

The vicar addressed him pleasantly.

"Sorry to trouble you, Tilbury, but the fact is Miss Andreyev can't be located. As she was last seen in or about your grounds, we want to have a look round. You've no objection, I hope?"

"Miss Andreyev, sir?" The blue eyes scanned their faces in bewilderment. "Seen abaht here? It's the first I've 'eard of it, and I didn't know she was missing, but then I've not stirred outside the place all day. Don't you suppose she's took a sudden notion to go away?"

"No, we don't—" Neil was beginning when Gisborne checked him.

"She may have met with some accident, or—" The vicar hesitated. "As a matter of fact, we rather fear suicide. So you've seen nothing of her?"

"Not a hair, sir; but you're more than welcome to search. Come inside, do. I daresay you'd like to start with the 'ouse itself? Plenty of odd corners 'ere, though I don't just see—"

Again Neil was about to interpose, but with a touch on his arm the elder officer assented.

"Thanks, Mr. Tilbury, we might as well go through the house, just as a formality. It won't take long to make sure."

Tilbury stood aside. As he held back the door Neil noticed that his fingers were stained black, with something which appeared to be paint.

The party trooped silently to the attic, and under the owner's guidance poked into every room and cupboard. Throughout the tour Neil kept his eyes on Tilbury, who, to his thinking, seemed to overstress his anxiety to help. He also betrayed a surreptitious interest in the front windows, never passing one without glancing outside. Once at the honk of a motor horn he listened acutely and checked a movement towards the stairs. Was he expecting some one? Inconspicuous trifles in the conduct of a person wholly obliging—yet they seemed somehow significant of unrest. Mild as the fellow appeared, he had undoubtedly got possession of something either intrinsically valuable or else incriminating—contrived it, moreover, by trickery. If he were successfully hiding one thing, why not another? Standing behind him Neil felt an overpowering desire to seize him by the throat and throttle him into confession, but realising the futility of such tactics, held down the impulse.

"Well, that's that," pronounced the senior constable, as they wound up their fruitless exploration in the back lobby. "But it's the grounds we're chiefly interested in. Mind if we poke about a bit?"

"Go wherever you like, sir. There's a wild bit towards the far corner I've not been near for days. Sort of ravine, with bamboos 'anging over. If you'll step this way, I'll just show you."

As they set forth on to the terrace a deafening clamour broke from the kennels. It came from the two Alsatians, who were not only barking with might and main, but hurling themselves against the doors.

"Dogs making a rare noise, eh, sir?" remarked the younger officer.

"Yes, they're a bit troublesome, owing to me chaining 'em up. They've taken to going for the tradespeople."

They never used to do that, thought Neil, with a sidelong glance. Insufficient exercise was probably their grievance. The racket grew positively hysterical as the five men filed along a gravel path. Tilbury leading the way.

Suddenly a woman's voice screamed breathlessly. "Alf! Alf! Where are you? What's it all—oh!"

A small, panting figure rushed round the corner of the house, hat pushed awry to show sagging braids of treacle-coloured hair. At sight of the visitors she let fall a Gladstone bag and clapped one hand over her frightened mouth.

It was Connie Tilbury. But she had gone to Cornwall! What had brought her back, after only a day's absence?

## CHAPTER THIRTY-SEVEN

EVEN as Neil was wondering whether her departure was a hoax, Tilbury strode rapidly towards her. Impossible to say if any wordless communication passed between the two, but the woman's startled eyes glued themselves to her husband's face. In them was a still-born question.

Tilbury spoke quickly, and to Neil's ears there was relief as well as command in his tone.

"Got back, have you, old girl? That's all right, then. Don't let all this 'ere upset you. Fact is, Miss Andreyev's gorn off, and these gentlemen are 'unting 'igh and low for her. Think she was seen somewhere in this direction. You go along in and get off your things. We'll tell you if we come across anythink."

Her stifled gasp made Neil think that she, at least, was ignorant of what had happened, though he could not be sure even of this. As though afraid to venture any comment, she gazed at her husband like a mesmerised rabbit, then slowly, her colour faded to a sickly tint, retreated indoors.

Letting the others proceed, Neil whispered to the younger constable: "Keep that fellow under your eye, and on no account let him get in touch with his wife. I'm going off on my own."

With this he turned back and sprinted towards the lodge. Behind him the dogs kept up their irritating hullaballoo. It crossed his mind they must have been shut up for many hours.

The lodge was locked. He managed to scramble in through the kitchen window, and upstairs and down made a rapid survey. Nothing seemed amiss, but on the living-room table he noticed a confirmation of Bert's story, in a collection of sticky rings, large and small, where two bottles and some glasses had been set down. So far, good, but there was no sign to suggest anything connected with Natasha.

In the open once more he ran hot-foot along the right-hand wall to the top of the hill, and here cast his eye over the much-trampled ground in search of revealing footprints. If those he sought were here, they were trodden in by others of more recent date—a hopeless muddle.

His attention was caught by a sign, freshly painted, and still only partly dried—a big board, on which was daubed: *"Private Property.—Trespassers Keep Off."* Had this been here two nights ago? He thought not. Paint in this weather did not take long to lose that glistening newness. All at once he recalled the paint on Tilbury's fingers. That suggested the man himself had done this—probably to-day. Was he merely annoyed at the influx of holiday prowlers, or had he some other reason?

He peered in at the window of the tool-hut. Amongst various implements was a ladder which he fancied he had formerly seen inside the garage. With a sudden cold fear in his heart he bent over the well-kerb and dropped a lighted match down the black shaft. No, nothing here to substantiate his morbid dread. Then another idea came to him. He turned back towards the gaping entrance to the crypt and, stooping, let himself down the sloping planks. There was just sufficient light to see the place was empty.

But what was this? On the rough door shutting off the slimy stairs, a new staple and padlock had been fixed, making access into the opening impossible. This precaution had been taken since Thursday night, but how much later? With a vivid recollection of the cramped descent ending in black vacancy he pressed his ear against the boards and listened. Silence, unbroken, equivocal. . . .

Why need such fantastic horrors seize on his imagination? If Natasha did visit this place, it was in broad daylight. She would never have ventured past the danger-point on these steps. No, whatever happened, she drove the car to the bridge, a quarter of a mile away, got out and—what then?

All the same, he felt vaguely dissatisfied. The new padlock was one of several queer things which called for immediate investigation. For that matter, what accounted for Connie's sudden reappearance? If she went to Cornwall only yesterday with the intention of spending the Whitsun holidays, how was it she had returned in barely more than twenty-four hours? She must have turned round at once to come back.

By Jove! that was the oddest feature of all. Not only had she rushed in with great excitement, but judging from her reception she had been expected. Either she had not been any real distance, or else'—here was an idea!—she had been hastily summoned home.

In a twinkling he was outside again, scanning the garden below for the search party. The sunset had faded to ashes of rose; high overhead in a clear, pale sky sailed the moon, like a fragment of pearly shell. Still light to see by, but in another half-hour it would be night. . . . Those infernal dogs! Would they never let up with their noise?

Far off, amongst flowering shrubbery, he caught sight of a blue coat moving along. He started towards it, not noticing the small figure just making for the kennels; but midway the descent he heard the clank of chains, a scrambling rush, and the next instant two tawny forms, frenzied from confinement, swept past him like a tornado.

Instinctively he turned to watch them—Bistre and Tiger, mad, drunk, their fierce eyes scanning the ruin as they circled round, and then with one accord plunged into the crypt. He was after them like a shot.

There they were, muzzles pressed against the crack beneath the door, whimpering and sniffing the dank air from within with the force of suction pipes.

Good God! Could it mean—? Icy horror gripped him at the thought of what might lie below in that tomb-like void. The dogs knew—straight as a die they had come here. He seized the staple, wrenched at it with all his might. It held firm as a rock. Never mind, he would break down the door. One of those tools in the shed would do the trick.

Smashing the window-glass with his fist, he tore out the flimsy frame and reached a broken pick. A moment more, and he was raining blows upon the stout boards which cracked, but did not yield.

As he swung back the pick for the fourth time, there was a muttered curse from the rear, and at the same time the entrance-way was blocked by a man's figure. Tilbury, a wild light in his eyes, caught at him with one hand, while in the other he levelled a glinting object.

"Get out!" he snarled, his spiky moustache stiff above his back-drawn lips. "Don't you see that sign? My property, this is. I'll not have busybodies mucking abaht and damaging it." As he spoke he thrust himself bodily between Neil and the door.

"Stand back!"

The pick poised aloft, but even as the guardian of the door raised his right hand, a *contretemps* occurred. The dogs, not to be thwarted, shoved between their owner's legs, upsetting his balance. He kicked at them savagely, and with a powerful surge they sprang for him. The revolver thundered. When the acrid fumes cleared, one of the assailants quivered on the floor, with blood pouring from his side.

"That'll show you!" The falsetto voice cracked on a note of hysteria. "The next'll be yours, unless you make tracks out of 'ere, you—you—"

Again the pick described an arc above the sleek head, but the frantic man dodged in time. Before he could take fresh aim a steel grip closed on his throat, and when the second shot roared the bullet only grazed Neil's leg. Undeterred by the red-hot shock, Neil tightened his hold. Through a blue haze he saw his victim's eyes standing forth like glass marbles from a purpling face. . . .

The crypt had grown dark as though a curtain had been drawn. From behind a sobbing thing that bit and scratched flung itself on Neil. Sharp nails dug at his eyes, a foot encircled his injured leg with such unexpected violence that he was thrown to the ground, dragging his prey down with him.

The next events crowded hard on each other's heels. Two greasy braids dipped in his face. Connie clutched him by the hair and with her free hand swooped down blindingly. Somehow she had got hold of the revolver. The cold ring of metal drilled into his forehead, and he knew the game was up.

Yet he must have given a lurch, for when the deafening report volleyed it was not his voice which shrieked. He struggled up with a confused impression of being entangled with seething bodies, one of which—a demon in the shape of a dog—worried and tore at something underfoot. He was drenched in a warm, sticky fluid—blood, though whose it could be he had no idea. A croaking whisper gave the first intimation of the truth.

"You bitch!" The sound came from Tilbury's choking lungs. "You let the dogs out, blast you! And now you've done me in . . ." There was a cough, and more blood belched from the speaker's mouth.

Three running figures appeared at the opening. Gisborne bent over the prostrate owner of Stoke Paulton, while the policeman wrenched the furious Alsatian away from Mrs. Tilbury's mauled person.

"Help me clear them all out!" panted Neil. "The woman'll want tying up, but don't waste time over her. It's our job to smash in this door and see what's down in that hole."

Already he was back at his task, slashing at the boards, while one of the constables found a rope in the tool hut and with it secured the screaming Connie, whom he laid on the grassy slope beside her husband. The latter needed no attention. A bullet through the jugular vein had finished his career.

The wood gave at last. Gisborne seized a loose plank and ripped it away. In a minute more the rectangle yawned before them, with the muddy steps stretching down into the black chasm. The ladder was fetched and lowered cautiously from the last foothold. Would it touch bottom? Just—but it was necessary for some one to steady it at the top, and another man to hold on to him before a third dared venture a descent. Neil pushed forward, but the younger constable thrust him back.

"Not you, sir, with that wound in your leg. I'll go—though I don't believe there's anything in this idea of yours."

"Look at the dog," answered Neil grimly. Bistre, whining and bristling, was peering over the brink with every manifestation of terror.

"Well, sir, we'll have a squint. Just you hold on to the top rung firm as ever you can, for this ladder's not any too safe. Haul the dog away first. . . . Yes, I've got a torch. . . ."

He sank from view into the dripping darkness. No one spoke during the interval while Neil, his heart strained to bursting, gripped the insecure ladder from above and tried to see into the hole. After long minutes a hollow voice came up.

"There is something, sir." A pause, while the shaft of white light played below. "Yes, it is the young lady right enough—crumpled up in a heap. I'm much afraid she's done for. . . ."

## CHAPTER THIRTY-EIGHT

NEIL, reaching the bottom, was dimly aware of a rubble-strewn cave produced by an interior landslide. In a disc of radiance he saw a blanched face with sunken eyes lying in what he took to be a pool of blood, but which turned out to be the scarlet beret. He lifted one limp hand. It was icy cold. A dry sound came from his lips.

"That swine killed her!"

The policeman nodded slowly. "Maybe. There's a nasty mark on her temple. We'll get her above ground, and see if anything can be done."

Neil was not clear as to how the difficult ascent was managed, or for what length of time the motionless form lay, wrapped in his coat, while he and Gisborne employed every known device to achieve an apparently impossible task. Brandy had been sent for, the doctor summoned. For long minutes—or was it hours?—the two men laboured in the stillness of the blue dusk, watching with bated breath for signs which never came.

Then something happened. The dog, Bistre, pushed past them, thrust out a warm tongue and licked the girl's cheek. A trick of eyesight? The moon passing under a cloud? Neil could have sworn he saw the lashes faintly stir. Gisborne must have had the same delusion, for he relaxed and mopped his forehead.

"Yes," he muttered. "Barely alive. God be praised! It's more than I dared hope for. . . ."

It was one in the morning before Graves gave a definite pronouncement.

"She'll pull through, but it was a close shave. Another hour would probably have done for her. There's a slight concussion and her left arm's fractured, but if no complications set in from the exposure and damp we've nothing to fear. She mustn't be moved, of course. The nurse can manage very well with Miss Gisborne's help. That leg of yours fairly comfortable?"

"I'd forgotten it," answered Neil, but at the welcome news about Natasha he felt suddenly very weak.

"Keep off it—and take a stiff peg of whisky." The doctor paused, eyeing him with embarrassment. "Mr. Starkey, though it's no fault of mine, I feel I owe you an apology over certain things I said a few nights ago. There seems little doubt now that Tilbury engineered Miss Bundy's death. Whether he actually did the murder or not, I still don't know."

"Then the woman's said nothing?"

"No, but she'll talk, to save her neck. They've got her locked up in the county jail. I expect we'll hear something before long."

Towards daybreak Neil slept, and woke at nine to find Rachel beside him with a pot of steaming coffee. He could now see Natasha, if he would promise not to talk. His heart in his mouth, he pushed open the door of the adjoining room and stood looking down on the being he loved. The features were startlingly defined by a coif of white bandages. The eyes, dark and somnolent, strayed over him with slow recognition.

He knelt by the bed and pressed his lips against her hand.

For moments she lay still, and then, suddenly a tremor ran through her. She made an effort to sit up, her pupils strangely dilated.

"The papers!" she whispered in acute anxiety. "Where are they? Were they taken from me?"

"Yes, by me. I found them inside your blouse. Look, here they are." And he held up a long manilla envelope. "Now don't speak again. Everything's absolutely all right."

A deep sigh escaped her. She sank back, and before long drifted into sleep.

Presently he drew from their covering a sheaf of manuscript pages, and set himself the task of deciphering what till now he had assumed to be Theodore Bundy's hieroglyphic characters. Only the second portion, he found, was in the dead scientist's hand, the other being written in round, unfamiliar script. Each sheet bore a date, set down by Caroline Bundy, but this was no diary.

At first the meaning of it was totally obscure, but little by little the truth began to dawn on him. At the end of twenty minutes he realised with a shock that here in his hands was the key to an elaborate and amazing plot—that Caroline Bundy's illness, her extraordinary will, her death, all were explained by this semi-coherent mass of scribblings. Easy now to see why Tilbury was so frantically anxious to destroy a record which at one stroke would have overthrown all his carefully built plans and brought him to the gallows.

However, before going further, it will be well to give an account of Natasha's experiences from Friday afternoon onward. Here is the story she told as soon as she was allowed to speak:

When she parted from Neil, she was already turning over in her mind a tentative decision regarding Bert Stokes. If Neil's theory were correct, the boy had something in his possession which at any moment he might part with for the advertised reward, and while she had no clear idea what this treasure could be, she instinctively felt that it concerned her chance of clearing herself. As Neil had pointed out, if it were her aunt's bag which was sought, then the object inside it must be either of great intrinsic value, or else seriously incriminating to the murderer. Whichever it was, it meant a vital clue towards unravelling the tangle, and as such must be secured before it disappeared altogether.

Bert had always been well disposed towards her. She resolved to see him at once, and by cajolery or threats get the truth out of him. If she did no more, she might at least frighten him so badly that he would not dare enter into negotiations. She went to the garage, but he was not there. Finding out where he lived, she repaired to Briarcliff Villas, only to learn that he had put on his best clothes and sallied forth, evidently on some prearranged appointment. This definitely alarmed her. What if even now he were on his way to meet Tilbury and effect the exchange?

She drove slowly through the town, keeping an eye out, but the boy was nowhere to be seen. She did, however, catch sight of the two Tilburys, complete with luggage, just entering the railway station. Evidently the couple were setting off on a journey, which in a measure relieved her, since it showed that no immediate plan was afoot; yet at the same time the innocuous appearance of the bustling pair so shook her conclusions that she was ready to think the whole idea of their guilt was absurd. Very likely she and Neil were entirely wrong, the bag was not her aunt's, and all hope of clearing things up was doomed to crushing disappointment.

Damped and discouraged, she turned homeward, keeping to the by-lanes, and presently passed the rear boundary of her former habitation. Here she met the squad of workmen just returning from their labours, and knowing that the place must now be deserted she took a sudden determination to visit the ruin. Accordingly, she got out of the car by the stile and climbed the hill to look round.

The two Alsatians, roaming at large, spied her with an enthusiasm which warmed her heart. They followed her about for some minutes while she pried into the crypt and examined the stairs leading down into the earth, and presently their barking ceased and they ran restlessly out into the sunshine.

It was while she was still in the crypt that she heard voices approaching, and her heart stood still as she recognised one of them as Tilbury's. How was this? Had he not gone away after all? No, he was close at hand, coming straight in her direction. Peering cautiously out, she received a second shock. The person with him was Bert Stokes! Instantly she knew Neil had not been mistaken. Not only that, but in all probability the crucial moment was at hand, if not already passed.

She was not at all concerned over her own safety. The one idea which consumed her was that now, with any luck, she might witness or overhear something she could report to the authorities—perhaps even prevent the stolen object from changing hands. Quickly she hid herself just inside the muddy stairway and drew the door to. If the two men came upon her, what could they do? She had no physical fear of Tilbury, and Bert, who had the strength of a giant, was her friend. If she could remain concealed for as much as half a minute she might learn all that was necessary. Anyhow, she would take a chance on it.

The two came into the crypt. She heard a yawn, a stifled groan, and the sound of something heavy slumping on to the ground. Tilbury's protesting voice exclaimed: "'Ere, this won't do! Wot's come over you? Feeling sick?" There was a drowsy grumble, then silence, which lasted so long that she ventured to move the door an inch and peep through the crack.

To her amazement she beheld Tilbury, his back turned, stooping over the apparently unconscious Bert and going through his pockets. As she watched, fascinated, she saw him straighten up with a long envelope in his hand, glance at the latter's contents, and start to tear it across.

In a twinkling she flung wide the door and pounced upon him from behind. He was taken wholly unawares. Before he knew what was happening, she had seized the envelope and thrust it inside her blouse, buttoning her coat over it, but as she dashed for the exit, he uttered an oath and pushing her back, got between her and the opening. With a nasty gleam in his pale eyes he came towards her, reminding her of some mean-spirited animal which attacks only when cornered. She was not in the least frightened, certain she was a match for him.

"Wot's the idea?" he snarled with a vibration in his voice which indicated abject terror. "Give that back—see? I promise you, my girl, you won't get out of this 'ole with it. Give it back!"

He caught hold of her as she tried to dart past, tearing at her coat, but she kept her arms crossed over her breast, thus providing the best possible defence against his assaults. A struggle ensued. Once his loathsome face approached so close that, lunging swiftly at him, she drew blood with her finger-nails—two long angry scratches. Uttering filthy language, he tried to trip her up, but failed.

She continued to elude him, throwing him off each time he closed with her. If only she could get into the open, she could outstrip him in a race to the car, but every effort to reach the exit was prevented by his clutching hands. Never mind, she could hold out as long as he could. Sooner or later some one would come and he would then not dare continue the brawl.

What she did not realise was that in her enforced retreat she had edged towards the gaping doorway. Her first knowledge of this dawned when her foot slid on the slimy brink, but at that very moment there came the welcome sound of a motor cycle chugging to a halt at the foot of the hill! Help at last! She opened her mouth to shout, but it was too late. Tilbury, too, had heard the warning noise, and instantly clamped his hot, moist palm over her lips. At the same time with his right hand he caught up some object—a fragment of brick, she thought—and dealt her a violent blow on the temple. She was thrown backwards, slithered the length of the steps, and hurtled into blackness and oblivion.

During the hours which followed she had only brief intervals of consciousness. She remembered trying to scream, with a voice too weak to do more than rouse hollow echoes. Impenetrable, clammy darkness pressed in upon her. At one time she got to her feet and groping above just managed to touch the overhanging ledge, but the pain of her head and her broken arm was so excruciating that she sank again, spent with the exertion, and lay, like a rat in a trap, wondering how long it would be before her assailant came to finish her off. Perhaps he would simply stop work on the excavation and leave her to die in this foul, airless hole. She still had the precious papers, but they had cost her her life.

As Natasha came to the end, she checked a shudder to ask Neil a sudden question.

"Why didn't he dispose of me sooner? It must have been a terrible risk, leaving me there. Dead or alive, I had the evidence on me, and there was a strong chance of my being discovered."

"If you had seen the almost impossible feat it was to get you above ground, you'd understand what he was up against. There's not only a sheer drop of over seven feet, but no way of steadying a ladder unless some one holds on to the top. The bottom ledge shelves at a bad angle, and is all soft mud. If Tilbury had got down to you, he might have found himself trapped as well, unable to climb out and certainly powerless to get you out. I don't doubt he tried, and saw how hopeless it was. That's why he sent for his wife to come back at once and help him. He must have wired her immediately, but of course he couldn't explain why he wanted her here."

"So if she had reached the house before you did. . . . But even so, what would they have done with my body?"

"Hush! Don't let's talk of that."

"But there are still so many things I'm curious about. Bert, for instance. Was he drunk, or drugged?"

"The latter, I imagine. We've found an empty bottle at the lodge—chloral hydrate, which your aunt occasionally used as a sleeping mixture. Graves says that's what must have been put into the port. It would require only about a quarter of an hour to take effect. It's a stuff that's often used for doping people. Bert informs us that Tilbury himself drank stout—also that he did have the envelope in his pocket, intending it for the man he expected to meet. We've got the full story out of him now."

"But did he never guess Tilbury was the man?"

"He probably suspected as much, but the fellow was shrewd enough to give him nothing to go on. He knew that if he paid Bert money he'd be placing himself in his power for life, whereas if he drugged the poor idiot and took the papers from him, Bert could never state positively how he had lost them."

"But Bert might have gone to the police."

"Hardly. Don't forget, the papers were stolen in the first place. He wasn't in the least likely to make a complaint, especially as he could prove nothing."

She remained silent, thinking this over, but presently, with renewed eagerness, returned to the subject of the papers themselves.

"You've looked at them, but do you realise I don't yet know what they actually represent?"

"Automatic writings," he answered slowly. "Or rather, faked ones, conceived and executed by Alfred Tilbury—with my help."

"Your help? Whatever do you mean?"

"That if I had not come here, Tilbury would never have been able to imitate your grandfather's handwriting. The Bundy characters begin two days after my arrival—and I think I can tell you why."

He then related how Tilbury's intrusion into the study coincided with the disappearance of a page from one of old Bundy's letters, and how, when the page was returned, he had merely supposed it to have been picked up by the charwoman or Miss Bundy herself.

"We wondered, you and I, why your aunt was so fussy about locking everything up. I now believe it was because she wanted absolute proof that the spirit-messages were genuine, and if the person who produced them had access to her father's writings she could never have been quite sure. That explains why, when the character of the communications altered she questioned me so closely about the keys. My answer, unfortunately, set her last doubt at rest."

"Then Tilbury was never inside the study alone except on that one occasion?"

"On the contrary, after that date, he must have spent hours in there, poring over the diary and the lesser-known works. The later messages establish that fact, for not only are they couched in Bundy's typical phraseology, but they contain whole sentences, quoted verbatim. How and when he managed it, I don't know, but it has occurred to me he may have taken a wax impression of the keys, which were lying in full view on the table. My back was turned, and having no suspicions of him, I went on with my reading. As a matter of fact, I came near as anything to catching him in the room the night Miss Bundy was taken ill. When I found the door fastened—" He stopped, embarrassed.

"What did you do?"

"Nothing. You see, I wasn't sure the person in there was Tilbury—that is if there were really some one. It might have been you."

"Me! Why me?" she cried, astonished.

"Why not? You had a good chance that evening to borrow the keys, and after what you'd said about buried treasure and a possible clue among your grandfather's records—"

She smiled ruefully. "If that were the only thing you had against me!" she murmured, with a glance at him from her narrowed eyes.

He had barely time to press her hand, when there was a tap at the door, and the saturnine face of the doctor looked in upon them.

"That's enough for now," came the gruff command, and, at a signal beckoning him outside, Neil went into the passage to find Gisborne just returned from the town.

"The Tilbury woman has confessed the whole business," whispered Graves. "Mr. Gisborne, here, will give you the details, but as it's altogether a horrible affair, I'd prefer not to mention it just yet to the patient."

The three men descended to the drawing-room, where Neil listened to the story Connie Tilbury, in a complete collapse of morale, had finally disclosed. With illustrative excerpts from the document in Neil's possession, it forms a strange narrative, set forth in the following chapter.

## CHAPTER THIRTY-NINE

ALFRED Tilbury was on the brink of financial failure when at a charity performance in the town hall he first set eyes on the woman destined to be his victim. There was nothing in the dowdy, unimpressive person of Caroline Bundy to excite interest, but hearing some one whisper that the old girl in front of them was one of the rich land-owners of the district, he began to study her with respectful attention.

She had with her the lady later known to be Miss Emily Braselton. The two friends chattered, and Alfred, seated behind, listened with all his ears. The conversation he overheard was prompted by the programme, which consisted of pageants illustrating the famous Glastonbury myths. In the interval after St. Joseph of Arimathea was seen placing the Sacred Cup in a spring, Miss Bundy remarked hesitatingly, as though violating a confidence: "I don't suppose you know my father's private theory about that, do you? He seldom spoke of it, but it was his belief the Grail was hidden in the underground passage which used to run between our old Glebe House and the abbey here. I've often wondered if there were anything in it."

The handsome friend was sceptical, but Miss Bundy, on the defensive, gave reasons for the idea. As every one knew, the Mendip Hills were riddled with caves and springs. If, as many thought, the Grail was actually hidden hereabouts, the obvious explanation for its complete disappearance was that the spring covering it was underground, blocked up. Sometimes she had been troubled because she had never made an effort to follow up her father's cherished project of excavating the tunnel, but she had always been a little nervous about meddling with spiritualism, the channel through which his revelations had come. Miss Braselton strongly agreed, declaring that to her spiritualism and charlatanry were one and the same, whereupon Miss Bundy argued rather annoyedly that Theodore Bundy was too sound a thinker to have embraced any cause unworthy of investigation. Besides, how was one to dispose lightly of the abbey discoveries, the lost Edgar Chapel located by means of automatic writings? Here was something which no one could dispute. Eminent scientists the world over were turning their attention to the occult. Her father, if he had lived, might have shown the present generation a great proof of survival, as well as a valued symbol of the Christian faith.

The speaker's manifest hankering to probe into mystic matters gave the quiet listener his cue. Already in his mind he was summing Caroline Bundy up. Credulous, stubborn, shy, she had all the qualities which, properly handled, could be turned to account. He had struck oil with her sort before.

Several times in his photographic career Tilbury had superimposed the ghost-like form of a dead husband on the likeness of a living widow. Occasionally he had conducted mild seances and supplied alleged spirit-communications from the departed, always with remunerative results;

moreover, he possessed remarkable skill in imitating handwriting. This elderly woman had no husband, but she did have a pet idea which could be played upon. After hard thinking and discreet inquiries, he paid a call at Stoke Paulton, the sight of which greatly awed him, and humbly obtained leave to photograph the ruin.

After this it was a mere matter of preparing his combined negatives and re-photographing the result on new plates. The cup, cut from cardboard, was shown hovering over the hillside, diaphanous, but distinct enough for recognition. The effect was eerie and arresting. He then waited patiently for his dupe to make the initial move, knowing that if she were to be suitably impressed she must not imagine he had an axe to grind.

At last the hoped-for event happened. The old lady came into the shop and asked if the pictures had been finished. After a slight demur, he displayed them with apologies. She put on her glasses and looked spellbound. No doubt whatever, she was greatly moved—or, as Mrs. Tilbury put it: "Struck all of an 'eap." She questioned the photographer closely, got out of him a reluctant admission of his mediumistic powers, then took the views away with her. A week later she returned to suggest a tentative seance, but was met by stubborn objections, which showed Tilbury's understanding of her character. Eagerness on his part would have roused suspicion; diffidence stamped him an honest man, besides which Miss Bundy valued the favours eventually obtained in exact proportion to the efforts put forward to secure them. When the meetings ultimately began, both Alfred and his wife seemed to be giving way against their scruples, and both insisted they had no faith whatever in the phenomena evoked.

Connie remained throughout a passive adjunct, completing the circle and ensuring the proprieties. Alfred, simulating a partial trance, held a pen in his limp hand and transcribed messages previously prepared. The trio sat in the darkened study, chosen because of its associations with the deceased Bundy. When the lights were finally switched on, Miss Bundy would seize the written page, consign it to her handbag, and devour its contents in private. The conspirators then partook of an excellent meal, pocketed their pay, and departed, well pleased with themselves.

For a short time things went comfortably, but presently difficulties arose. Miss Bundy was openly dissatisfied with the nondescript handwriting and chafed at the total absence of the intimate allusions she would have expected from her father. She longed to believe, but ingrained caution restrained her. In short, she was unwilling to spend a great deal of money on an enterprise which might only bring down ridicule on her head, unless she had something better to go on than passages like these:

*"Jan. 2nd."* (Date in her own hand.)—*"Have waited long to reach you. . . . Ten years by your count. . . . Cannot rest till my earth-work is completed. . . . A.T. my chosen agent. . . . Be guided by me. . . . I send A.T. to you as my mouthpiece. . . . I always believed but was afraid to mention idea. . . . That's finished now I've seen Great Light. . . . His name be Praised. . . . Truth—every word. Your father speaking.*

*"Jan. 4th.—Spring. H.G. buried in spring by Joseph. . . . Why not found because under ground. . . . Hills. . . . Tor Hill direct line from house. . . . H.G. still there waiting to be revealed. . . . Photographs my doing. . . . Remind you duty. . . . Sacred trust. . . . Why doubt. . . . Dig."*

True, the references to the Grail were startling. Alfred Tilbury, an ignorant stranger, could not possibly know what she herself had never told to any living being save Emily Braselton. However, she had heard of telepathic thought transference, and could not be certain whether or not the medium was unintentionally reading her own mind. Was it really Theodore Bundy who guided the man's hand? The question haunted her day and night, but if she complained Tilbury instantly threatened to give up the seances—the last thing she wanted him to do. She presented him with her Ford car to make it easier for him and his wife to come to her, and tried to cultivate the patience continually urged by the communications.

The writings, still non-committal in the essentials, took on a scriptural tone, scattering Biblical quotations, and always emphasising the fact that A.T. was the author's unconscious channel, the only suitable one Bundy had been able to find. The Power was not yet strong and consequently could not give the wished-for results, but faith and perseverance would conquer all obstacles. The daughter was told that it was her mission to restore the Holy Symbol to a world lost in heresy, and that only by means of A.T. could the necessary revelations be achieved. She must keep A.T. with her, or the work would fail.

Tilbury, of course, was stalling. Unable at this stage to lay hands on so much as a scrap of Bundy's writing or any private details whatever, he could not better his present efforts, but to make up for this deficiency he found another method of consolidating his position. He resorted to flattery, made his employer see herself as a great woman hitherto unappreciated. Lapping up the unaccustomed adulation, Miss Bundy became more and more attached to the humble worshipper who alone recognised her true worth. Her soul had long been starved for admiration, and Tilbury knew how to feed her what she most wanted. As Mrs. Tilbury aptly worded it: "Alf 'ad a way with 'im."

Probably it was about now that Miss Bundy's personal ambitions were definitely stirred. First of all, she wanted to prove herself right and her old friend, the vicar of Bishop's Paulton, wrong, but soon she regarded the idea of finding the Grail as much more her own than her father's. Thanks to Tilbury, she saw in it a means of achieving fame. No longer would she be looked on as dull, uninteresting Caroline Bundy, overshadowed by greatness. No, she might yet earn distinction, if only she could summon courage enough to embark on the excavation.

Yet this was precisely what Tilbury wished to discourage. He was deliberately steering a cautious course, trying to keep his dupe interested, but at the same time holding her back from any decisive move. Once she started in to dig and found nothing, he and his wife would be shown the door. He had not as yet any intention other than to get what he could out of the living woman. It was only when he found himself gaining more and more influence over her that a new and bigger purpose began to form. Then it was that he said to himself: "Eccentric old ladies sometimes leave their money in strange ways. What's to hinder this one from making a will in our favour and popping off at the right moment?"

What indeed? There were two reasons in direct opposition to the project. First, the old lady's health was excellent, promising at least another twenty years of life, in which time her sycophants' hold on her would come to an end. Second, what likelihood was there of her making so preposterous a will unless she herself could benefit by it? Serious barriers, but Tilbury saw a possible means of surmounting both.

Into the automatic writings, two strong motifs were introduced—one warning the daughter of an early decease, the other impressing on her the means by which she could attain permanent glorification. Nightly these themes interlaced, and soon, in an uncanny fashion, Miss Bundy received confirmation of the former. Her heart began to behave queerly. She had spells of breathlessness, lost flesh to an alarming extent, and altogether became such a wreck of her former self that she was at last persuaded (by the Tilburys) to see her physician. Graves diagnosed high blood-pressure and prescribed accordingly. How could he guess what the patient herself was far from suspecting—that gigantic quantities of thyroid extract were being added to her soup, tea, coffee, and even the medicine she was ordered to take?

Tilbury, during his association with the chemist at Chester had acquired a random knowledge of certain matters, including the properties of thyroid extract. He knew that the preparation, though not a poison, could produce very frightening symptoms in given cases, and he rightly guessed that Miss Bundy did not require the stimulant and therefore would react in the desired manner. Her bad eyesight made her an easy prey, besides which Connie was usually at hand to divert her attention while the stuff was being poured into the cup or glass. The results were entirely satisfactory, except in one respect. The old lady, secretly terrified of dying, clamoured yet more importunately for convincing proofs of her father's authorship.

Tilbury realised that by hook or crook he must get in touch with the Bundy records. Playing a bold card, he announced his intention of quitting Glastonbury at once. Fearful of losing him, Miss Bundy offered him the position of bailiff, and so by one stroke he solved his present financial problems and brought himself a step nearer his goal. Even so, he was debarred from the actual study, which its owner shrewdly kept under lock and key. He would have had to burglarise it but for the happy chance which brought the American writer to the house on the morning following his own arrival. He himself had something to do with Miss Bundy's decision to get the biography executed without further delay, for it was her precarious health which made her afraid to postpone the undertaking any longer.

Exactly as Neil Starkey supposed, Tilbury obtained wax impressions of every key in the bunch, so that from now on he had only to leave the window giving on the rose-arbour unlatched after the seance in order to climb in, unlock the various cases, and browse to his heart's content. Seeing an opportunity to borrow a page of Bundy's writing, he took that along also to save time, photographed it, and after a few hours' sedulous practice, contrived to produce a creditable copy.

That very evening he wrote in the dead scientist's own hand. Miss Bundy, electrified by what seemed to clinch matters beyond a doubt, went at her project like a house afire. . . . The Power had reached its zenith. Who but Theodore Bundy himself could indite these strange and crabbed characters which scarcely any one could read; who, moreover, had ever addressed her with the stern voice of command, so that she inwardly trembled and dared not disobey?

Within a few days this passage appeared:

"*March 4th.*—'*Carrie, Hannah and I*' (note the Christian names, hitherto not mentioned) "*know that you are an ill woman. . . . Blood-pressure far above normal, heart failing. Your own stupidity, you were always stupid, though a good girl. . . . Still, not entirely your fault. Your mother died of high blood-pressure. . . . At any moment you may succumb to a fatal attack. . . . Death or paralysis—what then? The Sacred Sign will disappear for ever. Everything rests with you. Why can't you realise your responsibility? I am being put to great strain to show you what I want done. If you fail me, I shall be exceedingly displeased. Suppose you die without leaving any provision for the work to be carried on? Oxford antiquarians—bah! Irreligious lot, and not one sees beyond his nose. Fools—fools! It is your duty to help me confound them."*

And then the references to matters she alone understood: *"You recall Mrs. S.? A good woman—but less useful than A.T., who possesses a purer soul. Yes, your mother did come to encourage me in June, 1921. A clear demonstration. I even caught a whiff of the lavender-water she always used. . . . And the old men shall see visions. . . . I was right about many things in my youth. . . . You know Barnes disagreed with my original contention. . . ."* (Here followed a quoted passage from the work withdrawn from publication.)

The same effort continued:

*"It seems written that you will pass over to us, like Hannah, at the age of sixty-three. That is why it is so urgent for you to make arrangements at once. Keep your own counsel, but think, plan. . . . A.T. invaluable to success of enterprise. Without him you can do nothing, but he is not aware. . . . No one else will do your bidding with no thought of self. . . . The mists between us are often thick. Sometimes I fear the connection may be severed before . . ."*

Before what? Did this mean she might die before he could convey to her all he wished to say? The poor woman, now wholly obsessed by her desire for fame, began to see she might have to content herself with posthumous glory. Some one other than herself must be commandeered and equipped to carry out the work in her name, but where to look for suitable agents?

The writings themselves provided the clue. Alfred and Connie—who else? Those simple souls, selected by her father! They only would labour in her behalf, give all the credit to her. For that matter, they would be obliged to do so, if the will were properly worded. What a masterly idea! The obscure creature saw herself crowned by future humanity—a seeress, almost a saint. It must be so. She, humble daughter that she had been, would, by restoring the Holy Grail to the world, and incidentally furnishing a concrete proof that the dead still lived, become more renowned than Theodore Bundy himself!

What passed in her thoughts is, of course, only surmise. The plotters, knowing nothing, must have had some anxious moments while she hung fire, hampered by timidity and, perhaps till the last, fearful of incurring ridicule. Giles Gisborne's words had stung her badly. She felt she must run no undue risk. She continued to demand further tests, till, in a fit of anger towards the gardener—the latter's position undermined by Tilbury—she collapsed, and had to relinquish what was now her chief interest in life. The Tilburys were panic-stricken. Suppose she died without remaking her will? However, the attack was only a slight, premonitory one, which supplied just what was wanted to bring her to the desired point.

Luck again, but at the crucial moment Emily Braselton loomed on the horizon, threatening utter ruin to the skilfully laid scheme.

Up to the present Tilbury had counted on the continued administration of thyroid to bring about death from apparently natural causes. Now he was forced to seek other means, or abandon his idea. From the conversation which passed between Neil and the head mistress, Mrs. Tilbury learned that the latter was not only suspicious regarding the seances, but confident of freeing her friend from all delusions once she had her to herself. On no account must the two women be allowed to go away together; and yet it would be equally fatal to oppose the joint holiday, for in that case Miss Braselton would pounce on the conspirators at once and find means of exposing their deception. For a brief space there seemed no way out of the impasse, then a solution, perilous, but brilliant, flashed into Alfred's mind.

Miss Bundy herself played into his hand by insisting on a midnight seance. She sought her father's guidance—and got it. She was advised to go to Rome, but commanded categorically to put her affairs in order before she set off on what might be her last journey. Deeply agitated, she slept over the counsel, and next day, having agreed to her friend's proposal, was heard telephoning to her solicitor to come to Stoke Paulton that afternoon.

Acute tension. What did she intend to do? Those concerned must not show curiosity, yet it was essential for them to know the terms of the new will. They asked to go off on a jaunt, and while Alfred drove to Bristol to explore a certain wild region thereabouts, Connie got out of the car at the first bend and slipped unseen into the house. Hidden under the library sofa she listened to all that took place, and when her husband returned, triumphantly reported what she had heard. Yes, actually the old lunatic had left them nearly all her fortune—with conditions, it was true—but what did such silly conditions amount to?

They had to pinch themselves to make sure they were not dreaming. They, Alfred and Con, to inherit this luxurious estate! They joined hands and danced round the sitting-room in childish rapture. If only their old associates could know what was in store for them! What would that disdainful, interfering Andreyev girl say if she guessed what had happened right under her nose?

However, Connie had not quite foreseen what her Alf had in that clever brain of his. When he told her his plan she recoiled in horror. No, no! This was not what she'd reckoned on! She couldn't do it! Why, poor old Carrie had been good to them! Never, never, not even for him!

In a blind fit of revolt, she rushed out into the night—for what? She sobbed out something about telling Miss Bundy, warning her, but whether or not she meant to do this no one would ever know.

## CHAPTER FORTY

REASON—her husband's reason—reasserted its hold over Connie, who was speedily brought to heel. Impossible now to rely on their old, comfortable method. If they were to lay hands on their fortune they must do so at once, before Miss Bundy fell under her friend's influence. In short, their victim must not leave England alive—and they themselves must manufacture an iron-clad alibi to guard against the suspicions sure to fall on them when the astonishing will became known.

The problem bristled with dangers, but Alfred had a stratagem, ready prepared by his own forethought.

In order to prevent Miss Bundy from starting in on the excavation herself he had purposely kept the spirit-messages vague, but at the same time he had dangled a tempting bait before her in the promise of a final, spectacular revelation. Occasionally all she got after hours of waiting was something of this nature:

"*Must give you the required Sign. . . . You must know where to begin digging, otherwise much time and money wasted. . . . Hard, extremely hard. . . . Wait for Easter season . . . full-tide. . . . Maximum power. . . . Holy Week approaches. . . . Afterwards it may be too late. . . . Patience. . . .*"

It was this sort of thing which made her reluctant to break off the thread. A month in Rome seemed a calamity; but on the evening after the solicitor's visit she received the following communication:

"*March 18th.—Carrie, I am pleased with you. . . . Rome, rest—you may yet live to complete work. Also work safe if you do not accomplish in person. However, before you go you must have Sign from me. Not*

*in writing. . . . Photograph essential. . . . Like others, but more exact.
. . . Don't postpone, whatever you do. Obey me implicitly. Listen, I,
your father, speak to you. . . . If you put off the Power may not last to
reach you later on.*

*"Hill. . . . Ruin. . . . Night. . . . A.T. with camera. . . . Fire picture. . . .
Fire. . . . Fire—no, flash. . . . Flash-light, that is right. . . . Midnight. . . .
Supreme Test. . . . Am saving myself for it. . . . Try once, twice. . . . First
attempt may fail. . . . Ultimate triumph certain with God's help. . . . Now,
now is the moment. . . . By this Sign. . . . Millennium inaugurated . . ."*

How she must have stared at these familiar words known only to
herself! Ready now to swallow anything, she wished to try the photographic experiment that very night, but the pouring rain rendered a
flash-light impossible. On Thursday evening she was about to slip out
to join her friends, when Natasha stopped her—besides, it was drizzling
again. How was she to leave to-morrow with the task undone? It might
be she had lost her last opportunity.

The Tilburys, needless to say, were grateful for the intervention of the
elements, without which they would have had to risk the flash-light and
pronounce it unsuccessful. A hasty séance took place with great secrecy
after the household was in bed, and these instructions were issued:

*"March 19th.—One chance remains to us. . . . Friday, to-morrow
night. . . . Come back, come back alone—let no one know except A.T.
and C.T. Better thus. . . . Conditions ideal, never so good again. . . . The
Sign will be given you, the Great Being promises. . . ."*

Throwing caution to the winds, the infatuated woman asked the
Tilburys to help her. She must take this test photograph, but it was
unfeasible to remain home another night, since Natasha would be certain
to thwart her. The girl suspected something now. She was in league with
the doctor, and it was quite impossible to elude her vigilance. Besides,
here in plain language were her father's orders: *"To-morrow night—
come back alone."* That meant her difficulties were foreseen and this was
considered the one way out of them. Yet London was a hundred and thirty
miles away. How was she to manage the distance four times in a day?

Tilbury, appearing suitably indifferent, studied the time-table. If she
really wanted to come back, what about this six-thirty express to Bristol? He could meet her with the Ford, hurry her here without any one's
knowing, and she could reach London again at 2.40 a.m. A bit strenu-
ous, but she was right about Miss Andreyev, who never would permit
her to overtax her strength or to do anything the doctor didn't approve
of. The young lady had an eye like a hawk.

Miss Bundy balked slightly over the idea of arriving at Emily's flat at three in the morning. What would the servant think? Still, with great issues at stake. . . . While she fluttered like a distracted hen, Connie remarked irrepressibly: "I say! Won't Miss Braselton look silly when she hears how clever you've been? If you ask me, some of these know-it-alls wants taking down a peg."

It tipped the scales. What a tempting thought, to outwit Emily, that intellectual snob! The Sacred Treasure, when found, would prick the bubble of her friend's conceit. Yes, she would do it. After all, she was quite fit again now, and what was the loss of a few hours' sleep? The three put their heads together and mapped out the plan.

By tea-time, after her departure, Alfred let the whole household know he was afflicted with violent cramps, as, indeed, was the case. Since noon he had been swallowing minute doses of oxalic acid, left over from cleaning an old straw hat. From his chemist crony he had learned how much could be taken without serious risk, and the remedy, if things went too far. Chalk—that was the stuff—and he must be careful not to drink anything. The glass of brandy poured for himself he did not touch. Later in the evening he would take a little water, but he must save himself for what he had to do. Service-men, it seemed, used to knock themselves up with oxalic acid to escape a big push. The effects were superficially similar to those produced by food poisoning.

It was annoying to find Mr. Starkey about to quit the house. He had counted on him as an additional witness, but three would suffice.

At five-thirty Miss Bundy rang through to inquire about the weather, and after her first sentences the connection faded. If he had guessed what she was trying to tell him he might have been frightened to proceed, but as it was he confidently expected to steal the damaging documents from her and destroy them before morning. The old girl stuck to them like a leech, unwilling to let any one, least of all himself, see what they contained.

He now went to bed, and at eight o'clock had Crabbe and the cook fetched up to see his condition. While they were with him Connie made her pretence of telephoning the doctor, replacing the receiver as soon as she got through. She then switched on the radio to drown the sounds of her next action, which was to get the Ford stealthily out of the garage and into a well-screened spot behind the lodge. This consumed barely five minutes, and when she came upstairs again, the servants suspected nothing.

The instant Crabbe and Mrs. Hickson were safely back in the kitchen, Tilbury dressed with lightning speed and slipping out through the drawing-room door drove to Bristol to meet the eight fifty-seven express.

Miss Bundy was waiting as arranged, a short distance from the station, her near-sighted eyes peering anxiously into the gloom. With elated triumph she told him how well things had gone; how she had secured a first-class carriage to herself and been noticed by no one. Now for the Test! Was the camera in readiness? If only the Power would prove strong enough to show them what they wanted!

A moment later Tilbury received a staggering blow. She had lost her alligator bag—left it behind in the car. She had searched all over the West End, trying to find Natasha, only to be obliged to give it up.

Here was a predicament! Too late to turn back—the chance would never come again. He said to himself he must get hold of the bag before any suspicion arose, substitute some of old Bundy's letters for its enclosure, and hand the whole thing over to the bank. Unfortunately Miss Bundy neglected to mention the telegram sent to her niece. Her present thoughts were all on the weather. Rain threatened, therefore, they must be quick.

She did not notice the detour they made from the main road into the lonely waste, in the middle of which something went wrong with the car and she was asked to get out for a moment. The moment had come. Taking from under the seat a heavy coal-hammer and passing behind her as she stood by the roadside, Tilbury dealt her a savage blow. Without a sound she dropped, but he was afraid she was not done for. In a hysterical panic he struck at her head again and again.

He dragged the body quickly to the chosen ditch, removed the black bag, wrist-watch, and the tiny steel key from its chain, thinking he would need this to open the alligator bag. Heavy drops were now falling—a good thing, for a downpour would eliminate every trace. On, the way home he gulped down a final dose of oxalic acid, which took such rapid and dire effect that by ten o'clock, back in bed, he was racked by agonising cramps, and weak as water from the combination of illness and nervous reaction.

Fighting off approaching coma, he questioned his wife as to how her camouflage had fared. Perfectly, it seemed. When she was not bustling back and forth to the kitchen she was upstairs delivering her carefully rehearsed groans. As was expected, the servants had not come up again. If they had done so, she would have said the ill man was shut in the lavatory.

The doctor arrived in a quarter of an hour, found the patient in the lamentable state already described, and did what he could to relieve his sufferings.

Just before it was light, Connie replaced the Ford in the garage, cleaned it thoroughly, and burned the black bag with its contents in the lodge stove. The wrist-watch she buried deep under a hedge.

The one serious danger was represented by the alligator bag, but if they got hold of it on the excuse of carrying out Miss Bundy's telephoned instructions, there ought not to be any cause for alarm. Thank God the thing was locked, and they had the key! Connie made inquiries on Saturday and Sunday without success. Alfred, too worried to stay in bed, did the same on Monday, with the results familiar to the reader. When, from Natasha's lips, he learned of her own fruitless search, he was at first aghast, but afterwards concluded that the bag had been stolen in London, and its contents destroyed as worthless.

He bore with composure the minute investigation of his illness, confident his statement could not be disproved. Three reliable witnesses upheld his alibi, and when, slightly aided by himself, but mainly through an astonishing chain of circumstances, the dead woman's niece was arrested, he began to feel the fates were on his side.

All went smoothly till a fortnight before the trial, when at a chance meeting with the garage employee, Stokes, he suddenly had a terrifying inkling of the truth. Bert was the thief who had taken Miss Bundy's bag! Fool that he was not to have guessed it sooner! There was guilty consciousness in the boy's eye which assured him this was no wild conjecture. What if the idiot had had sufficient cunning to get rid of the bag, but keep the papers? The latter, almost indecipherable, would probably mean little or nothing to him, but he might easily show them to some one cleverer than himself. If so, it meant the gallows for Tilbury, whose one hope of safety lay in securing the manuscript and burning it.

From now on unending torment ensued. To sound Bert on the matter would be an open admission. The boy must not suspect that he had any interest in the bag one way or the other. So far Bert had made no move, doubtless because he was afraid, but if his fears were lulled and a reward offered he might part with his stolen possession. Tilbury therefore concocted an advertisement which he inserted in all the daily papers. If caught at the game, no one could criticise his zeal towards solving any part of the murder problem. He took pains to leave a copy of a newspaper, opened at the advertising section, at Saunders' place whenever he dropped in, but in spite of all, Bert remained unresponsive.

Meanwhile, the accused girl was acquitted—bad enough in itself, but infinitely worse because of the conditions which left her still under a cloud. He had seen enough of Neil Starkey to know the latter would not rest till Natasha Andreyev was cleared, but perhaps, if she left England, her admirer would follow. He tried to induce her to go, but only managed to rouse her distrust. Never mind, he reflected, neither of this pair could do anything unless they could lay hands on evidence of whose very exist-ence they were unaware. Probably his terror was entirely groundless. He came near convincing himself that Bert Stokes had never stolen the bag after all.

Immediately after his call on Natasha, he went up to London to make his usual inquiries at the Kilburn tobacco shop, and there found Bert's letter, which was at once a shock and a relief. He answered it on a borrowed typewriter, signed it "C. Lomax," and made an appointment to meet the writer at Glastonbury station. However, he had no intention of revealing himself as the unknown applicant. He had thought of a way to obtain what he wanted so adroitly that the slow-witted boy would have no future hold over him.

At this point Mrs. Tilbury's information ends, and we must turn to Bert's account to fill in the gap.

Tilbury, after seeing his wife off on the train, bumped into the wait-ing youth as if by accident, and hospitably invited him up to the house. Not once did he refer to the vital topic, and by the time the two reached the lodge, Bert's mind was in utter confusion. Was Tilbury the man he had expected to meet? All along he had had a tentative suspicion that he might be the real "C.L.," but perhaps he was mistaken. Anyhow, he did not refuse the port. He drank several glasses, and the stuff made him feel queer. His host suggested fresh air, whereupon they walked up to the ruin, but at the entrance to the crypt he sank down in a stupor, and knew nothing more till, on coming round, he found himself wretchedly sick and minus his papers. Although he was fairly sure what had happened, he dared not complain. When, on the next day, Neil came to interview him, he thought it was Tilbury, of whom he now had an overpowering dread.

The next bit is contributed by two motor cyclists, a grocer's clerk and his girl, who happened on Tilbury a few seconds after he had shut the door on his victim. What they saw was a pleasant-spoken man bending over a drunken chap. They laughed, joked for a bit, and went their way, totally unsuspicious of anything wrong.

Imagination must supply the rest. Tilbury, straining his ears at the bottom of the stairs, realises Natasha is unconscious, possibly dead. He drags Bert to the house, revives him, sends him off home, then dashes back to the crypt to listen again. The dogs know the girl is there. They sniff and bark to such an extent that he is obliged to shut them up. He discovers Neil's two-seater in the lane, drives it to the bridge and leaves it.

What is to be done? After desperate attempts to get down into the hole, he sees what an impossible feat it is, and sends a frantic wire to his wife. He must have her assistance quickly, or his victim will be missed and the neighbourhood ransacked. If she is found, the injury to her head will tell an ugly story, even if she cannot herself denounce him, and whatever defence he may put up, she has on her person the ruinous document.

During the long night he works busily, painting signs to keep off trespassers, padlocking the door, and stealing backwards and forwards from the house to the crypt. In the morning he sends the charwoman about her business, for no one must be here to witness what has got to be done. The body will have to be disposed of, but how? Burn it piecemeal, bury it in lime? If only Con would come! Her relations live six miles off the railway. No telling when his telegram reached her, or how long it will take her to get back. All day he waits, on pins and needles, and hour after hour the dogs keep up their noise. . . .

Connie Tilbury did her utmost, but even so she could not arrive home before early evening. The sight of the police turned her blood to ice, and though her husband's warning glance stayed the question on her lips, it could not explain matters. How was she to guess the true situation?

One of the few independent actions of her married life was to loose the Alsatians, whose barking got on her nerves—and by that simple deed she shipwrecked everything.

## CHAPTER FORTY-ONE

"WILL they hang Connie?" whispered Natasha when, days later, she had heard all the gruesome details.

"I imagine not. A life sentence, with something off for good conduct, seems the likely thing. No one doubts that she was entirely under her husband's thumb."

The girl shuddered as she thought of Mrs. Tilbury's abject subjugation and the maze of crime into which it had led her. She knit her brows and turned to her companion with a sudden question.

"Neil, what was it about that cold-blooded toad which gave him such power over women? He was not attractive in any sense we understand, not even very definitely masculine, and yet I'm convinced poor Caroline would never have fallen such an easy victim if he hadn't exerted an almost hypnotic spell over her."

"Well, there you are. Look at Landru and some of the other scoundrels who have preyed upon women. Many of them are physically repellent, but that doesn't seem to hamper them. Tilbury's main asset was that transparent naivete of his which made him somehow rather appealing. He was persistent, too, with a tireless capacity for taking pains. His wife, of course, must have known the utter brutality under the surface, which makes her devotion all the more amazing. When I was choking the life out of him she attacked me like a tigress. It's a strange irony to think her own bullet did for him in the end."

"Yes, in a way she's every bit as remarkable as he was. She has courage, you know. Picture what she must have endured during the two hours she was left here, knowing that at any moment something might wreck their scheme!"

"If she'd realised the risk her Alfred was running with the oxalic acid, she'd have been worse frightened. Graves declares the fellow might easily have collapsed on the way home. You remember how his muscles twitched even on Monday night and how his voice was almost gone? Typical symptoms of oxalic acid poisoning, though they could have come from other causes, which is what put Graves off. . . . But here—I'm forgetting your letters. Two of them. Want to look at them now?"

She perused the first with growing wonderment, and handed it to him without comment. The note, several times re-forwarded, ran as follows:

"Swan Lodge,
"Bedford.

"DEAR MISS ANDREYEV,—What I have to say will excuse me, a stranger, writing to you.

"On the evening of 20th March I motored my old father to Torquay, stopping for petrol at a filling station near Bristol. Our car is an eight-cylindered Getz, 1929 model, dark green, with wire tyres. My father sat inside, and as he was suffering from acute neuralgia, had his head wrapped in a woollen muffler. I wore a light tweed coat, a small beige hat, and carried a dark-red, rather shabby bag. I am neutral-blonde in colouring, aged twenty-four, and my features are quite a good deal like yours, to judge by your published photograph.

"As the filling station man had no change, I looked round to ask my father for some, but seeing he was asleep didn't disturb him, and gave the proprietor a pound note. I was anxious to get to an hotel, because the night air was bad for my father's complaint. Not until I read your defence did it ever occur to me that the two of us had been mistaken for you and your unfortunate aunt. I didn't dream, of course, that a car stated positively to be a Geisler

could turn out to be a Getz, or that any man, however muffled up, would be taken for a woman. I cannot tell you how bitterly I regret not waking up to this sooner. Thank God you had a clever Counsel, and that the tea-shop girl was so enamoured of your bag!
"Yours sincerely,
"JANET MACWHIRTER."

While Neil was shaking his head over this communication the second letter was put into his hand. It was neither more nor less than a stiff apology from Emily Braselton, who, up to the moment of Tilbury's decease, had continued to harbour suspicions against the acquitted girl.

Natasha lay back against her pillows and turned thoughtful eyes towards the open window. In a haze of sunshine the garden lay serene, with the black cedar casting a pool of shade, and the bordering syringa bushes a mass of waxen blooms. A peaceful scene—and yet, as her gaze fell on the ruined walls rising against the blue sky, a spasm of pain crossed her features. All this opulent beauty was now hers, but how could she ever enjoy it? No, Stoke Paulton must go to some one who could not tap its vein of dreadful memories.

"What's wrong?" demanded Neil, catching her faint sigh.

"Nothing that matters. I was thinking, that's all. . . . By the way, do you see what Emily says at the end—how even I must realise my conduct invited misconstruction? It's perfectly true. I could hardly have expected her to believe in me, when you yourself didn't quite think me innocent."

"Isn't it time to forget all that?" he said, flinching a little. "Though now you've mentioned it, I've never wholly understood why you couldn't tell me the truth."

"Can't you see how impossible it was? In the earlier stages, I couldn't have thrust on you the unwelcome responsibility of knowing I was scheming to evade the law. After all, you were little more than a stranger. Later on, when the evidence began to look black against me, it would have been positively fatal. In order to clear me, you'd have sacrificed Michael—oh, yes, you know very well you would!—and nothing would have convinced you that bringing him back here would have injured my case, as well as ruining him. Even now I don't see how I could have acted differently."

He was reluctantly obliged to admit logic in what she said. It seemed quite likely that Michael's movements on the night of the crime would never be revealed.

"Still, you might have taken my hundred pounds. Why on earth didn't you?"

She faltered under his direct gaze. "It's hard to explain the feeling I've always had about accepting money from men. I shrank terribly from applying to Serge Wassilieff. The thought of it was absolute torture. I've a sort of complex on the subject, I think, ever since some rather horrid experiences I had during the Paris days. You know what this Braselton woman said about the two positions I lost?"

"I'd hoped you'd tell me about that."

"I will. You see, I began earning my living at seventeen. I was employed in several French families as chauffeuse, and every time, without exception, the husbands, or the sons, tried to make love to me. I stuck it as long as I could, simply because jobs were hard to come by and my mother's hats didn't pay, but when I continued to hold out against these men's advances, an excuse was found to get rid of me. What could I do? If I'd made a row, the charges would have been denied, and the women would have been furious. So I held my tongue."

"The unspeakable beasts!"

"They were—beasts. One old general, with the Legion d'Honneur, used to lie in wait for me in dark corners. He—oh, I can't talk about it!" With a shaky laugh she pressed her fingers over her eyes. "I don't like posing as a persecuted maiden. Plenty of girls go through the same thing. My mother knew, though, and it made her very unhappy. That's why she was so anxious for me to come here."

Neil was at last beginning to see clearly, but with the wave of sympathy which swept over him came an uncomfortable suspicion.

"Natasha—" He stroked her smooth throat with a timid hand. "Is that why you told me I only wanted to make love to you? Did you think I was like those other brutes?"

"Not quite. You couldn't be," she returned with embarrassment. "But—well, I'd come to believe all men were pretty much the same. Either I'd had bad luck, or else there was something about me which invited the wrong sort of attentions. I'd begun to fear it was my fault. Oh, it's no credit to me if I didn't give in. I can't bear feeling cheap, that's all. . . . I think I've a sixth sense about certain matters. I was not mistaken over the Tilburys, was I? And I rather believe I was right about you too. I sized you up as the sort of man to whom conquests have come easy, who expected women to fall into his arms, and who had no desire to give up his independence. After all, why should you? Quite candidly, now, you didn't really want to marry me or any one else. Did you?"

He reddened under the question.

"Not at first, even though you drew me as no woman ever had done, and seemed to me the perfect companion I'd always been looking for. At the same time, you must see how this idea of your having a lover held me in check. No man wants to court a certain rebuff." He paused, to add in an altered tone: "I love you now, Natasha, every inch of you, in ways I didn't think possible. The kind of independence you speak of means nothing to me any more."

"When did it begin?" she asked, studying him with detachment.

"When I kissed you, of course—but something even more vital happened when I held that little green slipper of yours in my hand, that night at the inn. Queer, isn't it? After you were arrested and in danger, I tumbled headlong. There's been no hope for me since."

"In spite of half-believing me guilty?"

"In spite of everything. Never mind me, though. It's your feelings I want to discuss. I haven't bothered you, for obvious reasons, but now—well, the long and short of it is, what are you going to do about me?"

Those narrowed eyes of hers had never been more baffling than at this instant. It was without the least change of expression that she answered him slowly: "You saved my life twice. Doesn't that establish a sort of right over me?"

"No!" he cried with energy. "And let me tell you this! If you have any notion of marrying me for any reason other than because you'd hate living without me, I'll walk out of that door now and never come in it again."

Her gaze strayed lingeringly over his bronzed skin, the parting of his hair, the anxious lines which had formed round the mouth and eyes.

"Has it ever occurred to you," she said, "why, instead of letting Saunders send for the car I came all the way back to Somerset?"

"I supposed it was on your brother's account."

"No, he would have been as well off in London for the few days that were left us. I came because I had to see you again. Knowing how it would hurt, never dreaming I meant anything real to you, still I came. I couldn't help it."

Incredulous rapture surged through him. He slid his hands under her pliant body and caught her to him in a close embrace.

"Darling! It's a gorgeous, beautiful lie. Tell me more."

"Then listen. That evening we danced together—you remember? Up till that moment I'd been a little afraid, without knowing why. Well, when I felt your arms around me and your chin touching my hair, I realised the truth. It wasn't you I was afraid of. For the first time it was myself."

Their lips were together. Outside a breeze stirred the white syringa, sending up a waft of fragrance. Rooks cawed, and throughout the whole landscape there was a drowsy hum, but in the room itself, for long moments, there was neither movement nor sound.

THE END

Printed in Great Britain
by Amazon

81426594R00139